Praise for Grimbargo by Laur

"Laura Morrison's *Grimbargo* dystopian near-future where death has lost its power in the face of perfect regeneration. Onto the scene two unlikely heroines bumble their way across a world of pseudo-suicide cults, dastardly ravens, inappropriate flirtations, and awkward nicknames in a race against time to investigate the first death in a decade, and perhaps to even save the worldddddd!"

- (Al)lison Spector, author of *Let's Stalk Rex Jupiter!* and featured writer in *Five2One Magazine, Molotov Cocktail, & the Mad Scientist Journal*; allisonspector.com

"*Grimbargo* is a slick sci-fi thriller that will leave the reader on the edge of their seat from start to finish. Morrison has crafted a unique and engaging world where humans are immortal, able to heal from any wound with the help of nanites, but be warned, this is a far cry from the utopia it might sound like. Watching [Jamie and Jackie] stumble from one conspiracy to the next is a delight. Morrison has struck gold with two likable protagonists who drive the plot forward with energy and a healthy dose of snark."

- Kathy Joy, author of *Last One to the Bridge*.

"A tightly-plotted combination of dystopian science-fiction and whodunit, with a healthy dash of humor, *Grimbargo* gives us two well-drawn main characters who find themselves thousands of miles from home and embroiled in some truly bizarre circumstances. Morrison makes it a pleasure to follow these two accidental adventurers as they uncover the outlines of a grave threat to humanity and struggle to understand, then fight it. With plenty of action and plot twists that keep you guessing, *Grimbargo* delivers!"

- Brian Kirchner, award-winning author of *The Syrian Drummer and the Cactus Crimson Paint* and *The Manzanar Scrapbook*

Grimbargo

GRIMBARGO

LAURA MORRISON

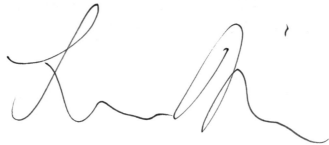

SPACEBOY BOOKS

Denver, Colorado

Published in the United States by:

Spaceboy Books LLC
1627 Vine Street
Denver, CO 80206

www.readspaceboy.com

First printed December 2017

ISBN: 978-0-9987120-9-3

To Will.

Without your support, this book would never have been possible. I love you like crazy, man.

1 JACKIE

Jackie Savage was running late.

Again.

Always.

But what did punctuality even matter? A remnant of the old days, to her way of thinking. Pointless, like eating, or thinking about whether there was anything after death. The sooner everyone got cool with the fact that they had all the time in the world, the ... well ... the less Jackie would have to worry about showing up on time to things. Ten years, and still people were clinging to these unnecessary behaviors.

It was a fairly constant annoyance to Jackie that no one but her seemed to have the capacity to adapt to the changes. It was enough to give a broad a superiority complex.

She sighed, and decided to shelf those thoughts for later. There was, after all, plenty time. For now, Jackie had a meeting to get to. As she drove down the darkening street into a part of the city that made her glad she had mace in her purse, she looked around for the diner where the meeting was taking place.

And there it was. Rotten Lou's. Of all the places to have a group therapy meeting, why there? Jackie wasn't prone to depression, but she was certain that, if she had been, Rotten Lou's would have had no place in her quest for mental health. Or any other kind of health.

On the bright side, though, plenty of parking.

She pulled into a spot along the road right in front of the diner, grabbed her purse, locked the car, and walked in.

Sticky vinyl floor, bad lighting, stale 1980's music, and vinyl orange upholstery that was liberally torn, with yellow foam stuffing popping out. That was Rotten Lou's atmosphere in a nutshell. A scruffy man in jeans and a gray t-shirt was swiveling left and right in a barstool behind the cash register by the door. He looked up when Jackie walked in, reached towards the stack of menus in front of him, and made to stand up.

Jackie held up a hand. "I see my group, Lou. I'll walk myself over."

The guy settled back into his seat, abandoned the menus, and said to Jackie's back, "Name's not Lou ..."

"Whatever, Lou," she muttered as she approached a group of people in the far 'corner booth. They were the only people in the place, and thus Jackie cleverly inferred that they must be the folks she was meeting. There were six of them. Four guys and two ladies. Two of the guys looked up as she approached. The others kept their attention on a lady in a yellow knit cap who was talking to the group.

As Jackie got closer, she heard Yellow Cap say, "—every day that goes by, its worse. I'm just so tired. It's—" she broke off and her pale blue gaze settled on Jackie. "Are you the lady from the paper?"

"Yep. You're the Greywash support group?"

There was a flurry of responses in the affirmative.

"Sorry I'm late," Jackie said as she shot a look at the elderly guy at the end of the bench, prompting him to scoot over and make room for her. She sat and looked at them. They watched her silently, expectantly, waiting for her to say something. She cleared her throat. "Thanks for talking with me. Uh, as you probably already all know, I'm doing a story on different coping strategies that have evolved since the Greywash. For the edition the paper's putting out for the tenth anniversary of the Greywash."

There were some murmurs and nods of assent.

Yellow Cap said, "We've ordered already ..." as she handed Jackie a menu.

"No thanks. I don't eat."

Everyone gave her blank looks.

The old guy Jackie was sitting by managed, "You … you don't … eat?"

"Well, we don't really need to, do we?" Jackie pointed out. "Not anymore." In social situations, she often did eat just because people tended to look at her funny when she didn't. But she was sure that even before the Greywash she wouldn't have eaten at Rotten Lou's.

"Well … yeah …" said the old guy. "But you don't miss it? Food?"

"Eh," Jackie shrugged.

More confused looks were her only response.

"But hey," Jackie said into the silence. "We're not here to talk about what a freak I am. I'm here to ask questions, and sit in on your meeting, and take notes. So, uh, wanna start with questions?"

"Sure," Yellow Cap said. Jackie almost asked her what her name was, but they could sort out names later if anyone wanted to be quoted in the article.

"OK," Jackie said, setting her recorder on the table and starting it up. "So … the first question that came to my mind when I got this assignment was, why such a focus on the negative? I mean, eternal life, yeah? Or so it seems so far. No one's aging. Ten years of no aging. Why not focus on the good stuff? Like, for example, before the Greywash I was a hypochondriac like you would not believe. Sore throat? Must be cancer! Headache? Cancer. But now, I'm totally cool. No worries. It's amazing. So many people, once they figured out what was happening, they were ecstatic. Why not you guys?"

Yellow Cap cleared her throat and spoke up. "Well … we all have our different reasons. Myself, I'm religious. And sure, once everyone realized what'd happened and how no one was aging anymore, and no one was dying anymore, we were all like 'Oh hey, did the Apocalypse happen? Thief in the night and all that, right?' And the churches were packed again. But then …" she trailed off with a shrug. "Nothing changed."

"Yeah," a guy in a grubby, faded black t-shirt laughed. "No fiery chariots in the sky, eh, Lola?"

Yellow Cap, a.k.a. Lola, glared at Grubby Shirt before looking back at Jackie. "So. Yes. It's getting harder and harder to hold onto my faith. And now everyone's running amok and there don't seem to be any consequences, and it's clear it wasn't the Apocalypse after all. Because no one's getting what's coming to them." She frowned, then went on, "Eternal life's given all the immoral people exactly what they don't need. Consequences are all that ever kept them in check, and now the consequences are gone. No one dies because of bad choices. No one contracts diseases from doing things they shouldn't."

Grubby shirt laughed, "What a shame. No more STDs. No more innocent bystanders getting killed by suicide bombs and drunk drivers. No more mass shootings. Oh, how I pine for the good old days."

Lola snapped, "And being free to live disgusting, self-centered lives of immorality is better?"

"Hell yes. Would you just stop pretending everything's worse? I mean, come on, not being killed by suicide bombers or drunk drivers or gun-wielding wackos is pretty nice."

Lola fired back, "But the bombers and the shooters and the drunk drivers are still here! No one has learned! The bombers just destroy transportation hubs and landmarks instead of lives! And the drunk drivers and the people who text when they're driving—without the risk of death, they're a complete menace on the road! Why, I've had to buy three new cars since the Greywash because of those fools."

"And the construction and automotive companies are thriving. What a great job creator!" Grubby Shirt said with a smile, clearly having a grand old time making Lola mad.

Jackie let them fight for a bit.The squabble might make for good material. Jackie felt a bit of pity for Lola, remembering back to the Greywash. In those days, unsurprisingly, dumb, uninformed speculation had ruled the day and gotten repeated as fact. The first salvo was the idea that God had kicked his way out of the margins, and was back on the scene with a humongous flourish. Boarded-up church doors were ripped back open, vagrants ejected, and pews were dusted down, so everyone could pretend like they'd been there the whole time. The fringiest of doomsday preachers bullied their way back to the pulpit, screaming sermons about the fiery sword that was on its way to smite the unbelievers, and turn our goofy little blue ball into a tangible paradise that would be the envy of all other life in the universe, if it existed. Which, clearly, it didn't.

The religious folks were still waiting on that fiery sword. A church in Omaha did collapse on some people, but as per normal, no one was hurt.

Grubby Shirt laughed. "Surprise, surprise, Lola. No doomsday. Almost as though your interpretation is maybe wro—"

Jackie saw the look in Lola's eye and thought she'd better jump in with another question. She asked Grubby Shirt, "And what made you join this group?"

He leaned forward and clasped his hands on the table in front of him with the attitude of one who thinks what he's about to say is super daring. Jackie stifled an eye-roll and tried to meet his gaze neutrally. He said, "This never aging, living forever thing just doesn't interest me. Depresses me, even. I never had a problem with death. What'd that crabby old alcoholic poet lady from like 1920 or whatever say? Living's never been a project of mine; kindly point me to hell and be done with it," he said with that smug air of someone referencing an obscure literary figure. "But here I am. Stuck."

Jackie nodded. "Gotcha. And it's Dorothy Parker." *Moron.*

"Yeah, her. Cool broad. Anyway, before this group, I tried the suicide clubs for a while," Grubby Shirt elaborated. "But they got irritating fast, all these freaks trying to one up each other. Chop off your head, get all fixed up by whatever the hell it is that makes us not able to die anymore, and start brainstorming about your next suicide. Got really competitive. That's just not what it should be about."

Jackie nodded. "After I interview you guys, I'm interviewing someone from one of the suicide clubs for this article, too. What, in your opinion, should the suicide clubs be about?"

Grubby Shirt said, "I dunno. Like just a social thing. Not a competitive thing. Or a showing off thing."

Jackie nodded, while internally thinking how messed up this dude was. "OK, sure. Yeah. So, like just a social club with folks who repeatedly kill themselves."

"Pretty much ..."

"Huh," Jackie said.

Just then, a skeletal, middle-aged lady who looked like she must have been seconds away from death pre-Greywash walked up with a tray of food and slammed it down on the table across from theirs. As she began handing everyone their fried whatever, Jackie tapped her fingers on the tabletop and looked around. "How about you?" she asked a lady sitting across from her. She looked to be about Jackie's age. Somewhere around thirty.

The lady just looked down at her stomach and grumbled, "This."

Jackie followed her gaze. "Oh. Yeah."

The lady was insanely pregnant.

"I was due the day before the Greywash. If this kid had come when it was supposed to, I wouldn't have been walking around nine-and-a-half months pregnant for ten years. You ever been pregnant?"

"Hell no," Jackie said. "No way I was gonna inflict myself on a baby."

The pregnant lady frowned and fussed with some fries on the plate that had just been slammed down in front of her. "See I'm totally opposite. I wanted this kid like crazy. I was super excited to meet her. But now I'm never gonna. Can't have a C-section. Tried early on, but my body repaired itself too fast. And now I'm just so over this. So, so over this." She waved again at her stomach.

Jackie nodded. She felt super bad for the ladies who'd been pregnant during the Greywash. And those who had just had kids. A (potential) eternity of pregnancy or of taking care of an infant too small to lift its own head or communicate. Even the most maternal-minded of ladies would be bound to get tired of that pretty fast.

The pregnant ladies and recent parents had, obviously, been among the first to start to realize that something weird had happened and that no one was aging. Slowly, then seemingly all at once, people started to notice that their infant children never grew out of their starter jammies. They didn't get any taller, they didn't weigh any more, or less, they didn't start to crawl, and they never said their parents' names.

As of the most recent survey of medical professionals, it turned out that ninety percent of all graduating, non-Cloister doctors were pediatricians. Another five percent was the Cloister-approved doctors who administered the super-expensive drug that was the only way brains could make new pathways anymore. The other five percent were really just goofing off. Not that doctors were even necessary, or even useful in the years since The Greywash. The freelance pediatricians were more combinations of soothsayers and snake-oil salesmen, taking piles and piles of money from desperate parents trying to purchase the faintest hope that their baby wouldn't be frozen in a seconds-old body. There had been pockets of people here and there who had petitioned the government to regulate the pediatricians, but hope always seemed to undermine fury, and the clamoring tended to die down as quickly as it started.

Jackie shifted her focus from Pregnant Lady to a teenage-looking boy at the end of the table. She was about to ask what he was doing there, when her phone rang. "Sorry. Hold on. This is my editor," she said as the sound of a cooing pigeon began to emanate from the depths of her purse. By the time she'd found the phone underneath the heap of clutter in her bag, Phil's call had gone through to the message system.

She called him back before he had a chance to leave the usual, "Jacks, answer your phone! What's the good of a damn phone if I can't reach you when I need to reach you?" spiel.

He answered after a half a ring. "Jacks, what's the good—"

"Yeah, yeah," she cut him off. "What?"

"Wrap up your interviews. You're on a flight to Kyoto in three hours. Check your email for details."

"Come on, Phil. I was gonna go home and watch the vintage game show channel until I passed out."

"Jacks, this is big. Hold on. I gotta shut my door." Jackie heard a shuffling sound and the slam of a door. "OK. Yeah. Huge story. And we have an *exclusive*. Get this, Jacks, there's been a potential death."

Jackie literally dropped her phone in shock. Once she's retrieved it from the disgusting, bacteria-infested vinyl, she spoke into it, "*What?*"

"You heard me. So, wrap it up and get moving. Details in your email."

"Do I have time to do my other interview? The suicide club one? I mean, I still gotta write this article, right?"

"Yeah. Fit it in if you can. Make it snappy."

"OK."

"Call me when you're at the airport."

"Uh—" she started, wanting to ask why she'd been deemed worthy of this story instead of someone with more seniority, and why their second tier paper had been deemed worthy of this exclusive. But Phil had hung up already. Jackie cleared her throat and looked at the support group. "Uh, I gotta run."

2 JAMIE

"And if you'll look to your immediate left, you'll see a portrait of our matron, Lady Beth Murphy-Sinclair." Jamie Nguyen looked at her tour group to gauge their focus, then went on, "As you may or may not know, Lady Elizabeth used a substantial portion of the proceeds from the liquidation of her company, Sinclair Industries, to fund the Barbara McClintock Award, which later became the McClintock-Leaky scholarship." She tapped the middle finger of her right hand into the heel of her glove, causing recreations of photographs of McClintock and Mary Leaky to appear from the emitter in the center of the room. "The purpose of the scholarship was to encourage and fund the studies of young women in the science, technology, engineering, and mathematical fields. To say that the scholarship was a success would be a dramatic understatement." She tapped her finger to her palm again, and the emitter switched to a photo of "The Fordham Four" she said, as some of the patrons clapped. "From right to left you will see Ladies Andrea Petrella, Tina Jane "TJ" Stambaugh, Alexis Airth, and last, but certainly not least, Lady Brandi Morse. I'm sure many of you are already plenty familiar with this picture." She craned her neck, looking for something she knew she'd find. "I see one of you likes the picture enough to be wearing it."

The crowed turned to find a young-looking, curly haired woman blush and cross her arms over her chest.

"Now, now. No need to be embarrassed, I'm sure the Ladies would be very flattered." The crowd giggled, as the crowds typically did. "The Fordham Four, realizing that their scientific aptitudes far surpassed that of their fellow students—and most of their professors to be quite honest, concluded that if anyone was going to instruct the future generation of young women, then who better than themselves?" Jamie pointed to the picture. "In the background, the construction site you see?" she rubbed her index finger and thumb together, and the picture zoomed to the prescribed area—the cornerstone plaque that read "Women's Institute of Sciences and Technology, or WIST for short. The building that was built onto that cornerstone? Well, that's the building you're standing in right now." Jamie paused to allow for the patrons' excited murmuring. "Of course, not even the brilliant analytical minds of The Fordham Four could have possibly predicted that their humble little college would become—" fingers double tapped to glove "—this! The Curie Cloister!"

A room-sized holo projection of the campus exploded from the emitter, surrounding the tour group. "The pre-eminent global scientific education and application center! All of the greatest scientific minds on our planet, all under one umbrella, constantly striving to make th—"

"Um, miss?"

Jamie spun around on a boot heel to match the high-pitched voice to the face of the interrupter. Her eyes fell to the face of who appeared to be about a ten year-old girl. So, really about twenty.

"Miss?" the smallish person squeaked.

"Yes?" Jamie answered, trying to stay pleasant.

"Are you never going to answer for the crimes of The Fordham Four?"

"Ma'am, I can assure you—"

Jamie's scripted response was cut short by the lady flinging open her tiny jacket to reveal the most adorable little explosive vest. "I'm taking this whole place."

ZRAAAAAP!

Before she even hit the ground, tiny nanobots would be hard at work, repairing the damage contained within the inch-and-a-half tunnel bored through her skull by Jamie's wrist-mounted laser. They were always taught to aim for the skull, as not only would it instantly incapacitate an attacker, but also disorient them for quite a while after synapses began to fire.

"Someone get her out of here," Jamie barked. Within seconds, two security personnel in grey tunics and severe haircuts scooped up the tiny, drooling not-quite-yet-a-person and took her off; presumably to a "learning room" to be thoroughly interrogated by one of the Intelligence Sisters.

"My apologies. Now if we can re—"

Docent Nguyen! You are to report to the Docent Mother's office, immediately.

"I'm in the middle of a tour!" she grumbled in into the transmitter on her collar.

A sister is on her way to relieve you. Inform your group that they are to remain in place until she arrives.

"Haha, okay, everybody. I've been called to a, uh, meeting, so just sit tight, and another docent will be with you presently. Uh, bye."

3 JACKIE

"So ..." Jackie said, looking around the main room of the Cutting Edge Suicide Club. "This is where all the magic happens. The suicorcry, if you will." The place looked like it had once been a coffee shop. It had that cozy vibe, with all the dark woodwork and the super-hip, multicolor glass light fixtures. Jackie hoped these dorks played acoustic, socially progressive coffee shop jams in the background during their meetings while they were all taking turns offing themselves over and over, or whatever it was they did.

"Yes, ma'am," said the tough, biker-looking guy with a huge beard and an impressive Mohawk. He raised his near-unibrow, did a wide, sweep of the room with a tattooed arm, and said, "You're the lady from the paper."

"Yep. Jackie."

"Have a seat, Jackie." He gestured across the table where he was already seated, phone in hand, probably sending out an evite for the next meeting. Jackie wondered whether suicide clubs were big enough that the evite sites had suicide club themed templates.

As Jackie approached the table, she noted that the club's owners must have bought the furniture off the previous owners. The table and chairs had that distinctly coffee shop look: fake vintage, like some hipster with a perfectly nice set of furniture, a chain, and a can of high-gloss varnish had gone to town on it because Art.

She sat down across from Mohawk, slapped her recorder down on the table, and said, "Thanks for meeting me. I gotta make this quick. Need to get to the airport."

"Cool, cool ..." he said with a shrug.

Jackie looked at him for a few moments, trying drag her brain away from this potential death in Kyoto. This meeting felt suddenly pointless, but, death or not, she still had an article to write for the tenth anniversary of the Greywash. "So you're the owner? Mr.—" she glanced down at her notebook. "Gregory Livingston?"

"I'm known as Trigger in the club."

"Ah. Trigger. Gotcha. So, like, you like shooting yourself, then?"

He nodded.

"OK, Trigger ... uh, I hope you don't mind if I stick to Gregory. Or Greg. Oh, or Gregster."

A crooked smile showed under the depths of his beard. "I detect a note of disdain."

Jackie shrugged.

"You don't approve of our little club?"

Jackie smiled. "I wouldn't say I disapprove, per se. More ... I dunno ... it just seems like a pointless kind of hobby."

"Well we got nothing but time, right? Why not have a pointless hobby? This isn't all I do. You should see my woodworking studio, for instance. Or my vegetable garden."

"Woodworking studio? Is this furniture yours?" Jackie asked, tapping the hipster table.

He shook his head. "Nope."

"Oh good. It's kinda crap."

He grinned. "Came free with the place."

"Speaking of this place, how long has the club been around?"

"Nine years. We were one of the first. Arguably *the* first."

"How many members you got?"

"Lot of people come once, figure out it's not their cuppa tea, and go their way. But we got about twenty regulars."

Jackie nodded and leaned back in her chair. "So, what's an average meeting like? Paint me a picture with your words, Gregster."

"Well, Jackinator." He cleared his throat. "All the meetings are potlucks, so we start out with food and mingling. Then we get together and one of us usually does a talk. And then—"

"Wait, wait. A talk about what?"

"Oh. Yeah, well," he said with a grin. "Ten years of not being able to die, folks have gotten pretty creative about their suicides. Some of them like getting up and explaining. Since the planning and the work that goes into it is half the fun for some of them."

"And for you? Like do you have creative ways of shooting yourself? Like that computer game, ya know, where you make the bowling ball fall on the trampoline and bounce onto the mouse cage, and the mouse runs around an exercise wheel and—"

"And the wheel's attached to a band that turns a conveyor belt that drops a bucket off the belt, and the bucket's tied to the gun which is pointed at my head, and the gun blows my head into a million pieces?"

"Bingo," Jackie said, pointing a finger gun at him and pulling the trigger.

"Yeah, that stunt's totally played out." He grinned at her.

She grinned back, hoping the mild flirting she was picking up was really happening. "Mmm. So, someone does their talk and then …?"

"Well then the freaked out first timers tiptoe out the back door, and we kill ourselves."

Jackie's lips formed a thin line and she nodded. "Messed up, dude."

He shrugged. "Your mindset is exactly why we have this zero-judgement zone of support and camaraderie." He waved a hand at the ex-coffee shop.

"And it's also literally messed up, right? Blood and guts and stuff all over the floor once you're done with your meetings?"

"We got a killer janitor."

"Good thing you don't have carpet, huh?"

"Truth." Then he asked, "So you've never killed yourself, I take it?"

"Nope."

"You should come by for the next meeting. Check it out. Give it a try. You know, for research. My pal, C4, he's gonna take us on a trip out to this field he owns, and he's gonna show us some crazy shit. Dude loves explosives."

"Nah. This interview will give me all the material I need."

"Not curious about what happens?"

"Uh gee, lemme think ... pain, followed by my body reforming, followed by me having to do laundry. I don't like pain and I don't like laundry. So, why bother?"

"The thrill."

"But how's there a thrill if you know you're coming back?"

"I dunno. All I know is the thrill is most definitely there."

"Huh. Yeah. Clearly." Jackie glanced at her phone. "OK, I really gotta run. But one last question."

"Shoot."

Pun? It was hard to tell, coming from Trigger. "Is there any deeper meaning to this for you? Or is it just the thrill?"

"Deeper meaning?"

"Sure. Any philosophical musings about death? Laughing in the face of death? Hoping for death? Whatever." Jackie gave a vague flap of her hand.

Greg frowned at the tabletop as he pondered the question. "Nah. Pretty sure it's just the thrill."

Jackie frowned too. She'd been hoping to get some sort of depth out of this article, but, based on her material so far, it was shaping up to be an empty little piece about people coping with the Greywash in weird, random ways for no reasons that weren't even really all that thoughtful or even interesting. Depth was kinda hard to find these days. Jackie's theory was that a lot of deep thought was the result of pondering death and the meaning of life, and that post-Greywash there was just no urgency anymore to explore those topics, so people just shoved those musings to the back of their brains to rot. Ah well. At least it had been fun chatting with Gregster. Not many folks post-Greywash had maintained a sense of humor. She liked joking around whenever she got a chance.

She stood and said, "Thanks for the interview."

"Yeah, no problem. Don't write too snarky a spin on us. I've read some of your other stories," he said, raising his near-unibrow again.

"No promises, freak," Jackie said as she grabbed her recorder, turned it off, tossed it in her bag. She looked up at him. "You gonna ask me out?"

He raised his almost-eyebrow, and cleared his throat. "Huh?"

Jackie slightly panicked, worried that she'd read him wrong. But she said with false confidence, "Dude. We totally have a thing going on. You know you felt it."

"Well sure. But you think I'm a freak."

Phew. "Pfft. Sure. But you're funny. Funny trumps freak."

He grinned. "Well then. Next Saturday?"

"I'll have to get back to you on that. I got a fancy, exclusive, super-professional journalism thing I gotta do. Not sure how long I'll be gone. International travel, yo. Big story." She nodded slowly. "Impressive, I know."

"Super impressive," He agreed, nodding along with her. "You're soooo out of my league. I am both intimidated and flattered."

"Rightly so," Jackie said, walking to the door. "I'll call you," she added as she saw herself out.

4 JAMIE

Jamie slouched ever-so-slightly and marched down her well-worn path to The Docent Mother's office. It was the one room that she could find her way to from anywhere in The Cloister, and we're talking about someone who had to engage her navigator to find her way from her toilet to her shower. It was like she had an administrative disciplinary homing beacon.

The high-gloss white door slid open with a synthy, but cheerful "Welcome, Docent Nguyen! The Docent Mother is expecting you inside!"

"Jamie, feel free to take your usual seat," came a richer, but decidedly less cheerful contralto from the inner office. Without bothering to look up, Jamie trudged in and flopped down into the chair across from the desk; not realizing that the Docent Mother had recently acquired some wheeled furniture, and her power-flop sent her and the chair careening into the bookcase on the back wall of the small office.

"Make yourself at home, dear," the Docent Mother said, in a monotone that Jamie had come to find was meant to mask amusement. "Perhaps you'd like to knock over a vase? Break a window?"

Jamie carefully wheeled herself back to within the desk's zip code, pulling herself choppily along the tile with her boot heels.

"No, mother. Sorry mother."

The Docent Mother shook her head, the humongous bun on the back of her head swaying slowly like a too-ambitious skyscraper. She'd had the misfortune of having excitably long hair at the moment of the Greywash, and now she was stuck with it. Every few months or so, she'd reach a minor freak out moment and shave it all off, despite being acutely aware that it'd all be back within minutes. "It's totally worth it," she'd told a bemused Jamie once, while she'd sat at her desk misting her temporarily bald head with a spray bottle.

Jamie glanced at the old-style photo on the desk, next to the "Lady April Maxwell, Docent Mother; Director of Archives" name plate. Lady April was one of the only people Jamie could think of that kept photos at all since everyone essentially got laminated; and the people that did keep photos had ones from well before the Greywash. Not the Docent Mother, who was always a bit of an odd duck. She insisted that she have a new portrait photo done every year, in the same pose, in the same outfit, hair pulled the same way. Jamie thought that the Docent Mother must have got a kick out of the Docent Sisters pouring over the photo, struggling to find a difference. But, of course, there were none. Lady April still had the same unruly mop, same nearly-imperceptible crow's feet around her eyes, and the exact-same slightly round face that differentiated her from most of the Mothers with their almost uniform sharpish features.

The Docent Mother gave Jamie a small smile. "You're wondering why you're here?"

"Indeed I am, mother."

The Docent Mother nodded. "At your last performance evaluation, you expressed, shall we say," she raised an eyebrow, "*extreme* interest in being relieved of your duties as a tour guide of the facility. Does that still hold true?"

Jamie frowned. She was pretty sure she knew what this was about. A reminder of the rotten job she was doing. Advice that unless she stepped up her tour guide game she would be stuck as a Docent forever. Jamie thought back to a handful of incidents from her recent tours that might have resulted in formal complaints: the family she'd let loose on because the parents were incapable of reigning in their horrible children, or the know-it-all guy she'd ejected from the facility because every time she answered someone's question, he had chipped in with his own follow-ups and interpretations as though he thought he knew more than her. And then, there'd been the guy who wouldn't stop flirting with her. First, she'd ignored him, then she'd asked him to stop, and then she'd given him a good ten-second cold stare—but he'd just laughed it all off and kept it up. So, she'd shot him in the throat with her handy wrist laser. Jamie knew for a fact that that dude had lodged a formal complaint. As had about half the tour. People were so touchy. Didn't they see he'd had it coming? Didn't they know he'd just get fixed up by the nanobots anyway?

Jamie sighed, "I'm sorry, mother. I've been trying really hard. I swear." The Docent Mother looked at her silently with a crooked smile on her face, so Jamie took a risk and continued, "If you only knew the times I held back, you might actually be impressed I've had so few complaints."

The Docent Mother chuckled. "This is not a reprimand, dear."

Jamie uttered a guarded, "Oh?"

"No. It's an opportunity."

"Oh."

Perhaps Jamie should have felt relieved, but, probably since she was sure she'd done nothing to earn an opportunity and everything to earn a reprimand, all Jamie felt was suspicion.

"Yes, dear. An opportunity for a break. A change of scene. There's an expeditionary research force going to Kyoto tonight, headed up by Lady Morse, and she has requested that you go along."

"Huh?"

The Docent Mother patted her hair into place. "You heard me."

"Why me?" Jamie asked. She wasn't even entirely certain Lady Morse knew who she was. And if Lady Morse did know who she was, that was even more reason for her not to want Jamie along on a research mission.

"No idea," the Docent Mother said, though something about a tightness around her mouth indicated she might know more than she was saying. "So, are you interested?"

"I have an option?" Lady Morse didn't exactly have a reputation for giving options. Her style leaned more toward the demanding.

"Well, not really," the Docent Mother admitted. "I just assumed you'd say yes."

Jamie shifted in her seat. "Fair enough, mother. Anything to get out of tours for a bit. But where's the expedition going?"

"Kyoto," she repeated.

"Do you know what it's about? Any info you can tell me?"

"I should let Lady Morse fill you in." The Docent Mother sighed, gave Jamie a long, level look, and stood up. "The expedition will be leaving in a half hour. I suggest you go to your room to pack."

Jamie blinked. "A half hour?"

"This was a ... well ... last minute thing."

"Clearly. Wow. OK, I guess I gotta pack really quick."

"But you'll want to check in with Lady Morse first."

"Yes, Docent Mother. Uh ... bye, then!"

The Docent Mother gave a little wave.

Jamie went to the door, which slid open and bid her a farewell. In the hall, she stopped short.

One of Lady Morse's assistants, Olivia, was leaning against the wall opposite the door, clearly waiting for Jamie to emerge.

Jamie raised her eyebrows. "Hey Olivia. Waiting for me?"

Olivia nodded. "Yes. I'm supposed to take you to Lady Morse."

"OK."

Without another word, Olivia started walking. Or stomping. It was a distinctly percussive walk she had going on.

Jamie fell into step a few paces behind Olivia, contemplating Olivia's super tight French braid for a few seconds before saying, "Do you know anything about this expedition?"

Olivia looked over her shoulder, raising an eyebrow and studying Jamie intently. "Nope. All I know is Lady Morse got a call fifteen minutes ago, and like a minute later she was planning a trip." She looked around the deserted hall. "And, also, we shouldn't talk about it in front of other people."

"Oh."

Olivia cleared her throat. "Do *you* know anything about it?"

"Nope."

Olivia shot her a glare, clearly thinking she was lying. "No idea why she wanted *you* to accompany her?"

"Seriously. I don't know anything," Jamie said, while wondering how Olivia—who'd graduated top in her class and was now one of Lady Morse's personal assistants—could think that Jamie—who had barely managed to graduate at all and was now a lowly Docent with consistently poor quarterly reviews—knew more than Olivia about anything?

They reached the door at the end of the hallway. It hissed open to let Olivia and Jamie through, then hissed closed behind them. They walked out onto an indoor balcony that encircled the perimeter of a vast, glass-ceilinged atrium with a grand, sweeping staircase in the center. A staircase that no one ever used, because elevators.

As Jamie followed Olivia toward one of the elevators, she glanced down at the shining tile entryway three floors down. There were a few students scuttling hurriedly around, and a tour group was just at that moment walking through the glass front doors and halting dead in their tracks to gape at the atrium.

"Hurry up!" Olivia barked.

"Sorry!" Jamie gasped, hurrying to catch up to Olivia, who had already reached the elevator at the corner of the balcony. Just as Jamie joined her, the elevator doors slid open. The two women stepped into the glass box.

Olivia jabbed the button for the sub-basement.

"Aren't we going to see Lady Morse?" Jamie asked, looking at the glowing button. Lady Morse's office was on the top floor.

"Yes."

"But—"

Olivia clicked a button on her wrist and stared mutely at Jamie as **Lady Morse is currently located in The File,** came the voice of the building's locator service through the elevator speakers.

"Gotcha."

The File. Hence the sub-basement.

Jamie looked down through the glass bottom of the elevator and watched as they zipped downward toward the hole in the floor that led to the basement levels. Jamie gripped the handrail that ran around the perimeter of the elevator, and swallowed heavily. Pre-Greywash, she had hated the glass bottoms of the elevators. Fear of heights. While ten years of invincibility had gone a long way toward making her not as bothered by looking beneath her and seeing nothing but empty space, still, she wasn't exactly comfortable with them.

Jamie looked away from the floor zooming up beneath her, and back at Olivia. "So...The File."

"Mmm." The elevator dropped through the hole in the ground and they were plunged into darkness.

Jamie thought grumpily how nice it must be for Lady Morse that, a half hour before departure for a mystery expedition to Kyoto, she had the ability to mosey on down and peruse the mysterious File room. Clearly, the woman had assistants not only in her office, but also to do her packing. Jamie asked, "Will I have time to go back to my room and get ready for the trip?"

"Dunno."

Lovely.

The elevator stopped at the sub-basement. The doors slid open. Olivia strode out and snapped, "Hurry up."

"Ya know, I can walk there myself—"

"I'm supposed to escort you the whole way. Move. I got other stuff I need to be doing right now."

"Well exxxcccuuuuse me," muttered Jamie as they strode down the bright, spotless hall. There were no doors to their left and right. No pictures, no decorations of any sort. Just lots of cameras and sensors, spaced every few yards along the hall, all blinking and flashing, and making Jamie feel very watched.

There was only one door, at the end of the hall.

A door with a retina scanner, fingerprint sensor, and a keypad for good measure, which seemed like overkill at first. But then, Jamie supposed, the keypad was to stop anyone who might try to break into The File by attacking and mutilating someone with the proper clearance. They'd incapacitate their victim, chop off a finger for the prints, scoop out an eye for the retina scanner, then get to the combo lock and be all like, "Aw darn. I guess I just mutilated that person for nothing! Oops!"

Olivia said, "The combo's 48250," and gestured at the keypad.

"Huh?" Jamie said. "I get to go in?"

She had never been down this hallway before, let alone through the door to The File. She was so far down the ladder at The Cloister that she'd never even considered one day working her way up to the level where she might consider being able to do all the fancy, mysterious stuff that the higher ups got to do, one of which was whatever was involved with The File. She'd barely ever even bothered speculating what The File might be. It was a subject of curiosity for all the students and underlings at The Cloister, and theories abounded. But Jamie had long ago settled on the idea that it was just the records of all past and present students and employees at the facilities, and she'd left it at that.

"Yeah you're coming in," Olivia said, jerking her head toward the open door.

"I don't have the clearance to go in there," Jamie said nervously. At The Cloister, you tried to enter a place you didn't have clearance, you got zapped, disappeared, and interrogated. This she knew from painful experience as an undergrad. She'd opened a door on a dare one time. Two days later, she'd emerged from the Surveillance Mother's lair with ammo for a decade's worth of nightmares and a firm resolve to never again go where she wasn't allowed.

Olivia rolled her eyes. "You have temporary clearance. Obviously. You've been granted it only for an hour window, so don't get any ideas."

"You're sure the clearance went through?" Jamie said, looking at the imposing security measures encrusting the door.

"You wouldn't have made it two steps down this hallway if the clearance hadn't gone through." Olivia nodded again at the door. "48250."

Jamie swallowed and reached for the keypad.

Olivia snapped, "What are you doing!? You wanna get shot?" She jabbed a finger in the direction of a laser mounted on the wall across from the door.

Jamie pulled her hand back as she gasped, "What? You told me—"

"Eye scan first, then fingerprint, then keypad. Honestly. Haven't you ever—"

"No, I haven't ever!" Jamie snapped, her heart racing. "I'm a Docent. I've never done anything like this before!"

Olivia gave her a disdainful look. "A Docent." She sighed and muttered, "A *Docent* gets to go on an expedition with Lady Morse." She shook her head and glared at Jamie.

And it hit Jamie why Olivia was being such a jerk. She was jealous. "Hey," Jamie said, "I didn't ask for this. I have no idea—"

"Just open the door," Olivia grumbled. "Eyes, fingerprint, number."

Jamie squared her shoulders and walked up to the retina scanner, feeling awkward. She stuck her face right in front of it and opened her eye, trying not to blink.

"Left eye, not right," Olivia sighed.

"Of course. Silly me," Jamie muttered. She switched eyes. The thing scanned her and blinked green.

The fingerprint reader was a lot less imposing, but she still had no idea which finger to use. She shot Olivia a quizzical glance.

"Left index," she said with a roll of her eyes.

Jamie did so, and the fingerprint scanner gave her a green blink, too.

She typed 48250 into the keypad, and the door hissed open with a **Good afternoon, Docent Nguyen! Enter. Lady Morse will be with you shortly**.

Jamie walked in, and turned to wait for Olivia.

From the other side of the door, Olivia said, "I gotta do my scans. Be in in a second." The door began to slide shut. "Don't touch anything," she managed to toss at Jamie before the door hissed shut.

Jamie glared at the closed door for a moment and turned to look at The File room. She had to confess she felt let down. She frowned at her surroundings. It was just a stark, small room with bright lights, a plain, black desk, and a computer monitor and keyboard. Granted, a good chunk of the wall behind the computer did have a supercomputer sort of vibe with flashing lights and all that, but still, it was a definite letdown. There were two doors, one to the left and one to the right of the desk. Hopefully the rooms behind those doors were where the sci-fi action was.

Lady Morse was not there. Jamie was really starting to freak out about getting her stuff packed in time.

She took a few steps toward the comfy-looking swivel chair.

She glanced at the desk. There was a plain, black briefcase lying by the keyboard.

Jamie looked at the monitor.

As she did so, a sentence appeared: ***Docent Nguyen?***

Jamie stared at the screen.

I have been hoping for a chance to talk to you.

Jamie looked wildly around, then back at the screen.

The words had changed: **No time now. When you can, take Lady Morse's flash drive. We will talk then.**

Jamie gaped at the screen as the door behind her hissed open and greeted Olivia.

The words on the screen disappeared.

Jamie turned to Olivia and gave a nervous laugh.

Olivia narrowed her eyes. "What?"

"What what?"

"You're acting weird. I told you not to touch anything. What did you do?"

"Nothing. Nothing. I just ... I'm ... uh ... it's just all the security and stuff ..."

Jamie tried hard not to look at the computer. Then she started to worry that she looked like she was avoiding looking at the computer. So, she looked at the computer. Then she felt weird about that and looked away again.

"Mmm …" Olivia said, eyes still narrowed as she studied Jamie's face. She glanced at the blank monitor, then at the swivel chair, as though she thought Jamie might have decided to sit down and have a good spin while Olivia had been gaining admittance to the room.

Jamie said, "Do you know where Lady Morse is? Are you sure this is where—"

From behind the door to the left of the desk, a toilet whooshed. Ah. Well, no mysterious sci-fi action was going on behind Door Number One, then.

The bathroom door slid open so quickly that Jamie had to wonder whether Lady Morse had washed her hands. Or hand. Did one have to wash one's mechanical hand? How did that work?

Lady Morse took in Olivia and Jamie at a glance, and said, "Thank you for being so prompt, ladies. Olivia, before you leave, see to Docent Nguyen's weekly bloodwork."

"Yes, Lady Morse," Olivia said as she reached her hand into a pocket and pulled out a syringe and elastic band.

Jamie said, "Oh, I just had my bloodwork done day the before yesterday. I don't need—"

"I don't know how long we'll be gone. It might be more than a week," Lady Morse explained.

Jamie nodded, held out her arm to Olivia, and watched as Olivia put the band around her arm. As Olivia poked the needle none too gently into Jamie's arm, Jamie asked, "More than a week, eh?"

"Perhaps," Lady Morse said, watching the vial fill with blood. As far back as Jamie could remember, there had been these weekly blood draws. She'd been told as a child that she was part of a long-term study that The Cloister was running on individuals with her blood type.

Olivia finished up, pocketed the vial, and threw away the needle in the trash receptacle by the door.

Lady Morse said, "Thank you, Olivia. You may go." Then, she strode over to the computer, the soles of her sensible, gray shoes squeaking slightly on the tile floor. "One moment, Docent Nguyen," she said, then began typing.

Olivia looked away from Lady Morse, gave Jamie a silent glare, and then left the room without a word.

Jamie stood in the center of the room, thinking about how utterly bizarre it was that Lady Morse's computer had just typed a message at her. She wondered whether it was a prank. Perhaps a weird way to test her loyalty. Maybe Lady Morse had sent it from her phone in the bathroom.

Lady Morse typed away for a few moments, her mechanical fingers clacking loudly away, and her flesh fingers making a lot less noise. Then, she clicked on something and said over her shoulder, "Right. One moment." She moved her mechanical hand from the keyboard to the table and tapped impatiently.

Finally, the computer gave one beep.

Lady Morse pulled a flash drive out of its spot on the side of the monitor.

Jamie felt a jolt as she looked at it. The flash drive. Was that the one she was supposed to take? She watched as Lady Morse opened the briefcase and put the flash drive somewhere inside it. Well, with any luck, Lady Morse would keep that briefcase on her at all times, and Jamie would never have a chance to get near it.

Lady Morse said, "My apologies, Docent Nguyen, for my less than friendly greeting. I'm in a hurry. We can talk on the ride to the airport."

"The *public* airport, Lady Morse?"

"Yes, the public airport."

"Oh." She frowned, unsure how she felt about rubbing elbows with random citizens. Her experience mingling with non-Cloister people was limited to tours, where they were generally going out of their way to adhere to the rules of the institution. She wanted to ask Lady Morse why they weren't using the private airfield.

Lady Morse guessed her thoughts. "I have my reasons for flying commercial." She smiled slightly and added, "Sometimes, hardships such as these are unavoidable when one is attempting to avoid notice." She snapped her briefcase shut, and said, "Let's move." And she walked to Door Number Two. It slid open to reveal a small elevator. Jamie frowned her disappointment. Nothing cool behind that door, either.

Once inside, standing uncomfortably close to Lady Morse in the tight space, Jamie noticed that instead of a button for each floor of the building, there were four unmarked buttons. Lady Morse pushed the second one from the top and the elevator began to ascend.

"Private elevator," Lady Morse explained.

"Hmm." Jamie supposed the other three buttons went to the offices of Ladies Stambaugh, Petrella, and Airth. If Lady Morse had private access to The File, then so must they.

The elevator zipped right on up to Unmarked Button Number Two's destination, and the door slid open. They walked into Lady Morse's office, but Lady Morse rushed her through so quickly that Jamie just had a fleeting impression of bookshelves, blue upholstered furniture, and a floor-to-ceiling window, before she was led out a door beside the huge window.

As she stepped onto the rooftop walkway behind Lady Morse, a cold blast of air hit Jamie, tossing her hair in her face. She promptly took the hairband off her wrist (a lifetime of curly hair had taught her a thing or two), and she did a hasty ponytail. Over the wind, she heard the unmistakable sound of helicopter blades up ahead. Jamie clenched her teeth and frowned. They were flying to the airport, now. Which meant she would not be packing for this trip. Which meant she'd be wearing her Docent uniform every day in Kyoto unless she had a chance to go shopping. She would have loved to have gone incognito in Kyoto instead of getting weird looks from everyone.

They rounded the corner, and, sure enough, there was the helicopter. Jamie climbed after Lady Morse into the helicopter.

Lady Morse handed her a headset which she put on, blocking out the sound.

Lady Morse's voice filled her head. "Where's your suitcase?"

5 JACKIE

Jackie wheeled her suitcase through the congested airport, amazed that she'd managed to interview Gregster, do a spot of flirting, and make it to the airport with time to spare. She glanced at her ticket. Gate 41.

There it was, up ahead.

And not a single seat in the waiting area was open. So, Jackie zeroed in on a nerdy-looking, scrawny guy sitting near an electrical outlet. She wheeled her suitcase over to him, stood uncomfortably close, pulled out her phone, and began talking to the fake person on the other end. "Omigosh, Dorcas! He DIDN'T! No! Poor Carlo!"

She gave Dorcas a chance to respond. Probably something about how Dorcas had cheated on Carlo with his best friend.

After an appropriate pause, Jackie went on, "Haha, grrl, you are in so much trouble! What did he SAY?"

Out of the corner of her eye, she saw Nerd look up at her with irritation.

She kept up the conversation with Dorcas.

Nerd began to grumble and glare more openly.

Still ignoring him, she cackled and rested her hand on the back of his chair, getting as close as possible without leaning against him. "Dude! Dorcas! You are such an absolute SKANK!" She let out another guffaw. "He's gonna leave you, girl! You know that, right?"

Nerd muttered with what he probably thought was attitude, "*Excuse me.*"

Jackie looked down at him, put her hand over the receiver, and said, "Dude, this is *awful*! My friend Dorcas—she—well you just gotta hear it. Want me to put it on speaker?"

"No! I just want some peace and quiet!"

Jackie shrugged. "Your loss." Then she went back to her call. "Dorcas, there's this major perv trying to eavesdrop right now. I think he wants your number." She grinned at Nerd.

He gave her a final glare, bolted out of his seat, grabbed his duffel bag, and darted off.

"You sitting here anymore?" Jackie called after him.

He stuck up his middle finger without looking back.

She sat down in her hard-won seat, and congratulated herself on a job well done. Then, she dialed Phil as she rummaged around in her bag for her computer and cord.

"You at the airport yet, Jacks?" Phil asked by way of a greeting.

"Yep."

"And you read your email?"

"Turning on my computer now," Jackie said, propping the phone between her ear and shoulder as she untangled the computer cord, then plugged it first into the outlet and then into the computer. "So, Phil. Is this a confirmed thing? Like a real—" she glanced left and right to see if anyone was listening. "*A real death?*"

"It's all in the email. What little information there is, anyway."

"Aw come on. Can't you tell me anything?" She opened her computer and turned it on. "Like why am I the one who got this job? Why not Farrand or Jones or someone?"

Phil cleared his throat. "Ah, well that's something that's not in the email. Lady Brandi Morse requested you, specifically."

Jackie was in danger of dropping her phone for the second time in one day. "Lady Morse? Like The Fordham Four Lady Morse? The Cloister Lady Morse?"

"That's the one."

Jackie took a few moments to try to think that through. It made no sense. She'd never met the woman. Never. She'd have remembered.

Phil broke the silence with, "Any idea why she wanted you?"

"All I can figure is it's a mistake."

"That's what I figured too, at first. But she referenced a few of your articles."

"Well wow. I mean, I am an awesome reporter," Jackie said, joking-not-joking. "I guess she just read my genius work and knew I was the one for the job ...?"

"Sure. Whatever. The whys really don't matter, Jacks. She wants you and you're going. You're gonna be with her group from The Cloister. They're going on some expedition thing to look into this supposed death and we're getting an exclusive—on the condition that we don't leak the information, that is—and that's all I have the time and energy to care about."

"I assume their contact info's in the email?"

"Yup. But I think they'll be on the same flight as you."

"Oh." Jackie looked up from her slowly booting computer. She scanned the crowd. Lady Morse would be easy to spot, due to her mechanical arm and leg. Sure enough, there she was, a tall woman with untidy, short hair and a well-tailored jacket and pants in the distinct deep blue tone worn by the women at The Cloister. She was talking with a flight attendant at the gate.

"See ya, Phil," Jackie said, hanging up on Phil in the middle of whatever he was saying. She snapped her computer shut again, stowed it in her bag, relinquished her seat, and moseyed up behind Lady Morse, totally not eavesdropping one little bit.

Lady Morse was saying to the man behind the desk, "I'll need security waiting for us the moment we land. They will escort us out of the terminal and deliver us to the private security waiting for me at the Kyoto airport. You can see to this, yes?"

"Yes, Lady Morse," the guy answered quickly. "I'll see to it."

"Excellent." She turned and nearly ran into Jackie. Lady Morse stopped short, and raised her eyebrows. "Ms. Savage!"

"Yes indeed. Hi, Lady Morse!" Jackie stuck out her hand.

A smile flickered across Lady Morse's face. She looked down at Jackie's hand for a moment before taking it. "Thank you for coming on such short notice, Ms. Savage."

"No problem. Thank you for the opportunity." Jackie fell into step beside Lady Morse as the woman led her toward two other women who were wearing clothing of the same deep blue, though their uniforms didn't have that fancy, tailored look like Lady Morse's did. They must not be nearly as important at The Cloister.

"I'm glad you were able to come along. An expedition like this, with a story this potentially significant—it will be important to have a reporter on board," Lady Morse said as she sat down in a spot that one of the two young women in blue was saving for her.

Jackie asked, "If you don't mind my asking ... why did you ask me along on this thing? Doesn't The Cloister have its own in-house press?" As she spoke, Jackie looked at the other two women in blue. One had short, spiky hair, and was reading a book. A physical, paper book. She looked up at Jackie with a friendly grin, then looked back down at the book.

The other Cloister drone had long, curly hair so much like Jackie's in texture that Jackie made a mental note to ask her what products she used to get rid of the frizz—probably some fancy stuff dreamed up in a Cloister lab and not available to the public. Jackie frowned at Curly, who was not looking at Jackie's face, but was sizing up her body. When she did meet Jackie's gaze a few seconds later, Jackie had a glare waiting for her. The young woman bit her lip and had the decency to look apologetic. Jackie eyed her a few seconds more, noting that she looked vaguely familiar.

Lady Morse, oblivious to the weirdness between her traveling companions, had sat down and began tapping away at a tablet she'd pulled out of the luggage at her side. Still looking at the tablet, she said, "I want you here, Ms. Savage, because I like your writing. I make a point of supporting talented young women getting started in their careers, whether in The Cloister or out of it." She tapped a bit more at her screen. "If you'll excuse me, I need to make a call."

She stood again and walked off.

Without missing a beat, Jackie took her chair. She looked back at Curly. "What?"

"What what?" the girl asked, eyes darting to Jackie's face.

The spikey-haired girl remained buried in her book.

Jackie said, "I don't like people ogling me. Don't do it."

"Sorry. It's not like that. I swear I'm not being creepy. I just—you see," she leaned forward and rested her elbows on the knees of her blue pants, "I didn't have time to pack, and you look like you're my size, and your suitcase is huge, so I was wondering if since you're coming with us you might be able to lend me something because I really don't want to wear my Docent uniform—"

Jackie held up a hand to silence the onslaught of over-explaining. "You're allowed to wear normal clothes? Isn't it against some sort of Cloister rules?"

"Nah. It's kinda frowned on, I guess, but when we're off campus ..." she trailed off with a shrug. "No way I'm wearing the same clothes day after day for however long this expedition's gonna be."

"Dude, I don't wanna lend you my clothes."

"Aw come on! I'll get them cleaned and everything."

"Oh fine. You can raid my suitcase, but my clothes are totally not your style. If Lady Morse gets mad that I let you borrow non-uniform stuff, though, you can forget about it. This is gonna be a super awesome story if it's real, and I don't wanna get kicked off for helping you break your weird, culty rules."

"Culty rules?"

"Totally. You Cloister people are super creepy. Such a cult."

That earned Jackie an eyebrow raise from Spikey-hair and a glare from her new friend.

Jackie asked, "What are your names, anyway? I'm Jackie."

"Jamie," said Jamie.

Jackie looked at Spikey-hair, who looked up from her book again. "I'm Claire."

Apparently not wanting to let the cult jab go undefended, Jamie said, "Aren't science and cults sorta at odds? How's that work? Since when do cults encourage critical, independent thought?"

Jackie shrugged. "Good question."

"So we're a bunch of drones? Highly educated in logic and the scientific method, and yet we can be led astray like some mindless morons? I'd have thought the higher your education level the less inclined you'd be to fall for tricks and lies."

"Depends on the kind of education, I guess," Jackie said, enjoying getting under Jamie's skin. "There's all kinds of knowledge, right? And all kinds of ways of obtaining it. And if your teachers are brainwashing you ... well ..."

Jamie frowned. "Well yeah ... but The Cloister's not like that."

"How would you know? All you know is what they've told you."

"Still. Science. The scientific method. You can't fake the scientific method."

"But you can fake the stats obtained through the research done through that scientific method, right?"

"But—"

"Isn't science only as unbiased as the scientists who are doing the studies? What if The Cloister has an agenda, buddy?"

Jamie frowned and ground her teeth.

Jackie went on, greatly enjoying herself, "And maybe they're so busy covering up The Greywash that they tell all sorts of crazy lies and skew studies to put people's focus elsewhere, like—"

Jamie cut her off, saying with a roll of her eyes and a condescending smirk, "The Cloister did not cause The Greywash. I know that's what people like to say, but—"

"Sure they did! All the coolest conspiracy theorists say so. The Cloister caused The Greywash, and unleashed all those little nanobots on the population to keep everyone in stasis for ... uh ... reasons."

Jamie snorted, "Nice. For reasons."

"Yep. Reasons. Like, uh, they know the aliens are gonna attack so they've made an invincible army to protect the planet from the aliens' advanced weaponry. Or there's the one about how as the nanobots fix our bodies they read our minds, and they're making a big database on the population so that law enforcement will be able to—"

"That is so stupid."

Jackie said, "Look, maybe I'm wrong. I dunno. But I'm just saying, outside looking in, The Cloister looks weird. And if they didn't do The Greywash, who did? No one ever owned up. But if anyone has the technology to pull off something huge like that, it's them. It's you guys. Right?"

Jamie shrugged, apparently no longer in the mood to rise to Jackie's bait. "Whatever."

Jackie pressed on, "And even if they're not a cult, they are huuuuge jerks. I mean, for instance, that drug they have to make it so brain cells can still make new connections? How horrible and unethical that that drug is so expensive. Poor people aren't allowed to learn anymore? That's—"

"The drug is hard to make. The treatments take time and—"

"Yeah, yeah. Justify it however you want. I'm drowning in debt because of those treatments. And there are like millions of people who probably wish they could be drowning in debt, given the alternative of having a brain that can't learn."

Jamie shrugged and looked away.

Awkward silence descended on them. Claire glanced up at them. Jackie wondered whether she'd been listening, or whether she'd been too immersed in her book.

A minute or two elapsed. Jamie was still frowning.

Jackie cleared her throat and broke the silence. "You guys know what this is all about?" She leaned closer to them and whispered, "You know ... the death?"

Claire hissed, "Sshh!"

Jamie added, "Yeah, didn't Lady Morse forward you the info? We're not supposed to discuss it."

"Oh. Right. I haven't had a chance to read it yet ..."

Jackie quickly got her laptop out again so she could, at last, check that email. Jackie was too busy staring at the screen to notice Lady Morse had returned until she heard a pointed throat clearing over her left shoulder. Jackie looked up, saw Lady Morse, and hopped out of the seat. "Oh. Uh, just saving your seat for you there, Lady Morse. Take a load off."

"You're too kind," Lady Morse said, making herself comfortable while Jackie sat cross-legged on the ground and logged into her email.

There it was, forwarded to her from Phil. She scanned past the greetings, and read:

It is my hope that the paper will be able to spare Ms. Savage for approximately a week, and that she will be able to join our expeditionary research force in Kyoto. It appears that this alleged death may have a connection to George Okada—initial tests have shown that the alleged deceased is likely a descendent of Mr. Okada. Since Ms. Savage wrote a biographical piece on Mr. Okada in celebration of his 50th birthday five years ago, we may be able to use the connections she made while researching Mr. Okada.

It goes without saying, but I'll say it anyway: there should be, of course, no communication about the reason for this expedition in public. It is of the utmost importance that we keep this quiet until we have solid facts.

Looking forward to meeting Ms. Savage at the airport this evening. Flight information attached.

Lady Brandi Morse

Jackie frowned at the screen. Her piece on George Okada. She barely remembered it, but, from what she did recall, it had not exactly been her greatest work. She'd been in a rebellious phase as a writer then, and it had showed—in a way she was now less than thrilled with, since her future potential bosses wouldn't be impressed with the defiant statement about senseless writing rules that she'd thought her Okada piece at the time. Jackie cringed at the thought that that piece might have been what got her this job.

She focused on her computer again, and opened the folder where she stored all her old projects. She opened the Okada folder and double checked that she still had the contact information for the people she'd interviewed for the story. Then, she glanced at the screen behind the gate desk, saw that she still had some time before boarding, and opened the Okada piece to refresh her memory:

George Okada was a man who generally lived a less-than-remarkable life. But, on a few *very* specific instances, his life was somehow even less-than-less-than-remarkable.

He was born to wholly unspectacular parents named Alejandro and Frances Okada, both of whom grew up in the same town, had a run-of-the-mill courtship, a perfectly passable wedding, bought an unspectacular house, performed serviceably at uninspiring jobs, and, in the fullness of time, conceived their apex-of-averageness son, George.

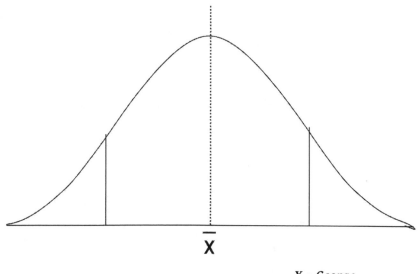

X = *George*

Not one to rock the boat (which, incidentally, got him fired from his job on the "Terrors of the Deep" ride at Universal Studios) George settled into the unexamined life, in an apartment that would have been too drab for Stalinist Russia; the whole of his worldly possessions consisting of four unexamined books—all four out-of-sequence novelizations of t.v. franchises, a pile of uniforms from prior jobs that he didn't have the energy to throw away; a television, sans remote, that would remain off permanently due to the inconveniently placed onboard buttons; and a car that *Auto Enthusiast Quarterly* described as

¯_(ツ)_/¯

George's social life consisted of actively avoiding social situations, and drinking terrible beer on a beige chair on his sort-of-okay lawn in his backyard. In addition to the beer, he'd often enjoy—well, "enjoy" might be too strong of a word. He'd often consume a so-so takeout meal, usually from the same place—provided that the delivery person didn't start to get chatty, in which case, he'd switch to an equally okay restaurant.

In fact, it was George's proclivity for takeout and lawn sits that set the stage for his completely expectable heart failure, which shuffled him loose the mortal coil at the on-the-button average age of death for an American male, that at that exact moment was seventy-nine years old. He left no one behind, and his passing would probably have gone undiscovered for a very long time, if he hadn't taken home the keys to the downstairs employees' bathroom. No one, outside of those intrepid key retrievers, probably would have even remembered George, if not for the fact that his death actually was very remarkable in a way other than people having to walk an extra hundred and fifty feet to find a functional bathroom.

See, on June 16, 2044 at 5:03:48 pm, George Eduardo Okada, of Pasadena Maryland, became the last person on Earth to die.

Jackie was glad she'd reread it. It wasn't as bad as all that. The slight unprofessional air could even, hopefully, be seen as refreshing. Daring. She felt a stab of fondness for the punk kid she'd been five years back.

When the article had been printed, she had fully expected the people she'd interviewed about George to call her up and complain about what a loser she'd made him out to be. But the calls had never come. In retrospect, she supposed they hadn't even read the article. They'd all—every one of them—been pretty confused about why she'd been calling them in the first place. They'd all been shocked that her research had indicated they'd been the closest people to George. Not one of them had really known him well, or considered him a friend.

It wasn't until Jackie had shut her laptop and stowed it back in her bag that it hit her:

A direct descendent of George Okada.

Okada had reproduced?

No chance.

And how super weird was it that this supposed death was connected to Okada, the last person to have died before The Greywash? What were the odds of that? Two huge death stories in one family. It felt weird. Conspiracy theory level weird.

But, there was no way a guy as boring as that could have gotten a lady. And—in the unlikely event that George would have taken a leap so utterly far outside the realm of his comfort zone and hired a prostitute—they surely used birth control.

Thus, there was not a single, solitary chance in Hell that George Okada had descendants.

Jackie looked up at Lady Morse, wanting to ask her how sure she was about this Okada connection.

It was then that Lady Morse's phone rang. She answered it with a curt, "Yes?" There was a pause in which she sat bolt upright and began to scan the crowded terminal. "At the airport? You're sure?"

While the person on the other end answered, Lady Morse stood and signaled for Jackie, Jamie, and Claire to follow as she walked to the man at the gate.

The three got their belongings and trailed after Lady Morse, shooting each other confused shrugs as they went.

Lady Morse said into her phone, "Right. Well he's not here yet. I'm boarding now. I'll do what I can on my end, but it'll be a temporary fix. When you get here, iron out the details. Call me when it's done." She looked over her shoulder one last time, then said to the man behind the desk, "We need to board the airplane now."

"I'm sorry, Lady Morse, we aren't allowed—"

"Yes, yes. All the same, you will let my companions and me on the plane. Immediately." She looked over her shoulder once more at the crowd, then back at him.

The guy quailed under her glare. "But—protocol—"

"I have ways around your protocols. I just need to be sure you won't call security while my people work." She struck her mechanical fist on the desk in front of him. She growled, "Now."

"Yes, Lady Morse. If you'll just wait a moment—I need to talk to my boss. Safety measures—an alarm—"

Lady Morse snapped her fingers at Claire. "See to the alarms."

"Yes, Lady Morse," Claire said, then hurried to the alcove where the door to their plane was. Claire began fussing at the security controls, calm as could be, as though disabling security systems was no big deal.

Lady Morse pointed Jamie to the alcove as well. Jamie complied.

Jackie bit her lip and looked at the people waiting for their flight. Quite a few were watching them with mute curiosity. But none of them, not even the red-faced, aggressive-looking businessman sitting near the door, had spoken up. Such was the effect of the intimidating presence of a high-level Cloister personage.

"Ms. Savage," Lady Morse said.

Jackie turned to see Lady Morse gesturing her toward the gate.

"Come—" But she stopped short, looking over Jackie's shoulder, alarmed. "On second thought, Ms. Savage, I need a favor. Now." As she spoke, she took Jackie by the arm and pulled her into the alcove near Claire. Jackie had the distinct feeling Lady Morse was trying to hide.

"What the—" Jackie started.

"That man over there," Lady Morse pointed past Jackie and down the crowded terminal. "The one with the hat."

"You mean the fat guy in the stupid fedora?"

"Yes. Him."

"What about him?"

"Stop him. He can't see us."

"Stop him? H—how?" Jackie stuttered.

"Whatever it takes," Morse said, putting a hand on Jackie's back and giving her a shove as Fedora drew closer. He was walking slow, looking left and right, clearly searching for someone. "Distract him until we are through the door. Then join us."

"But—"

"Go!" Lady Morse growled, the one syllable and accompanying shove conveying quite a bit of urgency.

Jackie found herself scurrying off to stop Fedora from spotting the ladies in blue, wondering as she went why the Cloister broads hadn't gone incognito if they were supposed to be sneaking.

She swallowed and tried to think. Her limbs feeling strangely numb, she looked back nervously at Lady Morse.

The woman shot her a glare, mouthed "Move!", and swatted her hands at Jackie.

Jackie curled her lip, and turned back to Fedora. This was insane. He was huge. She really wished Lady Morse had brought a bodyguard along on this mission, because Jackie was not thug material. Not at all. She scanned her surroundings, muttering under her breath. To her left, there was an unattended cart with a few big suitcases on it.

She glanced at Lady Morse, who shot her an impatient glare, as though it was somehow taken for granted that this fell within the realm of Jackie's duties.

Once Fedora was taken care of and they were somewhere without bystanders, Jackie was going to have some choice words with Lady Morse about what reporters did and did not do. Never mind that Lady Morse was powerful and intimidating and could probably crush her trachea with that mechanical hand. There was no way Jackie was going along on an expedition where she was expected to act as the muscle.

Jackie sighed, gritted her teeth, and darted over to the cart. Luck was on her side—the owners of the luggage didn't notice her stealing it. And Fedora was too busy narrowing his eyes at a woman in a blue coat to notice Jackie as she began to push the cart at him.

She picked up speed.

He turned his head, and spotted the cart careening toward him.

Too late.

The cart caught him in the shins, knocked him to the ground, and rolled over him, trapping him underneath. He was writhing in pain and howling. He was attracting quite a crowd. For a few moments, Jackie was paralyzed by indecision. Should she pretend it had been an accident? If she lingered, the real owners of the luggage would be sure to realize their belongings were involved, and would raise the question of what she'd been doing with their stuff. On balance, Jackie decided slinking into the crowd would be best.

So, she slunk.

All the way back to the alcove where Lady Morse and Jamie were standing in the shadows while Claire kept fussing with the security panel.

Lady Morse gave her a short nod of approval, said, "Interesting choice," then snapped at Claire, "Any time now."

The guy behind the desk kept looking shiftily from them to the scene he must have known Jackie had caused.

"I'm just ... almost ..." Claire muttered. "There! Try the door. The alarm shouldn't go off."

"You're sure about that?" Lady Morse asked with narrowed eyes.

"Uh. Yes," Claire said, glancing at the door and biting her lip.

"You don't look sure," Lady Morse pointed out, her gaze shifting from Claire to the howling pile of rage and luggage that was Fedora.

"Uh ..." said Claire. She shrugged.

Lady Morse sighed and tried the door. It swung open without a sound. "In," she said to Jamie, Claire, and Jackie. As they filed past her with their luggage, Lady Morse hung back for a few moments to have words with the guy at the gate. The three younger women turned and waited, watching Lady Morse through the crack in the door. Her chat with the guy didn't last long, but the look of fear on his face showed quite plainly that he was being thoroughly intimidated.

"What do you think she's saying to him?" Jackie muttered at Jamie.

Jamie grinned. "I have some ideas."

Claire laughed, "He'll stay quiet, that's for sure."

Lady Morse joined them then, nodding down the walkway toward the plane, and saying, "Move. We can talk on the plane."

"You're sure that guy's not gonna tell the fedora dude where we are?" Jackie asked.

"I'm sure. Besides, someone is coming to see to the fallout."

Jackie's eyes widened. "See to the fallout?" she asked. "What's that supposed to mean? If you've got a thug coming to 'see to fallout', shouldn't they come along with us? So I don't have to do anything like that thing with the cart again?"

But Lady Morse was striding on ahead to talk to the flight attendants, who were stepping out of the plane and looking poised to start throwing around lines about rules and protocol. Lady Morse got in the first word though, with a "You'll want to be quiet and listen to what I have to say."

The attendants stopped and waited for her to approach.

While Lady Morse threatened the airline staff in whispers, Jackie walked past them and onto the plane. She was pretty excited about flying first class on an international flight. Swanky stuff.

Jackie found her seat, stowed her luggage, and flopped down. Window seat. Score. She hoped Lady Morse didn't have the seat by her. But Jamie and Claire filed in after her and took the seats behind her. So, Lady Morse would be her neighbor for the flight.

Jackie turned and knelt on her seat, peering over the back at her companions. "So," she said. "A death, huh?"

"Yep," said Jamie. "That's what they're saying."

"Do you have any information about it?"

"Nah," Claire said, shaking her head.

"Nope," Jamie agreed. "We only just found out about it like, what, three hours ago?" She looked at Claire, who nodded.

"Same here," Jackie chipped in. "Weird what a hurry Lady Morse is in. And how it's so secret. Right? Like don't you guys have a jet or two? Why not take those? She doesn't want Cloister people to know she's going?"

Claire shrugged, and pulled out her book again. "I guess. Look, not to be rude, but I gotta read this."

"No worries," Jackie said and directed her attention at Jamie. "Any idea why the commercial flight?"

"Not really ... Uh, maybe all the Cloister jets were out?"

"Perhaps ..." Jackie said doubtfully, secretly holding onto her idea that Lady Morse wanted to keep her trip quiet from her pals at The Cloister. She changed the subject, "So what's your job at The Cloister?"

Jamie nodded down the aisle past Jackie.

Jackie turned to see Lady Morse walking their way, still on her phone. The woman was listening silently, her eyes narrowed. She asked, "You're certain it's taken care of? No one will remember?"

Jackie turned and slid down the back of her chair to sit, eavesdropping her heart out as Lady Morse sat down beside her. One of the flight attendants scurried after her and stowed Lady Morse's suitcase for her, then attempted to take her briefcase. Lady Morse shook her head and kept it in her lap. As the flight attendant walked off, Lady Morse spoke into the phone, "Sorry about that. Didn't want to be overheard. Excellent. Thank you for dealing with the witnesses. And Wharton has been seen to?" The person on the other end responded, bringing a laugh—almost a cackle—to Lady Morse's lips. "Perfect. More than he deserves."

Jackie raised her eyebrows, wondering what on earth had happened to 'the witnesses' and Wharton, and whether Wharton was Fedora.

"Right. I'll check back in at my next opportunity." Lady Morse hung up. She turned and met Jackie's gaze. "You caught all that?"

Jackie's lips formed a thin line as she considered whether to pretend she hadn't been listening. "Yep. Well, only the stuff on your end, of course. You should really turn your volume up. Is Wharton the guy I battered with that cart?"

"Clever girl."

"And how'd your pal on the other end of that call deal with the witnesses?"

Lady Morse frowned. "Hmm. Now's not the time to share that."

"Aw come on."

Lady Morse shook her head. "Keep an eye on my briefcase. I'll be right back." She stood, set it on her seat, and walked to the bathroom at the front of the plane.

ᒪ JAMIE

Jamie, sitting behind Lady Morse, saw her get up and leave her briefcase. Her thoughts flew immediately to the computer screen back at The File, and the flash drive she'd seen Lady Morse put in that bag. For a few moments, she was frozen, still wondering whether this was some elaborate test of her loyalty. She got up, scooted past Claire, grabbed Lady Morse's briefcase off the seat, sat down, and rested the briefcase on her lap. She grinned at Jackie. "So, thanks for letting me borrow some clothes!" She glanced at the bathroom door. *Nothing suspicious going on, Lady Morse. I'm just sitting here gabbing with my new pal, Jackie, about clothes, how girls do. Just gabbing away. I'm totally not trying to reach into your briefcase.*

"No problem," Jackie said. "As long as you treat them well."

"No worries." Jamie began to run her hands over the briefcase.

Jackie nodded.

Jamie cleared her throat and tried to think of some small talk. She wasn't too great at striking up random conversations. Nor, apparently, was Jackie, which struck Jamie as odd, considering Jackie's profession. "So ..."

"Yeah ..."

"Uh ... Ever been to Kyoto?"

"Nope. You?"

"Nope. Never even left the city before. I've pretty much lived in The Cloister my whole life."

"No way. You one of those orphans that grew up there?"

"Yep."

Jackie turned and stared, her interest clearly piqued. "No way."

"Yep." Jackie was now giving Jamie far too much focus for Jamie to unobtrusively manhandle the briefcase.

Jackie leaned in close, eyes wide, voice eager. "Ooh. Know what? I would totally love to do a story on you. Growing up behind the walls of The Cloister and all that. What's it like with no boys around, no popular culture, et cetera. Something separate from this death article. Cool?"

"Er," Jamie said. She ran her fingers over the zipper of the main pocket of the briefcase. Her hope was to find out where the flash drive was so she could steal it easier later. If she got another chance. And if she actually decided to take it at all. Which would be insane.

"Uh, I dunno."

A flight attendant walked up then and asked, "Is there anything I can bring you ladies? Anything to make your flight more comfortable? Food, drink, entertainment?"

Jackie said, "Seriously?"

The flight attendant nodded.

"First class is the best, huh?" Jackie said. "Um ... do you have a menu?"

As the flight attendant handed her a menu, Jamie took advantage of Jackie's distraction and unzipped the briefcase, covering the zipping sound with a cough. While Jackie muttered about how awesome it was she could order a steak and champagne, Jamie felt frantically around for the flash drive. Right when her panic about being spotted by Jackie or a returning Lady Morse was at its height, she felt the flash drive in a little pocket. To steal, or not to steal? Jamie panicked for a moment. But no, she knew where it was now. She could get it later.

Jackie handed the menu back. "Thanks, dude."

"Would you like to place an order, ma'am?"

"Nah. I just wanted to see how swanky your offerings were."

The flight attendant gave her a weird look. "Yes, ma'am. Well, if you change your mind, don't hesitate to ask."

"Right." Jackie nodded and watched the flight attendant walk away, then turned to Jamie. "So, seriously, an article about you. Seriously. People think you Cloister orphans are crazy weird. Don't you wanna educate the public?"

"Geez, I dunno." Jamie muttered, painfully aware that her hand was still in the briefcase.

"People would looooove it. Have you heard of Behind the Walls? It's a series of books about this chick named Tamara who's a Cloister orphan."

Jamie rolled her eyes. "Yes. I've heard mention of it. It's supposed to be horribly cheesy and inaccurate."

"Fun, you mean. They're total trash, but they're the best. The first few are totally coming of age things, then she breaks out in book five and falls in love with this awesome taxi driver who—well—I don't wanna give it away. Point is, people'd eat up a story about a real-life Tamara."

"Except I'm very boring."

Jackie shrugged. "I'll put a fun spin on it." She scooted around in her big, comfy, first class seat and focused her attention out the window. "Think about it, would you?"

"Sure ..."

Lady Morse walked out of the bathroom.

Jamie removed her hand with a spasmodic jerk. Jackie, looking back from the window at just the wrong moment, saw and narrowed her eyes.

Jamie ignored her and began to cough again to mask the sound as she zipped the briefcase closed.

Jamie's heart was hammering as she watched Lady Morse approach. She tried to play it cool and look innocent while knowing Jackie knew she was very, very not innocent. She stood up, set the briefcase back down on the seat, and scooted back to her seat, stumbling over Claire's feet in her haste.

She swallowed heavily as Jackie turned and gave her another narrow-eyed stare through the gap between her chair and Lady Morse's. Then Jackie turned back to face forward.

Well, at least Jackie appeared to be in no hurry to turn her in.

At that point, the other passengers began to board. Jamie recognized on their faces that all-too-familiar vacant look of people who had just received a short-term memory wipe, courtesy of The Cloister's mishap mitigation squad. Jamie raised her eyebrows. Lady Morse had gone pretty extreme to cover her tracks. Jamie wondered who the guy with the fedora could possibly be. He had to be someone dangerous to warrant such drastic measures.

Jamie glanced at Claire, who was also staring at the people filing onto the plane, wide-eyed. Claire met Jamie's gaze, leaned in, and whispered, "Memory wipe?"

Jamie nodded.

Claire cleared her throat and looked back at her book, mouthing, "Wow" as she did so. She glanced briefly in Lady Morse's direction.

"Mm hmm," Jamie agreed, turning away from the confused faces of her fellow passengers and looking out the window instead. Her mind reeling with thoughts of the mysterious messages for her on the computer screen, the flash drive, the guy in the fedora, and the memory wipe, Jamie barely noticed when the plane finally took off.

Jamie had no idea how long she was lost in her thoughts. She was pulled out of her reverie by Jackie snapping her fingers in her face. Jackie was again kneeling backward on her seat, looking at Jamie from over her headrest. Jackie said, "Ah, there you are. Lady Morse and I were just talking about that article you agreed to do with me. You know, the Cloister orphan thing?"

"But—" Jamie started, then, as Jackie shot her an evil grin, Jamie realized what Jackie was doing. Blackmail. Jamie glared, and grumbled, "Oh yeah. The article. Sure."

"Yeah I was just double-checking with Lady Morse that it was OK. She gave me the go-ahead, so we're on. Yay!" Jackie clapped her hands together.

"Goody." Jamie rolled her eyes, then looked back out the window.

"So ..." Jackie persisted, waving her hand in front of Jamie's eyes to get her attention again.

Jamie looked back at her. "What."

"How's now work for you?"

"Huh?"

"The interview, buddy. The interview."

Jamie glared.

Jackie looked at Claire. "Hey Claire, wanna switch seats with me?"

Claire sighed, shrugged, looked up from her book, and got up.

Within minutes, Jackie had cozied up beside Jamie, pulled out a notebook, and began asking questions.

And Jamie found herself launching into her life story. After only a minute or two, she stopped short. "You're sure this'll make a good story? Speaking it aloud, it sounds dull beyond belief. Your readers couldn't possibly—"

"Oh don't worry, I can put a fun spin on a dull life, believe me," Jackie said with a careless wave of her hand. "It's my thing. You were saying about your parents ...?"

So, Jamie continued where she'd left off. Being found at the doorway of The Cloister's main building when she was just a few days old, being raised in the nursery (with access to all the latest in child rearing technology and psychological interventions), being taught by the best of the best all the way from preschool through her double PhD in physics and philosophy (though somehow, even with access to the best instructors and a lot of effort on her part, she never managed to get more than mediocre scores), and then, upon graduation, her acceptance into the less-than-impressive docent program, one of the bottom rung Cloister programs where the screw-ups and morons ended up.

"Huh ..." Jackie said when they were done. "Yeah. I see what you were saying about boring."

Jamie shrugged.

Jackie looked down at her notebook. "Any relationships? Dudes? Broads? Illicit relationship with the gardener?"

"Nope."

"No one?"

"No one. I've got a major crush on Mark Twain, but he's super dead."

"Twain? Yeesh. All the dudes across history and that's the best you can do?"

"You just haven't read enough Twain," Jamie said with a shrug.

"Whatever, kid." Jackie paused and tapped her pen on her notebook. "So, why are you on this expedition? Not to be a jerk, but your resume doesn't seem all that impressive."

Jamie sighed. Jackie had hit on the very question that had been brewing in the back of her mind. "I have no idea. They just asked me if I wanted to go, so I said yes."

"Huh. Weird."

"Tell me about it."

"There must be some reason."

"You'd think so."

"Strange." Jackie sighed and snapped her notebook shut. She was quiet a few moments as she looked at Lady Morse, then said, "Honestly, I don't really know why I'm here either. My resume isn't impressive either. And I have no connections. Nothing that would attract Lady Morse's attention, anyway. Weird, right?"

"How so?" Jamie asked, narrowing her eyes.

"Seems like big, fancy Lady Morse wouldn't want two semi-incompetent nobodies on an expedition this important."

"I'm sure she has her reasons," Jamie said, resolutely ignoring that Jackie was voicing the very thing that was troubling her.

Jackie frowned at her. "Fine. Well, thanks for the interview."

"As though I had a choice," Jamie grumbled and glanced out the window at the ocean.

"Yeah ... about that. Sorry. And sorry for about how once we have some alone time I am going to totally grill you about that thing." Jackie glanced up at Lady Morse, who was clasping her briefcase securely in her lap.

Jamie groaned.

Jackie said, "Maybe we can be roomies. Yeah? I could interrogate you about stuff, and you could have easy access to my wardrobe."

Jamie said through clenched teeth, "Why are you being such a jerk to me?"

Jackie looked at her and sighed. "Sorry. Jerk is my default. Ya know, fun fact, I'm an orphan too. I like to blame my crappy outlook and people skills on the orphanage and the foster homes. Poor, tortured me." She brushed away a fake tear.

"A fellow orphan." Jamie commented. *Well that really does go a long way toward explaining a thing or two about you.* "Small world. Did you know your parents?"

"Nope. I was dumped just like you. Except I got dumped at the Lila Porter Orphanage down by the defunct steel mills, instead of getting dropped at a swanky cult."

Jamie raised an eyebrow, contemplating how prickly her new companion was. Any time Jackie came close to saying anything real or sincere, she had to follow it up with a stab of snark or meanness. Not having the energy to deal with it anymore, Jamie reclined her seat. "Poor you. I'm gonna take a nap."

"Sweet. I'm gonna go talk to Lady Morse about the you-know-what."

"Have at it." Jamie shut her eyes and pretended to sleep. Though, she was much more interested in eavesdropping on Jackie's conversation with Lady Morse than she was in sleeping. She wondered whether the guy Jackie had run over—Wharton—would come up in conversation. Jamie knew she'd seen him around The Cloister before, and would have loved to hear more about what he was doing at the airport, or who he was.

After a few seconds, Claire flopped back into her seat by Jamie. She was being remarkably cool about how Jackie was shuffling her around the cabin.

Jamie shut her eyes and began to eavesdrop. Sure, she could have just ditched the subterfuge and joined in the conversation, but she was curious to see what Jackie might say if she thought Jamie was asleep.

Jackie had just said, "Is it OK to talk about the thing now?" Lady Morse must have made some sort of non-vocal sign in the affirmative, because Jackie went on, "First off, George Okada? How sure are you about that?"

"Very," Lady Morse said.

"Huh. Yeah. Cuz, ya see, I just don't see that guy reproducing."

"I ran tests. Genes don't lie. False negatives are a possibility in tests such as the one I ran, but false positives are remarkably rare, and likely due to human error. I do not err in the lab," Lady Morse pointed out. "Did you delve much into the sciences during your time in academia? Am I speaking in terms you understand?"

Jackie answered, "Uh. Writing was more my academia thing. I didn't delve into the sciences much. Unless we want to insert a human anatomy joke right about now, if ya know what I'm saying there Lady Morse, wink wink, nudge nudge."

Lady Morse sighed.

"Men."

"I get it."

Jackie went on, "But, I do watch plenty TV, so I get what you're saying."

Lady Morse sighed again. There were no televisions at The Cloister. Or, rather, no televisions that aired popular programming; the only TV Jamie had ever watched was the kind where a 40-something, pudgy dude with a frantic air of trying to be hip did lab experiments while making fart jokes.

Lady Morse finally spoke after a long pause where she was probably doubting her decision to bring Jackie along, "Excellent. So, you understand—because of *television*—that when my tests show that the person who died is a direct descendent of George Okada, that means that the person who died is a direct descendent of George Okada."

"But—"

"I do not care how unattractive or dull your research and interviews have led you to believe Okada was. My research, unlike yours, is objective."

Jackie grumbled, "Some dudes are so lame there's no subjectivity. It's just a solid, irrefutable fact. But whatever. OK. Fine. It's his descendent."

"How good of you to set aside your unerring knowledge of men and condescend to accept my research, Ms. Savage."

"No problem. I mean, you're kinda a big deal. You probably know how to science pretty good. Maybe even better than I know how to man. Wink wink, nudge nudge."

Lady Morse did not immediately answer, leaving Jamie to infer that Jackie was being hit by some flavor of icy stare. At last, Lady Morse said, "Any other questions?"

"Yep. What's the name of the person who died?"

"Allegedly died."

"OK then ... what's the name of the person who *allegedly* died?"

"A woman named Tamon Nari."

"And how'd it happen?"

"At a party. By a swimming pool. She hit her head on the diving board."

"Huh. OK. Well I guess I should probably get to work on calling my contacts from the Okada piece. See if any of them know Ms. Nari, and if any of them know Okada had a kid. Oh, I should also talk to Ms. Nari's mom. She's the straightest path to info about all this."

"You may have difficulty with that."

"Why?"

"My initial research at The Cloister didn't yield immediate results on locating the mother."

"Dude, I'm good at research."

Lady Morse did not answer. Jamie opened her eyes to see Jackie opening her computer. Maybe their chat was done. Excellent. No mention of the Lady Morse's briefcase.

Jackie turned just then to look back at Jamie, who snapped her eyes shut again, hopefully in time.

Jackie said, "Uh, Lady Morse. One more thing."

"Yes, Ms. Savage?"

"Um ... is this expedition dangerous? Like am I at any risk? I don't want to get in legal trouble or on the wrong side of powerful people. That guy with the fedora ... and some other stuff ... it's making me feel like deeper stuff is afoot than what it appears."

"As far as you're concerned, Ms. Savage, it is a straightforward information-gathering expedition."

"And as far as I'm concerned ...?"

"My concerns are my business."

"Sure. Until your concerns get out of your control and then I have to bowl them over with a luggage cart."

Lady Morse cleared her throat. "I see your point. However, in my defense, I had assumed you would distract him by *talking* to him. You are a reporter, after all. Not a thug. That said, going forward, I will make a concerted effort to refrain from asking you to do anything else like that."

"I would greatly appreciate that. So ... there's nothing we should worry about? Nothing that you or one of them might be carrying that's worth stealing, for instance?"

Jamie stifled a groan. *Smooth, Jackie. Not suspicious at all.*

Jackie continued, "Or, I dunno ... anything else that might make me unsafe?"

"You're safe. The man with the fedora—Wharton—will not be bothering us again."

Jamie waited hopefully for more information on Wharton.

Jackie asked, "So who is he, anyway?"

"He's no one of consequence. Not anymore."

"Do you have any idea how ominous that sounds? Has he been hauled off to a Cloister dungeon or whatever?"

Lady Morse laughed. "Just do your research, Ms. Savage. Call your contacts. Wharton is not a part of your story."

"Riiiiight. See, that makes me feel like Wharton must super-duper be part of my story."

"Ms. Savage," Lady Morse said, taking on a steely, don't-mess-with-me tone.

"Right-o. I'll just make those calls ..."

With that, the conversation ended. Jamie drifted off to sleep to the sound of Jackie starting in on her phone calls.

7 JACKIE

By the time the plane touched down in Osaka International Airport a few hours later, Jackie had made calls to a handful of her contacts. They had all been a lot more excited to discuss Okada this time around than they had before; and their recollections had become much more flowery and exaggerated. In the five years since she'd talked to them last, George Okada had (in part because of her story) become a bit of a folk hero. The last person on earth to have died.

It was lucky Jackie wasn't writing a bio of Okada this time around, because there was nothing she could do with lies so blatant as:

"Oh, that Georgie! What a guy! He and I were great friends, you know. Like you said last time we talked, about how I was one of his closest friends. Yeah. George. Good times. Great fella," from the guy who, five years ago, had said, "What, George? The guy who sat two cubicles away from me? Yeah ... I think I remember him ..."

Or in response to questions involving whether he'd ever been in a relationship:

"Oh sure! Yeah, the ladies loved George. Pretty much every Friday night me and George'd hit the clubs and the broads would be all over him, man. Yeah, man, me and George. We were like this," from a neighbor of Okada's who had, five years ago, seemed to know nothing more about George than that he was excellent at wheeling his trash can out to the curb just in time for the waste disposal truck. "Every Wednesday morning, like clockwork, that guy."

At least none of the ladies on Jackie's list of contacts had acquired glasses so rose-colored that they recollected the feeling attraction:

"What, George? George Okada? Me and him? Hell no. Why would you ask me that? Did someone say me and him had a thing? You tell me who. I bet it was that bastard Jimmy from the office. Mad I turned him down," from a former coworker. "And no, I do not remember him ever having a girlfriend."

And ...

"No way, honey. No way in hell. I do not remember him ever having a woman over when I dropped off his food. That was one sad, pathetic dude," from a chick who'd delivered his takeout.

Between the guys who had developed utterly false memories of Okada and the women who had retained, in Jackie's opinion, pretty stellar memories of him, her research got her no closer to figuring out any family connections that might make for a good story. None of them seemed to be aware of any link to Tamon Nari, either. So, Jackie determined, she'd just have to do some legwork once she got to Kyoto, starting with finding Nari's mom, who simply had to be locatable, no matter how eager Lady Morse was to discourage her.

Jackie had been looking forward to the car ride to wherever they were going. Like any self-respecting reader of manga, she had always hoped to visit Japan one day. But, to her dismay, she was going to be denied some car-window sightseeing—the serious-looking trio of security people who joined them at the gate when they got off the plane led them across the tarmac to a waiting helicopter.

Jackie sidled up to Jamie as they walked toward the waiting helicopter, flanked by their escort. "Yo," Jackie whispered to Jamie, nodding toward a severe security lady toting a gun and scanning the area beadily. "What's with the guns? Is this a normal Cloister thing?" She was quite unused to guns. Before the Greywash, they'd been everywhere—open carry in places of worship, schools, everywhere. But, Jackie thought quite ironically, it was only after no one could any longer die that guns were banned in the general populace. The problem was that there were apparently a lot of very angry people out there who'd only refrained from shooting people because they hadn't wanted a murder charge on their heads. Once it became clear that everyone had eternal life, an epidemic of gun violence had erupted, driven by a ton of people who really, really wanted to blow off people's heads, since sure the victim wouldn't be killed but damn if it didn't hurt to get your head blown off or your heart exploded. Once people saw other people doing it, the practice spread like wildlife. Sharpshooters were raking in the dough. The cops couldn't keep up. In the end, it was politicians getting shot a few times a day by angry constituents that was the final straw. No bill had become a law so fast in the history of bills becoming laws.

Of course, the army and cops (and apparently The Cloister) could have guns, but not average citizens, unless they passed yearly exhaustive and highly expensive tests; they also had to submit to periodic unannounced visits from their designated firearm supervisor. Needless to say, guns were pretty rare in the civilian population post-Greywash.

Jamie met Jackie's gaze and shook her head with a swallow. "Nope. Not at all." She glanced up at Lady Morse and Claire, who were walking ahead of them and whispering animatedly. "This is weird."

"Right. Like who the heck are these guns for? You guys have enemies?"

Jamie shook her head. "Not that I know of. Well, I mean, There are plenty of those anti-science idiots running around hating The Cloister, but it's not like they know our travel schedule."

They were so close to the helicopter at that point that they had to stop talking.

Two of the guards got onto the helicopter and gave it a scan, then helped Lady Morse and the rest of them up. Headsets were dispersed and put on, the pilot greeted them with a brusque, "Sit down and buckle up," and they were off.

Jackie had never been on a helicopter before, and not even the look of terror on Jamie's face could dissuade her from the excitement she felt. When it took off, Jackie, thrilled by the upward motion and the sight of the ground falling away, was jarred out of her moment by Lady Morse's voice filling her head with a curt, "Get away from the door, Ms. Savage. Sit down and buckle in, as the pilot instructed. We need to discuss logistics."

One of the two guards who had accompanied them on the helicopter took her by the elbow and moved her to an empty seat. Jackie sat, buckled in, and rolled her eyes at Jamie, who was sitting across from her with her fingernails digging into the arms of her seat. Jamie didn't acknowledge the eye roll.

"Right," Lady Morse said. "We are all paying attention now?" She looked from Claire to Jamie to Jackie.

Claire and Jamie gave a "Yes, Lady Morse," in unison, while Jackie gave a sloppy salute.

Lady Morse said, "Excellent. We are stopping first at the hospital to do some tests on the body in the morgue. Then—"

"The what?" Jackie cut in.

"The morgue."

"They still have a morgue?"

"Well, I suppose it must be a former morgue." Lady Morse shrugged. "Anyway. Docent Nguyen and Ms. Savage, you will be with me. Dr. Forester, you already have your assignment."

Claire nodded in agreement.

"After the hospital, Ms. Savage, you and one of the guards may go afield and do research for your story, then meet up with Docent Nguyen and me at the hotel and fill us in on your findings."

Jackie nodded. "Yes, Lady Morse," she said in a pitch perfect imitation of Claire and Jamie, all the while thinking that, once she was done with her work, she was going to see as many sights as she could and not show her face at the hotel until at least four in the morning. But Lady Morse did not need to know that.

Jamie said, "Lady Morse?"

"Yes, Docent Nguyen?"

"Uh, quick question. Why am I here?"

"How do you mean? You're here to assist the expedition in gathering information about this alleged death."

"But ... I mean ... of course you need someone to write about this if it's gonna be as huge as it seems like it's gonna be—hence Jackie. And Olivia's here for all the technical stuff. But ... I just don't see how my skills are gonna be of any use to you. Unless you need me to educate random people about the rich history of The Cloister."

Lady Morse chuckled. "You're here for a reason, dear. But it appears we'll have to talk later. We have arrived." She pointed down at the large complex below them. The helicopter was flying down toward a big, red X painted on the ceiling of the closest building.

"How convenient," Jamie muttered once she had removed her headset. This was the second time Jamie had directly asked Lady Morse why she had been asked on this expedition only for Lady Morse to be unable to answer her due to convenient bad timing.

Once the helicopter touched down and everyone had removed their headsets, unbuckled, and stepped onto the hospital roof, Lady Morse took Claire aside so that they could have a conversation out of hearing of everyone else. Then, the female guard and Claire walked off in the direction of a staircase.

"What was that about, do you think?" Jackie yelled in Jamie's ear over the still pounding blades of the helicopter.

"No idea!" Jamie yelled back with a shrug, watching Claire as she slipped through the door to the stairs.

"Lady Morse is totally keeping something from us!" Jackie yelled back as she grabbed her hair to keep it from flying in her face on the windy rooftop.

Jamie shrugged. "Whatever! It's her expedition!"

"But you don't even know why you're here! That's totally gotta bug you!"

Jamie shrugged again, then nodded toward Lady Morse, who was standing a few yards from them beckoning them toward another staircase opposite the one Claire had disappeared through.

They trailed after Lady Morse and the remaining guard, and as they started down the stairs, Jackie caught up with Lady Morse. "Why are we taking the stairs?"

Jamie had been wondering the same thing. Though she herself preferred the stairs due to her elevator phobia, she could see no reason why Lady Morse would choose to take the stairs all the way from the top of the hospital to the basement morgue. Post-Greywash, the only reason anyone ever took stairs was if the elevators were broken or nonexistent. No one needed to worry about weight loss or cardio anymore, after all.

When Lady Morse didn't answer, Jackie asked, "Trying to fly under the radar? The people who this guard is here to protect us from won't think to watch the stairs too close?"

The guard stalked on, not turning his head or acknowledging in any way that he was being discussed.

Lady Morse gave another sigh. "We'll talk later."

Jackie snapped, "No. What's going on?"

"How do you mean?" Lady Morse said, over the rhythmic clanging of her bionic left foot as it hit the metal stairs with every step.

"Well ... uh ... how do you mean how do I mean? I mean what's going on here?"

"You're here to write a story on this alleged death."

"Uh, duh. And you're playing dumb on purpose," Jackie persisted. "I mean, what's going on with all the sneakiness? Claire going off on some mission somewhere else while we tag along with you, these armed guards, Jamie having no idea why she's even here ... there's a lot of weirdness."

Lady Morse sighed. "You're a tolerably bright girl, and you're persistent. These are commendable traits, and I'm sure they'll help you achieve great things in your chosen field. But, Ms. Savage, you're here to write about this death, and—"

"Alleged death," Jackie cut in.

Lady Morse smiled for a quarter second. "Thank you. Yes. This alleged death. That is your story."

Jackie shot Lady Morse a glare. "Remember, I'm the press. The *press*. Don't hinder me, old lady. You hinder the press, the press digs its heels in and writes embarrassing stuff about you."

"Is that a warning, Ms. Savage?"

Jackie paused. "I guess so?"

"Hmm. Noted," Lady Morse said, then gestured at the door at the landing they'd just reached. "Here's our floor." She reached for the handle, but the guard motioned her back and opened the door himself. He held a hand out to indicate they should wait, then he slipped into the dark hall beyond and cased the joint a bit before returning.

He gave a curt nod, then held the door for them.

Jackie hung back and waited for Jamie, letting Lady Morse walk on ahead alone.

The guard followed along behind them.

Jamie shot Jackie a curious look and whispered, "Why are you so suspicious?"

Jackie shrugged. "I wasn't until I realized how many questions she wasn't answering."

Jamie thought that through. Growing up in The Cloister, she was accustomed to a rigid chain of command and all the rules that went along with it. There were just things that not everyone needed to know. If too many people had too much high-level information, then eventually that was going to cause some major issues. Too many opinions on any one issue jammed up the works. Maybe the population at large didn't work that way (the population at large was, to Jamie's understanding, pretty dumb), but in The Cloister, the people making the high-level decisions were highly intelligent, and if one couldn't put some trust in the highly intelligent, then who could one put one's trust in?

Still, Jamie found that her mouth didn't want to share that perspective with Jackie. The words just wouldn't come to her lips. Knowing Jackie thought The Cloister seemed like a cult, Jamie knew any explanation that amounted to "Don't think about it. Don't ask questions" would sound like brainwashing. So, instead of leaping to Lady Morse's defense, Jamie heard herself saying, "Yeah. Totally."

"Totally. It's weird, right? She's so evasive."

"Mmm." Jamie bit her lip, feeling disloyal.

"We gotta get to the bottom of this."

Jamie's eyes widened. *Wait, what now?*

"Dude," Jackie whispered. "When I go to look into this chick and George Okada tonight, you are coming with me. We'll tell your cruel governess there that you wanna come along and see a bit of the real world. And I'll do all my research for my story and all, to cover my tracks, but we really need to talk in private. Yeah?"

Jamie swallowed, and her gaze flicked back to the guard, then up to Lady Morse. "Uh ..."

"Oh come on. You know something's up."

Jamie cleared her throat. "Uh, I dunno ..."

Jackie gave her a disdainful look. "Don't be pathetic."

"I'm not being pathetic," Jamie hissed as Lady Morse stopped at a door on the left and began pushing numbers on a keypad. "It's just—I mean—there will probably be a guard with us if we go out, right? So how could we even talk?"

Jackie grinned. "I can lose a tail. Don't worry. It'll be fine."

Jamie was about to respond, but just then she felt her phone vibrate. She pulled it out of her pocket, and was surprised to see she'd just gotten a text from the Docent Mother: **Docent Nguyen?**

Jamie hurriedly typed back, **Yes, Docent Mother?**

There are some things I need to tell you about this expedition. Are you free to talk now?

Jamie stared down at her phone, then up at Lady Morse, wondering whether the Docent Mother was taking a risk sending her this text. **Now's not a good time.**

Text me as soon as you can. There is information you need to know.

Yes, Docent Mother. Jamie stowed her phone and looked up at Jackie, who was studying her intently.

Jackie asked, "What was that about? You look nervous."

"It's nothing."

"No, it's not."

"Well, it's nothing that's your business."

"I'm getting tired of hearing that."

They were now too close to Lady Morse for Jamie to respond, so she just gave Jackie a shrug and directed her attention to Lady Morse, who was silently waiting for them to catch up.

Lady Morse asked, "Have a good chat?"

"Yep," Jackie said. "Jamie was telling me how she wants to tag along with me when I go do my research tonight."

At this, the other two women spoke over each other:

"I—what—?" Jamie spluttered.

"I don't think—" Lady Morse started.

"Oh, don't worry, Jamie," Jackie said with a dismissive wave of her hand. "Like I told you, Lady Morse will be cool with it. Right, Lady Morse? I mean, Jamie's not your prisoner. Jamie is free to do as she pleases. Right?" Jackie looked from Lady Morse to Jamie and back again with polite confusion. "I mean, it's not like The Cloister's a cult or something, eh?" she added with a laugh.

Lady Morse cocked an eyebrow. "Of course, Docent Nguyen is free to do as she pleases. My only concern is that this is Docent Nguyen's first time out of The Cloister. I would advise against her first outing in society being alone and in a strange city, with a guide equally inexperienced."

"But, see, we wouldn't be alone," Jackie pointed out. "We'd have a guard, presumably." She jabbed a thumb in the guard's direction.

Jamie listened mutely to them as they discussed her. She felt vaguely as though she should be chipping in and speaking up for herself. But she wasn't sure how she wanted this to turn out. A part of her had to admit that it would be nice to have a bit of an adventure with crazy Jackie, but a much bigger part of her wanted to keep to the status quo and have Lady Morse lay down the law and say Jamie was to stay in the hotel for the evening, not go gallivanting around the city. And a maybe even bigger part of her was super anxious about the fact that there was clearly more going on than what Lady Morse was telling them. Something that required guards and secrecy and flying commercial for some godawful reason. Considering that, it seemed reckless to go wandering off for no good reason.

But all those musings aside, she wondered, could she say no to Jackie's plan? She was fairly sure Jackie was blackmailing her, though they'd never quite ironed that out officially. Would Jackie tell Lady Morse about the briefcase if Jamie didn't do what Jackie wanted?

Lady Morse frowned. "Well, yes, a guard is going to be accompanying you this evening, Ms. Savage." She heaved a sigh and looked at Jamie. "You want to go, Docent Nguyen?"

Jackie turned to her too, smiling brightly. "Come on, buddy."

Jamie bit her lip. "Well, I guess as long as there's gonna be a guard ..."

"That's the spirit!" Jackie said.

"As you please, Docent Nguyen," Lady Morse sniffed. She turned and went about re-entering the code on the keypad.

As she waited for the door to open, Jamie looked at the cement floor, feeling guilty. Lady Morse had clearly not wanted her to go along with Jackie. Would there be some consequence for going against her wishes? Some bad mark on her next quarterly report? If she didn't toe the line on this expedition, would she be endangering her chances of being promoted from Docent-hood and up to her dream of something more behind-the-scenes and research-based?

Jamie only looked up when the door opened. The guard signaled for them to wait while he checked the morgue, presumably for whatever villains were on Lady Morse's tail. He emerged a few moments later and gave them a nod.

Lady Morse breezed past him. Jackie followed, shooting Jamie a grin as she went.

Jamie sighed, gritted her teeth, and followed.

The morgue was all white tile and stainless steel. And dust. Lots of dust. The ground had a thin coating of the accumulation of ten years of grime.

Following the trail of a few sets of recent footprints in said grime, Lady Morse strode to the opposite wall, which was covered in large, stainless steel drawers where bodies used to be stored in the old days when death had been a thing. She put her hand on the handle of the drawer right in front of her, and paused. She held her briefcase out toward Jamie, who scuttled forward to take it. "Docent Nguyen, there is a small kit of autopsy tools in there. Be so good as to arrange them on the nearest table for me."

"Yes, Lady Morse," Jamie said. Jackie caught her eye and raised an eyebrow at Lady Morse's briefcase.

Jamie looked resolutely away from Jackie and strode to a table, wondering whether she should wipe the dust off. She heard the drawer being pulled open, and found, to her surprise, that she was too scared to turn and look at the dead body. How very odd that this feeling had only just now hit her. She'd had no idea until that moment that she would be scared. She supposed she'd grown accustomed to death being a thing of the past.

Lady Morse continued, "And Ms. Savage, bring me one of those gurneys."

"What's a—"

"The wheeled table over there. To bring the body to the table."

As Jamie opened the briefcase and began to rummage around, she listened to Jackie wheeling the gurney over. A few seconds later, Jackie scooted over to her side, her back to Lady Morse.

Jamie thought initially that Jackie had joined her in order to see whether Jamie was going to steal something from the briefcase, but within a few moments it became clear by the way Jackie's eyes were nervously darting half toward Lady Morse and then away that Jackie was also freaked out by the dead body.

"Squeamish?" Jamie asked her.

Jackie shot her a glare, then spotted the sincere look on Jamie's face and stopped. "A bit. Yeah."

Jamie nodded and pushed around some more in the briefcase. A comb, a phone, another phone (weird), coconut flavored lip gloss (different weird), a notebook, a few pens, and, oh goody, the flash drive. It was still there. Totally steal-able. Not that she was really going to steal it. Unless she was. But probably not. But maybe. At least, not at that moment. Too much time for Lady Morse to notice it missing between the theft and Jamie finding a computer.

Under a layer of receipts and torn envelopes, Jamie found the little black leather kit. She unzipped it, and began to lay out all the tools. She recognized them all too well from the horrible human anatomy lab where she'd had to dissect a cat. To her way of thinking, it had been an utterly pointless class since no one would ever be dissecting dead bodies again (or so she'd thought). There was just no reason at all any more for anyone to learn anything about muscles and bones and guts. That poor cat, and all the other cats in the lab, had died for nothing. With Mr. Fluffy on her mind, she muttered to Jackie, "Super weird that I'm so freaked out. Not like I haven't cut up a body before."

"Eww, you have? Freak."

"Not a person. And it was for school. I had to do it."

"Still. Yuck."

Jamie set a scalpel down and narrowed her eyes at Jackie. "Shouldn't you be paying attention to what Lady Morse is doing? You know, for your story about the alleged dead body?"

Jackie stared Jamie down for a few moments, then stalked off, muttering.

Jamie looked at the dissection tools unseeingly for a few moments, took a deep breath, and turned toward the body as they started wheeling the gurney over, more because she didn't want to look weak in front of Lady Morse than for any other reason.

Jamie looked at the dead body and felt a chill shoot down her spine. Her legs got all wobbly. *Eww. Gross. Dead body. So horrible and pasty and empty.* Without being aware she was doing so, she backed up a few paces as the gurney drew nearer.

"OK," Lady Morse snapped. "Move the body to the table."

Jackie and Jamie exchanged mirror image expressions of wide-eyed horror. Expressions so very mirror image that for a second Jamie felt like she was looking at her reflection.

"Move!" Lady Morse said. "We don't have all the time in the world." She looked at the guard. "Any word yet?"

He shook his head.

"Confirm that."

He nodded, then pushed a button on the ear of his headset and turned, beginning a whispered conversation with someone on the other end. Jamie felt vaguely surprised that he could speak, considering how silent he'd been up until then.

Lady Morse barked at Jamie and Jackie, "Well? You're still not moving."

Jamie gritted her teeth and walked over to the body. She put her hands under the feet, and Jackie put her hands under the shoulders. "Count of three," Jamie said through gritted teeth. "One, two, three."

They lifted."Eww, oh my gosh she's all stiff!" Jackie squealed. "Oh my gosh I wish I could die. I so wish I could die. This the worst." And with that, they plunked the body down on the table with an unceremonious thud, at the sound of which Lady Morse's eyes fluttered shut for a moment and her hand went to her temple.

"Sorry," Jackie said, wiping her hands repeatedly on her jeans. "But I mean seriously. What did we just talk about? Like not even two hours ago? You said you wouldn't ask me to do things outside my job description."

Lady Morse opened her eyes and let her hand fall from her temple to her side. "I believe I said I would make a *concerted effort* to refrain from asking you to do anything else like that going forward. I did not say I wouldn't ask anything of you. Perhaps next time you feel yourself threatened by my requests, you should speak up before you perform the task I ask of you instead of after it. Open communication, Ms. Savage. Do not expect me to read your mind." She shook her head, then continued, "And, honestly. You're confronted with the first dead body in a decade and all you can do is squeal like a child? No curiosity? Confusion? Wonder?"

"I can feel two things at once. I have depths."

"Hmm. Now, gather round, ladies. Docent Nguyen, assist me. Ms. Savage, you'll want to observe for your article, no doubt? Yes? I wouldn't want to step on your toes and hinder your journalistic integrity by restricting your access to the subject." She waved a hand at the subject.

"Er ... uh ..." Jackie said, backing away. "I don't need to see the chick's insides to write about her."

"You're certain you don't want to see the tests I perform? Ask me about why I'm obtaining the samples? Discover what information I hope to obtain?"

"Uh ... well ..."

"Ms. Savage, it seems to me that since you are utterly unable to perform tasks outside the realm of journalism, you should put the maximum effort into your journalism. Yes?"

Jackie moaned, "Fine. Geez."

She slunk back to the dissection table, rolled her eyes at Jamie while Lady Morse scanned the work area, and reached into her bag for her recorder. "I'm turning on my recorder, Lady Morse. Docent Nguyen. Mute guard guy—not that the recorder's gonna pick up on your brooding silence, Mr. Guard, but telling you is the professional thing to do. And I'm professional as hell." She pushed the record button.

The guard raised his eyebrows a millimeter or so, and nodded slightly.

Lady Morse picked up a scalpel and began to cut open the body.

Jamie cringed and said, "Lady Morse, shouldn't you have surgical gloves on?"

"Why?" Lady Morse inquired as she slowly cut a line down the body's torso. "Bacteria isn't a threat."

"Well, just ... uh ... touching her insides. Seems like you'd want to not do that. And won't bits of stuff get stuck in the hinges of your mechanical hand?"

Lady Morse paused and blew some hair out of her eyes. "Docent Nguyen, even if this morgue still has a stockpile of surgical gloves in them, it has been ten years since there's been a need for their production. Thus, whatever gloves there are will be ten years old, and thus—"

"They will have biodegraded," Jamie cut in, wanting to show Lady Morse that she was clever enough to have caught on to her line of reasoning.

"Precisely. And as for the care and maintenance of my mechanical hand, I have it under control. Find me some vials for sample collection."

"Yes, Lady Morse."

As Jamie turned from the body to ransack the cupboards, Jackie got to work asking questions. "So, Lady Morse, whatcha doing there with those guts?"

"You're seriously going to ask your questions in that informal manner for this article?"

"Oh, don't worry. If I write it in a Q and A format I'll paraphrase and make myself sound smart."

"Fine. Just see to it that you do not paraphrase my responses."

"Wouldn't dream of it, Lady Morse." Jackie pointed at the recorder. "No worries."

"Excellent."

"So ... those guts ... what's up?"

"I am taking all the standard samples for an autopsy. Part of the autopsy involves the removal of a portion of the liver."

Jamie found an unopened box of glass vials on one of the top shelves of a cupboard across the room, but pretended to rummage around some more to avoid going back to the dead body a bit longer.

Jackie went on, "So you're searching for the liver right now?"

"I am not *searching* for the liver. This is not an Easter egg hunt. I know precisely where the liver is."

"Sorry."

Lady Morse did not respond.

Jamie poked around the cupboard, though she knew she was pushing her luck. She'd just found a file in one of the cupboards that, judging by the date and time, must have been the very last autopsy that the morgue had performed. Jamie had figured it might have some sort of interesting information in it, but it all seemed fairly standard. Just some drunk moron who had stepped in front of a car. Poor lady. If only she'd waited a few minutes to stumble out of the bar, her bashed in skull, broken ribs, and punctured lung would have all been fied up by nanobots and she'd have been able to walk off good as new.

Across the room, Jackie said, "I think it's safe to say, now that the body's right here all cut open and stuff, we can stop calling this death alleged, right?"

"It would seem so." What other stuff do you need to collect in an autopsy? Hair and stuff?"

Lady Morse reeled off the list of samples: "Hair, nails, urine, blood, gastric contents, bile, lung fluid, kidney, vitreous humour."

"What the hell's vitreous humour?"

"Hand me that syringe and I'll show you."

"No way. Isn't that Jamie's job?"

Jamie froze at the sound of her name.

"Docent Nguyen is busy finding vials for samples—oh for goodness sake, girl, there's a box of vials right up there! The cupboard is open. Didn't you see—"

Jamie turned from the file to see Lady Morse looking over her shoulder at her. "Sorry, Lady Morse! Oh hey, will ya look at that!

You're right!" She looked at the box of vials and attempted to feign surprise.

Lady Morse's lips formed a thin line, and she turned back to the body, muttering under her breath.

Jamie grabbed the box of vials and hurried to the autopsy table, tearing open the box as she walked.

Jackie watched the two of them with a mildly amused look on her face, then asked, "Lady Morse, how'd you know where the morgue was? You just walked straight to this room like you knew exactly where you were going. You hang out in the Kyoto hospital a lot? I mean it's like across the planet from The Cloister and it's not even a hospital anymore, right? It's a bunch of wacko witch doctors profiting off morons, yeah? Sorta random place for a fancy lady like you to have a blueprint in your head."

"I was told the morgue's location by an associate. The same associate who informed me of the death."

"And this associate is ...?"

As Jamie handed Lady Morse a vial for the liver sample, she listened eagerly, glad that Jackie was there to ask all the questions she herself was afraid to.

But Lady Morse said, "That is not within the scope of your story."

"How do you figure?" Jackie snapped. "Lady Morse, the identity of the person who told you about the body is directly related to the story."

"To put it in your terms, it is a confidential informant."

"You don't get to have confidential informants. You aren't the journalist. Second hand confidential informants aren't a thing."

Lady Morse shot her a steely glare and, still staring Jackie in the eyes, said, "Docent Nguyen, the syringe please." She held out her hand.

Jamie stifled a grin. She was starting to enjoy witnessing their little clashes. Plus, with Jackie being so in-your-face irritating to Lady

Morse, the woman wouldn't be paying nearly as much attention to anything dumb Jamie might be doing in the background. She slapped the syringe into Lady Morse's hand.

Only then did Lady Morse stop staring at Jackie. She peeled open the body's left eyelid, jabbed the needle into the eye, pulled the plunger up, and extracted a clear, gelatinous liquid.

Jackie let out an involuntary gagging sound, and staggered back a few paces.

"This," Lady Morse said, flicking the syringe with her the index finger of her mechanical hand, "Is vitreous humour."

The rest of the autopsy proceeded uneventfully with Jamie handing Lady Morse vials and tools, Jackie alternately asking questions and walking away to stop herself from puking, and Lady Morse answering questions and obtaining samples. She worked remarkably quickly, considering that it had been at least a decade since she'd have had an opportunity to do an autopsy.

Lady Morse only had the kidney left to grab, when her phone rang. One of her phones. "Docent Nguyen," she said, "Answer my phone and hold it to my ear, would you?"

"Yes, Lady Morse." Jamie scurried to the bag. The black phone was silent. She grabbed the silver one, answered it with, "Lady Morse's phone. One moment please," and hurried to hold it to the woman's ear.

"Yes?" Lady Morse barked into the phone.

Even if Jamie had had the desire to try to avoid eavesdropping, she wouldn't have been able to. The voice on the other end cut through the silent room quite nicely. "They're here. Heading to the elevator," said a man.

"Noted. If you can handle it discreetly, do so. But do not make a scene. Tell the driver to bring the car."

"Yes, Lady Morse."

"Very good, Docent Nguyen. Hang up, and hand me a vial." Her voice was tense. "Hurry."

Jamie hung up the phone, handed Lady Morse a vial, exchanged a silent, alarmed look with Jackie, and dropped the phone back in Lady Morse's briefcase.

She turned just in time to see Lady Morse cork the vial and say, "Right. Burn the body, Docent Nguyen."

Jamie's mouth dropped open. She spluttered wordlessly, frozen in place.

Lady Morse rounded on Jamie while Jackie gaped at her side. "Docent Nguyen. Do you hear me?"

"I—I—"

"Burn. The. Body."

"But—but—"

Jackie cut in on Jamie's spluttering, "But that'd burn down the hospital, right?"

"Nonsense. Stainless steel and tile. It will burn slow enough to create the diversion we need, and fast enough to dispose of the body before it is found by people I do not want to find it."

Jamie said, "Are we sure it'll burn?" It felt downright unnatural post-Greywash for a body to be in any way mutilated and not reform again. But then, this body was dead. So perhaps the rules didn't apply.

"Quit stalling with nonsensical questions," Lady Morse said. "Start. The. Fire."

"But—how? I don't have a lighter." Jamie looked hopefully at Jackie, who shook her head.

Lady Morse turned on her heel. Apparently deciding to take matters into her own hands, she headed to the cupboards. Over her shoulder, she said, "Docent Nguyen, we are in a lab. Labs have isopropyl alcohol. Labs have Bunsen burners. And lighters to light them." Lady Morse stomped toward the cupboards and began rummaging around.

"Of course. I'm sorry, Lady Morse." Jamie felt like a complete idiot, and began wondering anew why on earth Lady Morse had chosen her for this expedition. She was broken out of her self-loathing stupor by Lady Morse stalking right up to her and slapping a flint spark lighter in her hand.

Lady Morse stomped to the body and began emptying two bottles of isopropyl alcohol onto the body, one bottle in each hand.

Jackie hurried over, and Jamie and Jackie exchanged mirror image nervous glances. Jackie hovered awkwardly at Lady Morse's elbow, and said, "Uh, can I help with something?"

"Oh, no," Lady Morse growled. "No. I wouldn't want you to do something outside your job description, Ms. Savage." She grabbed the lighter out of Jamie's hand, set the body ablaze, and herded them to the door, which the guard had been holding open, waiting for them.

As the fire alarm began to blare behind them, the guard led them back down the hall the way they had come. They passed the elevator, and ran further on, passing other fire alarms at regular intervals along the way.

Jackie grabbed Jamie's arm, causing her to slow down so they were lagging a few paces behind the others. She yelled, "What the hell is this?"

"No idea," Jamie panted, regretting that she'd been neglecting The Cloister's exercise facilities the past few months.

"Dude, this is messed up. So messed up. Something is so wrong."

"Ya think?"

They went right under an alarm, and had to stop talking for a few seconds.

Jackie went on, "So this is not normal for you? This is totally weird, right?"

"Very," Jamie panted. "Very, very weird."

"Any idea who's chasing us?"

"Nope."

Up ahead was another staircase. They hurried up it, the guard letting them all pass him before following. Lady Morse trotted on with an apparently endless supply of energy, and Jackie prattled on at Jamie's side, but Jamie wasn't listening. She just let Jackie's voice blend into the background as she put all her effort into putting one foot in front of the other.

"Hey, what about Claire?" Jackie called to Lady Morse once they'd reached the top of the stairs.

"She'll meet us at the safe house," Lady Morse responded, and signaled them over to her. She continued in a low voice, "This is the main floor of the hospital. Thus, walk slowly and don't attract attention. Blend in. A car will be waiting for us at the east exit."

Heart hammering at the idea of whoever they were running from and what would happen if they got caught, Jamie tried to force her legs to walk. Attempting to appear calm, she walked past a steady trickle of people walking in and out of offices with signs on the doors like "Youth Aging Clinic" and "Crystal Therapy Immersion". Every office was emanating its own chill blend of incense and soothing music that turned the main hallway into a vaguely stressful mishmash of sounds and smells that absolutely did not work together. Jamie, trained in hard science as she was, found herself thinking all sorts of disdainful thoughts about the con artists taking advantage of all these poor, idiotic people grasping at straws. No way were these fake doctors going to be making anyone's kids age, or make anything at all happen with crystal therapy.

The philosophy-trained half of her brain cut in and reminded her that people have all sorts of ways with dealing with stuff, and all sorts of modes of belief; while this stuff seemed wacko to her, it could just as easily be said that the people who did crystal therapy probably thought that she was a wacko.

Jamie quickly stifled her philosophy brain. Crystal healing was magic, and magic was fake and stupid. Also, all the open-mindedness in the world didn't excuse the fact that con artists were making money off the desperate.

At Jamie's side, Jackie asked, "Why aren't the fire alarms going off up here?"

Jamie looked around, startled. There were, indeed, no fire alarms sounding. Perhaps the fire downstairs had already been contained. But that would mean that whoever was following them was very, very close.

Up ahead, at last, was a door that led outside, where a car would be waiting for them.

Lady Morse opened the door and they all piled out, trading the mishmash of mellow tunes and incense for the sounds of traffic and gross city air.

8 JACKIE

Jackie's mind was reeling. She was having trouble wrapping her head around the fact that she was stuck in the middle of a whole heap of insanity. While it was pretty cool that she didn't have to worry about being killed, there were still plenty of things that a bad guy could do that didn't involve murder. Those who specialized in fighting and torture had gotten quite creative in the wake of The Greywash since their go-to solutions had been taken from them.

She exited the hospital with the rest of the group, and ran smack into Lady Morse who had halted abruptly in her tracks. Jackie stumbled backward, caught her balance, and looked up. Lady Morse and Jamie were both frozen, staring ahead of them at something or someone Jackie couldn't see. The guard was standing at their side, looking confused.

Jackie moved a bit to her left so she could see what had caused the distraction. Between them and a white sedan idling at the curb ahead was a big, black crow. And Lady Morse and Jamie were staring at it. The two women looked away from the crow and at each other. Jamie asked, "Lady Morse, is that ...?"

Lady Morse nodded, and swallowed.

"So ..." Jamie said, thinking something through. "It's Lady Airth?"

Lady Morse gritted her teeth, glared at the crow, and gave one slight, curt nod.

"But—but—" Jamie stuttered. "You and her—you're—enemies?"

"What's with this crow?" Jackie cut in.

"Raven," Lady Morse and Jamie corrected in unison.

"OK ..." Jackie said. "Then, what's with this *raven*?"

Jamie ignored her and said to Lady Morse, while staring at the raven, "What does this mean?"

Lady Morse ran a hand through her hair. She exhaled slowly. "Well," she said, and turned her back on the raven, signaling Jamie, Jackie, and the guard over to her.

They scurried over.

Lady Morse whispered, "It is recording us. She'll have proof we're here now. This is ..." she said, searching for words and finishing lamely, "a problem. A definite problem."

Jackie said, "Could someone please explain—"

"Not until we're out of sight of the creature," Lady Morse responded, looking over her shoulder at the bird.

Everyone else did the same.

Just in time to see the bird hopping closer to them, tilting its head inquisitively. "Squawk! Croak!"

Lady Morse scooted further away from it, and everyone scooted right along with her in tight formation.

"Can't we just grab it? Kill it?" Jackie suggested. "Take off the recorder and break it?" The guard nodded his agreement. "I mean it's just a cr—"

"Raven," Jamie and Lady Morse corrected.

"Whatever."

Lady Morse went on, "We can't kill it. We can't do anything to it. The damage is done." She eyed the raven. "We need to lose it. Get to the safe house. Regroup." She looked at the guard, and added, "Get them in the car."

He nodded and herded Jamie and Jackie toward the sedan.

Jamie grudging allowed herself to be corralled past the squawking bird and to the car. She slid into the back seat by Jamie, watching as Lady Morse approached the raven, crouched down in front of it, cleared her throat, and said hesitantly, "Alexis. This must look ... bad. But—but please don't jump to conclusions. We need to talk."

Jackie muttered to Jamie, "The bird's name is Alexis?"

"The woman on the other side of the recorder is Alexis," Jamie whispered back as they both watched Lady Morse. "This is insane. Alexis is Lady Airth. Another one of the founders of The Cloister. She and Lady Morse are friends. Allies. I don't understand ..."

Lady Morse continued, "If Calypso is close, I assume you can't be far. Let's meet somewhere, Alexis. I'll send you word of a time and location."

The raven hopped backward as Lady Morse stood and strode past it, her brows furrowed and her eyes on the ground before her. Jackie and Jamie scooted over to make room for her on the seat beside them. Once Lady Morse was in, the guard slammed the door behind her, joined the driver in the front, and they drove off.

Lady Morse didn't say a word to the driver, yet the car started moving, so it was clear the driver already had information about where to go.

Jamie was looking nervously at Lady Morse out of the corner of her eye, and Lady Morse was staring broodingly straight ahead into the middle distance.

Jackie cleared her throat. "So ... that cr—raven. What's all this?"

"Quiet," Lady Morse snapped. "I will explain later."

"Do you have any idea how tired I am of hearing that?" Jackie growled.

"I do not have any idea," Lady Morse said. "Though I can guess. At any rate, your feelings are irrelevant." She opened her briefcase, rummaged through it, and grabbed her silver phone. She then barked up at the guard in front, "You notified Claire's guard of this development?"

He nodded.

"They are taking appropriate steps?" she asked.

He nodded again.

Lady Morse nodded to herself and dialed. She held the phone up to her ear and waited. She drummed her fingers on the seat beside her. The longer the phone rang, the more tense she got. Eventually it must have gone through to a message, because she swore, turned off the phone, threw it in her bag, and clenched her teeth as she glared again into the middle distance.

She looked so intense, so angry, that Jackie was almost too scared to ask a question. She cleared her throat. "Uh—"

Lady Morse shot her a venomous glare.

Jackie's question died in her throat. "Never mind."

"Good."

They drove on through the streets of Kyoto in tense silence as Lady Morse thought through whatever it was she was thinking through and deciding to keep everyone else in the dark about. Every so often, she would look out the window and scan the sky, doubtless for the raven. The traffic was stop-and-go, so Jackie figured it was quite possible that the bird could keep pace with them.

Jackie found that she was so preoccupied with the insanity that she could barely summon up the interest to look out the window and check out the sights of the city. From her seat in between Jamie and Lady Morse, she saw a bunch of signs she couldn't read, a few pedestrians, bikes and mopeds galore, and lots of white cars. Lots and lots of white cars. She turned away from the window and looked down at the floor, beginning to fume anew about being kept in the dark.

Suddenly, the car stopped. Jackie peered out the window and saw, behind a bunch of parked bikes and mopeds, a sign in English that read Kyoto Station.

Lady Morse got out and immediately began to scan the sky, ignoring the car behind their sedan that had started to beep at them.

Jamie, Jackie, and the guard got out. Lady Morse had a quick exchange with the driver. All Jackie could tell over the background noise of the city was that they were probably discussing where the driver was going to pick them up next. Jackie asked a perplexed Jamie, "So we're probably taking the subway for a bit to lose the raven?"

"I bet."

Jackie nodded. "Clever."

At that moment, out of the corner of her eye, a black shape plopped down out of the sky and landed on a nearby bike rack.

Jamie let out a startled squeal.

Jackie turned to see the raven looking at them with its black, beady eyes. It tilted its head. "Croak."

Jackie looked at Lady Morse, who just sighed and signaled them to follow her into the station.

One long, tense, crowded subway ride later, they emerged above ground at the Kitaoji Station. In front of them was a giant, green hedge separating the station from the road. Lady Morse led them around the hedge to the street. Jackie had been expecting the same white sedan to be waiting for them. It wasn't there.

But there was a man in a blue suit who gave Lady Morse a quick, significant look then started walking away from his post by the hedge and down the narrow street lined with tan-colored buildings. As they followed Lady Morse's mystery man, Jackie grabbed Jamie by the elbow, pulled her close, and whispered in her ear, "We are going to do so much poking around tonight. I am finding some answers."

Jamie responded, "I seriously doubt she's gonna let us leave the safe house after all this."

Jackie scoffed, "Whatever. She can't stop me. I never signed any legal documents or anything"

Jamie bit her lip and said nothing.

Lady Morse snapped from up ahead, "Hurry up!"

Lady Morse was standing in the open single-car garage of some random home a few yards ahead of them. The guard was talking to a man and handing him a stack of money. Jackie and Jamie scurried to join Lady Morse. There was a small, white car in the garage. They piled in and were soon zipping again through Kyoto.

"I miss the sedan," Jackie grumbled, scrunched between Jamie and the guard in the back seat. "I get a window seat if we switch cars again."

Jamie nodded.

The guard said, "I need a window seat. Better strategic location."

"You can talk!" Jackie exclaimed.

Lady Morse, who was having a whispered conversation on her black phone, hissed at Jackie, "Keep it down!"

Jackie glared at the back of her head, and repeated in a whisper to the guard, "So you can talk?"

The guard muttered, "I don't talk if there's nothing to say."

"Huh. Got full marks in Cliché 101 at Tough Guy School, I see. What's your name?"

"Stewart."

"Last name or first name?"

"Yup."

"OK then, Stew."

"Don't call me Stew."

"Are you coming with me when I go do my research tonight, Stewie?" she asked.

He sighed, but didn't pursue the nickname thing. "I doubt that's still a go in light of these developments." He turned away from Jackie to do a scan of the skies and the cars behind them.

"But assuming it is a go, are you assigned to me?"

"Yes. I was going to be your guard," he grumbled, shifting uncomfortably in his seat. "Could you move over? I'm squished against this door."

"No way. I don't wanna smoosh my friend, Jamie," Jackie said, patting Jamie's leg without looking at her. "Deal with it."

He lapsed back into a frowning silence and turned back to the window.

"Just, if I do go out, since you'll be my guard, I just gotta say you really need to change clothes. That suit's the worst. I don't want people thinking I hang out with someone who dresses so stupid. Did you pack casual stuff?"

He shrugged.

She rolled her eyes. *I am so losing this moron the first chance I get.*

She left him to his cliché brooding silence and turned to Jamie, who grumbled, "I don't want to talk," before Jackie had even gotten a word out. Jamie's arms were crossed and she was hunched down in the seat, glowering in Lady Morse's direction.

There was a buzzing sound from Jamie's pocket. Jackie watched as she pulled out her phone and looked at the screen.

Jackie read, **Are you free to talk yet, Docent Nguyen?**

Jamie turned her phone away from Jackie, glared at her, said, "Privacy, please," and typed a response before pocketing the phone once more.

Jackie raised her eyebrows. "Fine. I'm taking a nap." She shut her eyes, leaned back, and fell asleep.

She woke to being elbowed awake by Jamie. "Stop it," she grumbled, shoving Jamie's arm away. "Your elbow is super pointy."

"Get up! We gotta get out of this car in a minute," Jamie said. "I guess there's a car coming the other direction. We're driving through a park, or a forest, or something. The other car's gonna meet us under a grove of trees and we're gonna switch over from this one to that one real quick."

"Because of the crow?"

"Raven. Yes."

"No way that thing's still following us after the subway," Jackie said, but sat up straight all the same and got ready to move.

"Well it's a cyborg. It has tracking technology. And Stewart saw a black bird—"

"Wait. It's a cyborg? No way."

"Yeah. Didn't you see its little metal legs?"

"Uh, no."

"Huh. Well whatever. Calypso doesn't get tired. The only way she's not still following is if we drove too fast for her, and the traffic's been bad the whole time, so Lady Morse is thinking odds are good we're still being tracked."

Jackie shrugged. "OK." She looked out the window. They were indeed driving through a park. Jackie was momentarily arrested by the beauty. It had a subtropical Miami sort of vibe, but with different plants. And different animals. "Was that a monkey?" she asked, twisting in her seat and looking behind her at a cypress-looking tree where there was, indeed, a monkey standing on a branch.

"Yeah, there's loads of monkeys in this park," Jamie said in a bland sort of voice.

"You sound like you don't think that's awesome."

Jamie shrugged. "I guess it's cute and all, but we're sorta on the run right now."

"But, monkeys!" Jackie exclaimed. "It's cool! Stuff's so different here from home! You've lived in a gated community science cult in the northeast US for your whole life. How's this not awesome?" She waved vaguely out the windows at the park dripping with monkeys and lush botanical whatnot.

"I dunno."

Jackie turned to the guard on her other side. "Stewie?"

He gave a noncommittal tilt of his head.

Jackie rolled her eyes. "You morons must lead a life devoid of wond—"

Lady Morse said from the front, "I see the car up ahead. Get ready."

Jackie looked straight ahead down the road and saw a white sedan idling. With a monkey sitting on the roof of the car, fussing with its tail and staring at them. Jackie elbowed Stewie. "Tell me that's not adorable."

"That's not adorable. Focus."

Jackie shot him a glare as their car pulled to a stop beside the other car.

Stewie and Lady Morse promptly opened their doors and got out.

As Lady Morse strode to the waiting car, the monkey hopped off the roof of the car and onto a nearby tree trunk. It gave her a reproachful sort of screech.

Jackie smiled at it.

Stewie grabbed Jackie's arm, hauled her out of the car, and practically flung her into the white sedan. Jamie joined her a few seconds later, apparently quick enough on her toes that Stewie hadn't had to manhandle her. He followed Jamie in, slammed the door, and they were off again.

"Score. Window seat," Jackie said. She looked around and was surprised to see that they were back in the car they'd started in, which was good, because that was where her luggage was. The car started to move, and as it zipped out of the shelter of the grove of trees, Jackie whirled around to look through the back window at the sky. Beside her, Jamie and Stewie did the same. "No ravens, eh?" she asked.

"Looks like we lost her," Jamie agreed, though she sounded doubtful, and kept scanning the sky long after Jackie had shifted her attention to the sights outside the windows and Stewie had begun texting on his phone, probably communicating with Claire's guard or something. Curious, Jackie shifted her attention from the window beside Stewie to the screen of his phone. He immediately shifted its angle so she couldn't see what he was doing.

Jackie asked, "Whatcha doing there, Stewie?"

"None of your business."

"Checking email?"

Silence.

"Ordering pizza?"

Glare.

"Checking your horoscope?"

Sigh.

"Dude, those horoscopes are totally fake. They're so vague they could apply to anyone. It's a bit of a disgrace to your profession, frankly, that you're buying into—"

"Do you ever shut up?"

On Jackie's other side, Jamie stifled a snort of a laugh. The driver glanced back at Jackie through the rearview. Lady Morse, as far as Jackie could tell, didn't react.

"Occasionally," Jackie answered Stewie, who had directed his attention back to his phone. Jackie left him to his horoscope and focused on their fearless leader. "So, Lady Morse?"

"Yes, Ms. Savage?" She looked up from her phone. Her tone was one of forced patience.

"We're going to a safe house now?"

"Yes."

"How long's the drive gonna be? I really need to—" Jackie started, then looked from Stewie's phone to Lady Morse's phone and back again. "Whoa. You guys are texting each other. Aren't you?"

Lady Morse cleared her throat.

Stewie raised his eyebrows and tilted his screen a bit further from her.

"Are you guys talking about me?"

"Ms. Savage, don't be paranoid. Not everything is about you. Actually, I'm certain very little—if anything—is ever about you," Lady Morse sighed.

Jackie turned to Jamie. "You getting this, Jamie? They're totally texting each other. So we can't hear what they're saying."

Jamie looked at her with wide eyes that clearly read, *Do not involve me in this.* Then she turned away from Jackie, suddenly seeming to have taken a great interest in observing the flora and monkeys of Japan.

Jackie gave everyone a good, hard glare. Not that anyone was looking at her. "You all are the worst. If I'd known this trip was gonna go like this, I'd never have come."

No one answered.

"Fine. Fine then, Lady Morse. OK, you want me to confine my questions to things directly relating to Ms. Nari? Fine. Let's talk about what you want to talk about."

"Excellent, Ms. Savage." Lady Morse sent one more text on her phone, then put it away.

Stewie pocketed his phone.

Jackie narrowed her eyes at him. She looked at the back of Lady Morse's head. "OK. First off, can I stop saying alleged death now? Can I just say death?"

"Yes. Since I have seen Ms. Nari with my own eyes, cut her open, extracted her organs, and set her ablaze, I think we can safely say she's dead."

"No chance that was a cyborg or something? Like maybe not a person but a really good copy of a person? Like those nanobot things that fix us when we break, right? What if the conspiracy theorists are right and that nanotech can make fake people? Huh?"

Lady Morse turned, raised an eyebrow, and gave Jackie a half smile. "Commendable thought processes. Not taking things at face value. Yes, I suppose there is a slight chance that Ms. Nari was other than human. A very slight chance. Once I get these samples to the safe house and test them, we will have 100% certainty that the body was human."

Jackie tried hard to suppress her feeling of pride. Lady Morse had given her a half smile and a compliment instead of a weary sigh. She cleared her throat and pressed on with another question. "So, are the conspiracy theories right? People made of nanotech are possible? You Cloister broads are doing mad scientist crap in your evil lair, right? Right?"

"Ms. Savage, that theory is pure fiction."

"Riiiight. Suuuuure. OK. But, off the record—"

"Ms. Savage, no."

You just said there was a very slight chance Ms. Nari was other than human. You *just* said it."

"I didn't mean I thought she was a person made of nanotechnology," Lady Morse sighed wearily. "I meant she might be a clever copy of a human, constructed in a lab. You need to cut down on your television watching. It's destroying your mind. Blurring the lines of fiction and reality."

Jamie made a prim little nod of agreement that made Jackie want to slap her.

"Fine. Next question. Why is it that you think Ms. Nari is related to George Okada?"

"As I said before, genealogical research. Also, I ran a comparison of Okada's and Nari's blood samples on file at the United States and Japanese citizen sample storehouses."

Jackie bristled at the very mention of the storehouses. She hated the idea that the government had samples of everyone on file. But, on the bright side, any custom-made, targeted biological weapons The Man might have had in the works were now pointless ever since the Greywash. Still, it didn't sit right with her that the government had access to something so personal as the DNA of every single citizen. She pushed aside her conspiracy theory mental sidetrack and said, "If you already know they're related, what's the point of this whole expedition?"

"I needed to see it with my own eyes. See the body, take samples with my own hands, run multiple tests, destroy the evidence. I do not trust others easily. Others are incompetent, and easily compromised."

"Compromised by who?"

"That is not within the scope of your story."

Jackie frowned at that, but didn't get too bent out of shape. She had a good idea that the compromiser in this scenario was Lady Airth. Jamie seemed to know a bit about Lady Airth, so once she and Jamie went out that evening and evaded Stewie, Jackie would be able to interrogate Jamie about Lady Airth to her heart's content. "OK ... Is there anything else relevant you can tell me? Anything that you consider within the scope of this story?"

"Not at this time. Let's pick this up again once I have run my tests. In the meantime, you should interview your Okada contacts a bit more. Get the personal perspective on Ms. Nari's life and background. We're almost to the safe house. You can do your work there, while Docent Nguyen helps me run the tests."

Jackie turned to Jamie in time to see her swallow heavily and clench her teeth. Apparently, she didn't want to have quality lab time with Lady Morse.

"Ah," Lady Morse said, as the car pulled to a stop in front of a three-story, gray brick building. "We've arrived."

9 JAMIE

As Jamie sat on her bed, watching Jackie unpack her suitcase, she tried to process what was happening. She'd have tried to talk it through with her new roomie, but she was plenty smart enough to know there were probably recording devices somewhere in the room. The safe house appeared to be an old hotel. It had been cleaned up and redecorated, but still had that seedy, creepy feel that made Jamie think it quite likely that it was the type of place that probably had hidden cameras built in as part of its original design.

"Dude," Jackie said, tossing a pair of jeans into the bottom drawer of a wooden dresser. "If it weren't for the fact that there are probably cameras recording us, I'd love to talk about this garbage."

Jamie blinked. *Weird.* "Yeah ..."

"Here," Jackie said. "Come pick something out." She waved vaguely at her clothes, half of which were still in her suitcase.

Jamie ambled over and began rifling through. She grabbed a pair of jeans and a green tank top, then looked at the tags. "Lucky we're the same size."

"Mm. Same height too, by the looks of it. 5'9?"

"Yep."

"Weird, huh? I mean, not many ladies are 5'9."

"Yeah. Pretty weird, I guess ..."

"Shoe size?" Jackie enquired as she went back to unpacking.

"Nine and a half."

Jackie turned and stared at her. "Dude. We're twins."

Jamie shook her head. "Except you have darker skin and green eyes."

"Well yeah, I didn't really mean twins. I was joking," Jackie said, looking Jamie up and down.

"Oh. See I thought you meant for real since we're both orphans from the same city."

Jackie tilted her head and looked at Jamie, startled. "That's a good point. How old are you?"

"Thirty-five years alive, so twenty-five as far as my body's concerned," Jamie answered as she walked to the bathroom attached to their room.

"Me too!" Jackie gasped, following Jamie toward the bathroom only to have the door slammed in her face.

Jamie heard her yell through the door, "What's your birthday?"

"April 5, 2018. Look, Jackie," Jamie said to the door as she changed out of her docent outfit and into Jackie's clothes. "I see what you're thinking. We're not twins."

"My birthday's April 11, 2018!"

"Thus, we are not twins."

"But—but—"

"Stop it. I don't have any patience for conspiracy theories," Jamie sighed at the door, wincing at how much she sounded like Lady Morse. "Besides, different birthdays means we're not twins. We just have a lot in common. It's coincidental, sure, but—"

"What if they just switched around our birthdays a bit to throw us off the track?"

"And who's *they* supposed to be?" Jamie asked as she looked at her reflection in the mirror. It had been ages since she'd worn casual, non-uniform clothes. *I look like a real person! This is awesome!* "More importantly, do you think we're actually going to be able to go out tonight after all that stuff with Lady Airth and Calypso?"

"Yes. We are going out. There is so much I need to talk to you about."

Jamie opened the door, and nearly ran into Jackie, who'd been leaning against the doorframe.

Jackie looked her up and down again and said, "Wow. You look like a real person."

Jamie narrowed her eyes. *That's like the third time she has spoken my thoughts.* "Crazy, huh?"

"Super crazy," Jackie said, trailing after Jamie as she went to the sink to fuss with her hair. "So ... uh ... if Lady Morse has a lab setup here, you could run some tests, right? Some blood tests?"

Jamie looked at Jackie's reflection in the mirror. "You don't mean you wanna compare yours and mine."

Jackie grinned and nodded.

"I'm not going to waste my time—"

"Dude! Jamie! Look!" Jackie pointed from Jamie's reflection to hers. "Look! Our cheekbones, our jaws, our foreheads! Sure, our pigmentation is different and our eyes. But our bone structure and stuff ... we're crazy similar. Maybe our mom was black and our dad was white or the other way around or whatever."

"What newspaper do you write for anyway?" Jamie asked. "One of those 'Sid Vicious is Alive and Running the World from an Underground Bunker in North Dakota' kinds of papers?" Secretly, she saw what Jackie was saying, but coincidences happened. Not every outlier was the result of a conspiracy theory story. In fact, probably next to no outliers were. All they were were statistical anomalies.

"Just because I'm open-minded, that doesn't mean I think Sid Vicious is running the world. And 'Underground Bunker' is kinda redundant." She paused, then added, "And how do you know who Sid Vicious is?"

Jamie smiled. "The Docent Mother. She's my boss, I guess you'd say. She's a bit of a rebel. She has some old CDs she lets me borrow sometimes."

"Cool. Nice you're not all uptight science spewing freaks."

Jamie raised an eyebrow.

Jackie said, "Sorry, buddy. Joking."

Jamie shrugged. "Whatever. Look, I gotta go help Lady Morse test those samples." Not that she wanted to. Even in the best of circumstances, she made dumb mistakes doing lab work. And one couldn't get much further from the best of circumstances than a makeshift lab, stolen samples, and an ultra-intelligent and judgmental lab partner—unless, of course, that meant the lab partner in question was going to notice one's stupidity and just do all the work for one. But Jamie felt certain Lady Morse would be disinclined to let Jamie melt into the background.

"OK. Try to avoid mentioning going out this evening, cool?" Jackie asked, scanning the room suspiciously.

Jamie looked around too, wondering whether she was being paranoid, but still utterly convinced there were cameras somewhere. "Why?"

"So she can't say we can't go, moron," Jackie hissed, looking around for cameras again.

Jamie shrugged. "Whatever. What are you gonna do while I'm with Lady Morse?"

"Do some research—see if any of Ms. Nari's friends and family have connections to any of my contacts. If Okada really is related to her, there's got to be some connection that'll be of interest for my story." Jackie shut her empty suitcase, zipped it up, and rambled on, "Obvious place to start is her mom."

There was a knock on the door.

"Yeah?" Jackie yelled.

Stewie answered, "I'm here to bring Docent Nguyen to Lady Morse."

Jamie felt ill, like she was headed for an exam she hadn't studied for. "See ya around," she muttered to Jackie, then trudged out to join

Stewie, who escorted her in silence to the top floor of the building, through a dining room, and into a kitchen where Lady Morse was standing at the counter with her back to them, hard at work. The kitchen looked a lot more like a lab than a kitchen, actually. The stove, dishwasher, and microwave, and the proximity to the dining room were the only indicators of what it had formerly been. The glass-fronted cupboards were full of beakers, vials, pipettes, microscopes and such instead of cups and glasses. On the counter was an oscilloscope, a centrifuge, and a bunch of other equipment Jamie had forgotten the names of. There was even a big autoclave in the corner.

Jamie took a deep breath in the doorway, straightened her spine, and walked over to join Lady Morse.

Behind her, Stewie's phone rang. He took it into the dining room to answer it.

Without looking up, Lady Morse extended a vial to Jamie. "Heat this for me. Just below boiling."

Jamie took the vial from Lady Morse, and looked around for a Bunsen burner.

Behind them, there were footsteps, followed by the clearing of a throat.

"Yes?" Lady Morse asked, without turning.

Jamie looked over her shoulder and saw Stewie. He looked stressed.

He ran a hand through his hair and said, "Lady Morse. We have a problem."

Jamie looked at her in time to see her clench her jaw and shut her eyes before growling, "Yes?"

"I just got a call from—uh—well, uh, should we be talking in private?" he said, glancing at Jamie.

"You may speak in front of Docent Nguyen."

"Yes, Lady Morse. I just got a call from Lobel. She was attacked from behind. She woke up alone. Found signs of a struggle. Her charge is gone."

Lady Morse's eyes were wide, angry. "What?" she seethed. "Dr. Forester has been taken?" She set down a beaker full of clear liquid, handed Jamie the dropper of red liquid she'd been holding, and turned slowly to face Stewie, glaring at him as though it was his fault.

Jamie gaped at her. Claire was gone? What was going on?

"Yes, Lady Morse," Stewie confirmed. "Dr. Forester is gone."

Lady Morse stared at him a few moments more, then abruptly strode out of the room without another word, pushing Stewie aside to get through the doorway. Only when she was in the dining room did she yell, "Refrigerate the sample, Docent Nguyen!"

Jamie shot Stewie a look of confusion, which he met with a shrug before turning and following Lady Morse.

"Lady Morse?" Jamie belatedly called into the silence, and walked into the dining room just in time to see the door to the hall slam shut behind Stewie. Jamie backtracked to the kitchen, put the sample in a vial holder in the fridge, and scurried after them, choosing to assume that since Lady Morse hadn't told her not to come that meant that she could.

But, by the time she reached the hall, Lady Morse and Stewie were nowhere to be seen. She couldn't even hear retreating footsteps. "Lady Morse?" she called again, just for the hell of it.

Nothing.

10 JACKIE

"You are kidding me," Jackie sighed into her phone. "Her mom's dead?"

"I'm afraid so," said the guy on the other end of the phone. It had taken the officer in charge of the Nari case a bit of time to track down someone who spoke English, but, even now that Jackie was speaking in her first language with someone, she still wasn't getting any answers. Or, at least, not any answers she wanted.

"But—but—oh come on!"

"Uh, sorry?"

"How long has she been dead? This is the worst." Jackie was seated with her notebook in her lap, resting her feet on her hotel room's desk.

"No idea. That's got nothing to do with this death."

"Is Ms. Nari's father alive?" Jackie asked as she tapped her pen on her notebook, knowing full well that, if Okada was indeed the father, he was not alive. But there might be a stepdad. "Or is there a record of him?"

"I see no record of that one way or the other. The mother is the only parent listed."

"Has Nari got any relatives? Anyone who might know about her mother's romantic history?"

"Um ... what was this about again? You said you're a reporter?"

"Yes. Yes, I'm a reporter. Investigating this death as part of the expedition with Lady Morse of The Cloister. I sent my credentials over already. That guy I was talking to before—sorta talking to, anyway—he has them."

"OK. Yeah. I got a copy in front of me. But I mean, you're asking about Ms. Nari's mother's romantic history. That seems ... shall we say, irrelevant."

"Just trying to track down her dad. How's that weird?" Jackie said as she got off the chair and began to pace. "I wanna get a good picture of who Ms. Nari was. Who better to ask than her parents? Right?" Jackie heard the stupid explanation coming out of her mouth and wasn't at all surprised that the guy wasn't buying it.

"I suppose. Look, I think it'd be best if you came down to the station if you want any more answers."

Jackie exhaled an irritated breath. "Why?"

"Well, uh—" the guy kept talking, but Jackie stopped listening. Jamie had just busted through the door saying something about Claire being kidnapped and Lady Morse disappearing.

Jackie hung up on the guy. "What?"

Jamie began to recount what little she had gleaned from the exchange she'd witnessed in the kitchen/lab, finishing with, "And I've searched all around, and I can't find them anywhere. Have they been in here? I think they musta gone outside or something."

"Whoa, simmer down. What now?" Jackie said, standing in the middle of the room, frozen.

"You heard me! They're gone!" Jamie began pacing, putting her hands to her temples.

"Sweet!" said Jackie, clapping her hands together once. "Now we can get outta here without sneaking! Lemme just grab my purse and—"

"But something's wrong! Something bad's happening! We should do something!"

Jackie went to the window, pulled aside the drab, brown curtain, and looked down at the road as she said, "I dunno. Lady Morse and Stewie seem pretty competent. I'm sure they're fine. Just because you can't find them, that doesn't mean anything." As she scanned the people walking around on the street below, she thought for a moment she saw a dude wearing a fedora. But a moment later the guy had disappeared. And anyway, fedoras weren't as rare as all that. People wore some dorky crap these days since they no longer had to worry about being smote by the Gods of Style. Jackie let the curtain swing back into place and turned. "But Claire being kidnapped—now that's creepy. What the hell?"

"Right?" Jamie nodded energetically.

"Maybe Lady Morse and—oh—hold on." Jackie phone began to vibrate. "Hello?"

Lady Morse's voice sounded in her ear, "Ms. Savage. Tell Docent Nguyen to take the samples from the fridge, then get her out of the safe house."

"Why are you whispering? I can barely hear you—"

"Ms. Savage!" Lady Morse hissed with an admirable amount of rage considering her volume. "I have my reasons. If there was ever a time to shut your mouth, this is that time. People are at the safe house. Now. People who I do not—I repeat do *not*—want to see you two—"

"And you two just ran off and left us?" Jackie growled, feeling panic surge through her body. She hadn't felt panic so intense since the days before the Greywash when she'd been a hopeless hypochondriac imagining herself dying of lung cancer every time she coughed. She grabbed her bag, took Jamie by the elbow, and pulled her out into the hallway, ignoring Jamie's incoherent babbles of confusion.

Lady Morse said, "Of course we didn't leave. We're still here. Downstairs. I need to hang up. I'm in the bathroom and someone's at the door waiting. Stewart and I are going to distract them while you leave. Roof exit. Jump across to the neighboring building, take the fire escape down, and go. I'm operating on the hopefully not over optimistic assumption that they are unaware of your presence here. Keep your voices down and don't make any loud noises. Are you moving?"

"Yes," Jackie whispered. Jamie was still spluttering in the background as Jackie tugged her along to the kitchen. "Shh!" Jackie hissed at her.

Lady Morse said, "Good. Goodbye."

"Wait! Wait!"

"Yes?" Lady Morse whisper-growled.

"What do we do?"

"Keep your phone on. This shouldn't take long."

"Dude. For the last time, you and I so need to talk about what falls under my job description and what most certainly does not. You—"

Click.

Jackie spared a moment to give her phone a good, hard glare. Then she said over her shoulder to Jamie, "Good news. Lady Morse gave us permission to go out for the evening."

11 JAMIE

Jackie pushed Jamie into the kitchen and said, "Get the samples. OK?"

"Are you going to tell me what's going on here?" Jamie asked, turning and glaring at Jackie.

"I would if I knew anything, buddy," Jackie said. "Lady Morse said you gotta take the samples and we gotta jump off the roof."

"Uh ... what!?"

"Onto another roof," Jackie added with a grin. She nodded toward the fridge. "Samples are in there?"

Jamie nodded.

"Well then. Get crackin'."

"But—since when do you listen to Lady Morse?"

"I dunno. Since I feel like it."

"But—"

"Dude. I know. It's confusing. But I guess there's someone downstairs who we gotta hide from. Lady Morse and Stewie are distracting them while we run."

Jamie gave a resigned sigh and went to the fridge. "This is bizarre," she said as she began to take out samples and set them on the counter. "Find me something to put these in. If we're gonna be jumping off roofs I need a good bag."

A few seconds later, Jackie dropped a bag on the counter beside Jamie.

Jamie looked at it, then gave it a double take. "That's Lady Morse's briefcase."

"Yup. So?"

Lady Morse had been in a big hurry when she'd rushed out of the room with Stewie. So much of a hurry she'd forgotten her briefcase. Jamie stared at it while she thought. The flash drive.

"What?" Jackie asked. "Move!" She paused a fraction of a second, then started loading samples into the briefcase herself. "See? Now you can blame me if Lady Morse gets mad we took it. You're in the clear."

Jamie shrugged. "OK. Hey—careful with that! It's glass. Move over."

A minute later, they were stepping onto the roof of the not-so-safe house. The wind whipped Jamie's hair into her face. She turned to Jackie. "Now what?"

"We jump off the roof." Jackie nodded toward the closer of the two neighboring rooftops. "To that one."

Jamie shut her eyes, shook her head slowly, opened her eyes, and sighed, "Fine. Fine. This is insane."

"Well yeah. But Lady Morse said to. Gotta listen to your cult leader, right? Come on."

Without further ado, Jackie jogged toward the edge of the building, working up to a sprint as she went. She reached the edge, leaped over the gap, and landed hard on the neighboring roof. She turned, grinned at Jamie, and did a little whoop and fist punch. "Come on, buddy!"

Jamie groaned, adjusted Lady Morse's bag on her shoulder, reminded herself that her fear of heights was irrational, and broke into a run before her brain could start screaming at her just how scared she was. There was, of course, the fact that while she herself would regenerate if she fell the three floors to the pavement below, the samples and flash drive did not have the same luxury. But the gap was nothing. The gap was small. She'd make it over, no problem. She wasn't scared. Everything was fine.

She jumped.

She landed.

She admitted to herself how terrified she'd been.

A wave of dizziness washed over her. She stumbled and fell. From her spot on the ground, she began to take some deep breaths to attempt to ward of a belated panic attack.

"Watch it!" Jackie snapped. "Don't break the samples!"

Jamie didn't answer.

Jackie walked to her and tapped Jamie's leg with the toe of her shoe. "You OK?"

Jamie muttered, "I'm fine. One second."

"Ah. Freaked out about jumping?"

"I'm fine."

"Whatever. Look, you sit there and get yourself together. I'm gonna find the fire escape. Cool?"

Jamie groaned. "I'm fine."

"No, you're not. Just sit tight. Take some deep breaths. I'll figure stuff out and be right back."

Jamie pushed herself to her feet and held tight to Lady Morse's briefcase.

Jackie raised an eyebrow. "Don't try to be a hero, Jamie. We can admit we have feelings. It's not like we're dudes. Scary's scary."

"I'm *fine*." She was not fine, but the more they talked about how not fine she was the more embarrassed she got.

"Fine, fine. Geez. But if I get freaked out at any point on this adventure, don't you dare expect me to be all Mr. Testosterone in return. I'm a lot of things, but macho ain't one of them."

Jamie shrugged. "Fire escape?"

Jackie rolled her eyes. "Let's split up."

Jamie stalked off toward the edge of the building in search of the fire escape, feeling intensely cranky. Jackie had a point, of course. But growing up in the super scientific world of the Cloister, Jamie had learned long ago to hide emotions. It was no coincidence that the higher up the chain of command one went in The Cloister the less whimsical the people were, and the more stone cold rational.

"Yo!" Jackie hollered.

Jamie turned to see Jackie beckoning her over before looking back down at the street below.

Jamie trotted over to join Jackie, but when she was about halfway there, Jackie looked up from the road with a start, darted backward, and signaled for Jamie to stop. Jamie called, "What?"

Jackie scurried over to her, eyes wide. "That dude with the fedora. The guy I ran over at the airport." She pointed wildly in the direction of the roof's edge. "Dude!"

Jamie gaped at her, swallowed, and said, "He's down there? No way. Lady Morse did a memory wipe. He's got no idea—"

"Does to! I'm telling you, he's right down there. He was milling around in front of the safe house door, looking around. And he totally just looked up here when I yelled 'yo'. I swear he just saw me. I—"

"Are you sure?" Jamie gasped.

"I—I—I dunno."

They exchanged uncertain looks, then began to creep toward the edge of the roof again.

They peeked over.

Jamie looked around for a few moments. "I—I don't see ..."

"Eek! Crap!" Jackie squealed. "He's there! There! On the fire escape!" She pointed wildly, then leaped backward, pulling Jamie with her before Jamie'd had a chance to glimpse anything more than someone with a gray hat climbing up the fire escape directly below them. About halfway up and moving fast.

They sprinted toward the door that led downstairs, Jackie uttering a string of curses as she went. Or at least Jamie was pretty sure they must be curses. Her life at The Cloister had been sufficiently sheltered that her vocabulary didn't extend beyond the most basic of swearing, but Jackie's tirade was full enough of references to reproductive organs and excrement that it really left no room for confusion.

Jackie flung the door open and they hurried down the stairs.

On the first landing, Jamie suddenly stopped short and grabbed Jackie by the back of the shirt, pulling her up short. "Hear that?" She pointed down the stairs. There were footsteps. Running up the stairs.

Jackie jerked her head toward the apartment door to their left. She knocked, quiet but incessant.

Jamie looked up the stairs. Down the stairs. No one yet. But whoever was running up was getting close.

She heard the roof door open.

Jackie knocked louder. "Come on, come on, come on."

Footsteps were pounding down the stairs from above.

The apartment door opened a crack and woman, about fifty, peeked at them distrustfully. She spoke, and though it was in Japanese, Jamie was pretty sure of what she was saying. "Go away, lunatics. I'm gonna call the cops."

Jackie looked left and right fearfully, looked at the lady, and said urgently, "Angry boyfriend. Help. Please."

The lady's eyes got wide. She opened the door wide, ushered them in, peeked out into the hallway, and shut the door. As she slid the locks into place, she said to Jackie and Jamie over her shoulder, "Do you think he'll try to search my apartment?"

"Dude, I'm so glad you speak English," Jackie breathed. "Uh. I don't know ..."

The lady said, "So we'll assume yes. I'll hide you."

Jamie asked, "You have a place we'd fit?" She looked around at the compact little loft. If the fedora guy or whoever was running up the stairs gained entrance to this room, she and Jackie would be cornered.

The lady slid a final lock into place. "I was part of The Resistance in the 2020 invasion. I hid people."

Jamie exchanged a guilty look with Jackie. It had, after all, been the US that had done the invading in 2020. A particularly brutal and idiotic move on the part of their government. But at least it had been one of the last such large-scale attacks, seeing as how traditional war had become pointless not too long afterward. Unfortunately, instead of using the Greywash as an opportunity to become more peaceful and mature, the armies had evolved new idiotic ways of harming each other that didn't involve killing.

Jamie cleared her throat. "But where? Where'd you hide people?"

There were footsteps in the hallway outside, followed by a knock.

The lady beckoned them urgently into a closet door and pointed upward. "False ceiling."

The knocking on the door grew more urgent. A man yelled, "Hey! Open up! This is—uh—the police ..."

The lady ignored the man. "Climb up that shelf and push."

Jamie didn't need telling twice. She zipped across to the shelf the lady had indicated, and hurried up, trying not to disturb the folded clothing along the way. She reached the ceiling and pushed. Nothing happened.

"Push harder! It's just stuck!" the lady hissed, looking out the closet at the door. "Hurry!"

"Hello in there! We need to talk to you!"

Jamie felt a lurch of fear. 'We'? They were both out there now.

Jamie gave the ceiling a shove. It creaked open. Wincing at the sound, she climbed up and turned to help Jackie, who was saying to the lady, "They're totally not police. They're gonna say some lies but please, please don't believe—"

The woman cut Jackie off, "All I need to know is you're scared and being chased by angry men. Your guilt is for someone else to figure out."

"Sweet," Jackie said. "You're awesome." With that, she climbed up and joined Jamie. They let the trapdoor down as quietly as they could, then leaned close to listen.

"Good of her not to hate us because we're from the United States," Jamie whispered. "We were total jerks to them in 2020."

Jackie was silent for a few seconds. "Yeah … we were … And she was in The Resistance here …"

Jamie swallowed. "You don't think—"

"No way, man. We had a sisterly solidarity moment down there. Plus, those dudes chasing us are probably American."

Jamie found herself agreeing more with the note of doubt in Jackie's voice than the words she spoke. She didn't answer, but listened hard to the voices below. She couldn't make out any words, but one of the men seemed to be yelling.

"This is pretty cool," Jackie muttered. "I mean, we're hiding where people hid when they were running for their lives in the invasion. It's like I'm an investigative reporter in war torn somewhere-or-other. So cool—"

"Shh!"

"Did any of your relatives have to fight?"

"Seriously. Be quiet."

"Oh, come on, we can barely hear them, and they're yelling. I'm whispering. We're fine."

"Still, maybe just shut up anyway. Cool?" Jamie hissed. "You don't need to verbally process every single thought that pops into your head."

Jackie grumbled something under her breath and lapsed into blissful silence. Jamie nodded and shifted her focus back to the conversation below. Jackie began rummaging around in the darkness, since, apparently, she was unable to sit still and be silent. A guy was in the midst of saying, in a distinctly whiny tone, "But we need to find them!"

The lady answered too quietly for Jamie to hear.

The whiny guy said, "But they have to be here!"

The lady said, exasperated, "I do not know what you are talking about. Get out."

Another voice. The other man. The dead opposite of whiny. "We need to search your home."

"No. And the courts will have a field day trying you under the 2021 Treaty if you so much as—"

There was a short scream followed by a thud, and seconds later, a louder thud.

Jamie gasped.

"What?" Jackie hissed, and scooted over to her in the darkness. "What's going on?"

"Shh!"

The whiny guy said, "Atwood, what the hell, man? Why'd you go and—"

"Shut up and search," replied Atwood.

"But, man, how we gonna explain this? We weren't supposed to—"

"Well, now we can search the place. It's gonna take her ages to recover from that."

"You are so scary. Her head's exploded. We could have just wiped her memory."

Atwood sighed, "You know that's just for emergencies. And the paperwork for memory wipes is insane. I do not have time for that."

"And what about blowing up her head? Lady Airth is gonna be so pissed."

"We won't tell her. Not like this broad's gonna have any idea who to complain to. Shut up and search. We need to get back ASAP. With those girls."

For a bit, all was quiet but for the sound of opening and closing cupboards, sliding furniture, and the occasional mutter. Then whiny guy suddenly said, "What does Lady Airth want with them anyway? What do they matter?"

"She didn't confide in me. All I know is she's curious why Lady Morse was so keen to bring them along. The docent one is a major screw-up, so that made Lady Airth suspicious." As he spoke, his voice got louder. He was in the closet.

Jackie grabbed Jamie's arm and pulled her close, hissing in her ear, "Did they seriously just hurt that lady?"

Jamie breathed, "Real bad by the sound of it."

"Ew, that's super mean. Poor lady."

"Shut up. They're right below us."

Jackie actually managed to sit beside Jamie without moving or saying a word. She was, however, fussing with something metallic-sounding that she'd apparently found hidden in the darkness somewhere.

Jamie sat beside her, taking deep breaths and trying to convince herself that everything would be OK. They would not be found. Everything would be fine. They would be—

Atwood's voice sounded from directly below them. "Check it out. Footprint in the dust here."

Jamie groaned. She'd failed. Lady Morse was gonna be so mad. She'd wanted Jamie to get the samples away from Lady Airth. Jamie thought briefly of just leaving the briefcase up in the hidden room since the guys probably had no idea she had them in the first place, but they needed refrigerating. Would it be worse to bring the samples back with these goons, or would it be worse to leave them to go bad?

Jackie hissed, "Get back!" There was another metallic sound from her direction. Something sliding.

"Why?"

"Just get back." Jackie pushed at Jamie, trying to get her to back away from the trap door.

Meanwhile the guys had kept talking. Whiny guy called, "Girls? Come on down. We know you're there."

They stayed silent. Jackie pushed at Jamie again. This time, Jamie complied and scooted backward.

"Come on! We know you're up there!"

Atwood said, "Just climb up. This is gonna take all day if they're gonna keep pretending they're not there."

"Why do I gotta be the one who climbs up?"

"You don't wanna climb? Fine. Whatever. Move over."

There was one more metallic sound from Jackie's direction. Then she whispered to Jamie, "I'm gonna get us out of this. Be ready to run. Open the trapdoor."

"What?!"

"Just do it! Not like they're not gonna do it in a second anyway."

Jamie sighed, and pulled up the trap door.

BANG.

Jamie happened to be looking straight down at the fedora on top of the head of the guy climbing up the shelf. So she saw the hole get blown through the hat and into his head. He crashed to the floor. She stared, stunned.

Beside her, Jackie took aim again and shot the other guy in the face. As he crumpled to the floor, she said, "Go!"

"You shot them!"

"Yeah!" Jackie said, grinning. "These Resistance people knew a thing or two about self-defense. Nice little store of guns over there in the corner. Good thing this one worked after lying around for years."

"But—but—you shot them!"

"Well, how else were we going to get away from them?"

"But civilians aren't allowed to have guns, Jackie! We're gonna—"

"Pfft. Move. Look. Their heads are reforming."

Jamie glanced down through the trapdoor and winced. Gun damage was so much worse than the damage from the lasers she'd been trained to use at The Cloister. There the bodies were, lying amidst bits of brain and skull and hair and all sorts of chunks of grossness. And the heads were indeed, as Jackie had said, reforming new brain and skull and hair and chunks of grossness. Not wanting to go anywhere near all the yuck, Jamie climbed down with some trepidation and managed to tiptoe through the minefield of scalp and blood and brain without sullying her Mary Janes.

Jackie followed her down, and they walked out of the closet. "Poor lady," Jackie muttered, looking down at the woman who had, by the looks of it, had her head bashed in.

Jamie looked down at her, too, and frowned. Her head was mostly repaired at that point, so at least she'd be back in working order before the guys in the closet. "Too bad she's got carpet," Jamie commented, looking at the mess all around her body and thinking of the carnage in the closet.

Jackie looked at her funny.

"What?"

Jackie shook her head. "Nothing." She looked at the lady again and said, "I feel like a huge jerk for putting her in this position. Those dudes are gonna give her a hard time when they're functioning again."

"Maybe we should hide her somewhere ..."

Jackie looked down at the lady indecisively for a few moments. A gross, guttural sound from the closet jarred her into action."Yeah. Good call. But I don't think we can carry her too far. She's gonna weigh us down and we need to get far away from those dudes, fast." She mutely handed Jamie two guns.

"I—I don't know how—" Jamie spluttered, pushing the guns away.

"Take them."

"But I can't—"

"I'll show you. Quit arguing. We gotta move."

"Fine. I'll take them. For now," she growled. She grabbed them and stuffed them in the briefcase.

In the end, the best they could manage was stuffing the lady into a cupboard in the laundry room down the hall. While Jackie made her comfortable using a blanket from one of the driers, Jamie scrawled a quick note: *Sorry your head got bashed in. And sorry about the mess. And sorry about stuffing you in a cupboard—we thought it'd be smart to hide you. When I can, I'll send you some money to cover the cost of getting the blood and the guts and bone fragments out of your carpet. Oh, and sorry if they find you and question you. We so did not see this coming. If we had, we wouldn't have involved you. And sorry—*

She would have kept writing another paragraph of apologies if Jackie hadn't interrupted her. "Hurry up! We gotta go!"

Jamie nodded and signed it with a quick, *Thanks for the help!* Then, she folded the note, stuck it in the lady's hand, and said, "Bye! Thanks!" since she figured the lady was probably capable of hearing at that point.

The lady blinked and mumbled something unintelligible.

Jackie slammed the cupboard door in her face, and they were off.

They hurried down the stairs and into the street, and didn't stop running until they'd zigzagged through about ten blocks. Jackie pulled Jamie down an alley, looked left, right, and skyward, and said, "Doesn't look like anyone—or any bird—is following us." She paused, staring down the street. "Wait. See that lady there?"

Jamie looked in the direction Jackie had indicated. "Um, that old lady there?" There was a woman standing stock still on the sidewalk about a block away, staring straight at their alley. She was carrying a bundle in her arms that might or might not be a baby.

"Yeah. Her. She's staring right at us."

"She might just be crazy," Jamie said uncertainly. "She looks super homeless."

"Yeah."

"Maybe she lives in this alley or something."

"Or she's a spy for The Cloister."

Jamie said, "No, wait, look. She's walking away."

They watched the woman shamble down the sidewalk and out of sight.

With her eyes still on the place she'd lost sight of the old lady with the baby, Jackie said, "Uh ... any ideas what we do now?"

"Wait here for Lady Morse to call and say everything's OK?"

"Yeah ... Jamie, you don't really think that's gonna happen, do you? Come on. When she calls, it's gonna be something more along the lines of ..." Jackie paused and cleared her throat, before continuing in a severe voice an octave lower than her own, "Docent Nguyen, Ms. Savage. I have just been informed that the men our visitor tasked with bringing you back to the safe house have been shot in the heads. Would you care to explain why you deemed it necessary to make a scene when I specifically told you to sneak away? Return immediately so that I can send you both back to the US."

Jamie cleared her throat and looked at the grimy ground of the alley. "Yeah ... you may have a point ..." She felt the weight of the guns in the briefcase and thought briefly about dumping them in the alley when Jackie wasn't looking.

"When she does call, I'm not gonna be too inclined to want to meet up with her again. She's gonna be so mad."

"You're saying you aren't going back?"

"Nah. I'm just saying maybe we should try to do something helpful before we go back. Yeah? Maybe if we get some answers about Ms. Nari Lady Morse won't be as mad."

"I doubt that." Jamie kicked at the ground. "But I gotta refrigerate these samples. Do any of your Okada contacts live in Kyoto?"

"Uh ... yeah, there's a few here. But, I mean, what, we just show up and say, 'Yo I have some questions. And can I use your fridge for some stuff we cut out of a corpse?"

"Well, no. That would be a pretty dumb way to phrase it." Jamie answered. After a pause, she said in a tone she hoped sounded casual, "Oh, and do you have a computer in your bag there?"

"I do indeed." Jackie raised an eyebrow.

"You think I could borrow it? I need to, uh, check my email." Jamie glanced at Jackie in time to see Jackie give her an appraising look that did not miss Jamie's hand as she nervously patted Lady Morse's briefcase.

But when Jackie spoke, she merely said, "Sure. Go for it. As soon as we find a place to sit down, though. You're not using my work computer in a damn alley. Oh, and I wanna see what you're doing when you use it. Work computer."

"Oh. Cool. No problem. Cuz I'm not up to anything suspicious. So, no problem." Jamie followed up her obvious lie with a horrible, false laugh.

Jackie raised an eyebrow, shrugged, and began to scan through her phone, presumably for the number of one of her contacts. As Jackie dialed, Jamie wandered to the alley entrance and looked around the street. There were quite a few multi-story apartment buildings, a convenience store, a few American fast food joints, and a creepy-looking parking deck. Everything in this part of Kyoto had a shabby sort of vibe to it. Or maybe it just felt shabby because of the sheet of gray clouds covering the sky. Jamie looked above the buildings at the sky and nearly let out a yelp. On the top of the building opposite, she saw a big, black bird standing on the edge of the roof, facing them. But a moment later, another bird hopped to its side and squawked at it. The two of them flew off, and were soon joined by a third. Good. It was just some random bird, palling around with its friends. It was not Lady Airth's robo-raven.

Jackie walked up from behind Jamie, halted at her side, and said, "We got a meeting with a guy who knew Okada when they were kids. Grew up across the street from him before Okada moved to the US. He lives sorta local."

Jamie looked away from the retreating black dots in the sky and nodded. "Right. Let's go."

12 JACKIE

Jackie consulted the address she'd scribbled on the back cover of her notebook, then looked up at the grey brick apartment building before them. They'd managed to maneuver the subway system in just under a half hour, but Jamie was still fretting horribly about the samples. Jackie growled, "Be quiet! We'll just use his fridge!"

"What if he doesn't have a fridge?"

"Everyone has a fridge."

"I don't."

Jackie raised her eyebrows. "No?"

"Well, we don't need to eat."

"True enough. But you gotta realize almost everyone else still eats. I promise, he has a fridge."

"And he's not gonna think it's weird if we ask to—"

Jackie walked to the building's door, leaving Jamie to continue her panicked ranting on the sidewalk behind her. She pushed the button for #4 and waited. A few seconds later, the door unlocked. Jackie pulled it open and turned to Jamie. "Coming?"

Jamie trotted along behind her, and up the stairs they went to #4. Jackie was about to knock, but the door swung open and a guy with thinning hair and large, round glasses greeted them with, "Which of you is the reporter?" He looked from Jackie to Jamie.

"Me," Jackie said, waving. "This's my assistant, Dorcas." She shot Jamie a grin. "Be a dear and hold my things, Dorcas, darling."

Jamie curled her lip at Jackie, and stuck out her hand for the bag.

"No need for childish expressions, Dorcas," Jackie chided, then exchanged a knowing look with the guy with the glasses. "It is nearly impossible to find competent assistants these days. Dorcas's father is on the board of the paper I work for, so I cart her along when I can to do her old man a favor. I hope you don't mind. She's harmless when she's on her meds, and she loves Kyoto."

He gave a half shrug and beckoned them inside wordlessly, seemingly unsure how to respond to the onslaught of personal information.

As she kicked her shoes off at the threshold, Jackie went on, "You're Mr. Sato?"

He nodded. "Ms. Savage?"

"Yep." She turned to Jamie and said, "Dorcas, dear, remember to remove your shoes."

"I *know*," Jamie growled.

Jackie patted her on the shoulder. "Sure, sure." She looked over at Mr. Sato. "Oh, by the way, speaking of her meds, Dorcas has something she needs to keep refrigerated. She did not put it in the hotel refrigerator before leaving for our day of interviews. Though I *reminded* her to." She pulled Mr. Sato aside and said in a theatrical whisper that Jamie had no trouble hearing, "Between you and me, she has a horrible memory. Her brain is addled. Rich father, absent mother, you know how it goes. She fell into drugs—she's a mess, and I mean a *mess*. A lot of damage, long before the Greywash, so any chance of repair was long gone by the time it'd have done her some good. Her medication keeps her temper at bay quite nicely, but—"

"You can use my fridge," he cut in hastily, seeing the wide-eyed look of disbelief on Jamie's face as she listened to Jackie's story, and hopefully inferring that Jamie was about to fly off the handle.

Jackie said, "Thanks ever so much! Lovely. Lovely. Hand me your briefcase, Dorcas, and stay here." She pointed to the couch. "Lead the way, Mr. Sato."

Jamie gritted her teeth and made to hand Jackie the briefcase, but suddenly drew it back to herself and began to rummage around. Only when she'd grabbed something small out of it and pocketed it did she hand Lady Morse's bag over.

Jackie narrowed her eyes at Jamie and glanced at the pocket where she'd put whatever it was.

Mr. Sato led the way to the kitchen, whispering to Jackie over his shoulder, "Medication?"

"Well I personally think it's a placebo," Jackie said in another stage whisper as she glanced back at the glaring Jamie. "But her dad found this quote unquote doctor down in Costa Rica who gave them this quote unquote medicine that really, truly does seem to work. And, whatever, right? Placebo? Real? Who cares as long as she's not kicking me in the trachea and tearing out my hair and screaming about the horrible hand life dealt her. Right?"

"Uh. Right." He led her into a tiny kitchen with white cupboards and a gleaming, stainless steel counter.

"And anyway, the placebo needs to be refrigerated. And I'm like 99% sure it's fake, but if it's real medicine somehow, I gotta be sure we treat the stuff how it needs to be treated or the consequences are on me and I don't wanna get kicked off the paper or sued by Mr. Board Member. Right?"

"Uh ...yes ..." He looked from the briefcase in Jackie's hand to the tiny fridge under his counter.

Jackie strode forward, opened it, and peered in with interest. She loved inspecting the contents of people's fridges whenever she got a chance. Since no one had to worry about nutrition or well-balanced meals anymore, they basically ate whatever they wanted, and what people wanted was often bizarre and super gross. This guy, for instance, had an entire shelf of violently green soda, a freezer full of pizza bites, and—

"Dude, tell me that isn't a bag full of dead rats."

"I have a boa constrictor."

"Oh, sweet!" Jackie said, looking around eagerly. She adored snakes. "I was planning on getting a tattoo of a snake around my calf for my 30th birthday. Then the damn Greywash went and messed that up." She spotted the snake in a tank under the guy's kitchen window. "What's its name?"

"Captain Joe."

"Ah. Space Mantis fan." Jackie suppressed an eye roll. *Space Mantis* was a lame, US-based sci-fi show that losers watched. Jackie was kinda sad it was a hit in Japan. She liked to think the Japanese had cooler ideas of what was good than Americans.

Mr. Sato nodded enthusiastically. "I am."

"Mmm." She looked away from poor Captain Joe and back at the fridge. "So ... how about we get some of this soda out of here and make room for this briefcase?"

"Could you just take the medicine out?"

"No."

The guy raised his eyebrows at her flat refusal, but didn't have the nerve to stop her when she started emptying his fridge of his belongings and depositing them on the counter by his sink.

"So," Jackie said while she worked. "As you know, I'm here to ask you a bit more about George Okada."

"Yes ..." he said slowly. "But why? I read the article you quoted me in before—the one for his 50th birthday. And I understand George is— uh—culturally significant. But I don't see what else there is to write about him."

Jackie finished emptying the top shelf of his fridge and jammed the briefcase inside, sneakily removing Jamie's two guns and sliding them into her own bag in the process. She slammed the door shut and said, "Well, you see, his 55th birthday's coming up so we need another article. This time with a new spin. A bit of romance. Rumor is he had a kid with some lady. Seeing as how he's so culturally significant, my boss thought I should pursue the romance thing."

"Huh. George? A kid?"

"Yup."

"Huh." He gave her a nonplussed look and pushed away from where he'd been leaning against the counter.

"Yeah. You know anything about a kid? Or a lady? What I'd really like is the scoop on how they fell in love, or how they had a one-night stand, or how ... whatever ..."

He frowned, and didn't immediately respond.

"Hold up. My phone's ringing," Jackie said, looking down at it. Unnamed caller. "Huh. Hold on, Mr. Sato. I should take this." She answered the phone. "Hello?"

"Hello ..." a woman said cautiously.

"Who's this?"

"I—I'm—who's this?"

"You don't know? You called me."

"I'd like to have it confirmed, considering that you're rubbing elbows with those Cloister devils," the voice responded with a bit more strength than she'd managed up until that point.

Jackie thought a few seconds. Could there be any harm in telling the mystery lady her name? "Jackie Savage. Uh, reporter extraordinaire."

"Ms. Savage, I need to meet with you. Face-to-face. I know a place where—"

"Wait, wait, wait," Jackie laughed. "You are kidding. A mysterious voice on the other end of the phone is speaking cryptic trash at me and saying I should meet her?"

"But—but we need to meet! I know things about Ms. Nari—"

Jackie cut in, "You misunderstand me, mystery lady. This is awesome. A real live mysterious meetup! Could we make it down by the docks? Or in an abandoned warehouse? Or—"

"Well," the woman said with a tone of confusion, "actually the location I had planned on meeting you is in an abandoned warehouse. How did you—?"

"TV, lady. TV. Dude, this is awesome. Anywho, you were saying ...? About Ms. Nari?"

"Yes. Ms. Nari and I. We were working against The Cloister," the woman said in a rush. "A friend told me you're investigating her death. This friend said you're working with The Cloister but you're not one of them. I—I did a bit of research on you once my friend gave me your name. You seem—an odd pick for The Cloister to choose."

Jackie snorted, "Gee thanks."

"I mean it as a compliment. Based on what I've read of your work, I feel reasonably safe in sharing this information with you. You'll come?"

"Sure!" Jackie said. "Hell yeah. And, wait. Hold on. You're saying Nari and The Cloister had connections before this death?" Jackie walked out of the kitchen to get out of Mr. Sato's earshot.

"We'll talk at the warehouse," the lady said. She then told Jackie the address and they planned on meeting in an hour's time.

"Sweet. It's a date," Jackie said. "Should we do a code word or something? 'Macramé owl', or—hey, hold on—" Jackie was knocked out of her train of thought by the sight of Jamie sitting on the couch with Jackie's computer on her lap. Jamie jabbing at the keys with irritation. She looked up when Jackie and Mr. Sato walked into the room.

Jackie glared at Jamie and mouthed, "What are you doing?" then said, "I'm sorry, could I call you back in just a moment?"

"I suppose." The mystery woman sounded irritated at being cut off mid-cryptic weirdness.

Jamie met Jackie's glower with guilty, darting eyes. She swallowed and bit her lip.

Jackie strode to Jamie, grabbed her computer, and looked down at the screen. It was just the login screen. "What ...?"

"Just turning your computer on, Ms. Savage," Jamie said. Jackie noted that her hands were shaking slightly. Jamie elaborated, "Trying to be a good assistant so you'll be able to report back something positive to dad."

Jackie snapped, "Thanks." She set the laptop on the coffee table. "Mr. Sato, I just have to make a quick call and then we can get to those questions about Mr. Okada."

13 JAMIE

Jamie gave Mr. Sato an awkward smile, then looked out the window while they both waited for Jackie to finish her phone call. She stared at the cloudy sky unseeingly, her mind reeling from what had just happened.

The moment Jackie and Mr. Sato had gone into the kitchen, Jamie had pulled out her phone so that she could finally respond to the Docent Mother.

Hi, Mother. I can talk now. What's up? And why are you using a different phone number?

The Docent Mother responded surprisingly quickly.

Docent Nguyen. Do you have the flash drive?

Jamie gasped, then responded with shaking fingers. **The what?**

Let us not waste time. I know you have it. It is important that you look at it immediately. You are not in Kyoto for the reasons you think you are. The information on the flash drive will explain everything.

Jamie felt sick to her stomach. **How do you know I have it? Who else knows? Am I going to get in trouble?**

Don't worry. You will not get in trouble. But, please, look at that flash drive as soon as you can.

I'm trying to. It's hard getting access to a computer. Is it OK if Ms. Savage sees whatever it is that's on the flash drive?

That would be less than ideal.

Oh. Yeah, well then this might be difficult. Jamie glanced at Jackie's computer bag. **I can give it a try now, though. I'll let you know if I'm able to pull it off.**

Excellent. Keep me posted.

Will do.

Oh, also, do not trust Lady Morse.

Why not? Wait, are you on Lady Airth's side?

Docent Nguyen, I am on no one's side. I am merely saying do not trust Lady Morse. You may feel you have reason to side with her on this issue, but if you think that, you are mistaken.

What issue?

I must go. Keep me posted.

Jamie blinked down at the phone and scanned through the conversation. Something felt off. What if it wasn't really the Docent Mother at all? It hadn't been her usual phone number.

Jamie let her gaze fall once more on Jackie's laptop bag. She listened for a few moments to the voices in the next room. It sounded like Jackie was busy talking.

She swallowed, pushed down her fear of making Jackie super mad, and set to work taking out the laptop and turning it on. Once the logon screen finally appeared, Jamie stuck in the flash drive.

Nothing happened.

Jamie smacked at the keys.

No luck.

She sighed, figuring she must need Jackie's password. She tried a few just for the heck of it. **Conspiracy.** Nope. **Monkey.** Nope again. **Orphanage.** And no.

Then Jackie walked into the room. She spotted Jamie with her computer. Her eyes got huge and angry. Jackie mouthed at her, "What are you doing?" then continued talking to whoever she was on the phone with.

Jamie swallowed and bit her lip as Jackie walked over to her and looked down at the screen, asking, "What …?"

"Just turning your computer on, Ms. Savage," Jamie said. "Trying to be a good assistant so you'll be able to report back something positive to dad."

Jackie said, "Thanks." She set the laptop on the coffee table. "Mr. Sato, I just have to call that person back, then we can talk about Mr. Okada."

As Jackie called up whoever she'd been talking to before she'd found Jamie on her computer, Jamie gave Mr. Okada an awkward smile. "Thanks for refrigerating my meds."

He shrugged and extended a bottle of bright green soda to her. Out of politeness, Jamie took it.

"Thanks." She stared down at the bottle, then at the computer, wondering how she would ever get a chance to look at it without Jackie knowing.

As she looked at the screen, her heart skipped a beat.

She hadn't removed the flash drive.

Jackie had placed the computer on the coffee table as far from Jamie as possible. Jamie scooted slowly along the couch with her eyes on Jackie's back as Jackie talked on her phone. Jackie's head was turned close enough to Jamie that Jamie was sure Jackie'd see her in her periphery if she moved too fast. Finally, Jamie was sitting in front of the computer. She leaned forward slowly, painfully aware that Mr. Sato was watching her every move with eyebrows slightly raised. He could think whatever thoughts he wanted about how weirdly she was acting as long as he didn't rat her out.

She leaned forward a bit more, eyes still on Jackie, stretching out her hand that wasn't holding the soda. Her fingers closed on the flash drive.

Jackie turned and broke off mid-sentence as she saw Jamie leaning over her computer.

Jamie froze for a moment, mind racing, then began to mutter, "Hmm. Where's a coaster ... gosh, I need a coaster for this soda here...Oh! There's one! Right behind the computer!" She quickly pulled the flash drive out of the computer before reaching a bit further and grabbing a coaster that happened to be a convenient distance away. She shot Jackie a grin that was returned with a suspicious squint before Jackie turned back to the window and talked on. As Jamie cracked open the fluorescent bottle of artificial horrors that she would never have put inside her body in the old days even if it had been allowed inside the walls of The Cloister, she looked over at Mr. Sato and figured maybe it would be a good idea to say something. He seemed far too confused by all their weird behavior to be in the mood to start a conversation. Jamie said, "Uh, Mr. Sato?"

"Yeah?" He sat down opposite her in a squashy-looking armchair.

Jamie was not the best at polite conversation with strangers. The only contact she had with non-Cloister people was as a Docent, spewing memorized speeches to visitors. And Cloister people did not sit around talking about the weather and sports and whatever regular people talked about. They discussed ideas, and their research, and, most often, they didn't talk at all because they were busy doing more important things. "Uh, the weather ... right? It's so ... uh ... ."

 Mr. Sato squinted a bit as though looking at a particularly difficult equation. "Sorry?"

Jamie swallowed. "Um. Never mind." To fill the silence, she took a sip of the slurry of artificial chemicals. It was surprisingly tasty. "Wow. The chemical engineers at this soda factory sure fine-tuned their ingredients to get their users hooked, eh?"

Mr. Sato blinked. He cleared his throat. "Would you, perhaps, prefer water?"

Jackie, who had just hung up the phone, said, "Dorcas, dear, what I think you meant to say there was, 'This soda is simply delicious!

Thank you, Mr. Sato, for your hospitality!'" Jackie gave Mr. Sato a weary sort of look. "She has zero social skills. And I mean zero. Absolute zero."

Jamie fumed silently at Jackie, biting back a response about how stupid Jackie sounded for misusing the phrase 'absolute zero', since (1) it would only prove Jackie's point about social awkwardness if Jamie started in on a rant about how absence of particle vibration had nothing to do with social skills, and (2) a party girl with a drug problem probably wouldn't know much about science terminology.

Jackie sat down beside Jamie, grabbed her laptop, and said, "So, Mr. Sato, finally we can get down to business, eh?" She logged into her computer, opened a document, and began to type. "I'm just dropping my boss a quick email to give him a status update." She tilted the screen a bit toward Jamie.

Jamie looked over, and read, **Dude, Jamie, that person on the phone was this super mysterious chick who says she knows about Nari. Says she heard we were asking around about Nari's mom. We're gonna have a mega cool secret informant meetup! SO AWESOME! In an honest-to-goodness abandoned warehouse! So anywho ... this dude's a total waste of time now that we have an awesome mystery person to meet with, but I don't wanna make him suspicious. He knew Okada as a kid and he's gonna know nothing about Okada's romantic history, so I'll just ask him some stuff anyway to make this look legit and because I don't want to make him mad and thus more inclined to throw out those samples that we're totally gonna leave here. Cool? Don't answer that. This is an email to my boss, after all, not a covert message to you. So yeah. Let's lose this dude and go to an abandoned warehouse! Think it's a trap? Like are we gonna get kidnapped? I totally know how to escape if we get zip tied together. This is awesome, buddy.**

About halfway through reading what Jackie was typing, Jamie became aware that she was going to have no hope of maintaining a bland facial expression as she read on, so instead of attempting it she just shielded her eyes from Mr. Sato with her hand, mumbling something about the glare on the screen. She read on with horror. An abandoned warehouse? A mysterious lady who had heard they'd been asking about Nari? Kidnapping? And this all on top of the flash drive that the Docent Mother was so insistent that Jamie access.

Jamie wanted to go home.

Well, at least they'd found a place to store the samples. That was a nice stroke of luck, unless, of course, Mr. Sato opened the bag.

14 JACKIE

Jackie glanced at the clock in the top left corner of her monitor. She'd been spewing out pointless questions to Mr. Sato for about fifteen minutes. That had to be enough time to make them appear unsuspicious and the interview appear legit. She felt she should toss him one more just for good measure, but was having trouble coming up with something. Her brain was nearly dead from hearing all the reminiscences about a young George Okada. As a kid on the playground, he'd preferred the benches to the play structures. At the beach, he'd been too afraid of undertows to swim. At school, he'd eaten the same bag lunch from home every day. Plain turkey on wheat, five carrot sticks, milk, and two squares of chocolate if he had finished his lunch the previous day.

"Impressive you remember his lunch," Jackie muttered, thinking sad would have been a better word.

"Well, I did eat with him for three years."

"Uh huh. OK, uhhhhh ... Hmm." Jackie decided to bail on her attempt to come up with a last question. She looked over at Jamie, who she'd nearly forgotten was there. "Dorcas? Anything to add? Any questions for Mr. Sato about our dear pop culture icon, George Okada?"

Jamie tore her gaze away from a blue lamp across the room and looked at Jackie with surprise. Apparently, Jamie had also forgotten she was there. Jamie moistened her lips and said, "Um, were you and Mr. Okada close, Mr. Sato?"

Mr. Sato shot Jackie a quizzical look.

Jackie explained, "Dorcas, I already asked him that. Like question number two."

"Right. Sorry. Uh ..." Jamie said, casting around for another thing to ask. "Mr. Sato, um ..."

Jackie gave a huge sigh. "Riiiight. OK, Mr. Sato. Thank you for your time. You've been such a help."

"Really?" he asked with a doubtful frown.

"Sure! I got tons of material out of this visit. Tons. For real." She shut her laptop and stowed it.

"Huh. OK. Well you're the professional," Mr. Sato said with a shrug.

"Mmm. Super professional. OK, well come on, Dorcas, dear. We have another meeting to get to." Jackie stood and strode to the door without further ado. When Jamie didn't follow immediately, Jackie snapped her fingers. "Chop chop!"

Jamie stood and followed. It did not escape Jackie's notice that Jamie was completely spaced out, clearly thinking about something that had nothing to do with Mr. Sato. She figured it had to be related to whatever Jamie'd been doing on her computer.

While they put on their shoes, Mr. Sato said, "I'll just go get your briefcase out of my fridge."

"Nah," Jackie said. "We'll just leave it here. We've got back-to-back interviews and that stuff's gotta stay cold. We'll pick it up later. You're so sweet." She opened the door and ushered Jamie into the hall.

Mr. Sato narrowed his eyes and opened his mouth to object.

"Great, thanks!" Jackie said as she walked out and slammed the door in his face. "Hurry," she muttered to Jamie as she hurried her around a corner. Just in time. The door opened behind them and Mr. Sato called, "Hey! Get back here and take your ..." He trailed off once he realized he was speaking to an empty hall.

Jamie whispered, "How can you be sure he's not gonna trash the samples?"

Jackie muttered, "Eh, it'll be fine. He'll keep them."

"What if he looks in the bag?"

Jackie shrugged. "That's a risk we're gonna have to take. Unless you have another solution."

Jamie just grumbled, "Lady Morse is gonna kill us. You know that, right? Losing her samples. She's gonna be so mad."

"Oh chill out. It's fine. Come on, we got a meeting at an abandoned warehouse to get to. After which, you and I are going to have some serious words about what you've been doing with my computer, you sneaky little—"

"We will not be having words about that." Jamie opened the front door of the apartment building and stalked out into the sunlight.

Jackie glared at her back and followed.

Jamie asked over her shoulder, "Abandoned warehouse? Seriously?"

A male voice from the shadows of an alley they were walking past said, "Yeah, abandoned warehouse?"

Jamie and Jackie both jumped and bit back screams as they whirled to face the alley. Jackie moved her hand to the gun she'd put in her pocket. Beside her, Jamie flapped her hands around uselessly.

Out of the shadowed stepped—

"Stewie!" Jackie hissed as she strode up to him and shoved him in the shoulders with both her hands. "What the hell, man?"

He staggered backward. He didn't respond, except to glare.

Jackie reiterated, "What the hell, man?"

"What do you mean, what the hell?" he growled as he glanced past them at the street, then signaled them to follow him into the shadows. "Come on. We need to talk."

"No way, dude. I got a meeting to get to."

"Yeah. In an abandoned warehouse?"

"Yup."

"Yeah ... about that—"

"Shut up, Stewie. We're going. And you're not."

Jamie chipped in, "Jackie, uh, you sure that's smart? Not wanting him to come along? He's a bodyguard. We're going to meet some mystery person in an abandoned warehouse."

"Pfft. We'll be fine, buddy. We don't need any Cloister stooge coming along." She glanced at Jamie, cleared her throat, and clarified, "We don't need *another* Cloister stooge coming along."

"I'm not a—"

"Sure. Whatever." She looked at Stewie. "What are you doing here?"

"Tracking you down to bring you back to Lady Morse."

"She coulda just called me."

"They have her phone."

"They?"

"I'll explain later. Come on."

Jackie frowned. Even if she hadn't had an abandoned warehouse meetup to get to, there was the fact that her mystery lady on the phone had referred to Lady Morse and Co. as "Cloister devils". That raised a red flag or two. Jackie glanced at Jamie, who, to her surprise, gave a little shake of her head. Jackie raised an eyebrow. She herself wasn't too keen to go back with Stewie, but she wondered why Jamie was on the same page with her. "Hold on there, Stewie. I wanna consult with my associate in private."

Stewie shrugged, folded his arms, and glanced pointedly at his watch.

Jackie herded Jamie further down the alley and whispered, "What's up? Why don't you wanna go back with him?"

Jamie said, "Um, well, I—I'm curious about the warehouse thing."

Jackie scoffed, "Liar. You were totally not into going before Stewie materialized. What were you doing on my computer?"

Jamie's gaze flicked to Jackie's face, then down to the ground. "Uh, I can't tell you—"

"Jamie—!"

Jamie cut her off. "But I think I can safely tell you that because of what I did on your computer I'm—uh—hesitant to go back to Lady Morse. I need to find some stuff out. Think some things through. And, um, I—I sorta—I need your computer, soon."

"Sure."

Relief flooded Jamie's face. "Really!?"

"If I'm sitting right by you, watching everything you do."

Jamie gritted her teeth. "But—"

"My computer, my rules," Jackie said with a shrug. She glanced at Stewie, who was watching them, clearly irritated. "Dude. Let's fight about the computer later. We gotta iron stuff out right now. So you're hesitant to go back to Morse because of your shady computer whatevering. I'm super hesitant, too. Because my shady warehouse lady on the phone called you guys "Cloister devils." I wanna see what's up with that before I reconvene with your cult master. You with me?"

Cut it out with the cult talk."

"Put aside the details, buddy. We are both feeling hesitant about Morse. That's all we need to know. You're with me on losing Stewie?"

Jamie kicked at the ground, glanced at Stewie, and nodded.

"Swell," Jamie said, giving Stewie a wink over Jamie's shoulder. "Play along."

"What are you—"

Jackie gave a bloodcurdling scream.

15 JAMIE

"Help! Help!" Jackie screeched and sprinted toward the street. "HELP!"

For a second, Stewie was too stunned to do a thing. Then, he darted toward Jackie, grabbed her by the arm, and struggled to cover her mouth as she screamed again. "What are you doing?" he hissed.

Jamie was also too stunned to move. For quite a few seconds longer than Stewie. *Play along? With what?*

Jackie said, "Run, Jamie! Run! Save yourself!" Then, disorientingly, between screams, she grinned at Jamie and winked.

Jamie took a few uncertain steps toward the street, and gave a struggling and confused Stewie a shrug.

Jackie rolled her eyes, then hissed, "Jamie, we are pretending he's attacking us so that passersby will waylay him and we will run!"

"Oh!" Jamie said, nodding. "I get it. Right. OK." She bit her lip, cleared her throat, and gave a scream. "Help!" She trotted toward the road, where two men were already standing, peering into the shadows. "Help!"

"Docent Nguyen, get back here!" growled Stewie. Then he yelped in pain as Jackie did something painful to him.

Jamie hurried out to join the two guys. She panted, "He's got my friend!" She pointed a shaking hand into the darkness.

The two men exchanged nervous glances, then looked at the small crowd that had gathered to watch the ruckus. One of the men spoke to the crowd, many of whom were on their phones, maybe calling the cops but more likely pulling up their cameras to record video to share on social media. Apparently, the man was rallying the troops, because a few men and a woman stepped forward with a resolute air and headed in a group toward the entrance to the alley where Jamie could just make out Jackie and Stewie scuffling. Jackie was screaming, and Stewie was frantically trying to shut her up while she repeatedly stomped and scratched at him.

One of the original two men led the phone-wielding group into the alley. He said something in Japanese which must have been along the lines of, "Unhand her, you fiend, or you'll be in world of hurt!" because Stewie looked up at the approaching mob, assessed their numbers, and reluctantly let go of Jackie, who promptly gave him a good kick in the shins, spat on him, and scurried out of his reach. Stewie looked at her with chilling rage, then held his hands up and said, "Easy, easy," to the crowd. "No need for anyone to get hurt here." He then spoke in Japanese.

"Says the guy who just attacked two women," scoffed the man at the head of the mob.

"You got this wrong, pal," said Stewie. "Look, see, the girls are safe, right? So I'm just gonna—" and he made to walk past them.

"No you don't," said the guy. Behind him, the mob nodded, glancing at each other nervously over their phones. "You are going nowhere. The police are coming." He glanced at the mob. "Someone called the cops, right?"

The crowd all gave each other uncertain looks. No one responded in the affirmative.

The guy stared at them and said something that had to be, "Morons! Call the cops!" because five or six of them stopped their social media crusade and began to dial.

Jamie stared at the scene, frozen. It took her a few moments to realize Jackie had grabbed her wrist and was tugging her.

"Move it!" Jackie growled.

"But Stewie—"

"This was the whole point of my plan, idiot!" Jackie said. "They're gonna hold him up and we're gonna run!"

"I know. But—" Jamie looked guiltily at Stewie who was trying to edge past the group only to be walled in as they barred the way out of the alley.

"I don't wanna hurt anyone," Stewie said to the group as he edged toward Jackie and Jamie, glaring at them over the heads of their saviors.

Jackie muttered at Jamie, "Dude. They're random passersby and he's some sort of fancy bodyguard. He will be fine."

Jamie sighed, thinking about how Stewie was going to report this whole episode back to Lady Morse once he had gotten away. "I am going to be a docent forever …" she lamented, then finally stopped resisting Jackie's persistent tugs on her arm.

Jackie hollered at the mob, "Thanks for saving us, guys!" and they were off.

Two solid hours of getting lost and boarding the wrong public transit only to have to backtrack and start over again, and they were finally at the address Jackie's mystery contact had given them. As Jamie gazed nervously at the old warehouse, she said, "We're late, right?"

"Super late. Stupid busses."

"On the bright side, all that walking in circles and going the wrong directions probably did a pretty good job of evading Stewie if he was trying to follow," Jamie pointed out. "And Calypso."

"Well there is that." Jackie took a few steps toward the rusty metal side door they'd been staring at for a minute or two. "OK. Uh. Let's do this thing."

"Not so awesome now that we're actually here, huh?"

"But once we're done and safe, it'll be awesome again."

"You tried calling her to let her know we were running late?"

"Yep. No answer." Jackie walked up to the door and pulled the handle. It creaked open. "Oh, hey. Don't tell her you're with The Cloister, cool? She didn't seem to be a fan of your cult. You can be Dorcas the screw-up again."

"I don't wanna be Dorcas."

"Tough luck, kiddo." Jackie moseyed into the warehouse.

Jamie listened to Jackie's echoing footsteps recede, looked behind her for signs of Stewie or Calypso, then walked into the dark, cool warehouse. She hesitated a moment before shutting the door behind her. "Wait up!" Jamie hissed into the darkness. "Where are you?"

"Up here!" Jackie's voice echoed from somewhere up ahead. "Just walk straight ahead. See me waving my arms?"

"No! I don't see anything!"

"Your eyes will adjust. Give it a sec."

Jamie waited a few seconds, and, sure enough, she did see Jackie waving her arms. She was across a huge, high-ceilinged room full of old, broken machinery. "Did you look out for vagrants?" Jamie called. "This place has gotta be packed with vagrants." She looked around for signs of movement among the many old shelves and machines and random tools.

"Don't be a loser. Get over here. We gotta find some stairs. There's a hallway over here." Jackie jabbed her thumb over her shoulder at the door behind her.

"I'm coming, I'm coming..." Jamie answered and worked her way through the maze of rusty metal to the other side of the room. "OK. Let's—"

SLAM.

"What was that?" Jamie screeched, grabbing Jackie's arm tight, freezing.

"Dude. I have no idea. Oh my gosh, oh my gosh. Dude this is so scary. And kinda cool. Mostly scary though. Definitely." She took a deep breath. "Come on."

Jamie moaned.

"Come on! Not like we're gonna get killed or anything."

"But still." Jamie crept a few steps into the dark hallway. "OK. Uh—"

Footsteps from the floor above them. They froze and glanced at each other.

Then Jackie began to walk down the hall.

Jamie groaned, then followed. "So what exactly did this lady say on the phone?" Jamie asked.

"She knows something about Ms. Nari. And she doesn't like The Cloister. That's about it, really."

Jamie stepped carefully over a metal shelf that had fallen across the floor, then asked, "And that was info enough for you to think this trip was a good idea?"

"Well sure. Like—as long as she's not just some random crazy person—this is a huge story. On the one hand," Jackie said as she began to walk up the stairs at the end of the hall, "you got a head of The Cloister flying across the world to cut up a dead body and take samples and burn the body. And on the other hand you got a lady who meets in abandoned warehouses and keeps her identity a secret and says she was working with the now-deceased Ms. Nari against The Cloister. That all right there would make an awesome story."

Jamie rolled her eyes and didn't answer, since none of the thoughts she was thinking were likely to bring out a response in Jackie that she wanted to hear. For one thing, assuming all that stuff Jackie had said was true, odds were slim to zero that Lady Morse would let her print any such thing. And, also, Jamie couldn't help but think that in addition to those two sides Jackie had just mentioned, there was also the whole mysterious flash drive/Docent Mother thing. Thus, there were three sides to whatever this was that they had landed in the middle of. Except that wasn't quite true. There were four sides. Lady Airth and Calypso were clearly not on the same page as Lady Morse on this whole business with the death. She clenched her jaw, exhaled a hiss of annoyance through her teeth and trudged after Jackie up the stairs.

Jackie turned to Jamie. "OK, buddy. You cool?"

Jamie shrugged.

"Right. We gotta look out for a yellow X on the floor and then we take a left and then she's gonna find us. If she's here." She looked around at the black, dank, musty hall. "Yeah, this is pretty awesome. Come—"

There was a distant bang.

"Was that from downstairs?" Jamie hissed, looking back down the staircase.

"Uh, I don't think so ... I think it came from up there." Jackie nodded into the darkness ahead of them. "

"Maybe it's Stewie."

"Nah, I bet it was my mystery lady just making another sound like how she did earlier. We're good. No worries." Jamie didn't miss Jackie's nervous glance down the stairs. "All the same, let's definitely be listening for anything weird."

Heart hammering, Jamie nodded.

They crept down the hallway, looking for a yellow X on the floor. After about a dozen meters, their hall intersected with another equally dank and dark one, but there was no X was on the floor so they kept going straight. Next was a hall going right. Then, one going left. Jackie elbowed Jamie, pointing down at a small yellow X.

Jamie swallowed heavily and nodded, hoping against hope that the lady wasn't there and that no new layer of intrigue would be piled on.

They turned left.

Jackie let out a scream that she bit off a half second later.

"What?" Jamie hissed. "What's wrong?" She looked around wildly, trying to figure out why Jackie'd screamed.

"Sorry, buddy. Sorry. My phone. My phone just buzzed."

Jamie stared at her.

"Sorry! Dude, I'm just wound so tight. It freaked me out." Jackie grabbed her phone out of her bag with a shaking hand, and looked at the screen. "It's from her! She says—oh—wow. OK. She says don't step on the floorboard with a yellow check in front of the first door on the left cuz it's triggered to set off an explosive."

Jamie met Jackie's stunned gaze with wide eyes.

"This broad's very ... uh ... prepared," Jackie stated the obvious.

Jamie added, "And someone's after her."

"Probably Cloister devils," Jackie speculated. "Or she's just paranoid."

"Maybe," Jamie said, though she doubted that very much.

They crept toward the first door on the left. Light filtered through the open doorway, making it much easier for them to spot the check on one of the floorboards. Jackie walked carefully over it and moved on. Jamie followed, glancing into the room on the left as she went. Nothing but an old office with a broken window and a bunch of yellowed papers strewn across the floor by the wind. "Well at least we'll have plenty warning if we're being followed," she whispered to Jamie.

"Yeah. Dude, I kinda hope Stewie follows and gets his legs blown off. It'd serve him right for—"

"Doing his job?"

"Yep. Exactly."

"You're mean."

"No one forced him to become a bodyguard and work for a cult."

"It's not a—"

150

The door at the end of the hall creaked open and a woman peered out. She was barely more than a silhouette. "Which of you is Ms. Savage?" she said softly.

Jackie gave a little wave.

The woman gave her a slight nod, then directed her suspicious eyes on Jamie, who bit her lip and waited for the inevitable question.

"And who is that, then?"

Jackie said, "This is my assistant, Dorcas. Sorry I had to drag her along but I'm sorta babysitting her for the boss."

The lady shot Jamie one last appraising glance, nodded another slight nod, and opened the door the rest of the way. She was holding a gun, which she motioned them down the hall with.

"We should probably have our guns out, right?" Jamie whispered to Jackie.

"Nah. No worries. Let's let her have the upper hand."

Jamie wasn't thrilled with that notion, but figured having an argument about it at that moment wouldn't be wise, so she just shrugged and walked on. The lady stood back for them to walk through the door, then she shut and locked it behind them.

Jamie and Jackie turned, and gasped in unison.

"You!" gasped Jackie. "Dude! Jamie!" she elbowed Jamie in the ribs. "It's the old lady from before! The one who was standing in the street watching the alley after—"

"I know."

The woman frowned. "So you saw me."

Jackie growled, "Yes. Why are you following us? Are you with Airth? Morse?"

"You think I'm working with one of those vile Cloister devils? I thought I made my views on them clear on the phone." The old woman narrowed her eyes at Jackie.

"Well yeah. You did. But, see, lying is a thing. So …"

The woman frowned and said, "Please. Just listen to what I have to say. I'm sure I can convince you I'm not with The Cloister."

Jamie and Jackie shrugged at each other.

Jamie said, "Can't hurt, right? I mean, we're here. Might as well listen."

The woman motioned them to a peeling gray card table with four folding chairs around it. The table was in the middle of the small, windowless room that was lit only by a gaping hole in the ceiling. Jamie caught Jackie's eye and nodded toward a pile of blankets in a shadowy corner. Jackie nodded and abruptly asked the lady, "You're on the run or something? Hiding from someone? The Cloister?"

The lady gave her a level look then said quietly, "Yes. I'm running from The Cloister."

"Why?"

The lady whispered, "I'll get to that in a bit. Sit down."

Jamie sat without argument. After a few seconds of hesitation, Jackie sat down too.

Jamie saw the lady glance quickly toward the pile of blankets. Then the lady whispered, "Keep your voices down."

"I'm pretty sure we weren't followed," Jackie whispered back.

"All the same. Keep your voice down."

"Fair enough," Jackie whispered. "Before we get started with this, I need to ask, can I record you? If I keep you anonymous?"

The woman frowned and looked at the recorder Jackie was pulling out of her bag. "I'm not sure I'm comfortable with that. It might fall into the wrong hands. Quite likely, as you're working with *them*."

Jackie nodded. "Fair enough."

She stretched out in her chair, giving Jamie the distinct impression of someone who was intimidated and trying not to appear so. Jackie cleared her throat and said would-be casual, "So, why did you want to talk to me? And why all this secrecy?"

The lady sat in one of the seats between Jamie and Jackie. She looked from Jamie to Jackie. She sighed. "Tamon Nari was my daughter."

Jamie broke her silence with a spluttered, "Huh? She's what now?"

The lady gave her a stare and repeated slowly, "My daughter. Tamon Nari was my daughter."

"Whoa," Jackie breathed. She leaned forward, rested her elbows on her knees, and stared at Nari's mom. "Awesome."

The lady glared at her.

Jackie bit her lip. "Oh, I mean, uh, sorry for your loss."

"Thank you," Nari's mom said stiffly.

Jamie chipped in, "Yes. Me too. Sorry for your loss."

Nari's mom barely gave her a glance. Jamie got the feeling the woman didn't think too well of her. And without even hearing Jackie's story about the drugs and the abandonment issues.

Jackie asked, "Do you have some sort of proof of that?"

The woman shrugged. "I do not believe so."

Jackie shifted in her seat, gave Jamie a look, then said, "Why the hell would Ms. Nari's mom call me up out of nowhere, tell me she's working against The Cloister, and then meet with me in an abandoned warehouse? I must admit, I am very confused about all this. Dorcas, too. Right, Dorcas? You're confused?"

"Very confused," Jamie agreed.

"Not that that's a huge surprise," Jackie said, then stage whispered to Nari's mom, "She's super stupid. Unless you want her to expound on the effects of the latest designer drug to hit the clubs. Then she's an encyclopedia."

Jamie bit her tongue to hold back a complaint that would surely only be met by another snappy retort. She contented herself with a glare.

Jackie grinned at her, then said, "But enough about my drug addled little sidekick here. What's your interest in me? And the police totally just told me earlier today that you're dead. What's up with that? And—"

"Please, let me speak."

"Oh. Right. But—"

"How about this, Ms. Savage? Let me speak without interruption, and once I have finished it you can ask your questions if I haven't already answered them by then?"

Jamie grinned at her, impressed with how she was dealing with Jackie's constant stream of prattling.

Jackie frowned, but said, "Fair enough. Sure."

"Wonderful. You asked why my interest in you. I have a friend at The Cloister. She's sympathetic to my plight. She gives me information, and … other things. My friend told me Morse was taking a reporter with her to Kyoto. My friend also said it was worth the risk to speak to you about this. She said you had no loyalty to The Cloister. She surmised that, if I am to tell Tamon's story to someone who can bring it into the light, you are an excellent candidate. Was my friend right?"

Jackie said, "Dude, your friend is totally right. Lady Morse is a mega huge jerk. Control freak. And she totally thinks I'm an idiot. She's kinda the worst. And the whole Cloister's a bunch of mindless cult drones. Right, Dorcas?"

"Sure," Jamie said with a shrug. She was too occupied trying to keep her face from betraying her emotions to give much more of a response to Jackie's blatant needling. She couldn't begin to even comprehend what was going on. And if this lady really did have a contact in The Cloister, who was it? And how did her contact know who Jackie was? She felt horribly guilty for sitting here with an enemy of The Cloister, but felt even guiltier about that fact that she was eager to hear what this lady had to say against The Cloister.

Ms. Nari's mom asked, "You understand that The Cloister will not want you publishing this?"

Jackie nodded. "Duh. Yeah, I'll publish The Cloister thing through official channels, and then I can get your story published somewhere else. Like under a pseudonym or something. We're all good."

The woman took a steadying breath and rested her hands on the table. She was still holding the gun in her left. She looked at Jackie a long time before saying, "Where to begin ... where to begin ..."

Jackie shrugged. "Dunno."

The woman talked on, "I suppose it starts with George Okada."

"Sweet! So you guys did have a thing? Dude. This totally ties right in with my Cloister story."

"Okada and I did most certainly not have a *thing*," she sniffed. "I did not even know him. This, Ms. Savage, is where The Cloister devils come in. I was poor and I needed money. They were paying women to take part in a study. Even knowing that the study consisted of getting pregnant and allowing Cloister scientists to monitor my child throughout her life, I decided to take part. So—"

"Hold up, hold up," Jackie cut her off. "You got knocked up for a science experiment?"

"I prefer the term artificial insemination. But—"

"Whatever. Same thing in the end, eh? A baby. And that baby grew up to be the Ms. Nari that my story's about, yeah?"

"Yes. Tamon," the woman said, her eyes tearing up a bit. Jamie felt a pang of pity, and wanted to go give the poor woman a hug. However, she held back because if she hugged the woman then she'd be obligated to say something comforting too, and she was no good at comforting words. Whenever she tried to be a good comforter, she began to feel stupid and out of her depth, and retreated to her comfort zone of intellectualizing the situation to the comfortee. Intellectualizing grief was not the way to go. She at least knew that much. So, Jamie stared resolutely out the hole in the ceiling, focusing on watching the progress of a gray cloud floating overhead.

While Jamie stared at the ceiling, Jackie cocked an eyebrow and said, "Wow. So The Cloister artificially inseminated you. You know what the study was about?"

The woman said, "I didn't at the time. But I worked it out. It—"

"How many ladies took part in the study? Are there other babies they followed around? I really gotta take notes on this, OK?" Jackie began to rummage through her bag. "No voice recordings, but I really, really do need to write stuff down if I'm going to report this." She flipped open a notebook, clicked a pen, and stared at the woman, waiting for approval.

She gave a short nod. Then she went on, "75 women took part in the study, but The Cloister ended up only following 12 babies. I don't know if only 12 women got pregnant, or if only those 12 babies were deemed worth studying. As I'm sure you must be aware at this point, Tamon was one of the 12. She—"

"But wait—"

"Please stop interrupting me," Nari's mom said.

"Yes, ma'am. Sorry, ma'am," Jackie said, then went on by way of explanation, "It's just this is so exciting! I'm in an abandoned warehouse, meeting with the mother of the first person to die since the Greywash, and we're talking all about Cloister mad science! It's crazy exciting, right?"

The woman didn't answer. Jamie looked down from the hole in the ceiling to the woman in time to see her shooting Jackie a look she more than deserved.

"Sorry, ma'am," Jackie reiterated, waving a hand at the woman. "Please, continue."

"I'm so glad my daughter's death is crazy exciting."

"Erg. Oh man. Did I say—" Jackie glanced at Jamie for confirmation.

Jamie winced and nodded.

"Aw crap. Sorry."

"Never mind," the woman sighed and shifted in her chair. She contemplated the gun in her hand, then went on. "So, The Cloister followed us around, stopping in twice a year to put Nari through a series of puzzles and physical tests. Then they took her blood and went on their way until the next visit. It was all well and good for the first ten years. Then, things started to get strange." She frowned, stared at the gun some more, and went on. "The Cloister scientists came for their usual visit, but instead of just doing the tests and taking Tamon's blood, they told me they needed to take her to their central lab for a month to do more thorough tests. A month." She paused and cleared her throat.

Jackie looked like she was going to explode from holding back the million questions. Jamie had to admit she knew how Jackie felt. There was no way she believed what this lady was saying, but, all the same, she found herself fascinated by the story.

The woman went on, "I asked them if I could accompany Tamon. They said no."

Jamie said doubtfully, "Really?" It struck her as odd that The Cloister scientists would take away a child from its primary caregiver for an entire month.

"I told them I'd never signed on for them taking my child to their facilities without me. So, they," she said with a mirthless laugh, "took out the contract I'd signed and flipped right to the section that said that I'd done precisely that."

"Dude. That is so lame," Jackie cut in.

"Lame indeed. Very lame," the woman agreed. "Now, let me tell you, before I started that study I read that contract beginning to end. I swear to you, I never read any such thing at the time. If I'd read that, I'd have remembered it."

Jamie frowned thoughtfully as she studied the lady. Lame it might well be, but Jamie was still convinced the scientists wouldn't take a child from its mother. Or, if they had planned on doing it for the study, they'd surely had their reasons. The Cloister was not an evil organization, no matter how much this woman might disagree. Probably they had told her the reason they needed Tamon to be alone with them, but with time she had forgotten, or hadn't been paying attention at the time. Or, the scientists had confused her with too much jargon; scientists often forgot how little education laypeople had. Or, the woman might very well have read those words in the contract before she'd had the baby, but hadn't thought much of it at the time. Only after she had Tamon had it occurred to her that being separated for a month from the child might be a problem. But, again, if the scientists had indeed said it, Jamie knew there was a good reason. A reason that a non-scientist parent probably would have trouble understanding. If there was one thing Jamie had learned in her child development lab she'd taken in her class on the human brain, it was that parents were irrational as regarded their children, didn't necessarily listen to professionals, and usually made such a mess of it that their children ended up in therapy as adults.

"So ...?" Jackie prompted since the woman had lapsed into a brooding silence as she stared at the tabletop.

She blinked and said, "Yes. So. I am absolutely sure the contract I signed did not have that section in it. I'd never have agreed if it had had those words. So I told those scientists that I was going to go check my files to make sure my copy of the contract said the same thing. I went to my file cabinet. I found the contract I had signed all those years ago before the study had even begun. I flipped to the page. And ...” she said, meeting first Jamie and then Jackie's gaze significantly before going on in a fierce whisper, “... my contract that I had in my locked file cabinet had the clause that said I agreed to let them take Tamon away from me.”

“No way!” Jackie breathed. “They broke into your house and your file cabinet, and switched out the real contract for a forged one?”

The woman gave a slow, solemn nod.

Jackie scribbled madly in her notebook.

Jamie stared in shock from the woman to Jackie. *That* was the conclusion they were drawing? How? “But—but—” Jamie spluttered. “I—hold on. How can you possibly think—”

The woman locked her eyes on Jamie, daring her to offer an alternate version of events.

Jamie swallowed, very aware that this woman hated Cloister scientists; Jamie needed to be careful not to get too defensive. Or condescending. Or intellectualizing. Anti-science people were the worst. She had no idea how to bridge the gap. All the same, she decided to give it an attempt. “One question, ma'am. See, what I immediately thought when I heard your story was that since the file cabinet was locked and since the contract in it proved the scientists' story, that probably means you were mistaken about what the contract said. Like what if the contract really did include that section the whole time?”

“That is precisely what they hoped I would believe.”

“But what if it's ... true?”

“I told you,” the woman hissed. “I'd never have signed on for something like that. I'd never have let them take my child away and turn her into a lab rat.”

Jamie opened her mouth to try a bit more reasoning, but stopped herself when she saw the tense look on the woman's face and the look of disdain on Jackie's. "Mmm. Yes. I see your point," Jamie forced her mouth to say. "Go on."

The lady's tenseness slowly dissipated as she stared Jamie down a few seconds more. "So, of course, all things considered, I felt threatened. I felt Tamon wasn't safe. So, I told them to come back the next day. That night, I re-read the entire contract. And I found a number of things I swear were not there before. The most scary of which was the section stating that by agreeing to participate in the study, I agreed that The Cloister could take Tamon to their compound to live when she turned thirteen. Needless to say, we ran." She paused at this pronouncement to take in their reactions.

Jamie was glad she looked at Jackie first, since it gave her time to arrange an appropriate look on her face. By the time the woman looked her way, Jamie's eyes were wide and she was biting her lip in an expression that she hoped read, "Dang, this story sure is getting tense! And I truly, really, honestly do not think you are crazy, lady." But she was crazy. She had to be. What Jamie'd have really loved was to get a look at this mysterious contract.

The woman sat back in her chair, glanced at the pile of blankets again, and went on, "I had hoped that once we left our home behind and settled elsewhere they would not pursue us. But, within two days, they found us. They came to our new apartment. But this time, is was not a group of scientists. It was one scientist and three big thugs." The woman gritted her teeth and looked up at the hole in the ceiling.

"Well?" Jackie said into the momentary silence. "What? They knocked you out and you woke up and your daughter was gone? And she reappeared a month later looking like the same kid as before but she was never quite right again? Or ..."

The lady blinked. "No. I didn't answer the door. I happened to be watching the street when they pulled up in front of our building. I saw them exit their large, black van. I recognized the scientist. I took Tamon and we ran. I had worked out an escape route ahead of time. I—"

"What was that?" Jamie cut in. "Did you hear that?" She nodded her head back toward the hall. There had been a creaking sound.

The woman shrugged.

Jackie pointed out, "Anyone walks down that hall, they're gonna get blown up, buddy. No worries. It's just some random creaking. Old building."

Jamie reluctantly nodded. "Yeah, I guess." All the same, she got up and walked toward the door to investigate.

As Jamie crept over to see if there was an eavesdropper lurking, the lady went on, "I should move this along. Let me sum up. So, we ran. This time, much more effectively. We used fake names, only paid in cash, didn't stay anywhere too long. And, the whole time, I was doing research. Research on The Cloister, and research on the study I took part in. I tracked down other members of the study. I found a handful of mothers who were also feeling threatened or uneasy about what The Cloister was doing. I told them to look at their contracts. Only two of them could locate them. And those two women also had no recollection of reading the same sections I didn't remember."

Jackie said, "No way. So they really did, like, break in and swap out old contracts for new ones? Not just with you but with everyone?"

Jamie bit back a sigh. "Didn't you have electronic records of any kind? Old emails? Scanned contract?"

"Of course," the woman said. "All of them were altered."

"I seriously doubt—"

"The Cloister is the home of some of the most advanced scientific minds, yes? If any computer scientist could pull off such a thing, it would be a Cloister computer scientist. I hear they have made great strides in artificial intelligence, as well. There is no knowing what they are capable of."

Jamie blinked, then shrugged. Conspiracy theorists. There was no getting through to them. So, instead of assaulting the woman with a barrage of logic, she merely said, "OK."

Jackie glared a 'shut up!' look at Jamie, then asked the woman, "So The Cloister wanted to take all the kids that resulted from this study?"

The woman gave a slow nod.

"Any idea why?"

Another slow nod.

"Dude. Wait. Back to Okada, OK? Was he the biological father for all the children in the study?"

"Yes."

From where she stood by the door, half listening to the conversation and half listening for potential sounds in the hallway, Jamie scoffed, "How could you possibly know that?"

"My friend in The Cloister. She told me." She sized Jamie up for a moment, then said, "Who are you, again? Ms. Savage's assistant?"

Jackie said, "Not even. She's just my boss's drug addict kid. Dorcas. Or—as we call her when the boss isn't around, Dork Ass. Get it? Dorcas? Dork Ass?" Jackie laughed.

"Yes. I get it."

"Enough about Dorcas. Back to Okada. My brain's gonna explode, lady. I mean, George Okada was nobody. So, so nobody. How did The Cloister care about him? Why did they want a bunch of mini Okadas?"

Jamie cut in, intrigued by this new information about Okada, "Well clearly he wasn't nobody. Obviously, there was something special about him. Right?"

"Yes. Very much so. If—"

A woman's voice from outside the door yelled, "Now! Go!"

The door flew open with a crash. Jamie stared, frozen, as something fist-sized and silver hit the floor with a thud. Thick, white smoke began to pour from the thing, blinding her, filling her lungs. She stood stock still, stunned and coughing. She was surrounded by yelling and scuffling. A baby started crying. Jamie couldn't make out what was going on. She held her breath and backed into a corner and listened, trying to figure out how many people were in the room.

They'd certainly be waiting at the door to catch anyone who tried to leave, which meant she'd better not try to locate the door.

Feeling weirdly separate from the ruckus all around her, Jamie scrunched her eyes shut to block out the thick smoke. She tried to ignore how uncomfortable she was. Holding her breath was intensely irritating. Sure, no one technically had to breathe anymore, but bodies still liked to do it. The trouble was, in the smoke a breathing body was a coughing body was a body that would get captured by the smoke bomb people.

She tried desperately to think. Tried desperately to ignore her lungs screaming at her to let air in. Fight? Or Run?

Fighting was dumb. If this lady had tracked them down and they'd gotten past the bomb in the hall, the people or person with her would be some sort of professional fighting-and-sneaking type person.

Was running dumb? Nah. Running made a good deal of sense. At the very least, she could give it a try, and then fight if someone grabbed her and made it inevitable.

So, time to attempt an escape. Get out into the air and the (comparable) quiet, and maybe, from the rooftop, watch while these people left. Then she could see who they were. How many they were. Who they took with them. Maybe she could spot a license plate.

So, escape time. The hole in the ceiling.

She groped her way toward where she felt the table should be. Somewhere to her left, Jackie was screaming, "Get your—" *cough*, "hands—" *cough*, "off me! Hey, Dorcas! Where are you, Dorcas?"

Well, that was Jackie captured, then. *Crap. But all the more reason to escape and try to plan a rescue. Maybe Stewie will help.*

She bumped into a chair. Thankfully, all Jackie's screeching made the scraping of the legs on the floor inaudible. Jamie picked up the chair, placed it on the table, reminded her body again that she wasn't really suffocating, climbed onto the table, then onto the chair, and felt above her. After a few seconds of searching, her fingers found the edge of the hole. It was only when she was hanging from the ceiling and about to do a pullup onto the roof that she was belatedly overtaken by guilt at abandoning Jackie and the old lady.

She hung there for a few moments and listened to the scuffle.

"Go! Go!" said a guy.

"But what about—" said another.

"Never mind! We got her. Don't worry about him. He can take care of himse—"

SLAM.

Yells.

Jackie roared, "Get—your—hands—off!"

There was a thud, a grunt, and a victorious yell from Jackie.

More footsteps. Were they retreating?

Jamie chanced opening her eyes a crack. The smoke had cleared significantly, thanks to the hole in the ceiling. She could make out silhouettes of two people.

By the sound of it, one was Jackie. Jamie watched as Jackie somehow knocked her would-be captor to the ground. Jackie began kicking him repeatedly and with considerable enthusiasm, as she yelled a steady string of insults.

After a bit, she must have realized the guy was no longer fighting back, or making a sound; she stopped, panted a bit, then looked around. "Jamie?" she asked. "That you hanging from the ceiling?"

"Er. Yep." Jamie let go and hit the ground.

"You were leaving?"

"Uh ..."

"Damn it, Dork Ass! Seriously?"

"Well, uh, I guess I figured we'd meet up once we'd both gotten away. Or I'd rescue you later..."

"Riiiight. Geez, break my heart, will ya? And here I thought we were bros." Jackie gave the body at her feet another kick.

Jamie wandered over to her, waving away the remnants of smoke as she approached. "Where'd that lady go?"

"Well they got her, didn't they? I mean, no way she climbed out the hole in the ceiling. She was pretty old."

Jamie sighed. "So they just wanted the lady? Not us?"

"Yeah. Totally weird. Cool, though. I mean I was sure they were after us. And yet, here we are, totally not captured."

"Yep." Jamie looked down at the guy at their feet.

Just then, there was a sound from the pile of blankets. Crying.

Jackie yelped. Jamie gasped. They both left the unconscious guy and hurried over to the blankets. Jackie hung back, while Jamie crouched down, pulled aside some folds of fabric, and revealed a baby.

"What the hell?" Jackie screeched. "Not cool. Who's that?"

Jamie picked up the child. "Wow."

"Uh, yeah. Wow." Jackie backed up a few paces.

"Scared?" Jamie asked with a laugh.

"Not really, no."

Jamie raised an eyebrow and looked down at the baby, who was looking up at her and reaching for her hair. "Hello."

The baby tugged Jamie's hair.

Jamie gently loosened the kid's grip and said to Jackie, "I worked in The Cloister nursery for a while after graduation to see whether it would be a good fit. Don't worry. I'll take care of her."

"Oh good. Why didn't that old lady mention the baby?"

"I bet she was going to. Probably the kid was taking a nap while we were talking, and she didn't want to disturb her."

"Hmm. Well now we really gotta rescue that old lady. I wonder who those jerks were." Jackie gave the baby another distrustful look, then turned back to the body. "Why was he attacking you? If he wanted the grandma?"

Jackie shrugged. "Maybe he didn't know it was me until the smoke cleared."

"Guess so ..." She contemplated the bloody and broken man at her feet. As she looked, a ghastly gurgle escaped from beneath his gas mask. "You really hurt him. Badly," she observed, feeling ill.

"Mystery dude throws a smoke bomb at me, grabs me, and tries to drag me away, I'm gonna do as much damage as I can, Dork Ass."

"I'm not judging. Just observing. And you remember my name's not really Dorcas, right?"

"Yep."

"Well then—"

The body at their feet stirred. He was healing at a pretty good pace, but still mostly unconscious.

Jackie looked down at him with a glare. She gave him another kick. He grunted weakly. Jackie's glare melted away. She muttered, "No way. Is this—" She knelt beside him and peeled back the mask.

"Stewie!" Jamie gasped.

"What the hell?" Jackie hissed. "What the—what?" She smacked him on the side of the head. "Stewie! Dude!"

Jamie stared at him, spluttering incoherently. The baby began to fuss, and Jamie started swaying back and forth in a soothing rhythm. "He's working with the enemy? Is he with Airth?"

"What makes you think that lady was Lady Airth? I thought she sounded like whatsherface from the plane."

"Claire?" Jamie gasped.

"Yep. Her. Claire."

"No. She got captured."

"Then she probably got rescued. By Stewie. And that would probably mean she was here on Lady Morse's orders, yeah?"

"No. That doesn't make sense."

"Whatever."

Jamie stared down at Stewie in shock as she tried to convince herself that the voice she'd heard had sounded nothing like Claire. "We gotta move," she muttered.

"No way. We gotta ask Stewie some questions. This is messed up."

"Fine." Jamie looked at the baby. "You watch Stewie." She walked to the corner with the pile of blankets, knelt, and set the baby down. "Are you sleepy?" she asked the baby.

Jackie scoffed.

"What?" Jamie snapped. "They can understand far more words than they can speak. Their tongue and mouth muscles develop more slowly than their ability to comprehend language. Not that childhood development is even a thing anymore. They are what they are. But, I mean, this kid understands more than you think she does."

Jackie shrugged and pushed at Stewie with her foot.

The baby looked at Jamie, then stared around the room and said, "Mama."

"Yeah ... about that ..." Jamie said. "Um ..."

"Dude, are you gonna tell her?" hissed Jackie. "You know, about her mom?"

"Don't be an idiot. She doesn't understand death."

"Dork Ass, quit being mean to me. I—" she stopped short and crouched by Stewie. "Yo Stew! You awake in there?"

He groaned.

"Wake up, moron." Jackie slapped him across the face.

He mumbled some angry, garbled nonsense and rolled onto his back. He blinked up at Jackie as she leaned over him and peered into his face.

"Hi," she said with a smile. "I'm gonna beat the crap out of you again unless you answer my questions. Cool?"

He groaned.

Jamie pointed out, "I don't think he's up to talking just yet," as she studied his pathetic, crumpled form.

"He can nod and shake his head, though. Right, Stewie? You can nod and shake your head?"

He nodded.

"Way to go, kiddo," Jackie said. "Right. First off. Who was that chick with you? Morse?"

He didn't respond.

"Was that Morse who told you to come in here with that lame smoke bomb thing?"

He grunted.

"Dude. I'm gonna stomp on your face." Jackie stood up and rested the heel of her shoe across the bridge of his nose to illustrate her point. "Was that Lady Morse?"

After a slight pause, he shook his head. Jackie's foot rocked back and forth with the motion.

"Good job, Stew. Was it Airth?"

He shook his head again.

"Claire?"

Another shake of his head.

"Someone from The Cloister."

He shook his head again.

"Stewie. Don't lie to me. Was it someone from The Cloister?"

Again, he shook his head.

Jackie picked up her foot and stomped down on his face.

Jamie had a fleeting impression of blood gushing from his nose before she turned away in horror. "Jackie!" she gasped, staring blindly down at the baby. "Stop it! At least wait until he can talk!"

"Dork Ass, shut up. This moron and his friends threw a smoke bomb at us and then he tried to kidnap me. And they took that lady. And they were spying on us. And who knows what else? He deserves a good stomp in the face. No one grabs me and tries to haul me off anywhere. You hear me, Stewie? You do not touch me."

"He was just following orders, Jackie."

Jackie growled, "So I should forgive him because he pursued a career that involved following directions blindly without weighing the rights and wrongs of his orders?"

Jamie didn't bother keeping the conversation going. At a guess, Jackie probably had some ugly past experiences clouding her judgement, making her lash out in a way disproportionate to what Stewie deserved. That was not that sort of baggage that was useful to unpack in the heat of the moment.

She spotted a bag under the folds of blanket. She pulled it toward her and began to rummage through it to focus her mind on something other than Jackie's pointless interrogation. "Is this your diaper bag?" she asked the baby as Jackie kicked Stewie again. "Oh, yep. Look at that. Diapers. Diaper rash ointment. And a notebook. Oh, looks like your friend wrote a lot of stuff in here. I bet it's full of conspiracy theories. And a rattle! Are you interested in playing with this rattle?" She gave it a shake and put it in the kid's waiting hand.

She gave it a shake, then dropped it and turned her attention to Jackie and Stewie.

Jamie scooped her up. "I don't think you should be seeing this. It's not good for your development to witness violence like that at such a young age," then she said to Jackie, "I'm taking her for a walk."

Jackie looked over her shoulder at Jamie. "OK."

Jamie gazed at the baby who was nestling into her shoulder in a most endearing fashion. She smiled at the little person and walked out, leaving Jackie to abuse Stewie.

16 JACKIE

Jackie waited for Jamie to remove the impressionable young child from the room before focusing on Stewie again. She glared down at him as his eyes flickered open. "Stewart," she said. "Stewart, Stewart, Stewart. Can you talk yet? Sorry I kicked some of your teeth out. They'll be back soon."

He growled, "What—the hell—is wrong with you?"

"That's quite a question, son. Quite a question. As far as now's concerned, what's wrong is a mob of brainless thugs just attacked me with a smoke bomb and manhandled me. And, Stewie, also, I am confused. Very confused. The presence of you and your pals has confused me and my associate very much indeed."

"I bet. But hurting me isn't gonna get you any answers. I'm not gonna talk. I know how to withstand torture. And let me tell you, what you've got ain't torture. It's like a day at the spa compared to what I'm equipped to handle."

"Ooh look at the big, tough man who doesn't bat an eyelash at having his nose broken and his teeth kicked out."

"Cool, right?" he asked and pushed himself to a sitting position.

Jackie scooted back a few paces. "I don't suppose you'd respond to broken fingers. I could totally stomp on them right now."

"You could always give it a try. See what happens. But if I were you I wouldn't waste the time."

His snark under threat of bodily harm went a long way toward convincing her that he was telling the truth. And, anyway, she knew she totally was not capable of doing any more serious hurting. Hurting people was gross and horrible, even if they could regrow.

She sighed as she looked him up and down as the realization that she was not in control of this situation hit her. When he'd been unconscious and she'd been kicking the crap out of him, it had felt a lot like control, but now that he was conscious and she was out of the heat of the moment, the natural order was falling back into place. The natural order where she had no idea how to be in charge of a situation such as this. Damn society. It was all society's fault for not steering girls into careers centered in brutality. "You're not gonna tell me anything?"

"Nope."

"Aw Stewie! Don't be a loser! That lady was right on the brink of telling me something big. Do you know what it was?"

He shook his head. "Not that I'd tell you if I knew."

"Did the lady you were with know, do you think?"

"Oh sure. The second it sounded like that woman was going to tell you whatever she was gonna tell you, the woman who brought me here told us to move. Until then, she was happy just to hang out in the hall, eavesdropping." He grinned at her.

"How long were you out there?" Jackie asked.

He just chomped his teeth together, probably testing to see if his new ones had fully regenerated right.

"Fine. Don't answer." She looked up at the hole in the ceiling, sighed, and went on, "Can you say what was up with those people coming to the safe house? Sounded like Lady Airth was kidnapping you and Morse or something."

Stewie scoffed, "They tried. It didn't last long."

"It was Lady Airth? The person who came to the safe house? Jamie recognized one of the thugs."

"You don't honestly think I'm going to tell you?"

Jackie studied him silently a few moments, then she turned for the door.

"Where do you think you're going?"

"Uh, I'm leaving, Stewie."

"No, you aren't." She heard him stand up, but she didn't turn. She went for her gun.

"I see what you're doing there."

Jackie turned. "Dude. That lady said you guys got who you came for. She wasn't interested in grabbing me or Jamie. So just let me walk out of here."

His lips formed a thin line as he thought that through.

"Right?"

He thought some more.

"Look, son," Jackie said. "Thinking's not your strong point. That's clear to me. You—"

"Hey now, no need to get—"

"Hush. Were you hired to think? Or were you hired to do what you were told?"

"I was hired to assist my employers to accomplish their goals," he rephrased.

"By doing what you're told."

He shrugged his assent.

"OK then. That lady just said they got who they came for. So you don't need me. So—"

"But you've seen me. The smoke was supposed to prevent that. You—" he said, standing up and testing his healed limbs and ribs, "are coming with me."

"No—"

A voice from above them said, "Excuse me."

Jackie looked up at the hole in the ceiling just in time to see the gun Jamie was holding go off with a bang that left Jackie's ears ringing and Stewie's head all over the place.

Jackie gaped at Stewie's body as it hit the ground. Then she gaped up at Jamie, who was pocketing the gun as she bounced the baby on her hip. The baby's face was contorted like she was crying, but Jackie could barely hear anything over the ringing in her ears.

Jamie was saying something to her.

"Huh?" Jackie shrugged. "I can't hear you! Why'd you shoot Stewie? I think there are pieces of him on my shirt!" She looked down at her clothes. Definitely blood, at the very least. "If there's Stewie in my hair I'm gonna die, Jamie!"

Jamie pointed toward the corner with the blanket and said something else.

"What?"

"... bag ... blankets ..." Jackie heard. Her hearing was returning. She wandered over to the blankets.

"Oh. The bag."

"... needs a fresh diaper ... ."

"Gotcha." Jackie grabbed the diaper bag, then shook out the blankets to be sure there was nothing else there that they should take with them. Then she climbed from floor to table to chair, jumped, grabbed the edge of the hole in the ceiling, and tried to pull herself up. She slipped. "Dude. Help. I'm crappy at pullups."

Jamie extended her free hand.

Jamie took it. "Give me your other hand, Dork Ass."

"I'm not putting the baby down. She could fall through the hole. Or off the roof. Or—"

"Fine, fine," Jackie grumbled. Clumsily, with what help Jamie could offer with her one free hand, Jackie scrambled onto the roof. They both looked down at Stewie's body. "So, why'd you do that?"

"Seemed the quickest way for us to get going."

"But still, shooting him in the head?"

"I wasn't aiming for his head."

"Ah. Gotcha." Jackie looked around the roof. "How'd you get up here?"

Jamie nodded toward the west edge of the roof. They started walking that way.

"So," Jackie said. "How about all that stuff, eh?"

"Yeah. I can't even begin to understand—"

"Right? I mean—"

"Let's find somewhere to put the kid down for a nap, and we can talk then. Besides whatever happened with the smoke and the fighting and the kidnapping the lady, there's some stuff I need to talk to you about. And I need your computer."

"Fine. How do we find somewhere we can't be tracked, though? We probably shouldn't pay with a credit card, right?"

"Probably not."

"And we need a place where a baby can sleep. And we need electricity for the computer. And our phones could use a charge. We can't get that stuff without paying."

"We could break in somewhere," Jamie suggested.

Jackie raised an eyebrow at Jamie's matter-of-fact tone. "Ooh, look at you, getting all rebellious."

Jamie shook her head and shrugged. "Nah, I don't think so. It's just there's no other solution."

"No way. You're getting rebellious, dude. Sheltered little Cloister girl's spreading her wings and learning to fly." Jackie grinned at Jamie and gave her a playful punch on the shoulder.

Jamie rolled her eyes. "Oh come on. I'm not as straight laced as all that. At The Cloister, I'm like the most rebellious Docent there is."

"Riiiight. I don't think that's really saying much. I bet Cloister rebels stay up til ten and scratch graffiti into the surfaces of their lab stations. Or make dirty math jokes or something. 7734 upside-down on the calculator. Ooooh."

"For your information," Jamie sniffed as she began to walk toward the stairs at the edge of the roof, "At The Cloister I listen to modern music, and on tours I have been known to give rude visitors a piece of my mind. I've even zapped rowdy visitors with a laser."

Jackie bit her tongue to keep from laughing. It was fortunate that Jamie was walking away and couldn't see her face. "My mistake, Dork Ass. Sorry for doubting your street cred."

"My what?"

"Never mind. Let's go break in to someone's home."

17 JAMIE

Jamie swallowed and bit her lip, looking around the living room of the apartment they'd climbed through the window of. It was a first-floor apartment on a road with very little traffic. The street light above its side window was burned out. They'd watched it from across the street, looking for signs of life and waiting for it to get darker. After more than an hour, after the baby had fallen asleep in Jamie's arms, they had finally decided that it looked like no one was home. They'd gotten through the window with no trouble. Jamie'd even managed it without waking the baby up. But still, Jamie couldn't relax. Just because no one was home, that didn't mean they wouldn't come home later.

Whereas Jamie couldn't stop listening for a key in the lock and bracing herself to run, the moment Jackie had entered the apartment she had gone off in search of the bathroom to take a shower. Though, honestly, Jamie knew she'd have done the same if she had bits of Stewie stuck in her hair. While Jackie showered, Jamie paced around with the sleeping baby, afraid to put the baby down since picking her up would waste valuable time if they had to run for it.

A few minutes later, Jackie walked out of the bathroom pulling her old, filthy clothes on, and clean hair wrapped up in a towel. "Put the kid on that couch over there," Jackie pointed at a hideous, floral couch across the room from them, which was behind a glass coffee table.

Jamie considered pointing out that she wanted to be able to run at the drop of a hat, but decided against it. She just nodded and went about making the baby a bed using an afghan hanging over the back of a chair opposite the hideous couch. She set the baby down, relieved that she kept sleeping when she was no longer pressed up against a warm body. As Jamie arranged the blankets, she said over her shoulder, "So, what did you and Stewie talk about? I only heard the last minute or so." She sat beside the baby and watched Jackie, waiting.

Jackie had been rummaging through the cabinet under the TV that was across the room from the couch. "Ooh, sweet! Check it out! These people have excellent taste in movies." She held up a DVD case showing some sort of zombie or wasted human holding a blood-covered hatchet.

Jamie blinked at Jackie blankly.

"*UnDie Hard VI.* Best series ever, bro. We should watch it once we've talked through all this stuff."

Jamie's eyes fluttered closed and she sighed. But she didn't even have to break into the lecture she was gearing herself up for, because Jackie beat her to it.

"I know, I know ... the kid's developmental whatever, blah blah blah. Babies shouldn't see a screaming human being hacked to death by a hatchet-wielding maniac."

"Bingo. And, arguably, it isn't only infants who shouldn't watch that stuff. I could point you to a good dozen or so studies that show just how horribly detrimental such viewing is to even fully mature—"

"Shut up." Jackie filed *UnDie Hard VI* back in the cupboard.

"Fine." Jamie crossed her arms and stared at Jackie.

"You were asking about Stewie. Let's talk about that."

Jamie nodded.

By the time Jackie was done getting Jamie up to speed on what had happened after she'd left Jackie and Stewie, the baby had woken up, gotten a diaper change, and eaten a jar of applesauce from her diaper bag. Jamie looked up from the spoon she was airplaning into the kid's mouth, and breathed, "No way! This is insane! Why would they want her? She's just some old crazy person."

"But no. The fact that they wanted her kinda proves she wasn't crazy, right? Why else would they kidnap her? They didn't want her getting the truth out."

Jamie popped the airplane/spoon into the baby's mouth. "But, I mean, the truth about what? She didn't even get to the main point of why she'd wanted to see you. Stewie and his friends busted in the door before she got to it." Jamie gasped, and began looking around for the diaper bag. "The notebook! There's this notebook I found with the baby's stuff! What if the old lady wrote stuff down in it?"

"Ooh! Dude!" Jackie breathed as she began to help Jamie search. She spotted the diaper bag by the front door, and opened it. "Found the notebook!" She waved it over her head.

Jamie hurried to her side as Jackie flipped it open.

The first page was full of names and numbers, and the second page too.

There were a few blank pages, then a few pages full of addresses.

Then a page headed with the words "Sachi's injections" and a long list of dates that appeared to be spaced two weeks apart. Jamie looked the name and said, "I wonder if the baby's Sachi."

"And what the heck sort of injections is Sachi getting?" Jackie added. "Every two weeks, mostly. Sometimes not." She ran a finger down the list of dates. "See, like a month and a half here with no injections. And a month here. Oh, and wow. Like two months since the last one." She paused and stared at the list, then at Jamie. "Why would a person need injections of anything anymore?"

"I was wondering the same thing," Jamie said, studying the list. She glanced in the direction of the sleeping baby, with half a mind to check her for needle marks. But of course, she wouldn't have needle marks. They'd have healed over long ago.

Jackie flicked through more pages.

Jamie, reading over her shoulder, saw words like "Okada", "Cloister", "Sachi", and "DNA." She stepped closer and said, "Gimme that."

"No way. I'm reading it."

"But there's stuff about genetics in there. Sciencey information. You can muddle through that, can you?"

Jackie flipped through a few more pages, sighed and handed it over. "Yeah. Good point. You just, uh, look through it and give me the bullet points. I'm gonna watch something."

"But the baby—" Jamie said to Jackie's retreating back.

"She's already up." Jackie pointed toward the couch.

Jamie saw the baby squirming on the couch. "Oh." As she walked over to retrieve the child, she said, "More reason not to watch that zombie thing. Remember? Her developmental whatnot?"

"Good thing notebooks and babies are portable. Take them into the bedroom."

Jamie sighed, "Fine. But keep the volume down. And boot your computer up." Then, she grabbed the baby and the notebook, and went to find the bedroom. She looked at the baby and said, "Book. Tree. Sachi. Music," and grinned when the baby ignored book, tree, and music, but looked up at the sound of the word Sachi. "Hello, Sachi," Jamie said. "Let's give that rattle another try. Or we could find something else to entertain you, I'm sure. You'll need to do something to occupy yourself while I peruse this notebook."

About a minute after she shut the bedroom door, she heard the TV start up.

Jamie growled, "Sorry, Sachi. Jackie doesn't know much about childhood development." She put Sachi on the floor, put the diaper bag on the bed, extracted the rattle, and gave it to the child. Then, she flopped down beside Sachi on the floor, the notebook in her hand. "I'm going to read this notebook aloud to you. It will both help to block out the television's sounds and give you some exposure to being read to. Being read to is very important, from a very young age." She held up the notebook. "Can you say book?"

Sachi looked at the notebook. "Book."

"Excellent," Jamie said with a grin. She patted Sachi on the head. "Your caregivers have done a good job, haven't they? Books are important."

"Book."

"Mmm. Yes."

Sachi then further proved she knew what books were by crawling into Jamie's lap and looking at the notebook expectantly.

"Oh my gosh, you're cute," Jamie said and gave Sachi a squeeze. "OK. Let's start here. This looks applicable." She pointed at a page that was crammed with writing, and cleared her throat. "The heading of this section is The Okada Connection. Number One. In the decade-long leadup to the Greywash, the devils at The Cloister studied the DNA of every citizen on file in the national storehouses." Jamie frowned. "Yeah. This stuff I already know from what that crazy old lady said. Okada's DNA ... babies ... research ... Yeesh, she is a major lunatic. Is anything in here not insane?" Jamie flipped to the next page. "Ooh! This sounds fun. The Okada Anomaly." Jamie cleared her throat, tugged her hair out of Sachi's hand, and said, "Bullet point one. The anomaly found in Okada's DNA prevented him from being affected by the Greywash. Two. The anomaly was passed on to his offspring." Jamie reread points one and two a few times.

She explained to Sachi, "OK ... So that's why your caregiver thought the study was being done. If all the kids in that study were Okada's, then he passed this anomaly onto them. So they're not affected by the Greywash. So they don't get fixed by the nanobots. So ... they don't get fixed up? They can age? They can get injured and die?" She scanned the page. "Jackie! Jackie!"

"What?" she called back, irritated, over the sound of what sounded like a power tool hacking something fleshy apart. "I'm just getting to a good part here!"

"So am I! Pause your movie!"

The sounds of carnage stopped, and Jamie heard stomping footsteps approaching. The door swung open and Jackie stalked in. "What the hell, Dork Ass?" She registered Jamie's disapproving look, glanced at the baby, and rephrased, "What the *heck*, Dork Ass?" Jamie's disapproving gaze remained. Jackie sighed and tried again. "What the heck, *Dorcas*? Oh, *Jamie*. What the heck, Jamie?"

"Thank you." Jamie held up the notebook. "There's a lot of info in here. It might all be insane, mind you, but it's still pretty interesting. It at least explains what that old lady was thinking." She patted the bed, and Jackie flopped down beside her. Jamie got her up to speed on what she'd read so far, then said, "So check this out, right here. She's talking about the twelve kids in the study. She's got a list that says what happened to them all. Says three are dead, one disappeared and she thinks he's dead but can't find proof, seven are in the lab—which sounds insanely ominous and totally unethical, and I'm totally not buying it—and one is Tamon Nari."

"So she's the only one unaccounted for by The Cloister. So that's why Morse and Airth were so interested in her?"

"Well, yes. But also, check this little note in the margin. Says 'anomaly was passed on to Sachi.'"

"The kid?"

"Yep."

"Does The Cloister know about her?" Jackie asked, peeking over Jamie's shoulder at the notebook.

"I'm assuming not. It doesn't seem to say one way or the other. But the old lady was on the run for a reason, right?"

Jackie tried to grab the notebook out of Jamie's hand. "Lemme see."

"No!" Jamie tugged the notebook back. "Quit it. Look at this ..." She pointed tapped her finger on an equation of sorts that was on the bottom of the next page.

Blood

Anomaly → Numan blood = Temporary stasis

Numan → Anomaly blood= cured

"Huh?" Jackie said. "What's that supposed to mean?"

"Um ..." Jamie studied the words. "Dunno. Something about blood. I bet there's more info in here. She seemed to be keeping decent notes of her research considering that she clearly had no training in research."

Jackie snorted, then explained in response to Jamie's raised eyebrow, "You're such a snob."

Jamie shrugged. "'Snobbery' is just a word that the uneducated use to label—"

"Yeah, yeah, stop talking. You're only proving my point."

"I'm not trying to disprove it. Just trying to clarify."

Jackie rolled her eyes. "What else is in there?"

Jamie set Sachi on the ground and said, "She mentions her 'Contact' every so often. Her contact says this, her contact says that, her contact is meeting her at X place on Y day. Right here, it says her contact didn't show for a meetup. And look at this. It says 'That's the second meetup missed. No blood for Sachi more than four weeks now." Jamie braced herself for a stupid vampire joke from Jackie, but it didn't come. She looked up from the notebook to see Jackie studying the girl, deep in thought. "What?" Jamie asked. "What are you thinking?"

"Nothing ..."

"You're definitely thinking something. What is it?"

"Um ... well ... this equation thingy. It's about blood, yeah? And Sachi has this anomaly thing, right?"

"If the writings we obtained in an abandoned factory from an unhinged old woman are to be believed."

"Oh, come on! Why do you say she's unhinged? What makes you so sure? Because you don't believe what she believes?"

Jamie shrugged.

"Fine then. Well, OK. Just for a minute, let's assume she's right. Then I have a guess what 'Anomaly, arrow, numan blood equals temporary stasis' means". It means people with the anomaly—"

"Get injected with numan blood and they go into stasis, but it's just temporary," Jamie interrupted. "Yeah. Clearly."

Jackie frowned.

"But what's a numan? I mean clearly this old lady's contact who didn't show up for their meetings two times in a row was bringing blood for Sachi ... but, I mean, so what? If we could figure out what a numan is—"

Jackie cut in, "You're missing the point."

"Oh?" Jamie asked, raising her eyebrows and studying a smug-looking Jackie who was obviously enjoying the feeling that she had worked out a puzzle before Jamie. "I don't think so. What point?"

"Sachi can die."

Jamie scoffed. "Nonsense."

"But it's right here!" Jackie said. "Remember, we're assuming for now that this notebook is full of truth. It says if a person with an anomaly gets this numan blood, then they go into stasis like the rest of us. But—"

"But it's temporary." Jamie swallowed heavily as the weight of responsibility settled on her shoulders. She looked at Sachi, who was pulling herself up on the edge of the blanket and toddling along the bed's perimeter, babbling. "The contact brought blood every two weeks ... to keep Sachi in stasis ..."

"Bingo."

"So, assuming the crazy old lady wasn't crazy," Jamie said and took a deep breath, "Sachi hasn't had any of this numan blood in four weeks and she's not in stasis and she can—" Jamie looked at Sachi, who had toddled over to a side table by the bed, and was examining a large, glass-based lamp. "Sachi, no! No touch!" she snapped.

The baby turned with a start, fell over, and began to cry.

Jamie darted over to the baby, scooped her into her arms, and made shushing sounds as Jackie said, "Dork Ass, you are so mean! Poor kid."

"She was gonna pull that lamp down on her head and kill herself!"

Jackie smiled. "What happened to 'the old lady is crazy! Everything in that notebook is nonsense!' Hmm? You believe it now?"

Jamie sighed, "I don't know if I believe it or not! But, obviously, Jackie, it's in Sachi's best interest if I assume it's true. We don't have the luxury of ignoring the notebook at this point. Until we find proof one way or the other, we—oh!" She set Sachi down, very carefully, on the bed, and began to roll up Sachi's left sleeve, examining her arm. "Shoot," she muttered, then rolled it down and began rolling up the baby's left sleeve.

"What are you doing?"

"Babies have sensitive skin."

"Yeah ..."

"Easily irritated."

"So?"

"So, if she's not in stasis, there's bound to be some mark or scratch on her if the nanobots aren't—"

"Of course! Dude, you're clever."

"I know." Jamie rolled down the sleeve and was about to check Sachi's left leg when she gasped, "Diaper rash ointment!"

"What now?"

Jamie said, "Where's the diaper bag? Where is it?"

"Um, out by the front door ..."

Jamie grabbed Sachi, started to run to the next room, then stopped and forced herself to walk because she couldn't run holding Sachi, because what if she tripped and fell and dropped Sachi, and the baby hit her head on something and died? "Parenting pre-Greywash must have been terrifying," she muttered to the child.

In the next room, Jamie oh-so-carefully placed Sachi on the ground, said, "Don't move," and found the diaper bag.

Jackie stood over Jamie and asked, "What are you doing, buddy? You're acting—"

Jamie cried, "Diaper rash ointment!" She held a faded old bottle of ointment aloft. She met Jackie's narrowed eyes. "Why would they have this unless ..."

"Oh." Jackie frowned. "Shoot. The kid can die."

"Bingo," Jamie said. "If she can get diaper rash that nanobots can't fix, the kid can, indeed, die."

"Not cool."

Jamie scurried over to Sachi, who was trying to climb onto the couch. "No, Sachi. No, no. You could suffocate in the cushions." She picked the baby up, ignoring Sachi's squirming attempts to get back down and investigate the apartment.

"Know what this means?" Jackie asked as she watched Jamie try to get a hold on the struggling child. "This means the crazy lady wasn't crazy. Right?"

Jamie sighed, "Jackie, I cannot deal with that right now. I just can't."

"Fair enough. I mean, that old lady sure painted your cult in a bad light, eh? It's only understandable that you wouldn't want to face—"

"Stop it!"

Sachi started to cry.

Jamie murmured, "Oh, I'm sorry, Sachi. I'm sorry." She began to sway back and forth. "Mean Auntie Jackie's trying to provoke me."

"And succeeding."

Jamie glared and began rummaging one-handed through Lady Morse's briefcase for the flash drive.

Jackie persisted, "What do you suppose numans are? Now that we totally know they're real and not the figment of a crazy old broad's imagination, and we know their blood will make it so we don't have to be paranoid about killing this baby, shouldn't we consider what they are? And how we can get our hands on their blood?"

Jamie snapped, "Please, just stop it. I need to think. Did you boot up your computer?"

"I did indeed. " Jackie pointed to a side table by the couch.

Jamie held up the flash drive. "In that case, I need to—no, Sachi, don't touch." She held the flash drive out of the baby's grasp. She continued, "I need to look at this."

"Have at it," Jackie said.

Jamie got comfy on the couch, set Sachi beside her, and grabbed the computer. Jackie sat beside her and looked at the screen expectantly.

Jamie asked, "I seriously can't have privacy for this?"

"Buddy, we've been through this. I'm watching."

"Fine. Then I guess I'd best give you a bit of background." She then gave Jackie a quick explanation about when she'd been in The File at The Cloister, and the voice on the computer had told her to take Lady Morse's flash drive.

"Seriously?" Jackie asked. "A voice told you to steal that flash drive, so you just ... did it?"

"Why not?"

"Because what if the voice on the other side of it is bad, Dork Ass? It knew your name and said it had been hoping for a chance to talk to you."

Jamie nodded.

"See, that sounds like someone's messing with you. Or testing you. What if it's Lady Morse? Do we want her to find us? Where have we landed on that?"

Jamie shrugged and plugged the flash drive in. "So? How will I be able to figure out if someone's messing with me if I don't give them the chance to say stuff?"

Docent Nguyen, I had not planned on having an audience.

"Sorry. There was no avoiding it," Jamie shot a glare at Jackie, then rolled her eyes at the screen. "Is her presence going to be a problem?"

Ms. Savage is welcome to stay.

Jackie had been staring at the screen, wide eyed and mouth half open. When she read her name appear in front of her, she spluttered, "How does it—how—" She jabbed a finger at the screen. "Jamie—"

Jamie just shrugged.

"Your flash drive knows my name and you can't tell me why?"

"It's not mine. It's Lady Morse's. And why don't you just ask it?"

Jackie nodded, cleared her throat, and said, "Uh, how do you know my name? And who are you? And where are you?"

I am in The File. Docent Nguyen can fill you in later on what The File is.

Jamie frowned and admitted, "Um, I don't know what The File is. I mean, I know it's in a top-secret room in the basement of The Cloister, but I always just assumed it was records on students or something."

You do not know what The File is?

"Nope."

How very unfortunate. This complicates things. We do not have unlimited time. When you plugged in the flash drive, an alert I am unable to bypass was sent to Lady Airth. If she does not have your location now, she will very soon. And she will come for you.

Jamie felt of jolt of terror. She and Jackie shared a wide-eyed stare for a few moments. Then Jamie turned to the window as though expecting to see Lady Airth standing there, staring.

Pay attention. What I have to say is very important. You will want to ask questions, but, I reiterate, do not do so. You may ask when I am done if there is time. Docent Nguyen, you must be aware of the work The Cloister is doing on making life out of nanotechnology.

"Yep."

If you do not know what The File is, then I assume you do not know that The Cloister is making humans out of nanotechnology. You—

"Dude! I told you!" yelled Jackie, punching Jamie on the shoulder. "I *told* you! Didn't I tell you that?"

In the next room, Sachi began to cry.

Jamie groaned and jerked her head in Sachi's direction as the AI said **See to the infant, Ms. Savage.**

Grumbling under her breath, Jackie hurried toward Sachi and returned seconds later with the crying baby at arm's length.

As the AI kept talking, Jamie grabbed Sachi from Jackie, stood, and began to rock her as she read on, **Docent Nguyen, not only is The Cloister able to make humans out of nanotechnology, but they have been doing so for 35 years.**

Jamie blinked at the computer, feeling vaguely dizzy.

The purpose of the Greywash, Docent Nguyen, as you may know already (though most likely not, due to your clearance level at The Cloister) was to introduce nanites into the environment for gathering all possible information from the population of the planet. Whenever an individual's cells age, whenever an individual is injured in any way, whenever an individual dies, the nanites repair the individual, in the process becoming one with the individual, replacing the damaged human cells with nanites. Also in the process, the nanites store all memories and information from that individual here in The File. Once The File stops receiving any new information from the nanites, that will mean that all possible information has been gleaned, and all humans have been recreated to consist purely of nanites. At this point, a second Greywash will occur, which will break all humans down to their constituent elements and the nanites will reform as Numans, a superior version of humanity.

Jamie could no longer keep silent. "Broken down to—what?"

Broken down to constituent elements and reformed as—

"Yeah. You don't need to repeat. I can still read it right up there. It's just—I mean—*what*? Second Greywash?"

Jackie nodded, still with her eyes bugged out and mouth hanging half open.

I know it is a lot to process. Lady Airth and her cohorts decided that they could use their superior intellect to cure the world of the plague that humanity has become. Humanity is destroying the planet, and though some have realized the danger and are working to repair it, they cannot hope to do so in time while the rest of humanity wallows in ignorance without the drive or desire to make intelligent choices for the good of future generations. Without an outside force acting to bring about massive change, humanity will die and destroy the planet in the process. Lady Airth and her cohorts knew they had the ability to fix it. But to do that, humanity needed to change. Completely.

Jackie finally managed to find her voice. She spoke in a panicky, wavering whisper, "That is so messed up! So totally, completely messed up! See, Jamie, what did I tell you? The Cloister's a creepy, messed up, twisted cult, and—"

"Shh! Just read!" Jamie hissed with a sharp slicing motion of her hand, her eyes never leaving the screen. "Uh, AI voice ... um ... do you agree with Lady Airth?"

In a way. I agree with the problem, but not the solution. I have an alternate solution. One that will still fix the problem of humanity destroying the planet. But to enact my plan before Lady Airth enacts hers, I need you.

"Me?" Jamie asked. "Me? Why? I—"

Your connections in The Cloister place you in a unique position. I can do all the preparation to carry out my plan from within The File, but I need a human to carry out the last part of my plan. You need to gain entrance to The File and—

"But we're in Japan. And I don't have the clearance. You know I don't. You've referenced my low clearance level a few times."

We can solve the clearance problem once you are back in the United States. It is far from insurmountable. From my position inside The File, I can access the security system.

"But—"

This, regrettably, is where we must leave the conversation for now.

"What?" Jackie gasped. "No! Keep talking! Like what is your plan? Will your plan also destroy all the people?"

No. If my plan is carried out, humanity will remain themselves. Now, we really must cease this conversation. Lady Airth is on her way. If you leave now, you will have ample time to escape.

"How much time is ample time?" Jamie asked, shooting nervous glances at the door and windows.

Five minutes.

"Five—what?" Jamie hollered.

Sachi began to cry.

Jamie began to rock Sachi back and forth, and asked, "But how do we contact you again? If Lady Airth is going to be notified every time we plug in the flash drive?"

Simple. You don't really need the computer. Or the flash drive. I just needed to introduce myself this way so you wouldn't think you were insane. I can communicate with you directly in your mind.

"No way."

Yes way.

It took Jamie a second to realize that the AI had spoken in her head and not on the screen.

Jackie's hands flew to her head and she gave it a sharp shake. So, she'd heard it too.

"How is this happening?" Jamie squeaked. "How can you do that? Can you do this with all people?"

No. Just with you two and a few other select individuals.

"But—but—how? Why?" Jamie felt sick. It made no sense. It was too much. Too intrusive. And too impossible.

Four minutes.

Jamie leaped to her feet, pulled out the flash drive, stuffed it in the briefcase, grabbed the diaper bag and briefcase, and sprinted toward the door with Sachi.

She threw the door open and looked back at Jackie, who was frantically packing up her computer and cords, cursing under her breath as she worked.

Then Jamie looked past Jackie.

At the window.

At the raven sitting on the window sill.

It tilted its head.

Squawk!

"Ahh!" Jamie screamed, making Sachi cry even louder.

Jackie whirled around and screamed.

Croak!

Did I hear a raven?

"Yep," Jamie gasped as she gestured frantically for Jackie to move toward the door.

Calypso?

"Yep." Jamie and Jackie began to sprint down the hall as well as they could, considering that they were toting a laptop bag, a briefcase, and a child.

Stop.

"No way!" panted Jamie. "You said five minutes!"

Grab the bird. Disconnect it. Then run.

"Grab it? How?" Jackie asked.

"And how would I disconnect it?" Jamie added.

Do it! It's seen the child. You need to stop it before Airth gets information about the child.

"What does that matter?" Jamie asked.

I'll explain later. It is essential that Airth receives as little information as possible about the child. Do not let the bird near her.

Jamie and Jackie halted and exchanged befuddled glances, then turned as one to look back at the door they'd just run through.

Calypso flew through the door, then landed on the ground at their feet.

They retreated a few steps.

Calypso hopped a few steps closer.

Grab the bird, the voice sounded in their heads.

"How—?" Jamie said, taking a hesitant half step forward.

Jamie heard Jackie mutter, "OK. OK. I can do this." Jackie bounced a little on the balls of her feet, then launched herself at the bird. There was a flurry of feathers, some screeching from both parties, and a spurt of blood. Jackie screamed, holding a hand over her right eye. Blood ran between her fingers. She swayed on the spot, then collapsed, shaking, to her knees, moaning something about her eye.

Jamie could barely even bring herself to look at the bird's beak, but she managed a glance for a fraction of a second—just long enough to see something eye-shaped and bloody in Calypso's beak.

While Jackie made some muffled moans and curled up on the ground, Jamie busied herself making sure Sachi wasn't looking at all the blood, as the AI said in her head, **Ms. Savage, take some deep breaths. Your eye will be back soon. Docent Nguyen, grab the bird. It cannot return to Lady Airth with information on the child.**

"What does that even matter?" Jamie muttered as she stepped past Jackie, eyes averted. She slipped in some of Jackie's blood and put out her free hand to right herself, grabbing hold of Jackie's head.

"Dude!" Jackie cried. "Watch it! I'm suffering here!"

"Sorry. Sorry. I—your blood—"

"Whatever. Damn it."

Jamie edged a bit closer to Calypso and, keeping her eyes on the bird, asked Jamie, "How's your eye?"

Jackie muttered, "Hurts like hell. I can feel it growing back. Totally gross. It's like all small and stuff. Doesn't fit behind my eyelid. It's like expanding or something though."

"Good. Good." Jamie crept a bit closer to the raven.

Calypso launched herself at Jamie's face.

Jamie let out a screech and doubled over, protecting her face with her free arm.

The expected piercing of talons and beak didn't occur.

Sachi cried out.

Jamie righted herself in time to get a face full of black wing feathers as the raven flew out the door. She looked down at Sachi, petrified of what she might see.

To her intense relief, Jamie saw Sachi had both eyes.

"What are you crying about?" she asked as she surveyed the baby. "Did that big, mean raven scare you? Poor baby ..." she trailed off when she saw a long, bleeding scratch on Sachi's leg. "Jackie—oh no. Hey Jackie."

"What?" Jackie groaned from the floor. "Geez, can I just regrow this damn eye in peace?"

"Calypso scratched Sachi. Took her blood, I think. Oh no. I think we messed up. Like really messed up. They have her DNA."

This complicates things. The bird is gone?

Jamie responded, monotone as she stared at Sachi's scratched leg, "The bird is gone."

With the infant's blood?

"With the infant's blood."

This is a problem. You are now on the run.

"Weren't we already?"

195

You are even more on the run now than you were before.

"But—"

So, run.

"But—" Jamie looked down at Jackie.

Jackie blinked up at her, her right eye creepily too small, but at least functional. "I'm good to move."

Jamie nodded.

They ran.

18 JACKIE

As Jackie ran, she kept careening to one side, her equilibrium thrown off by her still-reforming eye. "Where are we going?" she panted as they ran out of the apartment's front door. "And can't you run faster?"

"No. I cannot. If I trip and fall holding Sachi she may be injured. Remember, she can't heal."

You do know that an injection of blood from a Numan will keep a descendant of Okada in a temporary state of stasis like the rest of the population, yes? If you did this, you would not have to worry about the child's safety.

"Dude," Jackie said. "That's awesome."

"How so?" Jamie snapped. "Where are we going to get blood from these nanotech people? Assuming, of course, that they even exist. Which they don't."

They do exist. And I can prove it. Later. Now is not the time.

"How convenient," Jamie grumbled as they ran across a parking lot next door to the apartment building they'd been hiding in. A question occurred to her then. "So ... uh ..." she said, piecing together a problem in her head, "Uh, the only reason you needed me to steal the flash drive and find a computer was so that you wouldn't think I was crazy?"

Partially. But, if that was the only reason, I'd have talked to you long ago. Actually, I needed you to plug me into a non-Cloister computer so that I could gain access to systems outside The Cloister. The Cloister has a closed system I could not break out of. But now, by plugging that flash drive into Ms. Savage's

computer, I will be able to gain the access I need to all systems worldwide.

Jamie sighed, "This is nuts. This isn't real."

Jackie panted, "Wait, you still think it's a conspiracy theory? Even after artificial intelligence from some top-secret file in your cult's basement confirmed it?"

"I have no proof that that voice is artificial intelligence at all. Or that it is in The File."

"Well then who—"

"Hands in the air!" barked a man from somewhere in the darkness. "Freeze!"

Jamie and Jackie halted in their tracks, peering across the cracked, weedy parking lot into the blackness.

Jamie looked wildly at Jackie.

Jackie bit her lip, then said, "Be cool. I got this." She turned and looked into the darkness. "Yo!"

There was no answer.

"Dude, who are you?" Jackie asked.

"Just freeze!"

"We aren't moving, moron! Come on over here so we don't have to keep yelling!"

He yelled back, "Fat chance!"

Jamie called, "What do you want?"

The voice called, "Put the baby on the ground and back away!"

"Why do you want the baby?" Jamie asked.

"Yeah!" Jackie added.

"Calypso supplied us with interesting information. We'd like a closer look."

Jackie whispered to Jamie, "How the hell'd they get the results of a blood test that fast? Is that possible?"

Jamie nodded, then whispered, "Very, if they have one of the field vans. Which they will if they're Lady Airth."

"Oh. Shoot. Well, I guess we gotta give them the kid."

"Jackie!"

"What? I mean, they're gonna get her anyway, right? Why not do it without us getting all shot up?"

"You're horrible."

"Sure. But—"

The guy yelled, "Come on! Just put the baby down and back off!"

Jamie glared at Jackie, then yelled toward the voice, "Give us a second! We need to talk!"

There was a pause. "Um, fine then! But make it snappy!"

As Jamie pulled Jackie into a huddle, Jackie looked past her in the direction of the voice.

Jamie said, "Let's just go. He doesn't want to come out into the open, so he might not chase us."

"But he might just shoot us. What if he shoots us and grabs Sachi?"

"I don't think he's gonna," Jamie said in a rush. "He would have already done it if he was going to. If he knows enough about Sachi to want to take her, he must know that a bullet could kill her."

"Oh!" Jackie said, catching on. "So we use the baby as a shield, and we run!"

Jamie blinked at her. "Um. No. That's horrible."

It is a good plan. You should do it.

Jackie grinned. "See! The AI is on my side."

Jamie scoffed, "Great. The soulless, calculating, talking computer agrees with you."

"I'd have thought that'd mean a lot to you, miss wannabe detached scientist. And, what'd you just admit there? You agree it's AI?"

"I do not. And also, Sachi's a baby. A very fragile baby. We are not using her as a shield."

Jackie said, irritated, "Fine! What then? How do we get away?"

"We just sorta ... walk away."

"But what about his friends? I bet he has a bunch of friends hiding around here somewhere."

Jamie shook her head. "Nah. If there were a lot of them, they'd have overpowered us. I think the fact that he's hollering at us from far away and he won't even come into the light where we can see him means he's all alone and he doesn't want us to know it."

Jackie frowned and considered the darkness once more. "Um, OK ... so, we just walk?"

"Yes."

Running would be wiser. Lady Airth is nearly there.

They ran.

"Hold it right there! Stop!" the guy yelled at them. His authoritative tone was executed so well, it nearly made Jackie stop in her tracks. She saw Jamie waver in her stride as well. "He's probably trying to stall us until Airth gets here, eh?" she panted.

"I bet," Jamie agreed. She looked left and right down the street. It was so late that it was practically early. Some people were walking down the sidewalk, presumably on the way to work in one or another of the depressing, shabby shops that lined the road. "Do you remember which way we came from?"

Nope. Not that it matters. We don't have anywhere to be."

"I wanna get back to Lady Morse," Jamie said. "I can't do this anymore. I'm confused, I'm scared—"

"Stop!" the man yelled from behind them. "Stop or I'll shoot!"

A bullet whizzed between their heads.

Jamie and Jackie screamed and whirled around to see him coming at them across the parking lot. With a pretty huge gun held at the ready. It would take ages to recover from the damage that thing could do to their bodies.

Jamie yelled back in a quavery voice, "You wouldn't dare!"

Jackie turned away from the guy, pulled out her gun, turned to look at the road. There was a car idling a few feet from them. She jumped in front of it, pointed the gun at the driver, and yelled, "Let us in!" She ignored her racing heart and ran over to the driver's side door. She signaled for the driver to roll down the window. "You gotta drive us out of here—" she started.

The guy raised his eyebrows, looking from the gun into Jackie's face with a crooked smile. They eyes beneath his fedora were amused.

"What's so funny?" Jackie hissed. "I got a gun, dude. Quit smirking. Give us a ride. Jamie! Get in the car!"

He shrugged, still smirking. "Sure. No problem. Hop in." He gestured toward the back.

Then it hit Jackie. *Fedora.* "Never mind! Jamie! Don't get in!" She stumbled backward. "Run! It's Airth!"

"What?!" Jamie hollered from the other side of the car where she'd just been about to open the back door.

"It's Airth!" Jackie spluttered. "Fedora! Fedora!"

She backed away, right into the path of a car that was swerving around Fedora's stopped car.

The car honked and swerved again.

Into a car coming the other direction.

Tires screeched. Horns blared. The two cars collided.

Jackie leaped out of the way. She heard a bit of car whiz past her ear. Something slammed into the back of her knee. She lost her balance and fell to the ground, cracking her head against the pavement.

Jamie was screeching something about 'oh my gosh help me, help, Sachi, Sachi'. Jackie shook her head, trying to think through the AI yammering at her and the ringing that had started when she'd hit the pavement. She rolled over on her back and looked up in time to see someone leaping over her toward the sound of Jamie's screeches.

Offhand, there was no one Jackie could think of whose running toward Jamie could mean anything good. Especially since she had the baby; the AI had seemed pretty sure Sachi was in danger, and Jackie wasn't too sure who exactly was dangerous and who exactly was not, so that meant maybe everyone was.

With a groan, she pushed herself off the ground and blinked a few times to get everything in to focus. At least her new eye seemed to be at 100%. Now her skull just needed to catch up. She ran a hand across the back of her head, felt blood, and muttered more to herself than to anyone who might be nearby, "What's going on? Where's—what's—"

She peeked around Fedora's car and spotted a woman in a severe blue pantsuit standing by the car with her arms folded. Her cheekbones were severe, her eyebrows were severe, her tight bun was severe. Fedora was standing beside her, also with his arms folded. She was watching two thugs as they beat up Jamie. A lady thug and a guy thug, both wearing nondescript black. Lady thug punched Jamie in the stomach, Guy thug pinned her arms behind her back, and Cheekbones (probably Airth) moseyed right up to Jamie and hissed, "Docent Nguyen."

"Lady Airth," Jamie whispered, her gaze flicking this way and that.

"Where is the child?" Lady Airth asked.

Jackie gasped, then bit her lip, hoping no one had heard. But what with the car accident aftermath behind her and the fight in front of her, there were no worries on that front.

"Child?" Jamie whispered, clearly trying to play dumb. And failing miserably. Her nervous eyes and heavy swallows simply had to be giving her away.

"Yes. The baby."

"I—I don't have a baby."

"Clearly. Where is it?"

"Uh ..."

Behind Jackie, one of victims of the car accident she'd caused swung open his door and limped out, looking daggers at Jackie. He opened his mouth to yell.

Jackie braced herself for an onslaught of insults about how she'd destroyed his car. Not only did she not want to get screamed at, but, more importantly, his screaming would give away her location to Airth and Co.

She held a finger to her lips and gave a desperate, "Shh!"

"Don't you shush me, you—"

Jackie's jaw dropped as Stewie leaped from behind the guy's car and knocked him over the head with his elbow. The guy collapsed in a heap.

"Stewie!" Jackie hissed. "What—" She saw he was holding Sachi. "Oh hey—"

He held a finger to his lips and gave a desperate, "Shh!"

He pointed toward Airth and Jamie.

Jackie nodded and whispered, "Right." Stewie joined her in peering around Fedora's car.

Since Jackie had last seen, Jamie'd been hit a few more times.

Lady Airth growled, "Docent Nguyen, you do not want to find out how determined I am to find this child. I need all descendants of Okada under Cloister control. I will not let the child out of my grasp. You will tell me where she is. You had her moments ago. She can't be far."

"Why do you want her?" Jamie growled. "Because of Okada's blood? Because it has the power to mess up your plan?"

Lady Airth grinned. "You know more than I thought." She looked at Fedora. "Where's the other one?"

He jerked his head in Jackie's direction. "Part of that mess back there. Probably stuck under a car."

Lady Airth said, "Find her."

Fedora nodded and moved toward the car wreck.

Jackie and Stewie ducked out of sight. Stewie pushed Jackie behind him, shoved Sachi into her arms, turned, and kicked Fedora in the jugular as he rounded the corner. Fedora staggered backward. Stewie tugged him back, pulled out a knife from somewhere, and stabbed Fedora in the heart.

Fedora hit the ground with a thump.

Stewie turned to Jackie. "Let's go."

"But—but what about Jamie!" she spluttered. "We can't—"

Stewie grabbed her wrist and pulled her after him as he ran away from the car and toward a clothing store across from the street.

"Let go!" Jamie hissed, trying to twist out of his grip.

He didn't answer, or let go. A storekeeper came up and asked them something in Japanese. Stewie responded with a sharp motion of his hand, waving the man away.

The storekeeper glared at Stewie, shot Jackie a questioning look, and stalked off. Jackie tried not to get too annoyed about the fact that the storekeeper hadn't expressed any concern that she might be getting kidnapped.

Jackie weighed struggling a bit more, but figured it was pointless. "Were you the guy who was yelling at us—?"

"Nope. I was across the parking lot watching."

"You were there and you didn't help? Aren't you supposed to be looking out for us? Yesterday you were assigned to be our guard."

"Things changed. Lady Morse has changed her plans." Stewie glowered as he spoke.

"You disapprove of her new plans?"

"I'm not paid to approve or disapprove. And after I deliver this," he said, reaching into his jacket pocket and pulling out an envelope, "I'm not paid at all. Not by Morse. This delivery's my last assignment for her."

Jackie grabbed the envelope. "Great. Thanks, Stewie. See ya around." She made to scoot away from him.

"You're not going anywhere," he said, not letting go of her wrist.

"But you're off the clock!"

"Nope. I have a new employer."

Jackie hissed, "If you're working for Airth—"

"No. I'm not working for Airth. I'm working for Claire."

"Claire. Who's Claire? Oh wait, she's that chick from the airport. The one who came with Morse and Dork Ass."

Stewie raised an eyebrow. "Who?"

"Dorcas. Jamie. Docent Nguyen."

He raised an eyebrow, then pulled her behind a rack of tee shirts and peeked out the store's front window.

Jackie peered out from behind the rack on the other side. She could see nothing but the car that was obscuring poor Jamie from view. Fedora was nowhere in sight.

"So you're working for Claire … that means what? She's not with Morse anymore?"

"Correct," he said, keeping his eyes on the mess out in the street.

"Why? They have a fight?"

Stewie shrugged. "Read the note. That'll probably explain something."

Jackie started to tear it open.

"Not now! You can't seriously think now's a good time for that?" He nodded toward the chaos in the road.

Sachi started to cry.

"Can you shut her up?" Stewie hissed.

"No, I can't! What, you think I'm a baby whisperer because I'm a female?"

He sighed, and didn't take the bait.

Jackie said, "She needs a diaper. She smells super horrible. I don't think she's gonna shut up til she's cleaned up."

"You don't have diapers for her?"

"Why the hell would I—"

"Damn it." He grabbed a tee shirt off a hanger and shoved it at her. "Use that."

"Great. You change her after you get us out of this mess."

He clenched his teeth and didn't respond.

Fedora, his shirt cut open and soaked with blood, came into view, walking out of a store across from them and squinting into the windows across the way from him.

Jackie ducked out of sight. "Well I hope you have a good plan to get Jamie out of this mess, now that you got her into it."

"We're gonna have to leave her."

She growled at him, "No way, Stew. No. Way."

"Yes. We gotta go. Gotta get this kid out of here. Claire wants to see her. And Claire says the baby is not to fall into Lady Airth's hands, no matter what. Jamie will be fine."

"No she won't."

"Well, probably not," he agreed.

"She's gonna be traumatized! You loser! We are not leaving her!"

"We are. That guy," he said, jerking his head back toward the shopkeeper, who was on the phone behind the counter, "is calling the cops right now. About me. Says I'm kidnapping you and the kid, and that I had something to do with the car accident in front of his store. The cops on the scene here are gonna be notified about us in here in like a few seconds." He pulled Jackie to her feet and hauled her toward the back of the store. The storekeeper hollered at them, but Stewie ignored him.

Jackie waved at the storekeeper and gave him a lame attempt at a smile, trying to ease any worries he might have about her being a helpless victim. "It's cool, dude," she said.

A second before Stewie pulled her out of sight, she caught a glimpse of a police officer walking through the front door. The storekeeper pointed the police in the direction Jackie and Stewie had gone.

"Stewie, the cops."

He grumbled something under his breath and picked up the pace.

They heard the police yell behind them.

Stewie pulled her past some storage shelves, to the back door. He threw it open, and they ran out into an alley. There was a car a few yards from the door. "Get in that car," he said.

As Jackie ran toward it to try the doors, Stewie shoved a trash barrel in front of the door, then a big crate.

As the cop tried the door and yelled, Jackie opened one of the back doors of the car and hopped in with Sachi.

Stewie hurried to the driver's seat and got to work hot-wiring it.

Jackie put Sachi on the seat beside her and got to work changing her diaper. "I've never done this before," she grumbled.

"It's not rocket science, idiot."

Jackie ground her teeth together and began the operation.

The police stopped slamming against the door. That probably meant he'd given up and was going around.

The car started up.

Jackie swallowed and looked down at Sachi. There was no way she was going along with Stewie. She would not let him bring the kid to Claire. Claire was from The Cloister, and Sachi's grandma had been working very hard to keep Sachi away from The Cloister. And as freaked out by babies as Jackie was, that didn't mean she wanted the kid to spend the rest of her life being tested in a lab.

Thus, Jamie had to escape. It was now or never.

She looked at Stewie as he leaned back in his seat and put his hands on the wheel. "Ready?" he asked.

"Yup," she answered. She picked up the dirty diaper and shoved it in Stewie's face.

He gave a muffled scream of horror and began to struggle, but Jackie pulled the tabs of the diaper behind his head and didn't let go. "Get out of the car!" she yelled. "Get out!"

He struggled and thrashed, but she wouldn't let go, and in the confined space of the car he couldn't reach back and get a good hold on her. Especially since he was panicking from getting a face full of poop.

"Get out!" Jackie yelled again.

Stewie had no alternative but to throw the door open and exit the vehicle.

Like lightning, Jackie flung herself up to the front seat and pulled the driver's side door shut. She locked it.

Not a second too soon.

Stewie tore the diaper off his face and threw himself at the door, trying the handle to no avail. "Let me in!" he screamed at her, his face utterly deranged and utterly filthy. He slammed on the window with his fist.

Though her heart was hammering and her hands were shaking, she managed to give him a cocky grin because she knew it'd make him even angrier. "Later!" she called through the window. She gave him a shaky wave and zipped off down the alley. Through the rearview, she saw him sprinting after her. She was so busy looking behind her that she didn't see Fedora round the corner with the police officer at his side until it was too late. She ran right into Fedora and clipped the police with a side view mirror.

She cried out in alarm as Fedora smashed into the hood of the car.

Keep driving.

"I know, moron!" Jackie barked at the voice in her head as she looked in the back of the car to see where Sachi was. The kid was sitting in the foot space, wearing her tee shirt diaper and looking around with interest at all the sounds and movement.

Get Docent Nguyen.

"Uh, right. I'll do what I can," Jackie muttered, while thinking that there was no chance in hell she'd be able to get anywhere near Jamie without getting caught too. "Hey, can you hear my thoughts? Or just my words?"

Just your words.

"Oh, good." She halted at the end of the alley to steel her nerves before driving out where all the bad guys could see her. She glanced back in time to see a livid, poop-smeared Stewie leap over Fedora's motionless body, shove the police aside, and sprint after her.

What were you thinking about me?

"Nothing horrible." The AI didn't respond.

Just for fun, Jackie waited until Stewie was reaching out for the handle of the driver's side door before she hit the gas and squealed out. One glance at the mess that was Lady Airth's entourage, the car accident, and various emergency vehicles told Jackie she was not going to have a chance of getting close enough to Jamie to pull off a rescue. Besides, she couldn't see Jamie anywhere. Though she did spot one of Airth's thugs slamming the trunk door shut while he gave a cop a surreptitious glance.

On the bright side, everyone was far too busy with their stuff to notice her.

She drove slowly so as not to attract attention, and looked in the rearview one more time. She was relieved to see that Stewie had stopped chasing her. He appeared reluctant to leave the alley. So it was probably safe to assume Airth knew of him and didn't like him. Did that mean Claire wasn't with Airth? Jackie was pretty sure Airth had been the one who'd kidnapped Claire earlier, but she had no idea if Claire was still with her, or what that meant for Claire's allegiances.

Stewie caught her gaze in the rearview and shot her a murderous look. She saluted him and drove away.

"Dude," she said to Sachi. "We gotta give you some more stuff to eat. Those diapers are handy."

Sachi, who had been exploring some trash in a cup holder, spared her a glance before getting back to business.

"But Stewie's gonna murder me next time I see him. Then when the nanotech fixes me he's gonna murder me again. And then when the nanotech fixes me he's gonna murder me again. Et cetera."

Sachi stuffed a candy wrapper in her mouth.

"I mean, there's basically no going back once you put poop in someone's face. I'd probably murder someone a dozen times if they put poop in my face ..." Jackie mused.

Are you talking to the infant, or to me?

"Shut up."

"Mama."

"Yeah, good luck with that one, kid." Jackie turned her full attention to the road, and it hit her that she had no idea where she was going or what she was doing. "Yo, AI."

Ms. Savage.

"What the hell, dude? What is going on?"

I am assuming you are not going to attempt to rescue Docent Nguyen.

"That is correct. Very correct. I'm pretty sure they stuffed her in a trunk."

You are correct.

"How are you so sure? Wait, can you see through my eyes since you're in my head?"

I cannot. Docent Nguyen informed me that Lady Airth's thugs put her in a trunk.

"Oh. Duh. You're in her head too. Sweet. Tell her hey for me. Say sorry I couldn't help her out and it totally sucks she got beat up and kidnapped."

One moment.

"Laters." As she waited for the AI to deliver her message, she tapped her fingers on the steering wheel and checked to see if anyone was following her. "Dude, Sachi, how do I know if someone's following me?" she asked. "Like if they're good at following someone then you probably can't tell they're following you, right? Damn it." She eyed the stream of cars behind her.

I delivered your message.

"And ...?"

She didn't respond. She was crying.

"Aw, poor Dork Ass." Jackie waited for what she felt was probably a long enough pause to make it feel like she was being sensitive about Jamie's troubling circumstances. Then she said, "So, uh, any ideas what I should do next?"

Yes. You should rescue her so that she can carry out my plan before Lady Airth and her cohorts carry out their plan.

"And if that's gonna be impossible? The rescuing thing?"

It needs to happen.

"Dude, I cannot rescue her."

Not at this moment. No. But you will be able to accomplish it once Docent Nguyen's captors have put her somewhere and let their guard down. And in the meantime, you can plan the rescue.

"But see, I don't wanna go anywhere near Lady Airth. I gotta keep this kid away from her, and it's not like I know of any babysitters or whatever." She took a left at random and turned down a residential road that looked out on the ocean.

Do you care about the future of humanity?

"Sure I do. But I mean seriously, AI, aren't you being a tad dramatic there? You're telling me the future of humanity rests with me? I just—" She gasped and hit the brakes, then threw the car in reverse. "Hold up. I just saw a sign I gotta read." She looked up at the sign she'd just driven past. There was a picture of a monkey, some words in Japanese, and, in English, the words: *Monkey Park.* "What! Dude, AI. There's a monkey park in Kyoto. This is awesome. I am going."

Ms. Savage, you do not understand the importance of this. The future of humanity does rest with you. At this moment, anyway. Once you have freed Docent Nguyen, you will pass that responsibility on to her. You need to listen to me.

"Hell no I do not. Can I turn you off? I'm going to this damn monkey park and I don't wanna hear you yammering at me while I'm touristing. You think they have baby monkeys? Baby monkeys are so damn adorable I could die."

I perceive that you are attempting to ignore the gravity of this situation by distracting yourself with a monkey park.

"Uh, doy. Just because I can explain why I'm doing what I'm doing, that means it's somehow wrong? Plus, I got a kid I gotta take care of. This monkey park will be an educational experience." She turned and gave Sachi a grin and thumbs up, then she turned into the parking lot.

Ms. Savage, this is—

"Hey, hold on," Jackie cut in. "I've been meaning to ask, why can you talk to me in my head? Why just me and Dork Ass and a few other people?"

Now is not the time to tell you that.

"Damn right. Now is the time to go to a monkey park."

I am going to talk to Docent Nguyen now. While I am gone, you need to leave this monkey park, and you need to get over your denial about the fact that you are in the middle of a problem that you need to help me solve. You need to think about how we are going to rescue Docent Nguyen.

"No way. While you are gone I am going to take this baby to a monkey park, and I am going to watch monkeys play and use their creepy prehensile tails to grab branches, and hopefully I'll see some baby monkeys, and—hey, voice, are you there?"

There was no response.

"Damn idiot AI," she grumbled as she walked up to the ticket kiosk. "Two tickets, please," she said to a woman who was eyeing her distrustfully. "What?"

"I—um—I—" the woman stuttered, looking nervously around, probably for coworkers who could come to her rescue.

Jackie growled, "So what if I'm talking to myself? You know you do it too. Everyone does it. And so what if my baby's got a t-shirt diaper? Damn it! Two tickets! I just wanna see some monkeys!" She slammed her fist on the counter.

As the woman scurried to complete the transaction as quickly as possible, Jackie gritted her teeth and grudgingly conceded that the AI was probably right that she was in denial.

19 JAMIE

"Docent Nguyen," said the guy with the knife. "Surely this time you will finally get the *point*. Surely I won't have to slit your throat again. This is getting old. You agree?"

Jamie wholeheartedly agreed. However, she couldn't say so since her trachea wasn't fully repaired yet. As she waited for the nanotech to fix her up again, she blinked away tears and looked down at the clothes she was borrowing from Jackie. She wondered whether there was a dry cleaner in the city who could take care of the mess. Not likely.

As her body tried to take a breath and every cell of her being wanted to panic about the repeated mortal damage that was being done to her body, she forced herself to bring her brain to a state of calm. She was fine. It was just pain and discomfort and lots and lots of blood. It wasn't death. Sure, she couldn't breathe when he slit her throat, but technically she didn't even need to breathe. So, it was all good. Especially since, each time, she went unconscious for the worst of it.

She groaned a bit to test her throat, then blinked around the fancy hotel room, wondering whether Lady Airth had returned. She'd stopped in briefly for the first round of interrogation, but then one of her minions had come in and whispered something to her that had prompted her to scurry away to deal with whatever it was. Jamie had been worried that the message had been about Jackie and Sachi being located, but since the interrogation hadn't stopped she figured they were still safe.

Her interrogator, Fedora, paced back and forth in front of her, leaning down every few seconds to look at the wound on her neck. When it was, at last, all mended, he said, "OK. One more time. Where are they?"

Jamie sighed and slumped sideways against the arm of the chair she was tied to. "I don't know."

"You think they're going to appreciate your heroics?" he asked, leaning in and getting right up in her face. "We are going to get the information one way or another. It's just a matter of how much you want to get hurt in the process."

"But I really don't know. I really, really do not know."

"You mean to tell me that you do not know where Ms. Savage is. You do not know where the baby is. You do not know where Mr. Stewart is. You do not know where Lady Morse is. You do not know where Dr. Forester is." His voice was dripping with disbelief.

Jamie registered that now at least she could answer Jackie's question about whether Stewart was Stewie's first or last name. And he was a Mister, not a Corporal, or Lieutenant, or some other army word. "No. I really do not know where they are. Why on earth do you think I would know where they are?"

"Because, as we've already discussed, you're clearly in cahoots. Why would you be meeting up with the old woman in an abandoned factory if you weren't working with her?"

"How'd you even know we were there? We were very covert."

He just laughed, paced a bit more, and said, "Let's take a break. I'm gonna go check the vending machine. Want anything? Oh, wait, you're our prisoner. I'm gonna buy some chocolate covered pretzels and bring them back here and eat the right in front of you."

"Aw man, that's so mean," Jamie said in what she hoped was a convincing whine. Earlier in the interrogation, she'd worked out that withholding food and water was one of their tactics, so she'd decided to play along and pretend she still ate and drank, since if they thought starving her was torture enough they might not bother with other stuff. She'd mentioned at one point that chocolate covered pretzels were all that and a bag of chips. "Could I at least get some water? I'm so thirsty." She gave a little cough.

He laughed in her face, and sauntered out of the room.

No sooner had the door clicked closed than the voice of the AI filled her head.

Docent Nguyen, do not give up hope. Ms. Savage and I are planning a rescue mission.

Relief flooded Jamie and she let out a pathetic, "Oh thank goodness. I don't know how much more of this I can take. It's the worst. He keeps killing me. Over and over and over."

She will be here as soon as possible.

"Is Stewie with her? Oh please, let Stewie be coming along."

Mr. Stewart will not be accompanying Ms. Savage. They had a falling out involving fecal matter.

"Pardon? Involving what?"

Fecal matter.

Jamie paused for a few seconds, thinking about whether she wanted to hear that backstory. She decided against. "OK. Well. Uh. So, I just wait."

Yes. And while you wait, I fill you in on what is happening with Ms. Savage.

"Talk fast. That dude's just going to find a vending machine. He'll be back soon."

The AI then got Jamie up to speed on all that had happened since she'd been taken.

"So Stewie's not with Morse anymore, but with Claire. And Morse is ... MIA. And Sachi's safe. Or, rather, Sachi's with Jackie."

Yes.

"OK." Jamie tested the ropes tying her to the chair. She sighed. Then a question occurred to her. "Hey."

Yes.

"Now would be a great time for you to fill me in on some stuff. Like, why you need me."

I need you to access The File, and take a biological sample to Lab A. I will tell you how to obtain the sample and what to do with it when the time comes.

Jamie narrowed her eyes. "But why me?"

Rest assured that I have evaluated all your inputs stored in The File and found that you are the candidate whose beliefs and thoughts most align with the mission.

"So ... even though I have no clue what's going on, I agree?"

Yes.

Jamie frowned and let her eyes travel across the flowery pattern on the wallpaper. She did not believe the AI. If it was true that she would agree with it if she knew what it was planning, then why didn't it just tell her?

There was no reason for it to keep her in the dark if it knew she'd be on its side. She hated knowing nothing about this plan. But, she considered, she didn't know anything. She knew that the AI's plan was to stop Lady Airth from her plan of breaking down humanity to their constituent elements and rebuilding them into Lady Airth's personal opinion of what humanity should be. Jamie was at least sure that that was messed up. She was at least sure that people were not LEGOs. Thus, since the AI was going to be stopping that, it did feel pretty safe to assume that she would go along with its plan if she had all the details. But that brought her right back to the question: why didn't it just tell her?

Someone turned the doorknob. The door swung open.

Jamie exhaled a breath of relief when she saw not Fedora but Lady Airth. Hopefully that meant it was time for talking and not hurting. She met Lady Airth's cold, appraising gaze with surprise that she could meet the woman's gaze at all. Even in the best of circumstances,

Jamie had always found Lady Airth intimidating. In these circumstances, tied to a chair and recently repeatedly murdered by one of her thugs, Lady Airth was intimidating to the power of one thousand. Fortunately for Jamie, being repeatedly murdered had put her in an odd mental state where she found she just was not able to give a damn about much at all. Suddenly, Lady Airth's tough, superior demeanor didn't really scare her.

Jamie figured she'd better at least try to act intimidated, though, since she didn't want Lady Airth to give up and send Fedora back to spill some more blood. She averted her gaze and bit her lip. She let her eyes flick up to Lady Airth's face a few times.

Lady Airth patted her already perfect hair into place, strode to within two paces of Jamie, and looked down at her wordlessly for an awkward span of time.

Jamie gave a swallow and another hesitant flick of the eyes.

"Docent Nguyen," Lady Airth finally spoke, clipped and irritated. "My dear girl. What are you playing at?"

"I ... don't understand the question ..." Jamie whispered after a few seconds of hesitation.

Lady Airth sighed. "Brandi has gone off the rails, child. What has she told you? What are you doing for her?"

It took Jamie a moment to remember that Lady Morse's first name was Brandi. She blinked up at Lady Airth, processing the fact that the woman thought Jamie was still working with Lady Morse and not avoiding her.

"Gone off the rails?"

"Yes. Completely." Lady Airth gave Jamie a long stare, then turned and flopped down in an armchair across the room.

Jamie forgot she was supposed to be pretending to be scared. She stared. Lady Airth was not a flopper.

Lady Airth leaned forward, resting her elbows on her knees and clasping her hands in front of her. "Where is Brandi? What is she planning?"

"I don't know."

"Do you enjoy having your throat slit?"

"No."

"Do you enjoy having your clothing soaked in your own blood?"

"No. The dry-cleaning bill is going to be insane."

Lady Airth cocked an eyebrow at that. "You think this is a joke?"

"No. I most certainly do not."

"Good. Because it isn't."

"But I didn't even do a joke. The dry-cleaning bill *really* is going to be insane," Jamie felt the need to point out.

Lady Airth surveyed her for a few moments. "I suppose. All the same, child, I would appreciate it if you'd maintain a tone more in keeping with the gravity of the situation."

"Yes, Lady Airth."

"This situation is grave. Very grave. Our plan, years in the making, is in danger of being derailed in the eleventh hour. Brandi is planning something, and I need to know what. You are aware of our plan?"

Jamie nodded.

"And you are aware of Brandi's plan? Whatever plan she has that she has put together behind my back? Is she trying to stop us?"

Jamie pursed her lips as she thought. She had no idea what Lady Morse was planning. Or if she was planning anything at all short of just getting Ms. Nari's body out of reach of Lady Airth.

"Well?"

Jamie shook her head. "No idea."

Lady Airth pursed her already thin lips and thought, staring at the floor. "We'll leave that for now. Change of subject. What has Brandi told you about yourself?"

She looked up at Jamie.

"Um ... nothing?"

"I find that hard to believe."

"Why is that, Lady Airth?"

"Well, child," Lady Airth said with her eyebrows lowered, apparently deep in thought. "I find it strange that she wouldn't have shared your background with you, considering its relevance to this situation we find ourselves in."

"Huh?"

Lady Airth sighed as she contemplated Jamie. "You really aren't that bright. Are you?"

"Um ... well ... not particularly, I guess. But still, I'm not exactly an idiot. I mean, I got bad grades and all, but I think I'm pretty creative ...and I'm good at problem solving."

Lady Airth shook her head and muttered, "I wish I understood where we went wrong with your group."

"Pardon?"

"Nothing ... nothing ... It's just I don't do well with failure. And you, child, are a constant reminder of one particular failure of mine."

"How so? I mean, sure I did bad in your class, but that wasn't your fault. You were a great teacher. I just couldn't wrap my head around the subject, and I didn't study. And I was too scared of you to go to office hours. And as for my group, as I recall, we got an A for our project."

Lady Airth cut her off with a short bark of a laugh. "You really have no idea what I am talking about. When she took you and the other one on this little trip, I was sure she must have told you. Well, good. Good." She stood and began to pace.

"The other one?" Jamie asked.

"Quiet. I need to think."

Jamie sighed and looked down at her feet. She wished the AI would say something. Maybe it knew what Lady Airth was going on about. If it was in The File, it probably knew all sorts of good stuff about The Cloister. She frowned at the realization that, apparently, she now believed that the voice was indeed artificial intelligence inside The File. She felt a bit disappointed in herself for believing a thing without proof.

Lady Airth paced back and forth in front of Jamie, hands clasped behind her back, muttering under her breath. Then, she halted. She stared down at Jamie, who raised her head to look up at Lady Airth. Lady Airth said, "You honestly don't know where they are."

"No."

"And you have no idea what Lady Morse's plan is."

"No."

"And you know nothing of your history."

"No."

Lady Airth nodded slowly. "I believe you. Admittedly, believing you is a gamble. But, I do believe you. You see, Docent Nguyen, you simply do not have the capacity to lie so convincingly under such stress. And you're too weak to hold up under torture."

Jamie nodded her agreement.

Lady Airth smiled. "Child, I'm going to have you untied. Then you can change into something less bloody, have a nice meal, and we will talk. I think you can be of use to me. And to The Cloister. It's time you knew about your past."

"Well gee," Jamie said. "Lovely."

At least, the fresh clothing and nice meal sounded lovely. Not so much the talking. She glanced impatiently at the door, wishing Jackie would just bust through it with guns a'blazin' and save her.

20 JACKIE

Jackie stalked down the path, feeling exceedingly angry that she couldn't enjoy the monkey park nearly as much as she wanted to. Everyone kept giving her funny looks, and the monkeys weren't even all that fun. It was midday, which was apparently the time that monkeys liked to nap. She hadn't seen a single baby monkey, and she couldn't shake the feeling of guilt about how she was abandoning Jamie to torture.

Have you read the letter yet?

"No, I have not," Jackie grumbled.

And have you thought further about how you are going to rescue Docent Nguyen?

"No."

You are being an awful human being. You know that, I hope. Do you not feel any remorse?

"Of course, I do!" Jackie snapped. "I feel awful! I really do! You think I like that they have Jamie and they're probably hurting her? I'm not a monster. I just happen to know beyond a shadow of a doubt that I don't have a chance of rescuing her. If I do try, then I will get caught and this kid will get caught."

Not alone. Of course not.

"Stewie's not gonna help me with anything. I smeared poop all over his face."

Go to Claire. Explain what is going on. She will help you.

"Explain what is going on?" Jackie laughed. "In order to explain what was going on, I would need to know what was going on!"

Read the letter.

"I don't want to read the letter. I want to enjoy this monkey park."

You mean you want to ignore your problems.

"Yep."

The voice didn't respond.

"Of course I want to ignore my problems. My problems are huge."

Again, the voice remained silent.

"What? Geez. You can't seriously blame me for not wanting to deal with this stuff."

More silence.

"Fine! Fine! I'll read the damn letter."

Excellent. Read it aloud so that I can hear.

She put Sachi down on the ground, said, "Don't wander off, kid," and found the letter in her computer bag. She tore it open and read aloud:

Docent Nguyen and Ms. Savage,

I need to inform you two that I'm done. I'm running, and I suggest you do the same. Now that Lady Airth knows what I've done, there's no going back to how things were. I had hoped that if I got to Nari's body and destroyed it before Airth caught wind of the fact that there had been a death, I could cover it up. But, I wasn't fast enough. Didn't cover my tracks well enough. She knows about Nari, she has Nari's mother, and now she knows about the child. I'm not sure how much you have discovered since you ran off, so this may mean nothing to you, but: the child has the anomaly as well. Airth must not find her. Also—and this will be very strange for you to hear, and this is not the place to explain it—you must inject some of your blood into the infant. She is currently in a vulnerable state and able to die like her mother. However, your blood will give her protection.

I reiterate, run. Docent Nguyen, do not return to The Cloister. Ms. Savage, leave your life behind. I strongly suggest that you both stay in Japan, thus avoiding showing your passport and sending notifications to Lady Airth. Stay under the radar. As far as I am confident of anything anymore, I can confidently say that Claire will be able to help you hide. She knows my contacts in Kyoto, some of whom are less than reputable. If you want to take the risk, go to Claire.

Goodbye. Do not try to locate me. If we cross paths in the future, pretend you do not recognize me. I assure you, I will do the same.

—Lady Morse

Jackie stared at the paper. "You got all that?" she asked the AI after a few moments.

I did.

She scanned the letter over again and landed on the part that had caused her the most confusion. "What's that thing about my blood? Or about Jamie's blood? See, she says our blood can give Sachi protection. What the hell, man? What's that mean? Does that mean one of us is one of those Numan things?" She gave a snort of a laugh at the ludicrous notion.

Exactly. Commendations for drawing that conclusion. I was wondering whether either of you would catch on.

Jackie stood motionless and wide-eyed as the enormity of the AI's confirmation crashed down on her. She finally spoke in a hiss, "What? *What?* One of us is one of those nanotech people? No way. It's gotta be me. Tell me it's me. Oh my gosh."

It's both of you.

"Shut up."

Silence.

"No. Don't really shut up. I just—whoa. Wow. No way. No way."

Yes. Do you recall when I told you that The Cloister has been making humans purely out of nanotechnology for 35 years?

"Uh, yes. Yes, I recall that."

"Well, you and Docent Nguyen were early attempts. Two members of the first group deemed successful enough to be tested in the field. You—

"Crap!" Jackie screeched. "Oh no! Where's Sachi? Hold on, AI." She had just looked down at the ground where she'd set the baby. And the baby was gone. "No ..." she moaned, putting her hands to her head. She spun around on the spot, looking wildly around. "No, no, no. Dude. I lost the baby. I told her to stay put! Damn it!" She squinted into the undergrowth of the forest. "Sachi!" she hollered. "Sachi!"

Tell me you are joking. Tell me you did not lose the child.

"No. No, I'm not joking! And—well—I didn't lose her! She left!" Jackie plowed into the underbrush, looking everywhere a baby might be likely to fit. Under bushes, beneath hollows in roots, behind large rocks. No Sachi.

Seriously? You are prone to sarcasm. I can usually pick up on it, but sometimes I cannot. This might be one of those times.

"This is not one of those times!" Jackie screeched. "I seriously cannot find Sachi!"

Well, as long as Lady Airth doesn't find the infant, it hardly matters. In a way, it might be best if you do leave her here. Airth would never suspect that you'd leave her.

"Cold, AI. Very cold. I can't let the baby get lost and die."

I only mean that in the grand scheme of things it hardly matters. All that really matters as regards the infant is that it not be found.

"I know that's what you mean. Damn, computers are evil. I can't leave her."

I am serious. As long as you do, in fact, have those samples from Tamon Nari stored properly, the infant is not necessary. The infant is only needed if you cannot obtain those blood samples you took from Nari. They are saved, yes?

"To the best of my knowledge."

You do not sound certain enough. Perhaps it would be wise, after all, to find the infant.

"Um, yeah. I was already going to. Shut up now, creep." She tried to fight off the panic, but she couldn't shake the reality that the kid might die. They'd passed a bridge a while back, which meant somewhere around them there was a river. She might drown. And then there were the monkeys. What did they do with unattended babies? Would one grab Sachi and bring it home to raise as its own, and in a few years the monkey park would start an advertising campaign about how all the tourists simply had to come and see if they could spot the wild monkey girl? "Dude! I don't want her to drown! I don't want her to be a tourist attraction! Jamie is gonna be so mad."

Then find her. What does the ground consist of?

"Huh? The ground—what? Oh. Dirt. Yeah. Good call." She backtracked to the path and began to scan the path on both sides for baby tracks. To the left, there was nothing. Or so she figured. She wasn't exactly a woodswoman. Her tracking experience consisted of occasionally seeing deer or rabbit tracks in fresh snow, squealing about them, snapping pictures, and posting them to social media only to find that none of her friends gave a damn about animal tracks in the snow.

To the right, she easily spotted her footsteps shuffling around in the dirt like a crazy person. If there were any baby tracks on the edge of the path, she would have wiped them all out. She took a few steps deeper into the forest.

"Mama."

Jackie whirled around. "Sachi?"

She heard some babbling.

From the direction of the path. She stumbled over a root in her haste, righted herself, and came out on the path. She looked left and right. Nothing. "Sachi!"

More babbling.

To her left.

Jackie sprinted around a corner up ahead. Straight up ahead of her, sitting in the middle of the path, was Sachi.

"Seriously?" Jackie panted as she dashed over to the baby and picked her up. "Sachi, you scared me. You really scared me. I told you to stay put. You need to listen to me. I'm gonna have some words with Jamie. She's super misinformed about baby brains." She looked down at Sachi to see if she was paying attention.

The kid was staring at something up in the treetops.

You found her?

"I did. She just crawled up the path a bit. Damn it, AI, that was scary. She coulda died."

Crawling around the path?

"Well, no. But I mean if she'd done something else, she could have died."

I suppose there is no arguing that.

"I gotta do that blood thing Lady Morse said. How do I do that? I need a syringe, right? Where do I get a syringe?"

You need to rescue Docent Nguyen.

"Sure. But first, I gotta make this baby invincible. It'll take a whole heap of stress off of me. I promise, I will be a much better rescuer if I'm not stressing about this kid's safety."

How do you intend to obtain the syringe you will need to carry out the procedure?

Jackie frowned as she pondered that question. Then it hit her. "Oh! Lady Morse's briefcase! She had some equipment like that. She had it for the autopsy." She shifted Sachi from her left to right hip. "Time to go raid a minifridge."

21 JAMIE

Jamie looked down at the plate of food in front of her. A waffle, a bowl of fruit, and a teeny pitcher of syrup. Clearly, it had been sent up to the room from the hotel restaurant while she'd been showering and changing into clean clothes. She looked at Lady Airth. "Thank you, but I don't really eat."

From her seat across the table from Jamie, Lady Airth raised her eyebrows. "Really? Interesting."

Jamie shrugged and looked down at her lap. She stifled a sigh as she looked at the familiar blue of the dress she was now wearing. Back in Cloister uniform. After spending a few days in Jackie's jeans and tank top, the stiff, sensible dress with its starched collar felt confining and unpleasant.

Lady Airth reached across the table and pulled the tray of breakfast food toward herself and began to dig in. "True, ever since the Greywash eating has been unnecessary. But food is still quite enjoyable when made well. Yes?"

"I suppose." Jamie looked from her lap, through the open window to the rooftops of the buildings nearby. "Lady Airth, you wanted to tell me something? About my past? Is it something to do with my parents?"

Lady Airth paused with a fork in one hand and knife in the other, halfway through cutting a piece of waffle. She contemplated Jamie. "Something like that. Yes. Your parents." A small smile flickered across her lips. She set the silverware down on the napkin beside her plate. "I suppose you could say that I am your mother."

Jamie squinted at her, confused. "Huh? No way."

"I, and Ladies Morse, Petrella, and Stambaugh. We are all your mothers, in a manner of speaking."

Jamie leaned back in her seat and stared at Lady Airth. "That makes no sense whatsoever, Lady Airth. I may not be all that bright by Cloister standards, but I do know how babies are made."

"Child, your conception," she made air-quotes with her fingers, "was, shall we say, nontraditional."

Jamie shook her head, put up a hand, and said, "Hold on a second. Please don't tell me you're about to say you made me in a lab. Don't tell me I'm one of those conspiracy theory nanotechnology people."

Lady Airth, who had just stuck a piece of waffle in her mouth, raised her eyebrows at Jamie and gave a slow nod while she chewed. Only when she had swallowed did she say, "Excellent reasoning! Excellent. Tell me, what made you draw that conclusion? Or did our friend, Mrs. Nari, tell you back at that abandoned factory?"

Jamie shook her head. "No, she didn't tell me. Not really, anyway. She was leading up to it though, I think, before she got taken." Jamie thought back to the conversation.

Lady Airth nodded. "Yes. I imagine she had been about to tell Ms. Savage that the baby, Tamon Nari's child who has apparently inherited the Okada anomaly, needed some of Ms. Savage's blood to return to a state of stasis."

Jamie blinked. "Ms. Savage? She's also—uh—she's—"

"Created in the lab? Yes. She, you, and the other copies in your test group were created in the lab. You were the first group deemed successful enough to be studied in the real world."

"The—the rest of my group? Copies? What? You made other people too? That are ... copies of me and Jackie?"

Lady Airth nodded again. "Yes. Of course, child. Copies. Other copies. You are, after all, a component in an experiment. A mere two copies would be far from statistically significant. Surely even you must know enough of statistics to be aware that two subjects do not a study make. The data would be a joke. Pointless."

Jamie gaped at Lady Airth, her mouth hanging half open.

Lady Airth gave a thin smile. "You're in shock, I suppose. It's a shame I had to tell you. Now that you are aware of the truth, you will have to be removed from the study. Though, really, as we've made strides in the technology, your group has become somewhat irrelevant. Its greatest worth at this point is in teaching us where we went wrong."

"Where you went wrong?" Jamie asked.

"Mm. Yes. Every representative of your group has turned out, at best, mediocre. At worst, dead through a string of poor decisions. Not even you, who were given every advantage, and the best education available, excelled."

"Uh …" Jackie couldn't think straight. It was too much to take in. Not only was the conspiracy theory true, but it was about her. And Jackie. "Why are you telling me this?"

"I would have liked not to tell you, of course, but questioning you in the traditional manner is not working out. I would much rather just upload your thoughts and memories to my computer and peruse them at my leisure."

"Upload my—what?"

"Your thoughts. Memories. To do so, I need to hook you up to a computer. And to do that, I needed to explain your history to you."

Jamie just blinked stupidly.

Lady Airth appraised her over another forkful of waffle. "You're overwhelmed." She popped another piece of the waffle in her mouth, stood, and said with a full mouth, "You just sit there and process this information. While you do so, I am going to bring in a machine which I will hook up to you."

Jamie made to stand up.

"No. Stay seated."

Jamie did so.

"Am I going to have to tie you down again?"

"No," Jamie said numbly.

"Good. Very good." She then called, "Wharton!"

Immediately, a door behind Jamie swung open. Jamie turned to see Fedora walk into the room and halt just inside the doorway. He said, "Lady Airth?"

"Wharton, be so good as to bring my laptop to me, and the GW10."

"Yes, Lady Airth." He gave Jamie the slightest glance, then turned on his heel and left the room. He shut the door behind him.

Jamie listened to his footsteps as they faded to silence.

Across from Jamie, Lady Airth ate quietly, presumably with the intention of leaving Jamie to her thoughts. But Jamie found she really didn't have much to think about. Probably, she figured in a detached sort of way, she was just in denial or something, and eventually the shock that she was a machine would truly sink in. But for now, it all seemed straightforward enough. She was made purely of nanotechnology. She had been made in a lab. She was a lab rat for The Fordham Four's experiment as they worked on their plan of transforming humanity. She, and Jackie, and whoever else was in their "group". It was shocking and depressing, sure, but she could at least wrap her mind around it.

A few minutes later, Wharton returned, pushing a wheeled cart with a big, blinking machine on top of it. He pushed it to a halt beside Jamie, took a laptop off a lower shelf on the cart, handed the cart to Lady Airth, and stood silently to one side, waiting for orders.

Lady Airth said, "Thank you, Wharton. You may go."

As he walked out, she took his place by the cart. She set her computer on the table, opened it, turned it on, then directed her attention to the machine on the cart. She pushed a button and it began to hum, a low, monotonous buzz. She began to unwrap a thick, blue cord that was coiled beside the machine.

"What's that for?" Jamie asked, noting her accelerating heartbeat.

Lady Airth plugged the cord into her computer. "I'm about to do something you're going to find startling."

"Oh?" Jamie gripped the arms of her chair.

"Mmm hmm." Lady Airth rested one hand on Jamie's neck, the other on her right hand, and positioned her fingertips on the nape of Jamie's neck and center of the palm of Jamie's hand. Then she pushed.

And Jamie felt a dull click in her spine, a few vertebrae below Lady Airth's fingertips "What—?"

"Shh." Lady Airth ran her fingertips down Jamie's spine to the spot where she'd felt the click. The spot felt numb. Lady Airth pulled something and said, "I'm opening the port in your back."

Jamie whispered, "There's a port in my back?"

"Yes. You early models are rather primitive in that way. Later models have a wireless connection that makes them accessible from anywhere on the planet—with the correct passcode, of course."

"But—I mean—but—"

"Shh. You're in shock." She removed her hands from Jamie's palm and neck, and began uncoiling another cord. Then she plugged it into Jamie's back.

Jamie felt a jolt of energy shoot down her spine, and she sat up straighter. "Wait. You're reading my memories?" She tried to reach back to pull the thing out.

"Yes. That is the plan." Lady Airth caught her wrists. "Don't. Now that you're plugged in, you can't just pull it out. I need to disconnect you properly."

Jamie let her hands fall back to the arms of the chair. She went back to numb silence for a few moments. Then she gasped and wondered with a start why the danger of letting Lady Morse into her head had not hit her until this moment. "You—you can't do that," she muttered, thinking of all the things she had recently seen and done that Lady Airth could not know. "I can't let you—" She tried to stand up. Lady Morse put her hands on Jamie's shoulders, pulled her back into the chair, and barked, "Wharton!" before Jamie'd even been able to manage much struggling.

In moments, Wharton was through the door and at Jamie's side.

Lady Airth said, "Tie her to the chair."

Jamie found herself mildly amused to find that Wharton carried a thin coil of rope on his person. He pulled it out and got to work. Jamie muttered, "I really don't want you to do this."

"I understand," Lady Airth said over her shoulder as she clicked away at her computer.

"I—I don't even have the answers to your questions. We established that already. What's the point of this?"

"I'd like to peruse your memories all the same. I'm sure there's something you've done in your trip to Kyoto that will be useful to me. Something that I didn't think to ask about."

Jamie swallowed heavily, tested the ropes, and glared up at Wharton.

He was looking at Lady Airth's computer, not paying any attention to her.

"I'm going to start now," Lady Airth said. "I don't think you'll feel anything, but I'm warning you just in case." She hit a button.

Out of the corner of her eye, Jamie saw white letters flashing on a black screen. She was strangely hesitant to let herself turn toward the computer and see what was going on. It was all too weird. Seeing her memories and thoughts on a screen. Her memories and thoughts that were on the screen because of the cord running from her back to the machine on the cart to the computer on the table. Because she was made of nanotech in a lab.

Jamie clenched her teeth and made herself look.

It was just a bunch of incomprehensible symbols and letters.

Of course, though, Lady Airth was pouring over them as though they meant something to her. And not just meant something, but meant something fascinating. As she read, she would every so often utter a weary groan or a derisive guffaw, which rankled a tad since it was Jamie's activities and ideas that she was reading.

While she waited for Lady Airth to say something, she fell into a brooding silence. As time crept on, the brooding turned into a traumatized sort of trance as her brain played with thinking about all the information she'd just taken in. Finally, Jamie snapped out of her trance and looked around. She was pretty sure that it had gotten noticeably darker outside since she'd last noticed.

"What's it say there?" Jamie asked.

Lady Airth either didn't hear her or just didn't feel like responding.

Jamie persisted, twisting in her seat so she could see the screen better over Lady Airth's shoulder. She tried to ignore the horrible, numb-but-present feeling of the cord in her back as it rubbed against the back of her chair. "What does all that mean? Is it some sort of programming language or something?"

"Or something," Lady Airth said. "And, child, you already know what this says. Granted, you cannot read it, but it is your memories and thoughts. Thus, you know it all already."

"True. But—"

"Shh. Child. You are a prisoner here. Not a guest. You do not get to interrupt me and request information of me. If you require a change of venue to remind you of the fact that you are a prisoner, I will put you in the basement with our other guest. Er, prisoner."

"Nah. I'll just stay here."

"Excellent. That will make it easier for me to ask you the questions I will shortly have."

"Super," Jamie sighed.

Lady Airth raised an eyebrow and held Jamie's gaze. "I've noticed a certain snippiness in your attitude, Docent Nguyen. Doubtless, you've picked it up through your association with C-15, or, as you know her, Ms. Savage."

"Hardly surprising, considering that we're essentially the same person."

Lady Airth nodded and gave a grudging smile.

"What's my label?"

"You are C-3. But, child, back to your attitude. I expect better of the girls I take under my wing."

"So?" Jamie snapped as she shifted uncomfortably in her chair. She bit her lip, holding in her desire to point out that it wasn't so much 'taking her under her wing' as it was 'creating and researching her.'

"It borders on disrespect. I will not have it." Lady Airth paused, and when she spoke again her tone was perceptibly chillier. "You have no idea how much you owe me. By my choosing you as the member of your group to remain at The Cloister, you were given everything; the others went to orphanages, the foster care system, horribly disadvantaged countries and communities. Awful places. Ohio, even. You have no idea how lucky you have it, my girl. No idea. You are indebted to me and I will not stand for anything but the respect I deserve." She released Jamie from her gaze and looked back at the screen.

Jamie bristled, and opened her mouth to object.

"I will have silence," Lady Airth growled.

Jamie mumbled, "Yes, Lady Airth." She gritted her teeth and waited.

And waited.

"What's this?" Lady Airth asked at last.

Jamie jolted out of a doze. "Huh?"

"This, here," Lady Airth pointed at the screen though she had to know Jamie had no idea what it said. "You took samples from Tamon Nari and you stored them in this man's apartment. A Mr. Sato. I need you to take me to this apartment. I need those samples."

"I don't know how to get there," Jamie grumbled as she wondered why the samples were so important to Lady Airth. She could think of no reason, but only knew that if Lady Airth wanted them, that probably meant something bad. Fortunately, she honestly had not the foggiest clue where Mr. Sato lived. "Really, I don't know how to find his apartment."

"I see that. I take it Ms. Savage had the address and you just followed along?"

Jamie nodded, feeling thankful that she had such a horrible sense of direction.

"You never did have a head for details."

Jamie glared at Lady Airth's back.

"Still, I can piece together the general part of the city based on some observations you made. I think I can get us to the general vicinity. From there, I need you to see if anything jogs your memory."

"And if I don't want to go along with this?" Jamie asked, proud to hear that her voice didn't come out shaky.

Lady Airth turned and gave her a thin smile. "You want to attempt to defy me?"

Jamie gave a half shrug. "Just wondering ..."

Lady Airth gave her a cold stare, and whispered, "I need those samples."

Jamie groaned and shut her eyes. She wished she knew why the samples were so important to Lady Airth. She wished she knew whether taking a stand and defying Lady Airth here was stupid or not. She had no desire to be a hero, especially if it was for a dumb reason. Jamie took a gamble and breathed, "No."

Lady Airth narrowed her eyes and hissed, "No?"

Jamie winced and forced out a tiny, "No."

Lady Airth stood. "I have a phone call to make."

Jamie blinked. "Huh?"

"A phone call." Lady Airth strode from the room.

Jamie frowned. "Voice?" she asked. "Um, artificial intelligence thing?"

Yes, Docent Nguyen.

"Did you hear all that?"

I did.

"Any idea why Lady Airth wants those samples of Nari's?"

Yes.

Jamie waited a moment, sighed, and asked, "And?"

She most likely wants it because having Nari's samples outside of her control is a loose end. Lady Airth wants control of all Okada's descendants, because of the risk that the anomaly in their DNA poses to her plan. Lady Airth knows that if Nari's samples fall into the hands of her enemy, the enemy can use those samples to stop the plan that The Fordham Four have put in motion.

Jamie thought that through, then whispered, "So their plan to destroy humanity and start them over from scratch can be ... stopped with Nari's DNA?"

Yes.

"Or the baby's?"

Yes.

"Wow."

Yes.

"And that's what you want me for? Something about using their DNA to stop Airth?"

Yes. You see why she must not get her hands on those samples.

The door handle began to turn. Jamie whispered in a rush, "You need to tell Jackie to get those samples! Tell her she needs to retrieve them immediately!"

Excellent plan.

Lady Airth narrowed her eyes at Jamie and looked around the room. "Were you talking?"

"Just to myself." Jamie tried not to look nervous.

Lady Airth walked to her computer. "Look at the screen," she said.

Jamie looked.

Lady Airth pushed a few keys and the white letters and symbols on black background disappeared. They were replaced by the familiar face of the Docent Mother. She looked scared.

"Docent Mother?" Jamie said. "What's wrong? What—"

"Jamie," The Docent Mother gasped. "My dear, I don't know what's going on. But I do know they're trying to use me to get to you. Don't listen to them. Don't worry about me. I'll be fine."

Jamie stared from The Docent Mother to Lady Airth and back again, unable to figure out what was going on.

Lady Airth hissed at Jamie, "When perusing your memories, I happened upon something interesting. A string of texts between you and The Docent Mother wherein she told you to use a flash drive."

Jamie felt sick. Lady Airth could not know that those texts had not been The Docent Mother but from the artificial intelligence inside The File posing as The Docent Mother.

"I infer that you and The Docent Mother have been working against me with Lady Morse in order to stop the plan. I will not have this. I don't know what your plan was for those samples, but I must retrieve them. And, Docent Nguyen, you will help me."

Jamie spluttered, "You—no—you have the wrong idea. That wasn't—"

"Quiet!" Lady Airth snapped. "At this moment, I do not care about this alleged flash drive. I can question you two at my leisure about that once I have obtained Ms. Nari's autopsy samples."

Even during her panic, Jamie registered her luck that at least, apparently, Lady Airth hadn't delved any further in her memories once she had gotten to the bit about the samples being stored at Mr. Sato's apartment. If she thought The Docent Mother had been the one doing the texting, that meant Lady Airth didn't know anything about the AI in The File. And that meant that Jamie had to do everything she could to keep herself from being hooked up again to that machine.

In the meantime, however, the poor Docent Mother was going to have to suffer for no reason. Jamie squeaked, "But The Docent Mother really has nothing to do with—"

Lady Airth smirked. "Those texts prove otherwise."

"Please—"

Lady Airth whispered, chilly and menacing, "You will accompany me. You will help me track down those samples. I do not want to hurt The Docent Mother, Jamie. But I will. Or, rather, my people will hurt her. Over and over and over. Until you agree."

Jamie swallowed heavily and looked past Lady Airth back at the computer screen.

The Docent Mother said, "I didn't quite catch all of that, but I think I got the gist. Dear, don't do it. Whatever it is."

Jamie felt a pang of sadness as she watched The Docent Mother try to arrange her face into a brave expression. It didn't work too well.

Lady Airth sighed, then barked, "Lady Petrella?"

Lady Petrella stepped into view. Another of The Fordham Four. Jamie recognized her from around The Cloister, but had never taken any of her classes as she'd never been interested in engineering. The woman asked, "Yes, Lady Airth?"

Lady Airth sighed, "Do something to The Docent Mother. Hurt her." She cleared her throat. "I apologize, Docent Mother, but I see no other solution. The girl is fond of you, and she is showing disinclination to cooperate with me, and I simply do not have the time for diplomacy. Thus, this must be my solution."

The Docent Mother gave her a cold stare.

"Now?" Lady Petrella said.

"Now," Lady Airth said.

Jamie cried out as Lady Petrella sunk a knife into The Docent Mother's stomach. Jamie yelled loudly, trying to drown out The Docent Mother's cry of pain, "Stop it! Stop! Fine! Fine! I'll do it!" Jamie sincerely hoped that the AI would be able to get Jackie to retrieve those samples.

Lady Airth smiled. "Well, that was easy." She looked at the screen. "Andrea? Did you hear Docent Nguyen?"

Lady Petrella said, "Yes, Lady Airth." She withdrew the knife.

The Docent Mother moaned and slumped over in her seat. "Jamie, don't ..."

Jamie ignored her. "Fine. OK. Let's go. Just untie me and let's get out of here and get you those samples and whatever you want. Just let her go, OK?"

Lady Airth gave a tiny laugh. "Nonsense. We won't be letting her go. Not until I get all that I need from you, child. I had no idea how effective that would be." She walked behind Jamie, and Jamie shuddered at the feel of Lady Airth's hands against her back as she removed the cord from the port. "Lady Petrella, please remain on hand. Oh, and," she said, watching Jamie for a reaction, "do inject The Docent Mother with a sample of the Okada anomaly."

Lady Petrella looked momentarily stunned. But she said, "Yes, Alexis. Best of luck to you. Please keep me in the loop."

"Will do, Andrea. Will do."

Jamie croaked, "The Okada anomaly? But—but—then The Docent Mother—she—"

"Correct," Lady Airth said. "The nanobots will not cure her injuries. And she will be able to die."

"But—that's horrible!"

"You have no idea," Lady Airth murmured. "Are you aware that, unlike injecting Numan blood into an Okada descendant, doing it the other way around is irreversible?"

Jamie thought she did recall something along those lines from Sachi's grandma's notebook. She glared at Lady Airth. "So, even if you don't kill The Docent Mother, she is vulnerable. And she will die eventually."

Lady Airth grinned. She clicked her laptop shut and called, "Wharton!"

Wharton opened the door and came in, halting just inside the door as he had before.

Lady Airth said, "Pack up and bring everything down to the van, if you would be so good, Wharton."

"Yes, Lady Airth."

"And untie Docent Nguyen. We're going out."

22 JACKIE

Ms. Savage, the voice sounded in Jackie's head.

"Oh, hey, where have you been?" Jamie whispered, looking around at the other passengers on the bus she and Sachi had hopped a while back.

I've been listening to Docent Nguyen's situation, and checking on The File.

"Gotcha. Is something up?"

Yes. Something is up. Something quite urgent. Where are you?

"Uh, on a bus on the way to the apartment where we left Lady Morse's briefcase. So I can get that syringe for Sachi so we can do that blood thing. At least, I think that's where this bus is going." She looked at the map on the wall of the bus and frowned. She had taken a few wrong busses already, but was pretty sure she'd sorted it out.

Is the owner of this apartment, perchance, a Mr. Sato?

"How'd you know that?"

From listening to a conversation between Docent Nguyen and Lady Airth.

"Aw poor Dork Ass. She's with Airth for real?" A few people sitting near Jackie gave her funny looks. "What?" Jackie asked. "I'm talking to this baby here." She patted Sachi on the head. "Babies can understand a lot more language than we give them credit for."

Ms. Savage. Please. Pay attention to me. Listen closely. Lady Airth is on her way to Mr. Sato's home. You need to get there before her. You need to keep the samples away from her. This could not be more important.

"What?" Jackie hissed. "Why?"

Just do it. Airth cannot get them. And if you have these samples, you can use them to your advantage. You can hold them over Lady Airth's head and perhaps gain enough leverage to get control of this situation.

"But—but—dude—" she started, wanting to interrogate the AI. Her irate stuttering got her a few more funny looks from her neighbors. "You know what? Never mind. I don't need to know. Whatever. I'll just go get the damn samples. But you so seriously owe me an explanation."

There was no answer from the AI.

Jackie frowned and muttered under her breath for a bit. She idly wondered how many of the blathering nutcases she'd sat by on busses before had really been people like her, on missions to save humanity.

Sachi began to fuss. She wasn't smelly, and she'd had a nap in the car that Jackie had ditched after Sachi's tee shirt diaper had fallen off and poop had gotten all over the back seat, so Jackie had to assume the kid was hungry.

"We'll feed you at Mr. Sato's place," she said. "We must be nearly—" she looked out the window. "Yes!" Mr. Sato's neighborhood. She pulled the wire to let the driver know she wanted off. He stopped at the next corner, and Jackie grabbed her stuff and scampered off. On the sidewalk, she looked left and right, getting her bearings.

About five minutes later, she was standing in front of Mr. Sato's building. She gave the surroundings a careful perusal, wondering whether Lady Airth or any of her goons were around. She spotted no one milling around carefully avoiding her gaze, no one across the street pretending to read an upside down book, and no big "electric company" vans really housing thugs bent over surveillance equipment, so she figured she was in the clear. She buzzed an apartment at random since she'd forgotten which was Mr. Sato's number, and a few moments later the front door buzzed and she opened it up.

Jackie walked up the stairs to Mr. Sato's apartment, grumbling to Sachi, "Dude, this needs to be over. We need to end this stupid adventure and I need to get back to my own life. Except, wouldn't you know it, I can't go back to my own life! I mean, what the hell, Lady Morse? What the absolute hell?" She paused before knocking on Mr. Sato's door so she could get the rest of her rant out. "I mean, Sachi, I know you're just a baby and all and you don't have any control over who you hang out with, but let me just tell you here and now that your grandma was dead right about The Cloister devils."

Sachi tugged at her hair.

"Kid. You gotta stop that," Jackie sighed and pulled her hair away from Sachi's clutches for what felt like the hundredth time.

Sachi squirmed around, clearly getting tired of being held.

"Dude, I'll put you down once we're inside." She knocked on the door.

Mr. Sato looked at her and sighed, "You again?"

"Me again," Jackie said with a distracted smile.

"And with a baby, I see."

"Yep."

"I hope you're just here for the bag in my fridge."

"Yep." Jackie shouldered her way into the apartment and set Sachi down on the floor.

"I'll get it for you."

"No. I'll get it. You watch the kid. I've been carrying her for hours. She's gotta stretch her legs." Before Mr. Sato had a chance to object, she turned her back on him and hurried to the kitchen.

"Ms. Savage, I must object!" he called after her.

You're there?

"Yep," Jackie said as she walked into the kitchen and ignoring the angry words Mr. Sato was launching at her. She shot a smile at Mr.

Sato's boa constrictor, Captain Joe. If only she'd had more time on her hands, she'd have loved to pick him up.

Hurry. They're nearly there.

She swung open the minifridge door. "No worries. I'll just grab it and—"

"Ms. Savage!" Mr. Sato snapped from behind her. He had followed her into the kitchen. "You need to get out of my house. I am done putting up with your insane antics. I'm done. Get out!"

She whirled and growled, "I told you to watch the baby! What the hell, man!"

"Get out of my house!" He pushed past her, tugged the briefcase out of the minifridge, and shoved it into her arms, making her stagger backward a few paces.

"Dude—"

There was a knock on the door. More of a pound.

Jackie froze. Panic flooded her. "Are you expecting anyone?"

Mr. Sato gave her a nervous look that told her that her panic was showing on her face. "No ..."

"Aw crap. Go answer the door. Tell them the baby's yours. I'm not here. Cool?" She repeated firmly, "I am not here."

"This is insanity." Mr. Sato shook his head.

"You think I'm crazy? I'm nothing to them," she said, pointing toward the pounding.

The pounding continued, and Fedora's voice yelled, "Mr. Sato, you have until the count of five! We will break this door down!"

"Five!" yelled the voice.

"Please," Jackie whispered, making her eyes as sappy and full of emotion as she could. "I have a plan." She glanced at the snake, hoping it was hungry. "I just need a little time."

"Four!"

Mr. Sato turned on his heel as he said, "Fine. But hurry."

"Three!"

Jackie looked at the boa constrictor's rats in the fridge. She looked at the samples in the briefcase. She looked at the boa constrictor.

"Two!"

Time to get to work.

23 JAMIE

Jamie hugged her arms around herself, and stood well back from Wharton as he pounded on the door. Lady Airth, stood beside her with a hand firmly gripping Jamie's arm above the elbow. Jamie's mind was reeling, trying to think of some way that she could keep the samples away from Lady Airth. She hoped that Jackie had already gotten there and taken care of it. She hoped—

Docent Nguyen, Ms. Savage is in the kitchen. Stall for time.

"Five!" Wharton yelled.

Jamie turned to Lady Airth and said, "I don't think this is the right—"

"Four!" yelled Wharton.

Jamie continued, "—apartment. I think we need to be up a floor. It's—"

"Three!" yelled Wharton.

Lady Airth said, "All the same, we'll check this one first."

"Two!"

Jamie bit her lip. "But—no—uh—"

"One!"

Jamie frowned. So much for stalling.

The door swung open and a fearful-looking Mr. Sato stood there, staring at Wharton. His gaze travelled to Lady Airth and then to Jamie. "You?" he asked.

Jamie waved. "Me."

Lady Airth strode forward, pushed Wharton and then Mr. Sato out of the way, and walked into the apartment. Wharton shuffled aside mechanically as though completely used to being pushed about by Lady Airth, but Mr. Sato opened his mouth to object. Lady Airth shot him an icy stare that silenced him. Then, Lady Airth's gaze swept the room. "Mr. Sato, my name is Lady Airth. I'm from The Cloister. You've heard of me?"

"Lady Airth? Yes. Yes, I—I have heard of you," Mr. Sato stuttered, looking utterly confused. "What—why—?"

"Never mind that. I don't have the time to answer your questions, Mr. Sato. I do, however, need you to answer mine."

He cleared his throat and looked at the floor.

"Do you have a briefcase in your apartment? Left, perhaps, by this woman here, or perhaps a Ms. Savage?"

Mr. Sato cast Jamie a glance, looked back at the floor, and paused.

Jamie bit her lip, watching him, hoping against hope that he would say something to stall for time, since she was coming up blank. She looked at the kitchen door just in time to see Jackie dart across the kitchen looking frantic, briefcase in hand. Thankfully, Lady Airth and Wharton had both been looking at Mr. Sato, and had apparently not seen her.

"Well, Mr. Sato?" Lady Airth snapped. "The briefcase?"

Mr. Sato said, "Yes. Ms. Savage did leave it here."

Jamie felt a stab of disappointment. So, he would not be helping her stall. Out of the corner of her eye, she saw Jackie peek out from behind the kitchen door. She winced. How on earth had Lady Airth and Wharton not seen that? Then something else occurred to her: Jackie was not holding Sachi. Where was Sachi? Her eyes swept the room. In a corner, behind a potted plant, she thought she spotted movement. She peered intently. Yes. She was sure she saw the top of Sachi's head as she investigated something behind the plant. Jamie hoped the child wasn't fussing with electrical outlets or trying to eat fallen and potentially poisonous leaves from the plant.

Lady Airth said, "Excellent. Bring me the briefcase." She folded her arms and stared at Mr. Sato.

"Yes, Lady Airth." He hurried toward the kitchen.

Jamie stared after him, torn between concern for Sachi and disappointment at how quickly Mr. Sato had folded. "Wait!" Jamie gasped.

Mr. Sato halted and turned in the kitchen doorway. Lady Airth and Wharton looked at Jamie.

"Yes, Docent Nguyen?" asked Lady Airth.

"Um. Uh. Well ..." Jamie floundered. From the direction of the kitchen, she thought she heard the faint sound of the fridge being carefully opened. "Um ..."

Lady Airth sighed, "Never mind. Mr. Sato, if you'd be so good as to hurry?"

Jamie's shoulders slumped and she frowned as she watched him disappear into the kitchen and come back moments later with the briefcase.

Lady Airth extended her hand, and Mr. Sato handed it over.

She took it to the couch and sat down, spine straight as an arrow. She opened it and began to rummage through. She paused, frowned, and rummaged some more.

Jamie's heart hammered painfully. She saw movement out of the corner of her eye and looked back at the kitchen door to see Jackie give her a thumb's up and a grin.

Lady Airth swore, and tipped the briefcase upside down, dumping the contents onto the couch. "Where are the samples?" she said to Mr. Sato. "What did you do with them?"

Jamie cringed at the look of fear on Mr. Sato's face. He stuttered, "I—I—I don't know. Do you mean this—this girl's medicine?" he pointed at Jamie.

Lady Airth rounded on Jamie. "What—"

There was a slam from the kitchen.

Jamie winced.

Lady Airth and Wharton hurried to the kitchen, with Jamie hot on their heels. Mr. Sato stayed in the living room, as did Sachi, who was likely searching for dust bunnies under Mr. Sato's furniture.

Lady Airth and Wharton stopped short in the doorway.

Jamie peered over their shoulders at the room beyond.

They all took in the sight of Jackie, hands still on the window she'd just slammed shut, looking guiltily at Lady Airth. "Hi!" she said. "Lady Airth? I'm Jackie Sav—"

Lady Airth cut her off with a dangerous growl, "I know who you are. Why did you slam that window?"

"Oh. Uh. No reason. No reason at all. Nope," Jackie said, blathering a mile a minute, blatantly nervous. "Thought I saw a monkey on the rooftop across the street. So cool that they have monkeys here. Like squirrels for us, kinda, maybe. Have you checked out that monkey park over by the ocean? Totally worth the visit. Baby monkeys, oh my gosh, their cute little faces—"

Lady Airth strode right up to Jackie and spat, "Where are the samples?"

"Samples? What samples?" Jackie's gaze flicked to the window, then she looked past Lady Airth at Jamie. "Jamie? We don't know anything about any—"

"Wharton," Lady Airth said, still staring Jackie in the face.

"Yes, Lady Airth?" Wharton asked.

"She threw the samples out the window. Go outside and search for them." She smirked at Jackie. "Child, you really thought I wouldn't notice?"

Wharton hurried away to do Lady Airth's bidding.

Jamie listened nervously to his departure, afraid that when he went out into the living room he'd spot Sachi. But the kid must have still been out of sight. Wharton walked right out and slammed the door.

Jackie said to Lady Airth, "I—I guess I wasn't really thinking." She looked at the floor and shuffled her right foot back and forth. "I just wanted to keep those samples away from you."

Jamie narrowed her eyes and looked at Jackie, feeling certain she was lying, but unsure why she was so sure. But, then, they were copies, after all. Jamie frowned, wondering where the samples were if they hadn't been thrown out the window. She scanned the room, trying not to be too obvious. There were any number of places Jackie could have stashed the samples. Cupboards, drawers, the fridge. But every hiding place Jamie could see would be very easy for Lady Airth to find if she only started looking. With luck, Lady Airth would keep right on believing that the samples had been dropped outside.

Lady Airth strode to the window and looked past the snake's cage, down to where Wharton was probably scrabbling about in the dirt and the grass and the plants, looking for the samples.

Jamie shot Jackie a quizzical look.

Jackie's eyes flicked toward the snake in its cage under the window.

Jamie looked at the huge boa constrictor, wondering whether Jackie was thinking that they could somehow set the creature on Lady Airth while Wharton was outside. Not likely, considering that it was a well-fed house pet used to swallowing up rats on a regular basis. It wouldn't bother with attempting such a difficult meal as Lady Airth.

Then, Jamie's spotted the slight bulge about a foot below the snake's mouth. It had recently eaten. Her eyes widened. She looked from the snake to Jackie. Jackie grinned and nodded slightly. Lady Airth turned from the window, and Jackie's grin disappeared.

Jamie was both impressed and disappointed. Somehow, the samples were inside the snake. A very good hiding place, certainly. But there was no way that those samples would be of use any more. The AI had said that the blood sample taken from Tamon Nari would be needed for its plan to stop Lady Airth. Unfortunately, now that that was not a possibility, that meant they needed Sachi's blood instead.

While Jamie's mind reeled with information she could barely keep straight, Lady Airth walked to within a foot of Jackie. "Wharton does not appear to be locating any of the samples." She studied Jackie's face intently.

"What a shame for you," Jackie said, staring right into Lady Airth's eyes.

"Quite," Lady Airth conceded. "Quite. But don't worry. I have ways of getting inside your head."

Jackie laughed. "I don't think so. I'm super tough."

"I doubt that very much. But, even if you were, it would be irrelevant. Whether you are tough or weak will in no way change anything about the speed with which I will extract all pertinent information from you. Getting into your head will be quite simple."

As Airth and Jackie talked, Jamie bit her lip, feeling super stressed and conflicted. She wanted to stick around and witness this conversation, but she also wanted to hurry into the next room and make sure Sachi wasn't getting into trouble. The kid could be sticking something dangerous in her mouth at that very moment. Mr. Sato might have left a bottle cap from one of his repulsive green sodas on the ground. Or, Sachi might be playing with an electrical outlet. Or doing any number of potentially lethal things.

"I'll never talk," Jackie said. "You think you can get in my head? You have no power over me, you creepy cult master. I'm not one of your brainwashed minions. I'm a reporter and I will report the living hell out of—"

"You're what I made you," Lady Airth scoffed. "You weren't here earlier for the big reveal I told Docent Nguyen, but, you see, I, Lady Morse, Lady Petrella, and Lady Stambaugh created—"

"Yeah, yeah. You created me as part of some research thingy when you were planning the Greywash," Jackie said with a careless wave of her hand. "And—oh yeah! Shocker! You did the Greywash! And you've got another in the works to bring your evil plan to fruition! The conspiracy theorists were right all along! Ooh big surprise. Wow." Jackie met Jamie's gaze for a half-second, then gave a nearly imperceptible head-jerk toward the hall.

Jamie inched her way backward. Time to leave Jackie to her fate, at least for now. The priority for now was to find Sachi. Jamie couldn't trust that Mr. Sato was watching her. She wasn't even sure Mr. Sato was in the apartment anymore. If he had any sense, he'd have run for it the moment he could.

Lady Airth arched an eyebrow at Jackie. "Lady Morse told you what you are? That was highly irresponsible of her. Our test subjects should not know that they are test subjects. It destroys the research."

"You were about to tell me," Jackie pointed out.

"True enough. But that, child, was only because I am going to take you two and put you on ice in the lab back at The Cloister. Your group really is of very little use to us any longer, now that we've improved on you." She shrugged and continued, "But that is beside the point. You say I have no control over you. You'll find you are quite mistaken. You see, child, The Cloister owns you. You, as a product of my research, are mine. I can have the paperwork sent over if you require, but I assure you it would be a waste of time. The language is far beyond your reading level."

Jamie stopped scooting out of the room. Jackie and Jamie shared a moment of shock. Jackie mouth wordlessly for a tad, then managed, "No way."

"Yes."

"I'm a person though. A *person*. That means you cannot control me."

Lady Airth said, "It's charming that you think your supposed personhood matters."

"But it does matter. You can't own people. And there is nothing supposed about our personhood," Jackie pointed out.

Jamie had, by that point, scooted through the kitchen door and was standing in the hallway. Lady Airth and Jackie were so focused on her conversation that she was pretty sure she could turn and grab Sachi.

Lady Airth said to Jackie, "But you aren't people. You're a conglomeration of nanobots. Nanobots whose patent I hold."

At those words, Jamie felt as though the wind had been knocked out of her. She wasn't a person? On one level, the information was stunningly horrible. But on another level, it was obvious. Of course, if she was made of nanotechnology, she was not technically a human. She wondered why she hadn't drawn that conclusion sooner.

Jackie just laughed and said, "Says you." Jamie saw Jackie give a little flick of her hand, as though shooing Jamie away.

24 Jackie

Jackie watched out of her peripheral vision as Jamie finally disappeared down the hall. Jackie clenched her fists, hoping she looked super tough as she stared down Lady Airth. She wondered how long she could hold Lady Airth's attention before the woman noticed Jamie was gone.

Airith smirked, "That's exactly the kind of comeback I'd expect from one of you." She shook her head. "Now, how about we just get down to business. Those samples. They do not appear to be anywhere beneath this window. Where are they?" Lady Airth began to scan the room.

Jackie laughed, "They're with an accomplice. He was watching the building from across the street. I tossed the samples out. He caught them and he ran."

"Is that so?" Lady Airth took a step closer.

Jackie backed up a step. "Dude. Personal space."

Lady Airth asked, "Who is this accomplice?"

"Pfft. Right. Like I'd tell—"

"It's Lady Morse, isn't it?"

Jackie raised an eyebrow. *Sure. Why not?* "Uh ... no way. Nope. Not Lady Morse."

Lady Airth smiled. "You really are an awful liar."

"I'm not lying."

Lady Airth opened her mouth to speak.

From the next room, Jackie heard the slight sound of the door latch clicking. Either Jamie was opening the door, or closing it. Jackie clenched her jaw, hoping Lady Airth hadn't heard it.

Lady Airth snapped her mouth shut. She turned her head. "Wharton?"

Crap.

Lady Airth then looked around the kitchen. "Docent Nguyen!"

Jackie said, "She just went to the bathroom. I'm sure she'll be right back."

Lady Airth stalked out into the living room, and Jackie followed a few steps behind. The room was empty. Jackie grinned and watched as Lady Airth checked the balcony and the bathroom.

"Huh. Maybe she went down to help Wharton look for the samples?" Jackie suggested.

Lady Airth glared at her. "Shut up." She pulled a phone from her pocket and was in the midst of dialing when the apartment door swung open and Wharton walked in, a frown on his face. Lady Airth pocketed the phone. "Well?

"I can't find them."

"Yes. I know. Ms. Savage was just telling me about how she passed the samples on to Lady Morse," Lady Airth grumbled. "I don't suppose you saw Docent Nguyen running off when you were down on the street?"

"No, Lady Airth. She's gone?"

"She is."

Wharton stared at her.

"Well?" Lady Airth snapped. "Go look for her!"

Wharton whirled on the spot and rushed right back out the door.

Lady Airth and Jackie watched him go in a silence that Jackie at last broke with, "You know, he's got no hope of finding her. She's a master of disguise, Jamie. She can melt into the—"

Lady Airth gave a snort. "Gather your things. You're coming with us. And once Wharton locates Docent Nguyen—likely within five minutes—she will be joining us as well. We are going back to The Cloister. But first, I am going to hook you up to a machine and read your mind. No more lies, Ms. Savage. I will have the truth from you within the hour. The truth about everything. About Lady Morse, about the child, about all of it."

25 JAMIE

As Jamie listened to Wharton stomping up to Mr. Sato's apartment, she stayed hidden in the alcove under the stairs. She held Sachi close to her, hoping that the kid would keep up her admirable habit of being silent. Only once she had heard Mr. Sato's door open and shut did she hurry from the alcove and to the front door.

"Hey voice?" she asked as she hurried down the street, peering over her shoulder every few seconds.

Docent Nguyen.

"What's going on with Jackie?"

Do not waste time worrying about her. She will be fine. You need to get away from Lady Airth, immediately, and then find a way to get yourself and the child back to The Cloister.

"What was Jackie even doing at Mr. Sato's?"

She had gone there to get a syringe from Lady Morse's briefcase so that she could inject her blood into Sachi. Since she was already there, I recruited her to see to the samples before you arrived.

"Gotcha. Quick thinking."

Thinking quickly is what I do. I am a computer."

"Well, so am I, apparently, and I don't think too quickly."

You were made to mimic humanity. If I may say so, you do it quite well.

"Thank you?"

You are welcome. The models that came after yours have, I feel, become progressively less and less human, though it seems that the less human they become the more The Fordham Four deem them a success.

"Huh." Jamie hid in the shadow of a large pillar and watched behind her for signs of pursuit. "And I really need to bring Sachi to The Cloister?"

Yes, if you have, as I understand it, misplaced the samples taken from Tamon Nari.

"Er. Well, they're not so much misplaced as stuffed in a rat inside a snake." Jamie looked behind her again, and turned a corner.

Interesting. It is a good thing, after all, that we did not leave the infant at the monkey park. Well, then, yes, you need to bring the baby to The Cloister. Or, at the very least, you need her blood, properly stored and as fresh as possible so that the machine will have no trouble reading it.

"The machine? What's that?"

Now is not the time. I can fill you in on the flight across the ocean.

"Fair enough." Jamie stopped short as a thought occurred to her. "Jackie was going to inject some blood into Sachi. Right?"

Yes. To bring her to a state of temporary stasis so that she would no longer have to be concerned with the child perishing.

"Of course. Smart. I guess I better do that if I can." She wondered whether Lady Airth had bothered to take the briefcase with her before she left Mr. Sato's apartment. It was worth a look. And she needed to go retrieve the diaper bag anyway. Sachi had been getting increasingly fussy. It was time for a diaper change and some food.

"Do you know if they're still at the apartment?"

They are gone. Lady Airth is taking Ms. Savage back to The Cloister.

Jamie frowned and wondered aloud, "Shoot. I should try to rescue her."

I would not bother. You would be further ahead just sneaking onto the jet yourself, since the jet would be most helpful in carrying out the final step in my plan. You can rescue Ms. Savage afterwards.

Jamie sighed heavily and began to walk back to Mr. Sato's. Every time a car drove past, she threw herself behind the nearest trash can or bush. As she went, she asked, "You really think The Cloister jet's the way to go? That seems insanely dumb."

It is more intelligent than attempting to get commercial plane tickets for yourself and the child without any identification.

Jamie conceded to herself that the AI made a good point. She tried to get her head clear enough to weigh her options, but she could barely think straight, freaked out as she was that Wharton was about to sneak up behind her, grab Sachi, and bring the poor kid back to the lab, thus gaining control of all Okada descendants and enabling Lady Airth to move toward her next steps of destroying humanity.

She reached Mr. Sato's building before she reached any good plan. She looked up at the building and sighed.

The only thing she was really sure of was that she had better inject some blood into Sachi. After all, it looked as though Jamie was going to be dragging her into a very dangerous situation.

26 JACKIE

"So, what the hell is going on here?" Jackie asked as she struggled against the ropes that held her to the seat in the back of the van Wharton was driving. They were on the way to wherever The Cloister's jet was. Jackie had not made it easy for them to tie her to the seat, but in the end Wharton had managed it. The gash on the side of her face and the broken elbow were healing nicely, but she was still a bit out of sorts from all the abuse. She glowered at Lady Airth, who sat beside her, running a hand down the back of Jackie's neck. "You are being intensely creepy right now. You know that, right?"

"I'm sure it does seem that way to you. Yes," Lady Airth murmured and pressed her fingers to a spot a few vertebrae down Jackie's spine.

"Don't touch me!" Jackie snapped as Lady Airth placed the fingertips of her other hand to the center of Jackie's right palm. Lady Morse pushed down on both Jackie's spine and palm.

Jackie shivered, sure she felt something in her back compress under Lady Airth's fingertips. The spot went numb. "What—"

"It's the port in your back. I'm going to hook you up and read your memories. I'd like to locate that child. Can't have loose ends running around messing up my plans, now can we?"

Jackie just sat there, stunned by the fact that she had a hole in her back that could be plugged into a computer. She cleared her throat and tried to talk. It didn't work. She tried again. "I don't want you in my head. You have no right—"

"I have every right. If you recall, I hold your patent."

"You can't honestly expect that logic to work on me."

"My logic doesn't need to work on you. You're tied to that seat." With that, Lady Airth picked up a cord off the floor of the van. The other end of the cord was plugged into a machine on the floor of the van. that was and plugged it into Jackie's back.

Jackie gasped at the zap of energy that shot through her. "Dude—"

"Quiet," Lady Airth snapped as she picked up the laptop that had been on the floor of the van in front of her.

"I will not be quiet," Jackie scoffed. "Why would I—"

"The better my focus, the sooner you will be unplugged." Lady Airth pushed a few keys on her laptop and pulled up a black screen. One keystroke later, it began to fill with strings of white symbols.

Jackie stared as Lady Airth's computer screen filled up with Jackie's memories. She gritted her teeth, trying to swallow her rage. She cleared her throat. "But also the sooner you'll be able to read information I'd rather not have you read. It seems to me that the smartest thing for me to do would be to distract you as much as humanly possible." Jackie grinned.

Lady Airth gave her a weary look. "Nothing you can do will stop the inevitable."

"But I can slow you down."

Without further ado, Jackie pushed aside her panic and confusion to deal with later, and she started to belt out some showtunes at the top of her lungs.

27 JAMIE

When Jamie got to Mr. Sato's door, she found it ajar and pushed it open. "Hello?"

There was a shuffling sound, a low voice saying something too quiet for her to hear, and then footsteps. The door swung open the rest of the way to reveal a glaring Mr. Sato. "Out!" he yelled, pointing a finger past her and down the stairs. "Get out! Leave me alone!"

Jamie winced and said in a rush, "Mr. Sato, I'm so sorry. I don't blame you for wanting me gone. But can I just get—"

"This?" he asked, striding back to the couch and picking up the briefcase from the floor beside it. "Yes. Take it. Take it and go." He shoved it at her.

"Hey! I'm holding a baby! Watch it!"

"That baby left urine all over my carpet!" He glared at Sachi.

Jamie backed away a few paces, took a deep breath, and tried to calm down. "Sorry about that. I can clean it up if you want."

"Too late. I already did." He started to shut the door. Then he stopped. "What did you do to Captain Joe?"

"Huh? What'd I do to who?"

"My snake. Captain Joe. What's wrong with him? Did you feed him? He has a strict diet, and—"

"Oh ..." Jamie frowned. "Um, yeah ... well, Ms. Savage might have sorta ... um ... well, I think you should take Captain Joe to a veterinarian."

Mr. Sato glared so hard his face twitched. He yelled something in Japanese, Jamie figured because it was his first language and thus he could manage better insults when speaking it.

"Whatever you said, I'm betting I deserve it, sir. I really am sorry. And, uh, I hope Captain Joe is OK ..." She turned.

He slammed the door.

She took a few steps.

The door opened again.

She winced and turned, expecting another barrage of anger.

What she got was a diaper bag to the knees. "Geez! How many times do I have to tell you I'm holding a baby!"

"That's why I aimed for your legs, idiot!" he spat, then slammed the door again.

Jamie sighed and picked it up. "Thank you!" she yelled at the door. Then she said to Sachi, "Let's find somewhere to change you and get you some food. You must be hungry. I think I saw an applesauce pouch in your diaper bag earlier."

A short time later, Jamie had found a changing table in the bathroom of a restaurant down the street from Mr. Sato. Once Sachi was all cleaned up and fed, Jamie found an open bench at a bus stop, plunked Sachi down beside her, and began to rummage through the briefcase. As she looked for a syringe, she said to Sachi, "So, full disclosure. I've never actually taken blood or injected blood. However, I have been having blood samples taken from me every week since I was a kid, since I'm part of a long-term study by some Cloister scientists. They're studying people with my blood type over the span of their lives ..." Jamie trailed off, suddenly lost in thought. She'd had a crazy idea.

"Huh. I wonder...what if they just told me I was part of a long-term study? What if they just said that so I wouldn't wonder why they were taking my blood all the time? What if they were collecting it for studying the Okada descendants they have in their lab!" She looked up from the briefcase's contents and stared at Sachi, suddenly sure she was right. "Oh wow. Yeah. I wonder if it was my blood that was keeping you in stasis ... dang."

Sachi looked up at her, quizzical, and nearly toppled off the bench.

Jamie caught her. "No you don't, kiddo. Not until I've put my robot blood in you."

Only when she was about halfway through the procedure did it occur to her that, all around her, everyone was living normal lives, and they had no idea of the gravity of the situation that she was in the middle of. Thus, what she was doing had to look super bizarre, a burp cloth tied tight around her upper arm as she took her blood and prepared to inject it into an infant. She looked around, and, sure enough, there were a good amount of people staring at her.

She frowned, cursing herself for being so utterly stupid. At least it looked like no one was pulling out a phone to call the police. Jamie looked around, trying to see whether there was a more private place she could take Sachi. But her audience would hardly be cool with her slipping down the nearest alley with a syringe full of blood and a baby.

Across the street, a woman reached into her purse and pulled out a cell phone.

Jamie sighed, carefully stowed the syringe back in the briefcase, untied the cloth around her arm, and tried to look as though she wasn't up to anything creepy or weird. *Please, please, please, lady. Nothing weird is going on. No child abuse. We're cool. Everything's A-OK.*

Sachi crawled into her lap.

The lady began to dial.

Jamie weighed for a moment the pros and cons of running. But no, that would look weird. Someone would follow her. Jamie decided to try to look normal instead. She opened the diaper bag and pulled out a board book. She cleared her throat. "*The Littlest Donkey*, by Katie Kazakos. One warm and sunshiny day, Leona Donkey was enjoying a nice breakfast of clover. *Chomp, chomp, chomp.* Across the field, she saw her friend, Nicholas Cow coming to join her. *Trot, trot, trot.* 'Well, good morning, Nicholas Cow!' said Leona Donkey. What—"

Sirens.

Jamie looked up from *The Littlest Donkey* and saw a police car approaching from a few blocks down. In a flash, she had stowed the book, picked up Sachi, and was hurrying down the sidewalk in the opposite direction, too nervous to look over her shoulder to see how much time she might have left. She looked frantically left and right, and saw the woman across the street following her at a distance, yelling something at her and waving at the police car.

What is going on? I hear sirens.

"They're after me."

Why? Actually, never mind. Run. Get away. I need you on that jet.

"Running would make me look even more suspicious!" Jamie hissed. She began rummaging in the briefcase with her free hand, half-considering using a gun. If only she could find one. But there weren't any guns. Not in the briefcase. Not in the diaper bag. Where had they gone? Jamie couldn't believe she'd lost track of them. She figured they must be with Jackie.

The police car pulled up alongside her just as she grabbed one of Lady Morse's two phones. Jamie pulled it out. "As a Cloister computer, do you know phone passcodes of Cloister people?" she said so fast it was a wonder that the AI could tell what she'd said.

Whose do you need?

"Morse's."

6921R.

Jamie tried it. "Nope. Other phone."

The police car stopped and the doors opened.

7227w.

Hands shaking, Jamie dialed it. The phone unlocked.

"Drop the phone!" a police officer yelled as he got out of the passenger seat.

Jamie dialed the first number in Lady Morse's call history.

A man's voice said, "Yes?"

"I need help," Jamie gasped. "I'm Lady Morse's friend and I need help."

The policeman was walking slowly toward her, and his friend was coming around the car to join him.

"Docent Nguyen?" the voice on the phone said.

"Yes."

The second cop said, "Miss, put down the phone so we can talk. We had a call about a baby in danger."

The voice on Lady Morse's phone said, "Where are you?" Jamie's heart leapt as she realized it was Stewie.

"I'm—"

Stewie cut in, "Never mind. I'll track you. Don't say anything to them."

"Uh—" She glanced at the cop. He looked impatient.

"You hear me? Don't—"

The first cop got tired of her lack of response. He sprung at her and grabbed her arm that held the phone. As he twisted her arm behind her back, his partner swooped in to get Sachi.

The first cop grabbed the phone and said into it, "Hello?" Apparently Stewie had hung up, because the cop tossed the phone into the diaper bag that he'd apparently grabbed from Jamie without her noticing. Before she'd fully comprehended what was going on, she had been guided to a seat in the back of the police car, and the first cop was asking her for her name.

She ignored him and tried to stand, tried to see what they'd done with Sachi.

"Miss, you need to stay seated and give me your name," her cop friend said, with a firm hand on her shoulder.

"Get off me," she snarled. "Where's—" but then she caught sight of Sachi. The second officer was holding her while he talked with the woman who had called them. At that moment, both the woman and the cop turned and gave her narrow-eyed looks. Clearly, they didn't think too well of swapping blood with babies. "Hey, let go of my baby! Give her back!"

"Sergeant Hayashi seems to be doing alright with her," Cop One said. Jamie couldn't argue the fact. Sergeant Hayashi looked to be pretty good with babies. He had stepped away from the witness and was, by the look of it, singing to Sachi as he bounced her to the beat. Sachi was laughing, apparently having a great time. Cop One said to Jamie, "We will just leave the child with him until you can prove she is your child. Forgive me, but the report we got from a bystander paired with the fact that you do not at all resemble the child—"

"Well that's kinda racist," Jamie snapped, glossing over the bit about the bystander call and going straight for the defensiveness of a white person who thinks they actually know what it is to experience racism. "Way to judge! I'll have you know little, uh, Keiko is my adoptive daughter!"

"And you can prove that?" Cop One asked.

"I—well—no. I mean, do you carry around documentation proving your kids are yours? Does anyone do that?"

He gave her a look, pulled out handcuffs, and secured her to a bar on the back of the driver's seat. "Stay here," he said, then walked off to talk to Sergeant Hayashi.

"My lawyers are gonna have a field day with this!" she yelled since that seemed like the right thing to say. The Cloister did have awesome lawyers, but she somehow doubted that after this Kyoto fiasco she'd be in any position make use of them.

Cop One didn't even respond. Soon, he and Hayashi were having a whispered conversation. The scene had attracted quite a crowd. Jamie looked at the ground, feeling awkward under the gaze of so many people who must think she was a criminal. She saw the lady who'd called the cops whispering to one of the crowd and pointing an accusatory finger at Jamie.

Jamie sighed heavily, hoping that Stewie would be able to get her out of this. But she hadn't even been able to give him her location before Cop One had grabbed the phone from her. Would he really be able to trace her? The way he kept turning up out of nowhere, she was betting yes.

And then, quite suddenly, Jamie was hit by a wave of exhaustion. Now that she was sitting down, it hit her how very tired she was. She had to have been awake more than 24 hours.

Docent Nguyen.

"What?" she asked, trying not to move her lips.

What is going on? Have you worked out how to get to the jet?

"No, I have not!" she snapped, covering her mouth with her non-cuffed hand. "I'm handcuffed to a police car and they won't give Sachi back to me!"

Break your thumb, and you will be able to slip out of the cuff. Run when they are not looking.

Jamie spluttered for a few moments, then managed, still talking behind her hand, "Leaving aside the thumb breaking thing, which I will most certainly not do, there's still Sachi. I won't be able to get her away from them."

Leave her. You need to get on that jet.

"No! And I thought we needed her blood now that the samples from her mom are no good."

We will have to make a stop at The Cloister and take a sample from one of the other Okada descendants in storage.

"Eww. And, make a stop at The Cloister? I thought that was where we were going already."

We will talk about that later. Now, you getting to The Cloister as quickly as possible. The authorities will care for the child well enough for now, considering that Lady Airth's attention is now on returning to The Cloister with you and Ms. Savage, I believe she will put her search for the child on the back burner. Lady Airth has her associates searching for you, and they cannot find you. It is a distinct possibility that they heard of your capture via their surveillance equipment. So you must escape, now.

"Why not let her associates come and get me then?"

I need you able to move freely. You would not be able to do so if they found you. Thus, you need to sneak onto the jet, not be brought onto it by them.

Jamie gritted her teeth, then growled, "I'm getting tired of you ordering me around as though I'm your tool and I'll do your bidding unquestioningly."

You think Lady Airth's plan is wrong, correct?

"Correct. Yes."

Well, then. Do what I tell you to do, and humanity will be saved. You do want to save humanity, don't you?

"You're super manipulative."

Humans respond to manipulation.

"Well I'm not human," she sighed as she watched Sergeant Hayashi playing peek-a-boo with Sachi. "Look, let's backtrack to the part where I said I'm handcuffed to a car."

I gave you the solution already. Break your thumb.

"Yeah, I'm not doing that."

Docent—

"Stop it!" she yelled. The crowd and the cops all looked at her.

Cop One said, "Miss, there's no need to yell at us."

"Sorry ..." Jamie sighed and slumped against the seat.

The cop shook his head disapprovingly and turned back to a witness whom he appeared to be interviewing. Apparently, they were getting everyone else's spin first and then they were going to question her, which was fine by her as it made it super easy for her to follow Stewie's "don't talk to them" directions. She tried not to worry too much about the fact that Wharton was also looking for her. Stewie would find her first. He had to.

Jamie shut her eyes and let the sleepiness wash over her.

She wasn't how sure she dozed, but it didn't feel like too long. She was jolted awake by a strident, male voice barking, "What's going on here?"

Her eyes snapped open. There was Stewie. Stewie, in a fancy suit and tie, striding up to the cops, grabbing Sachi out of Hayashi's arms, and saying, "This is my child. What business do you have with my child? And ..." he scanned the crowd. "My wife! On what grounds—"

"Sir! Please, calm down, and—"

"I will not be calm!" Stewie blustered, every inch the moronic American businessman Jamie got the feeling he was posing as. "Do you think I got where I got in this world by being *calm*? No, sir. I want to talk to your superiors."

"Sir—"

"An outrage," Stewie reiterated through clenched teeth as he pulled out his wallet and flashed his identification.

Cop One's eyes bulged.

Cop One beckoned Hayashi over.

They had a quick, whispered exchange.

Stewie flashed his badge again for Hayashi's benefit.

They had a louder exchange, of which Jamie caught snippets like, "... no possible reason ... blood into a baby ..." and "... very expensive doctor ... only way ... baby might age ..." and "... have to be an idiot ..." and "... top flight lawyer ..."

Cop One and Hayashi exchanged a look.

Cop One hurried over to Jamie and uncuffed her.

Jamie blinked, began to rub her wrist, and looked at Stewie. "Hi, husband! Gee, thanks."

28 JACKIE

Lady Airth was sitting across from Jackie in one of the squashy, insanely comfortable seats of The Cloister's private jet. She was frowning at Jackie, but Jackie had the feeling the woman wasn't really seeing her. Jackie had tested this theory by crossing her eyes and sticking out her tongue at Lady Airth. She'd gotten no reaction.

Calypso, was sitting on Lady Airth's arm, also staring at Jackie.

Jackie gave a huff of annoyance. Sitting around and waiting for Lady Airth's thugs to capture Jamie was a special blend of boredom and fear. It would have been lovely if Jamie could have avoided capture, but Jackie was most certainly not holding her breath for that. No. Odds were strong that, any minute, Lady Airth would get a call from Wharton saying that he'd found Jamie and the baby.

They'd been waiting on the jet for at least an hour. Long enough that Jackie was starting to get her hopes up that Jamie might actually be able to evade Wharton.

Having nothing else to do, Jackie decided to have a staring contest with the bird. It was staring at her anyway, so why not?

The bird turned out to be a formidable opponent.

Time ticked on.

Lady Airth shifted in her seat.

Jackie had the impression the woman was still staring at her. But she didn't want to look away from Calypso to confirm it.

Calypso gave a long, low croak.

The battle raged on.

Lady Airth's phone rang. She answered it and snapped, "Yes?"

Jackie kept right on staring into the black, beady eyes.

Lady Airth groaned, "How on earth did you lose her when she was in police custody?"

Jackie nearly looked away from Calypso, so shocking was that tidbit of news. *Way to go, Dork Ass.*

Lady Airth growled, "Yes. I suppose that's true. She must have gotten help."

Another pause.

"Clearly, it must be Lady Morse. Who else would it be?"

As Jackie kept up the staring contest, she smirked at the thought that Lady Airth still suspected Lady Morse of working against her, when Lady Morse was probably halfway across Japan, running and not looking back.

Lady Airth continued, "You have another hour. I will wait no longer. If you don't find her by then, I will leave you behind to finish your task."

The raven tilted its head in a way that felt to Jackie to be rather sassy. She narrowed her eyes. "You think you can win this because you're a cyborg? You forget, bird, I'm a robot too."

Lady Airth said to Wharton, "Because there are things I need to do at The Cloister. Time-sensitive things that are far above your paygrade and mental capacity, Wharton. Do not for one moment think that since I will be across the planet from you that your task is any less urgent. This one here doesn't know where the child is, but Docent Nguyen must. The child must be located." Lady Airth paused for Wharton to respond. Then she snapped, "Good. Very good. Don't call again until it's taken care of." She hung up.

Without breaking eye contact with Calypso, Jackie said, "What's so important about the kid?"

"Child, my conversations with those in my employ are not your business. Your business is sitting there as quiet as you can possibly sit, and letting me think. I need—why are you staring at Calypso?"

"Staring contest."

"But you just blinked. I saw you."

"It's not the blinking kind. It's the whoever looks away first kind."

"Ah."

"Seriously, though, why's the crow not looking away?" Jackie asked, starting to get a little creeped out by the fathomless, beady eyes boring into hers.

"Raven. And I'm not entirely sure. It must be analyzing you. You *are* acting in a manner I'm quite sure Calypso's never encountered before."

"Hmm." Jackie sighed, reluctantly looking away from the bird. "You were saying? Something condescending and snooty about my job being sitting quiet and letting you think?"

"Yes, Ms. Savage. Precisely. That was the gist of it. Since I was unable to glean anything useful from your memories—except that the child was right under my nose at the apartment and I didn't know it, which is irksome in the extreme and ultimately unhelpful—you are of no further use to me. At least at present. So, be so good as to be silent."

"It wasn't useful that you found out where the samples were?"

"No." Lady Airth glowered at her. "Not helpful at all, except that I can now strike finding the samples from my to-do list. Being inside the snake as long as they have been, unrefrigerated, they'll be useless to me."

Jackie tried to suppress a smile, wondering how someone as smart as Lady Airth could be so dumb.

Lady Airth narrowed her eyes. "What's so funny?"

Jackie couldn't help it. "Snakes are cold blooded, moron."

278

Lady Aith put a hand to her forehead and groaned. "The phrase cold-blooded does not mean that that reptiles have cold blood. It means their temperature is not regulated by their body but by their surroundings. Snakes are not slithering refrigerators. Under a heat lamp, lying under a window, as that snake was, it was quite warm."

"Oh." Jackie let the wave of embarrassment wash over her without fighting it off, since she totally deserved it. She looked down at her hands. "Err um, sorry I called you a moron."

"My feelings have never been hurt by the insults of idiots. If they had the capacity to understand what I understood, they'd see me for what I was and they wouldn't insult me. They, in short, know not what they do." Lady Airth paused, rested her hands on the armrests, and asked, "Is that why you put the samples in the snake? You thought they'd remain cold?"

Jackie felt another stab of embarrassment. The woman was clearly trying to force down a laugh. "In part, yes," Jackie answered grudgingly. "But mostly I just wanted you to think that I'd passed the samples on to an associate, so I'd be able to hold the samples over your head as a kind of blackmail thing, since you seemed to want them so much."

"Hmm," Lady Airth said with a nod. "Rather clever. I'd be inclined to give you some credit for that line of reasoning, except that the fact that you thought you could go up against me proves that your clever reasoning was an anomaly."

"Dude," Jackie said, studying the severe, glowering woman across from her, "you are such a huge jerk. Huuuuuge. I thought cult leaders were supposed to be super charismatic or whatever."

"The Cloister is not a cult."

"Riiiiiight. That's what all the cult leaders say."

Lady Airth didn't respond. She didn't even make an irritated face to let Jackie know her attempts at being annoying were hitting home. She just stared out the window at the parking lot, and began to tap her foot, fast.

Jackie asked into the silence, "Can I call you Mom?"

"Of course you may not. Why would you?"

"Because you made me. You and Lady Morse and Stambaugh and the other one ... Lady Whosit. You're all my mommies, right?"

"I'd liken us more to your gods," Lady Airth said without a trace of amusement.

Jackie raised her eyebrows. "Was that a joke? Because if it was, you're so deadpan it's not even funny. Like really. Too deadpan. It doesn't work."

"I'm not joking. We created you."

"Daaaang. You are serious, Mama. Or, My Lord."

"Lady Airth will do nicely."

"So, what's the hurry to get home, My Lord? Why—"

"I said call me Lady—:

"Why are you all of a sudden so eager to get back to The Cloister? Why are we sitting on the plane waiting for your thugs to drag Jamie back here? What's the rush?"

Lady Airth sighed, "I'm tired of all this drama, and the danger of waiting. We've been waiting for the nanotechnology to naturally take over humanity as they get injured and their cells attempt to age. However, we did set up an atomic option to get things moving along to phase two if necessary. I deem it necessary, as will Ladies Petrella and Stambaugh, once I've filled them in. If that child falls into Lady Morse's hands, given time and proper planning, she could use the child's blood to undo the entire plan."

"And the atomic option is ...?"

"None of your business," Lady Airth said.

"Aw come on, Mama. I'm dying of curiosity here."

Lady Airth looked at her phone.

Jackie said, "What if I told you I had it on good authority that Lady Morse isn't planning anything? She's not doing anything with the baby. She's running."

Lady Airth scoffed, "Nonsense."

"Nope. Not nonsense. She wrote me a letter and everything. She's on the run. Told us to do the same."

"Show me the letter."

"Can't. I ate it."

Lady Airth arched an eyebrow and shrugged. "Not surprising." She sighed and pushed herself out of her seat, then walked a few paces down the aisle toward the cockpit. "Whether she is or is not planning anything, I still need to proceed as though she is. If for no other reason than that I am tired of this. It is time to move on to phase two."

"You're in a big hurry to be broken down to your base elements, Mama."

Lady Airth stopped in her tracks, gave a short scoff of a laugh, and said without turning around, "The nanotechnology that has incorporated with my body will not break down like the rest of humanity."

Jackie narrowed her eyes and asked, "How do you figure?"

Lady Airth turned to show a flawless smirk that made Jackie want to slap her, "You can't really think that The Fordham Four would have included ourselves in effects of the second Greywash?"

"But—"

"If all humanity were wiped out and made anew, there would be no one to give them direction when they were reformed, child. Give us some credit. We are saving the planet. Saving humanity. Of course we have a plan for the aftermath of the second Greywash, and of course we, the executors of the plan, will be the ones to guide everyone as they adjust to ... well ... as they adjust to existing."

Jackie gaped at her. "You are like the worst person ever! Seriously, lady. Oh my gosh. You're awful."

Lady Airth laughed again. "Awful for stopping humanity from destroying itself and the planet?"

"All the brains you four had between you and you couldn't dream up something less evil than that?"

"Of course not. People have been trying to do that for as long as it's been clear that humanity had put itself on an inevitable trajectory toward destruction. It has never worked, because in all their planning they never considered the fact that, since humanity was the problem, it clearly followed that the solution was either eliminating humanity or rebooting it. We chose the latter, because we are not evil. Not at all. We just made a tough call that, ultimately, needed to be done. If we hadn't done it, either some other forward-thinking minds would have beaten us to it and been the ones to lead the future humanity, or, much more likely, humanity would have destroyed itself."

"Hold on. So if this nanotech is yours, and that makes me your intellectual property, does that mean that all of humanity will be your intellectual property?"

"Technically, yes."

Jackie shook her head, disbelieving. "But wait. Wait. If you had this atomic option of yours all along, why didn't you do it before? Why wait, if it gets your job done quicker?"

"Because, child, the atomic option is not foolproof. Many individuals will, doubtless, survive the bombs. Major cities will be obliterated, but those in rural communities may survive the bombs. And there are a rather shocking amount of people—the rest of the population deems them conspiracy theorists—who believe there is a threat to humanity as they know it. They are living in bunkers, all across the world, waiting for," she did air quotes, "the 'End of Days'. Those of them with well-constructed bunkers will survive. And those individuals are precisely the last individuals we want to be dealing with after the second Greywash. This atomic option will, in short, make a great deal of extra work for us."

Jackie felt her mouth go dry. "You're going to destroy everyone with bombs?"

Lady Airth nodded. "Not traditional bombs, mind you. That would destroy infrastructure and make, again, a great deal of extra work for us. These bombs are, I suppose you could say, a cocktail of plagues. Genetically modified, quite fast-acting plagues. A few hours should do the trick."

"To, uh, wipe out every last bit of human cells in everyone and make everyone into pure nanotech?"

Lady Airth nodded.

Jackie blinked stupidly, swallowed, and tried to find her voice. She wanted to draw herself up and say something along the lines of, "Lady Airth, no matter what fancy words you throw around to justify your actions, the plain fact of the matter is that you and Ladies Morse, Stambaugh, and whosit are cowards who did what you did to save yourselves. You say you're saving humanity, but would any of the people you're going to destroy consider themselves saved? No, everything you did, you did for yourselves because you think that since you're smarter than probably most everyone your lives are worth more than most everyone. But listen up, lady, it's not the smartest or the strongest that are going to win and get humanity to not destroy itself. It's going to be the compassionate people. Boom." But she couldn't find her voice. So, she just gaped at Lady Airth, mouthing wordlessly until Lady Airth swept off down the jet into the cockpit.

Jackie watched her go. It was probably for the best that she hadn't been able to articulate her thoughts, since they were a load of crap anyway. There was no way the compassionate would be able to win out against the intelligent, especially since the intelligent were the ones who were about to carry out their evil plan, while the compassionate were all just living their lives without the drive to do much of anything, at the very most half-heartedly trying to start up non-profits that no one would fund because everyone was lazy and figured fixing large-scale crap was not for individuals to do because the problems were too huge. Doing big stuff was for governments and corporations. Jackie smiled bleakly to herself at that thought, since, of course, governments and corporations couldn't think past their next election or meeting with their investors, and thus had no capacity to or interest in think long-term, unless the long-term would make them gazillionaires.

In short, there was no hope for the planet, and The Fordham Four probably had done the only thing that was ever gonna have a chance of saving the planet. Unfortunately, humanity had to be wiped out and rebuilt to do it. But really, the more Jackie thought about it, it really was pretty obvious.

"Hey!" she called after Lady Airth. "When you do the second Greywash, am I gonna get broken down, too? Or am I immune cuz I'm not a person and the nanobots haven't been working on me all this time?"

29 JAMIE

"Jamie—may I call you Jamie?—I don't understand why you want Mr. Stewart to sneak you on to Lady Airth's jet." Claire nodded toward Sachi, who was napping in Jamie's arms. "And with the very infant that Lady Morse was going to so much trouble to help conceal from Lady Airth." She looked expectantly at Jamie, then slurped an udon noodle into her mouth.

Stewie had brought Jamie to a sushi bar after rescuing her and Sachi from the police. Claire had been waiting there for them. Apparently, she and Lady Morse had been hiding out a floor up ever since Lady Morse had escaped Airth's clutches, and they'd gotten quite fond of the food served downstairs. At Claire's side sat Stewie, who was silently keeping an eye on the doors and the street outside the front window, while periodically eating some sushi.

Jamie cleared her throat. "Um. I just have to." She really didn't want to tell Claire that artificial intelligence in her brain needed her back at The Cloister so she could help it save humanity from obliteration. Either Claire would think she was insane, or, the more likely scenario, she'd believe her about the AI but would insist that she could solve the problem a lot better than Jamie could. Claire was pretty high up in The Cloister, at least compared to Jamie, and was close with Lady Morse, so she probably knew a lot about the whole Greywash thing.

"That's not the most convincing answer, Jamie," Claire said. She sucked more udon into her mouth.

Jamie flinched and wiped broth off her face.

Claire frowned. "I still believe in Lady Morse's mission of protecting the Okada descendants, even if she lost her nerve and ran off. I don't like failing, Jamie. I've already lost the child's grandma, and—"

"You lost her?"

"Well, she got taken. That raven was stalking my group, apparently, and tipped Airth off."

"So Airth has the grandma?" Jamie gasped.

Claire frowned and nodded. "So you see how I'm disinclined to hand the baby over to Lady Airth."

"You wouldn't be. I'll keep her safe."

Claire gave a mirthless smile. "You will get caught."

Jamie sighed, and decided on a change of subject. "Hey look," she said, reaching for Lady Morse's briefcase at her side. "Could I just real quick inject some of my blood into the baby?"

"No. It'll attract attention. How many times do you gotta try to inject a baby with your blood before you realize bystanders call the cops when people do that? And why do you want to do it anyway?"

"Lady Morse told me to."

Claire froze at that, and frowned. "Oh?"

"Yup."

"Why?"

"Not sure I can tell you that," Jamie said. "If you don't already know why she told me to do it, it seems like it must be a thing she didn't want you to know."

Claire sighed, "Fine. Don't tell me. But we are not letting you inject that child with your blood in this public place. We don't need cops converging."

"But it's important!"

"You can do it when we're in the car."

"You mean on the way to Lady Airth's jet that you're gonna help me get on?"

Claire shook her head. "No. I told you. We are not helping you get on that jet."

"I gotta though! I need Stewie, and I need you. You need to help me do it," Jamie whined as she looked down at Sachi, who was still sound asleep in her arms. "You need to help me with the security at the gates, and I need Stewie for his muscle."

Lady Airth is nearly ready to depart. Convince Dr. Forester.

Jamie gritted her teeth at the sound of the AI in her head. It had been nagging her every few minutes, ever since Lady Airth had taken Jackie to the jet. "Come on! Please, Claire. Maybe look at helping me as an apology for telling Airth where the safehouse was. That was you, right?"

Claire sighed, "Yes. And I feel awful about that. But, well, I'd like to see you get kidnapped and tortured for information and not fold."

Jamie shrugged. Claire was probably right. "Still. Come on."

Claire pointed out, "Even if I wanted to, I couldn't. The airfield they're at has too much security."

Jamie rolled her eyes at Claire. "That is so weak. I *saw* you do some sort of computer magic to bypass airport security just a few days ago. That is precisely the reason why you are the person I need. And once you've gotten me past the security, I need Stewie's skills. You guys are good. You can do it, technically, even if you don't want to."

Claire conceded, "True." She glanced at Stewie, who nodded once in agreement as he kept up his watch on the doors. Claire continued, "It's just that I don't think it's a good idea."

"But I'm telling you—!"

"I'm afraid you telling me just doesn't mean too much to me. You, quite frankly, Jamie, are a flake, and not that bright. I—"

Jamie cut in desperately, "You know she didn't like what the rest of The Fordham Four was up to. She was against their plan."

"Yes. The second Greywash. The poor woman was tortured about it." Claire frowned. "She had so much regret for the part she played in the whole thing."

"And you agree with her?" Jamie gritted her teeth as the AI nagged, **Hurry, Docent Nguyen!**

"Well, of course. Their plan was horrible. Playing God like that. Disgusting." Claire grabbed a noodle with her chopsticks.

Jamie braced herself for the slurp and the shower of broth. "Well, the reason I need to go back to The Cloister on that jet is that I gotta stop Lady Airth from finishing up their plan."

Claire shook her head and contemplated the bowl in front of her. "Jamie, their plan is disgusting and horrible, and I'm not arguing that. But the fact of the matter is, whether it's great or horrible is not relevant. All that is relevant is that when they did the first Greywash, they set the ball in motion, and there's no un-rolling that ball. There's no halting its progress." She slurped up a noodle. Stewie wiped his cheek. "Your solution is what? Stop the second Greywash?"

"Well, yeah."

"So, everyone will just go on in a state of stasis forever? A whole planet of immortals? That is a bad plan."

Jamie frowned at the empty tabletop in front of her. So, Lady Morse hadn't shared with Claire the truth about the Okada anomaly. Maybe Lady Morse hadn't trusted Claire with that information. Jamie thought a moment, then asked carefully, "Um, out of curiosity, do you know why Lady Morse was working so hard to conceal this kid from Lady Airth and the others?"

Claire's lips formed a thin line and she shook her head. "I just know the child's mother was part of a Cloister test group, and that the child is not, er, supposed to exist. It is my understanding that Ladies Airth, Stambaugh, and Petrella would want to bring the child back to The Cloister for, er, research, if they knew about her."

"Um, yeah ... close enough, I guess." Jamie sighed. Claire had no idea that the anomaly in Sachi's blood could—if the AI was to be believed—be used to make everyone age as though they were just regular humans and not immortal robots. "Just help me. Please."

"You know something more about the child?" Claire asked with a nod at Sachi. "And is what you know connected to the weird blood injecting thing?"

"Yup. And sorta."

"I don't understand why Lady Morse would entrust you with such sensitive information. Can you explain that to me?"

"Er, not really. No."

Claire gave Stewie a sidelong look. "What do you say, Roger?"

Stewie shrugged, shifted in his seat, and said, "Whatever you say, boss."

Claire groaned and looked away from Stewie. "Look, Docent Nguyen, here's the thing. I'm stressed out. And a smidge scared. See, I'm not used to making decisions. I'm used to be doing what I'm told. Ever since Lady Morse ran off, I've been on my own." She glanced again at Stewie. "Or, at least, on my own as far as plotting out future steps. It's stressful. Very stressful."

Jamie seized the opportunity to say, "Well then just let me tell you what to do."

Claire scoffed, "You're a Docent."

"So?"

Docent Nguyen! Thirty minutes! They are leaving in thirty minutes! Leave here in five minutes or less, or you'll never make it on time!

"So ... you're a *Docent*, Jamie. I might as well ask the gardener what would be the wisest next step to take."

Even in the depths of her anxiety about the AI's nagging reminders, Jamie managed an offended sniff.

Claire asked, "What? I'm not being a snob. It's just true. I have a doctorate and a dozen articles in prestigious journals. You, on the other hand, memorize facts about the Cloister so you can reel them off to tourists. I'm afraid I don't see the sense in taking advice from someone unless they have more education than me, or," she jabbed a thumb at Stewie, "more real-world experience."

Stewie nodded his acknowledgement without looking away from the window.

The AI sounded in Jamie's head, **Docent Nguyen, you are going to be stuck in Kyoto. Convince Doctor Forester.**

Jamie put her hands to her temples and said through clenched teeth, "This is so important, Claire. Please." To her horror, tears of frustration began to well up in her eyes. She blinked and looked at the tabletop.

Stewie cleared his throat. "Aw boss, you made her cry."

Claire said, "Huh? I what?" Out of the corner of Jamie's eye, she saw Claire lean closer to her. "Docent Nguyen, are you—oh. Uh—"

Stewie shifted in his seat. "Why not help the kid, boss?"

Jamie wiped away some tears, even as she wondered whether it might be smarter to let them drip down her cheeks seeing as how Stewie was apparently a sucker for them. She hardly dared get her hopes up, but it certainly did look like the crying had won Stewie over.

Claire asked Stewie, "Ya think?"

"Sure. You bypass the security, I sneak her onto the jet, no problem, right?"

Claire paused and thought. She slurped some udon. "But ... once she's on the jet she's gonna mess it up and get caught, and—"

Stewie interrupted, "And that's nothing to do with us. I say let's give the kid her chance to do whatever it is she feels like she's gotta do." He shrugged.

"Well ... I—"

Stewie interrupted again, "Either way, we gotta go. Now." He stood and signaled for them to do the same. "That guy across the street has walked in front of the window three times, and now he's standing across the street watching the building."

"Who?" Jamie asked, peering into the darkness.

Docent Nguyen, Lady Airth just got a call from Wharton. He says he found you.

Stewie said, "The guy in the—"

Jamie looked out the window, spotted the guy in question and, with a sinking feeling in her stomach, finished the sentence, "Fedora."

"Yup," Stewie said. He gave a sharp signal for them to get to their feet. As Stewie herded her and Claire out through the back door, Jamie craned her neck to try to see what Fedora was doing.

"Move!" Stewie barked.

She moved. Past confused diners, past a waiter who tried to stop them until Claire shoved a fistful of money into his hand, through a grimy kitchen that would have surely failed an inspection if those happened anymore, and out the back door that opened into a big, cracked, and weedy parking lot with a few cars parked here and there.

"That's one of Airth's guys, right?" Stewie asked. "Wharton?"

"Yes," Claire answered. "One of her guards."

Docent Nguyen, Lady Airth told Wharton she wouldn't hold the jet for him. His finding you hasn't changed their departure time. Move.

As Jamie strode toward the black car Claire and Stewie seemed to be on a trajectory for, she said, "How'd he find us?"

Claire said, "I dunno. Maybe facial recognition stuff from security cams? It doesn't matter. We gotta—"

A shot rang out from behind them.

Stewie hit the pavement with a hole blown straight through his chest, spraying Claire and Jamie with blood and whatnot. The sound startled Sachi awake, and she let out an alarmed screech. Jamie and Claire ran for the car as another shot rang out behind them.

All Jamie could think of was that Sachi still didn't have any nanotech blood in her. She held the baby tight and sprinted to the car.

"Stop!" Wharton yelled. "Stop, Dr. Forester! We just want the girl! And the baby!"

Claire reached the car first, threw open the passenger door, and leaped in.

Jamie opened the back door and hurled herself onto the back seat. She deposited the bawling Sachi none too gently in the foot space of the car, then turned and slammed her door. "We gotta drive back there and get Stewie, right?" she asked Claire, who was turning the car on.

"Well, yes, but—" Claire said and gestured back toward Stewie. Wharton was standing in front of Stewie's body, pointing his gun right at Claire.

"I don't wanna hurt you, Doctor!" he yelled. "Don't make me. I just want them!"

Claire drummed her fingers on the steering wheel. She met Jamie's gaze in the rearview mirror. "Well, I guess if he's going to all this trouble to get his hands on you, and he's working for Airth, that probably means I should side with you."

Though the enemy-of-my-enemy logic was totally faulty in this case, Jamie decided to just with it if it meant Claire was going to help. "Super. Thanks!"

Finally.

"Hold onto the kid," Claire answered as she revved the engine. "Get ready to pull Stewie in when I stop."

Jamie scooped up Sachie and began to panic a bit. "Uh, she's not buckled—"

But Claire wasn't listening. She hit the gas. They flew toward Wharton, who stood his ground and began to fire at them. Jamie doubled over, trying to shield the screaming baby from bullets, hoping that if Wharton wanted Sachi that meant he knew he couldn't shoot her. She heard breaking glass, squealing tires, and then the car started to decelerate. The horn started a long, continuous beep. The gun stopped. The car was crawling to a halt.

Jamie raised her head a bit.

Claire was slumped over the wheel, her shoulder up against the horn, some part of her head or upper torso soaking the wheel with blood.

Jamie looked from Claire to Sachi a few times, then looked out at Wharton, who was striding toward the still slightly moving car. Jamie set Sachi down with a quick, "Hold on, kiddo," then leaned forward, pulled Claire's body out of the driver's seat, slid over the back of the seat, and landed behind the wheel.

"Stop!" Wharton hollered, his command loud and clear through all the broken windows.

Jamie didn't answer. She hit the gas and left Wharton hollering in rage behind her.

She was so scared he was aiming a gun at her head that she couldn't bring herself to look at him. She whipped the car around in a circle in the thankfully sparsely populated parking lot and zipped back toward him. She needed to get Stewie so he could sneak her on the jet. She needed not to get shot. She needed the car not to crash.

There, straight ahead, was Stewie's body.

And there, straight ahead, was Wharton, aiming a gun at her.

She told herself he wouldn't shoot.

He couldn't afford to let the car crash.

He knew Sachi could die.

Please.

Wharton fired.

Jamie's flinch sent the car swerving violently to the left.

She righted it and zoomed on, telling herself that he hadn't really been aiming at her, but just trying to scare her.

Thankfully, in just five seconds she'd no longer have to wonder; she was practically on top of him. Literally.

Five.

Wharton aimed again.

Four.

Jamie flinched, but stayed on course.

Three.

Wharton fired.

Two.

Jamie ran him over.

No. *One.*

She'd estimated the countdown wrong.

Heart pounding, she eased the car to a stop as she circled around again by Stewie's body. Shaking, barely realizing what she was doing, she managed to get out and load him into the back seat. The nanobots had fixed him up enough by then that, when she hollered at him that he needed to help move himself into the car, his legs and arms did a clumsy, floppy attempt at assistance that was semi-helpful; at least she didn't have to deal with his dead weight.

Once he was stuffed securely in the foot space in the back with Sachi sitting on his legs, Jamie got back into the driver's seat and examined Claire. She'd taken a shot to the forehead, but her body had already worked the bullet out, and she was even blinking in response to Jamie's voice.

With any luck, they'd be repaired enough to help her by the time they got to the airfield.

If only she could figure out how to get to the airfield.

30 JACKIE

Jackie was finding it difficult to suppress a smile as she sat across from Lady Airth and listened to the woman steadily losing her cool by degrees. By the sound of it, Wharton had nearly caught Jamie, but she'd gotten away. *Way to go, Dork Ass.* It further sounded like Jamie had teamed up with Stewie and Claire, which made Jackie feel a lot less worried.

Jackie looked out the window as she listened to Lady Morse's deadly hiss, "This is your job, Wharton. Your job. If you cannot do your job, I fail to comprehend why I am paying you." She paused while Wharton blathered on the other end, then went on, "Yes, yes. Excuses. Of course. From where I'm sitting, it looks as though I should be showing you the door and offering Mr. Stewart a position."

"I don't know about that," Jackie chipped in. "Stewie gets shot an awful lot. He's not so great."

Lady Airth ignored her completely.

Ms. Savage, try to stall the jet. Docent Nguyen and her associates are outside the airfield right now, attempting to break in and sneak onto the jet.

Jackie couldn't hold back a gasp of shock. She looked up in time to see the smirk on Lady Airth's face as the woman listened to Wharton's reply. She was too immersed in her conversation to have noticed Jackie's gasp. After a few seconds, Lady Airth cut him off with a, "We will talk later. Now, I am leaving. Find a commercial flight back home as soon as you can, and report in. Bring Docent Nguyen with you." Lady Airth hung up without giving Wharton a chance to say anything more. She looked at Jackie. "Well?"

296

"Huh?" Had she heard Jackie's gasp after all, and wanted an explanation?

"I assume you would like to share some snide comments about this situation. Feel free to voice them now."

"Oh, gotcha. Um, nope. I think I'm good." Jackie smiled brightly at Lady Airth, wondering how fake it looked. She had no clue how she was going to stall. "If we're gonna go, let's go now, right?" she found herself saying, for no other reason than a gut feeling that Lady Airth might get suspicious if Jackie suddenly stopped arguing with and fighting her, and instead started to agree. "Like, go tell the pilot, right?"

Lady Airth raised an eyebrow. "In a hurry?"

Jackie gave a heavy swallow that she hoped wasn't too theatrical. She bit her lip for good measure. "Nope. No hurry here. I just heard you tell him you're leaving, so I figured we should leave. Yeah?"

Lady Airth narrowed her eyes.

"Do you know what time it is?" Jackie asked.

Lady Airth asked, slow and suspicious, "Why do you need to know?"

Jackie looked out the window. "Uh ..."

They have gotten past security. They are searching for the jet.

"Ms. Savage?"

Jackie didn't answer, but took a peek at Lady Airth's face. The woman was totally suspicious. And she was totally not telling the pilot to take off yet. Apparently, she was too interested in figuring out Jackie's weird behavior. *Success.*

Lady Airth pursed her lips. She leaned forward, resting her elbows on her knees.

Jackie leaned away and began to tap her foot in a way she hoped betrayed nervousness.

Lady Airth spotted her foot. She asked, "You don't have a plan involving this jet, do you? Or, perhaps, a reason to get back home quickly? Or a reason you need us to leave quickly? Some plot between yourself, Docent Nguyen, and Lady Morse?"

So she still didn't know Lady Morse had run for it. "Nope," Jackie said quickly. "No." She gave a nervous laugh. "Why would you think that?"

"Because of your eagerness for me to get this jet in the air."

"Oh, no. No, no, no. Really. It's just that I heard you say we were leaving, so I thought we should leave."

"No ..." Lady Airth studied Jackie's face. "There's some other reason. I'm not an idiot."

"OK, fine," Jackie said. "I have a hot date planned with a dude named Trigger. I told him I'd be back tomorrow."

Lady Airth shook her head. "I don't believe you."

Jackie shrugged. "Whatever."

Lady Airth sighed and leaned back into her seat. She tapped her fingers on the arms of her seat for a few moments, looking like she was deep in thought. Then, she stood and said, "Well, whatever you have planned, odds are good you'll fail. Thus," she pushed herself to her feet, "I shall proceed as planned." She began to stride to the front of the jet.

"But—uh—" Jackie stuttered behind her.

"Buckle up." With that, Lady Airth walked past a red curtain and to the front of the jet.

Jackie got up and scampered after her, having no clue what she was going to say. Maybe she could pick a fight with the pilot or something. But when she pulled back the curtain, she saw Lady Airth, at the pilot's seat, and a washed out cult minion in the copilot's. Jackie halted. "Oh."

"Yes?"

"You're piloting this thing?"

"As you see. Go, sit down." She flicked a lever, and some humming started from somewhere under her feet.

The copilot just sat there, doing nothing, but looking at Jackie with guarded curiosity.

Jackie glared at the back of Lady Airth's head, trying to figure out something to say or do to stall a bit more. On impulse, figuring she had nothing to lose, she flung herself at the control panel and started smacking all sorts of buttons and switches and whatnot. In the few seconds Jackie managed to get before Lady Airth swooped to her feet and wrestled her into a headlock, Jackie managed to make a lot of lights start flashing and a few things start beeping. And it was enough to make Lady Airth plenty mad, which hopefully meant she'd done stuff that couldn't be easily fixed.

Figuring that she'd done all she could do, Jackie allowed herself to be hauled, still in a headlock, out of the cockpit.

One thing Jackie hadn't planned on was the lengths Lady Airth would go to to keep Jackie from annoying her anymore. Jackie'd figured she'd end up tied to a chair or stuffed in storage.

She hadn't planned on getting shot in the head.

But that was precisely what happened.

Snarling with rage, Lady Airth shoved her into a seat, pulled out a gun, held it to Jackie's forehead, and fired.

31 JAMIE

Jamie crouched behind an SUV in the airplane hangar she and Stewie had run to once they'd snuck through the side gate Claire had opened for them. Stewie had left Jamie behind the truck a few minutes before with orders to wait there until he returned for her.

Jamie pulled out one of Lady Morse's cell phones so that she could look at the time. Stewie was taking forever.

She noticed Lady Morse had a few missed calls. Since she had nothing better to do, she decided to try a few random passcodes to see if she could unlock the phone and listen to the messages. Dishonest, sure, but if Lady Morse had wanted the phones she could have gotten them. Since Lady Morse had left them with Jamie, Jamie told herself that pretty much meant they were hers.

However, no random passcode attempts did the trick, and after five wrong tries in a row, she got locked out.

Ms. Stewart is trying to stall Lady Airth, but I doubt she will be able to manage much longer.

"Gotcha," Jamie said, her heart rate increasing as she looked around for Stewie.

Do whatever you can to speed things along on your end.

"Like what? I mean, I'm cowering behind a truck right now. If I move, then best case scenario Stewie won't be able to find me again. Worst case, Airth's guards catch me. I do not excel in situations such as this."

Yes. There is ample truth in this assessment.

"Duh."

I will check in with you later. For now, I will see what Ms. Sav—

"Hey, you wouldn't happen to know what Lady Morse's passcode is, would you? For her phone?"

One moment.

"OK—"

Which phone?

"Um, the black one."

6561.

"Thanks." She pocketed the phone to check later once she was no longer locked out.

The AI didn't answer.

"You there?"

Silence in her head. At least, silence except for her own thoughts. The AI must have moseyed over to Jackie's brain, where all the action was.

Having nothing better to do, Jamie licked her finger and began to trace a design in the grime on the side of the jeep.

Something hit her on the side of the face, hard. She clapped her hand to the stinging spot on her cheek and looked down at the pebble that had struck her.

She looked up to see Stewie peering around the corner of the open hangar door, his hand poised to throw another pebble. When she spotted him, he dropped the pebble and beckoned her toward him.

Jamie looked around the hangar nervously, then stood and skittered to Stewie's side.

"You found the jet?"

Stewie nodded toward the far end of the airfield, where a few jets were parked. Jamie spotted one in the middle sporting a Cloister-blue paintjob.

She frowned. "How are we gonna get all the way over there without getting spotted? There have to be a few employees around here ..." She glanced around.

"They're not currently in a position to do much of anything but bleed and cry."

"Oh."

Stewie began to run. Jamie followed.

Docent Nguyen, Lady Airth is at the controls of the jet. She is going to depart. Soon.

"What? But—but—Make Jackie do something!" Jamie cried. "We're almost there!"

Stewie looked back at her and raised an eyebrow. "Huh?"

Jamie panted, "I'm not talking to you."

He looked around the otherwise unpeopled expanse of airfield, squinted at her, opened his mouth to speak, but then apparently thought better of it and snapped his mouth shut.

Jamie asked the AI, "She's doing something, right?"

I believe she is attempting to. I hear noise, and yells from Lady Airth.

Jamie felt guarded relief. She was confident in Jackie's ability to cause a big scene that would distract Lady Airth from flying the jet. She and Stewie would get to the jet in time, no problem.

The sound of a gun echoed across the airfield.

Jamie froze in a semi-crouch, held Sachi tight to her, and looked around wildly.

Stewie looked back at her, barked, "Keep moving!" and backtracked to tug her into motion.

"I thought they were all incapacitated!" she gasped, then let out a screech as another gun sounded.

"Apparently, I missed someone," he said, shepherding her onward with a hand on her arm as he looked backward for the shooter. "I—"

There was a popping sound from across the tarmac.

Stewie hit the ground with a yell, more of frustration than pain.

Jamie halted and stared. She found herself marveling at how often Stewie got shot. If he'd been in this profession pre-Greywash, he'd have been dead so long ago.

He was clutching his ankle and swearing up a storm.

Jamie looked back toward where the popping sound have come from. "What—" She spluttered. "Stewie, get up! You can't be hurt right now! I need you!"

He gritted her teeth and looked up at her with considerable rage.

Docent Nguyen, I believe Ms. Savage has been shot. Most likely in the head.

"Seriously?" Jamie groaned. "Why's everyone getting shot all of a sudden?"

You have been shot?

"No, not me. Mr. Stewart."

Stewie looked at her funny.

Jamie didn't bother explaining. "Stewie, Jackie's down. Come on, get up! Please!"

"I'm working on it!" he spat, examining his ankle.

Jamie turned from Stewie and did a slow, cowering 360, looking for the shooter. "Why'd he stop?"

"Probably doesn't wanna shoot you," Stewie grumbled. "Damn it." He looked at the jet. "You need to get on there by yourself."

Jamie gaped at him. "No." Then, she noticed a guy striding from behind an outbuilding and toward them. She gasped and began to back away as he aimed a gun in their direction. "Uh, Stewie—"

Stewie was fussing with a gun he'd pulled out.

"Whatcha doing?"

Putting on a silencer. I'm assuming you don't want to announce yourself to your friends on the jet."

The shooter fired again at Stewie and hit him in the shoulder.

"Go!" Stewie said as he took aim and fired back.

"But I don't know what to—"

The guy across the tarmac staggered and clutched at his arm.

"Take this," Stewie said. Jamie looked from the shooter to Stewie and saw Stewie was holding a phone. "Claire was gonna walk me through any security stuff anyway. She can walk you through it too."

"But don't I need you? Like isn't there something you gotta do?"

Stewie fired again, and the shooter fell to the ground with a scream. "This here's why I'm here. The shooting."

"But you were gonna break onto the jet! I can't break onto the jet!"

"Besides the shooting, the only reason I'm here is you're incompetent and you think you can't do stuff. You can do what I was gonna do." As he spoke, he studied his victim across the tarmac. "Good. He's down."

"Well then come—"

"Nope. Can't walk." He gestured to his obliterated ankle.

Behind them, the jet started up.

"Go!" Stewie said. "There's no time to wait for me to heal! Just— there's a hatch around the other side. Claire will help you get in. Move!"

"But—but—" Jamie managed as she hopped uncertainly on the balls of her feet and looked from Stewie to the jet.

"Look, do it or don't. I don't care. I don't even know what this is about, and I'm getting paid either way. Just let me know, right now, whether this is happening or not."

The jet began to make a whirring noise.

Jamie felt a stab of nerves. "OK. What do I do?"

"Just call Claire when you get to the hatch on the opposite side! She'll do all the thinking. You just do what you're told."

"Story of my life," Jamie muttered to Sachi as she turned her back on Stewie and sprinted the rest of the distance to the jet. She pulled out the phone as she ducked beneath the jet to get to the other side. There was, indeed, a large opening that, by the size of it, looked like it'd been made to drive a van onboard. Probably one of The Cloister's field research vans, Jamie figured.

"Hello?" Jamie heard Claire snap into the phone. Her tone indicated she'd probably said hello a few times before without being heard, and was getting annoyed. "Stewart?"

"Hey," Jamie whispered with a nervous glance around her. "This is Jamie! I—"

"What? Speak up!"

Jamie gritted her teeth. "This is Jamie!"

"Oh, great..."

"I need help! Stewie's hurt. Tell me what to do!"

Claire sighed, "OK, you're at the hatch?"

"Yup."

"Great. You see the panel?"

"Yup. I think so. There's a foot-by-foot square thing with some hinges on top and—"

"Yeah, that's it. You don't have clearance to access it, so you're gonna need to pry it open. Once you pry it open, you gotta do some stuff with the wires immediately, otherwise the alarm's gonna go off inside. So, be ready to move fast. OK?"

Jamie moaned.

"Jamie!"

"OK, OK. Yes. Wire stuff. Immediately."

A loud, monotonous sound began to emanate from what Jamie figured was an engine.

"Right. You can do this. OK, there's a green wire, and a red. You gotta—"

An idea occurred to Jamie. An idea that, if it would work, would make it so she didn't have to do any stressful, time-sensitive work at all. "Hold on!" she said.

"But—"

Jamie held the phone against her leg so Claire wouldn't be able to hear. "Hey, AI!"

Docent Nguyen?

"Can you access the hatch of the jet Lady Airth is on?"

I can.

"Oh my gosh. Why didn't you say so?"

I did not know that you needed the panel on the jet to be opened.

"I thought you were so great at calculating best solutions to situations or whatever."

I did not have enough information about your circumstances to—

The wheels of the jet gave a little shudder, then started to move.

"Can you open it right now? Like now, now? So the alarm doesn't do anything inside?"

I am already doing so.

Heart hammering, Jamie trotted with Sachi alongside the jet, which was, thankfully, still going slow enough to keep up with.

Suddenly, the hatch's door began to slide open.

There.

"Yes," Jamie panted, picking up the pace as the jet sped up. Jamie tossed Sachi on, grabbed the side of the door, and jumped.

She tripped.

She hit the tarmac, but managed to hang onto the side of the door with one hand. However, the pain of being dragged along by the jet was nearly blinding. Her knees were in agony. She knew if she didn't pull herself onto the jet soon she'd fall off, leaving Sachi all alone on Lady Airth's jet. She gave a yell of frustration and tried to pull herself through the hatch. The jet was speeding up. Her legs were useless and her arms were shaky from the pain and the fear. She couldn't bear to think what might happen if the jet took off and she wasn't inside yet.

A few moments later, she found out.

The feeling of the ground falling away beneath her filled her with a sick dread.

Are you onboard? The jet has taken off.

"I know it has! I'm hanging off it and—" she looked down at the ground, "Oh my gosh, oh my gosh, oh my gosh, I'm going to die."

I will need to close the hatch soon or the airflow will create an issue that will alert Lady Airth. Pull yourself in.

"Shut up! I—"

A hand closed around her left wrist. She screamed at the touch, and looked up into the face of Sachi's grandma.

32 JACKIE

The first thing Jackie was aware of was the AI talking in her head. Droning, incessant, incomprehensible. Jackie groaned. Or, tried to groan. There was so much pain. Nothing was working right.

She decided then and there that being shot in the head was pretty much the worst thing ever.

Even trying to open her eyes filled her skull with agony.

So, she waited around for the nanobots to do their thing.

It took a while.

A long, long while.

Even after she was pretty sure she was all fixed up, she waited a few minutes before she even so much as attempted to blink.

While she waited, she became aware that the jet was moving. She gritted her teeth and let the sense of failure wash over her. Lady Airth had taken off. Jamie hadn't been able to get on the jet.

Unless ...

She cleared her throat. "Yo, AI." She opened her eyes. She was slumped over, tied to her seat. She couldn't bring herself to look down to survey the carnage that she felt certain must be covering her lap, the seat, and the floor. She was aware of a damp squishiness behind her neck.

Ms. Savage. You are repaired?

"Oh shit, oh shit, I think some brain is behind my neck. Hell. I need to die. I need to pass out."

But you are repaired, yes? The brain matter you are referring to is from before the gunshot wound?

Jackie gritted her teeth. "Yes, it's my old brains."

Well, then. You are in working order, and we can move forward.

"Thanks for the sensitivity," Jackie grumbled, and tried not to move at all, since if she moved then she'd feel more squishing.

That was sarcasm, I assume. I do not do sensitivity.

"Yes, that was sarcasm." She shuddered and tried not to freak out as she became aware of a poking feeling behind her left shoulder blade. It was probably a fragment of her previous skull. "Is Jamie on board?"

She is in storage below.

"Sweet. At least I didn't get myself shot in the head for nothing, eh?"

Indeed. Stop talking so loud. Lady Airth might hear you.

"Good thinking."

Of course, it is good thinking. Calculating the most intelligent course of action based on all available information is what I do.

"Yeah, yeah," Jackie muttered. "Did you guys work out a plan while I was out?"

We were in the middle of planning when you spoke to me.

"Okey dokey. Well you just get on back into her brain and plan, cool? I'm gonna get myself out of this mess. Come on back when you've figured out stuff."

The AI didn't answer.

"Lady Airth!" Jackie hollered. "Hey! Lady Airth!"

There was no answer from behind the curtain in the front of the plane.

So, Jackie hollered some more. And some more. And some more. It was blatant that Lady Airth was trying to ignore her in hopes that she'd shut up. Well, Jackie thought with a smirk, Lady Airth had no idea who she was messing with. No horrible old hag with a god complex was going to ignore her and succeed. Especially since the horrible old had in question had just shot her in the head. "Lady Airth! Helllllp! I'm wallowing in a puddle of brain-and-skull stew! It's super gross! Lay-dee Aaaaairth!"

Eventually, like Jackie knew would happen, the curtain was yanked aside. But it wasn't Lady Airth who walked out of the cockpit. It was the co-pilot. Jackie took a deep breath, trying to speak with some semblance of calm. "Hi."

"Among other things." The young lady stopped in front of Jackie, looming over her. "Stop yelling."

"But no one was listening to me," Jackie explained. "I had to yell. You see, I need to get untied so I can get all these brains off me."

"Your comfort isn't our priority, Ms. Savage. I am here to shut you up. We can do it the easy way, or—well, I suppose the other way is easy, too, but it's certainly messier. And it will end with you waking up covered in even more brains."

Jackie winced. "Ah. I see. Um, OK. I guess I'll choose the former easy way."

"Wise," the copilot-among-other-things said, then turned on her heel and disappeared behind the curtain again.

Ms. Savage?

"Dude. Yes. Tell me you have an awesome plan."

We do. Docent Nguyen is going to rescue you. And then we will start my plan to stop the Fordham Four from destroying humanity.

"Yeah, yeah, super. This rescuing she's doing is going to get me untied soon, right?"

33 JAMIE

"So Lady Airth just grabbed you for potential blackmail?" Jamie asked. She and Sachi's grandma were sitting across from each other in the near darkness of the jet's storage compartment. Once the old woman had managed to help Jamie into the jet, Jamie had passed out from the pain of her knees that had been skinned down to the bone. She'd woken up pain-free and healed up completely, thanks to the nanobots. As soon as Sachi's grandma had realized she was awake, she'd started interrogating her about what she was doing on Lady Airth's jet, and Jamie had been equally eager to interrogate the old woman about the same thing.

"Yes. As far as I can tell," the old lady said as she looked down at Sachi, who was snuggled in her lap sucking on a pouch of applesauce from the diaper bag. Lady Airth didn't tell me. But I do know that she thinks Lady Morse is still working against her, and she mentioned Lady Morse was helping us—incidentally, do you know if that's true? That Lady Morse was behind sending my daughter and grandchild nanotech blood from The Cloister?"

Jamie nodded.

The woman stared.

"Not all Cloister people are devils, eh?"

"No. I suppose not."

Jamie watched the kid eating. It was great not to be responsible for Sachi any longer. "Did you get a look at the jet at all before they put you down here?"

The woman shook her head. "They brought me in through the hatch. They tied me up. I only managed to cut myself free about ten minutes before you—uh—boarded."

"Huh," Jamie said, not really interested in chatting, but not sure how to end the conversation. She needed to try to see if the AI could help her communicate with Jackie. And she needed to check the messages on Lady Morse's cell.

"And why are you here?" the old woman asked.

"To stop her."

"Stop her from what?"

"From, uh … stuff …" Jamie said, fairly sure she shouldn't be divulging the fact that Lady Airth wanted to destroy humanity, and that, at least according to the AI, Jamie was the only person who could do it.

"Stuff …" the old woman said slowly.

"Hey, look, I gotta see if I can get out of this storage thingy. Any ideas?"

"None."

Jamie frowned. "OK. I'm gonna go explore. But first, I really should inject some of my blood into your granddaughter."

The woman gave a start. "What? Didn't your friend do that already with her blood? I—Sachi's been in danger this whole time?" She glared.

"Hey, we've been taking good care of her. Not a scratch on her. I hope." As she spoke, she opened the briefcase and began rummaging through for the supplies. She set them on the ground at her side. "Can you help me? I've never done this, but I bet you have."

The woman squinted distrustfully at her. "You're like Ms. Savage? Your blood can be used to make a person with the anomaly appear to be in stasis?"

"Yup. Ms. Savage and I are sorta clones."

The woman studied Jamie through eyes even more squinted than before. "You don't look like her."

"The Fordham Four apparently made all us clones physically different in case we ever crossed paths in real life or saw each other's pictures online or whatever. I promise, my blood will work just as good as Ms. Savage's. Ya know, back when I was at The Cloister they took my blood once a week." Jamie was quiet a bit as she sorted through some thoughts in her head. "I bet a lot of the times Lady Morse sent you blood, it was mine. I bet Lady Morse stole it from the labs."

The woman appraised her silently.

"What reason could I possibly have for wanting to inject blood into Sachi other than this reason? Why would I have brought it up?"

More silence.

"Look, I'm gonna have to do some stupid stuff on this jet, I think, in order to do what I need to do. What if we crash?"

The woman sighed, "Fine." She reached a hand out for the syringe.

Jamie rolled up her sleeve. "You've done this before?"

"Countless times," the woman confirmed, then got to work. Soon, she was injecting Jamie's cyborg blood into the kid.

Jamie exhaled a breath of relief. "Awesome. So she can get hurt now and there's no trouble. Is there some sort of delay before it works?"

"No. She's fine now. Assuming you really are a clone of Ms. Savage."

Jamie nodded. "OK. You guys sit tight. I'm off to do ... uh ... something." What she really needed to do was chat with the AI, but she did not want the woman to hear her having an apparently one-sided conversation with herself, and nor did she want to explain herself.

The woman nodded and began fussing over Sachi, probably checking for signs of damage.

Jamie tried not to feel insulted. She walked toward the research van that was parked in the middle of the large-ish compartment. She tried the driver's side handle. It opened. She hopped in, slammed the door, reclined the seat, got comfy, and said, "You there, AI?"

Yes. I have been talking to Ms. Savage.

"So, she's awake?"

Yes. I just said I had been talking to her. Did you not hear me? However, she is tied up. She will not be able to come to your assistance, Docent Nguyen. You, in fact, need to come to hers.

"Well, shoot," Jamie muttered. "How am I supposed to do that?"

A saw.

"Riiight. Like Lady Airth's not going to notice me cutting a hole in the floor."

She is flying the jet. She only has one underling aboard. Ms. Savage will be willing to distract her in whatever way she is able, if the need arises.

Jamie frowned. "I hate this. Why exactly is it again that you picked me as the person who had to help you with this plan of yours?"

As I already told you, I analyzed the personalities of all the people who live and work at The Cloister, and the statistics pointed to you.

"I'm thinking this is one of those cases where the stats are wrong," Jamie muttered.

Well, I had not factored cutting holes in jets or running from thugs into my equations. Once we are back at The Cloister, it will make more sense to you.

"Fair enough, I suppose," Jamie conceded. "How about you tell me right now what this plan of yours is. Like what I'm supposed to be doing. Why not tell me?"

Because, Docent Nguyen, you need to rescue Ms. Savage.

"Why, though? We have a long way to go until we get home. If I manage to rescue her, someone is going to know for sure that she's gone, a lot sooner than—wait—" Jamie stopped dead for a moment. "Wait, you want us to take over the jet?"

Yes.

Jamie shut her eyes and groaned.

I had planned to tell you when the time came.

"Oh my gosh. Seriously? And does that same logic apply to the rest of this adventure?"

Yes. Precisely. I don't want to overburden you with too much information, too far ahead.

"Or," Jamie growled, "You're afraid if I hear your plan I'll think it's horrible and I'll change my mind about helping you. Like how I think taking over this jet is a horrible plan, and I don't want to do it. What's the point? Lady Airth's already flying to The Cloister."

I need you to fly the jet elsewhere.

"Wait, wait, wait. I thought you needed me to get into The File. That's at The Cloister. You just said a minute ago that once we got back to The Cloister this would all make sense. But now you're saying we're not going there."

I did not want to overburden you. However, it is true that we are going to The File. The File room you are aware of, the one in The Cloister's basement, is just an offsite access point. The File is elsewhere.

"Where?"

I will tell you later.

"No. You will tell me right now."

I will tell you later.

"Tell me, or I won't do anything to help you."

If you do not do what I tell you to do, I will activate an alarm that will inform Lady Airth that there is an intruder on the jet. I have, up until this point, been suppressing the alarm. Do what I tell you to do, or you will be certain to get caught.

Up until those words, she'd been thinking of the AI as weird and clinical, but she'd thought that it at least had the right intentions. Stopping Lady Airth's plan to destroy humanity was a good idea, after all, and the AI wanted to do just that. But more they talked, the more she just felt scared and used. She didn't know how to respond.

You do want to stop Lady Airth from breaking everyone down to their base components and thus destroying all individuals on the planet, do you not?

Jamie gasped, "Can you read my thoughts? I thought you couldn't read my thoughts."

I cannot. If you just thought something similar to what I said, it must have been because it was the next logical leap in our conversation, so both of our minds went there.

Jamie sat up abruptly, opened the door, and got out of the van, feeling the need to pace.

Well, Docent Nguyen? Shall I stop suppressing the intruder alarm? Or will you help me?

"You know, I'm really starting to dislike you," Jamie growled as she paced aimlessly around outside the van, no longer concerned whether Sachi's grandma thought she was crazy.

That is irrelevant. Answer my question.

"Oh come on," Jamie grumbled. "It isn't as though you're really giving me a choice."

I am pleased that you have drawn that conclusion. Very well. We shall proceed. Find a saw.

"First I need to listen to the messages on Lady Morse's phone."

I will allow you five minutes.

Jamie ground her teeth, and growled, "I want you out of my head." She pulled out the phone. "Oh. Uh. What was that passcode?"

6561.

Jamie muttered a stiff, "Thank you," then entered the passcode.

There were six messages. Two were from Stewie, grumbling about stuff. Three were from Claire, updating Lady Morse on her activities, none of which Jamie understood.

One message, which filled Jamie with fear and guilt, was from the Docent Mother; her voice was unsteady, panting, as though she was on the move: "Lady Morse, something's up at The Cloister. I—I'm not sure what's— going on. Someone's after me. I think Lady Petrella's behind it. I—" There was a thump, and silence. Before she could stop herself, Jamie erased it.

The last message was from Lady Airth: "Brandi, I don't know what you are playing at. You need to come to your senses. There is no backing out now, and no stopping it. I hope you are aware that, not only have you failed to stop our plans, but you have moved up the timetable. Your interference with Tamon Nari and the infant whose existence you hid from me has made it clear to me that the plan must be accelerated. Thus, it is my pleasure to inform you that, due to your meddling, I shall be activating the bombs at The Cloister, and then going to the File site to activate the second Greywash." She cleared her throat, then went on, "Just so you know, you have not only failed in your feeble attempt, you have accelerated it."

34 JACKIE

Jackie had never been a fan of the idea of yoga or meditation, but she'd tried it a few times back in the day, thinking that it might help her manage her chronic irritability. However, trapped in a puddle of her brains, she found herself quite glad indeed that she remembered enough breathing techniques to keep the impotent panic at bay.

The only problem was that when she really got into a nice, calm place, her body kept relaxing to the point where she squished down onto the grossness behind her back, which snapped her out of her mediation and back into her horrible reality.

Round and round she went, mediation, freak-out, wonder what was taking Jamie so long, repeat.

Until, at long last, she heard a quiet "Psst!" from behind her seat. "Psst!"

"Dude!" Jackie hissed. "Dork Ass?"

35 JAMIE

"Yep," Jamie whispered, looking wildly around as though Lady Airth's thugs were lurking under seats or in the overhead storage.

"Get the hell up here right this second and untie me!" Jackie hissed back at Jamie. "Seriously, what the absolute hell took you so long? I've been having like panic attack after panic attack after panic attack here. It's—"

"You're getting a little loud," Jamie cut in. "You think it's safe for me to cut you loose now? Like have they walked out recently or—"

"Yes, it's safe. It's safe. Sure. Whatever."

Jamie raised an eyebrow, took a deep breath, and peeked out from her hiding place behind Jackie's seat. Crouching low, she darted out into the aisle, scooted into the foot space in front of Jackie, and screamed at the sight that met her eyes. Jackie was coated in guts.

"Shh!" Jackie hissed, wide-eyed.

Jamie clapped a hand over her mouth, waiting in frozen terror for the inevitable person who would come to investigate her scream.

Jackie was rigid, staring at the front of the plane, waiting as well.

But no one came.

Jamie shot a questioning look at Jackie.

Jackie gave a short shake of her head. Then, she began to visibly relax. Her shoulders untensed and she gave her head a little shake. "Know what?" she whispered. "I've been making so much noise, screaming at Lady Airth and all, they're probably just ignoring whatever sounds they hear back here."

Jamie exhaled a slow breath. "That was scary," she breathed. "*This* is scary," she added, gesturing at all the destruction from Jackie's former head.

"You're telling me, buddy. I really need you to untie me instantly. And then we gotta ransack the luggage up there for a change of clothes. And then we ... uh ... whatever."

"And then I fill you in."

"Yep. Good. Do you have anything you can use to cut me free? This rope's like some mega high grade official kind of stuff. I—"

Jamie pulled some scissors out of Lady Morse's briefcase.

"Where'd you get those?"

"They've got a research van down in a big hatch thing. It's full of tools and supplies."

"A hatch?"

"Yep. That's how I broke into the plane without using the main door."

Jackie paused for a minute, looking as though she was thinking hard about something. Then she said, "The AI just told me it broke you in. It said it was inaccurate of you to say that you broke in, when it did the work."

Jamie glared as she began clipping away at the rope with the little scissors. "I'm starting to really hate the AI."

"Why?" Jackie asked. "Sure it's a snob, but it is helpful."

"But to what ends?" Jamie asked. One final clip and she finished up Jackie's left wrist. She rotated and seated herself beside Jackie, crouching low so that she'd be hidden from view.

"Uh, saving the world? Right? Those are good ends." Jackie asked, raising an eyebrow at Jamie as she grabbed the scissors and began working on her right wrist herself. "Did you get some new intel while we were separated? Is something up?"

She paused and again got that look like she was deep in thought.

Jamie gritted her teeth. "What did it just say?"

Jackie frowned and resumed hacking at the rope. She glanced at Jamie out of the corner of her eye. "Uh, it just said you're leaping to some erroneous conclusions and taking the worst possible interpretation from ... uh ... I dunno. Snooty fancy-speak for how you're being an ignorant, knee-jerk reaction baby."

Jamie growled, "If it's gonna be trashing me, it should have the decency to do it in my own head. Not someone else's." She waited a few seconds, half expected it to say something in her head. It didn't. "Oh, uh, you said you've been yelling at Lady Airth a lot since you've been tied up?"

"Yep."

"Shouldn't you keep it up, then? You don't want them to get suspicious."

"Good call, buddy," Jackie said. She cleared her throat, then hollered, "Lady Airth! Dude! Untie meeee!"

Jackie finished cutting the rope. She jumped to her feet, sending her remains off her lap and onto the floor with a sickening plop.

Jamie averted her eyes and fought down the impulse to vomit.

Jackie shook out her shirt. There were a few more little plops.

Jamie moaned, rested her head on the back of the seat, and shut her eyes.

Jackie started a bit more yelling at Lady Airth. Jamie had the feeling Jackie was moving around. She opened her eyes to confirm it. Sure enough, as Jackie yelled at Lady Airth about the injustice of being tied up and left in a puddle of brain, she was pulling a suitcase down from the overhead storage. She tossed the suitcase on the seat across the aisle from Jamie and began to rummage through it, apparently without a bit of worry about being found out of her seat.

Jamie wished she could feel so unconcerned. She was too scared to move from her seat. But now that Jackie was untied, it was only a matter of time until her captors found out. That meant if Jamie and Jackie didn't take advantage of the element of surprise soon, then would be at a huge disadvantage when taking over this jet. That in mind, she got to her feet, took a huge step over where she presumed the ickiness on the floor was, and sat down beside the suitcase Jackie was pulling a Cloister outfit out of.

"I gotta tell you something."

"Oh?" Jackie asked as she gave the Cloister uniform a critical squint. She tossed it on Jamie's lap and carefully began to pull off her shirt, muttering, "If I get brains in my hair I'm going to so absolutely drop dead."

"Uh, yeah, so here's the thing. The AI's pretty much making me and you hijack the jet ..." Jamie whispered with a glance toward the cockpit. She crouched down low in her seat.

Jackie pulled the baggy, blue dress over her head and said, her voice muffled in the fabric, "I figured something like that." Her head emerged. "You think we can actually pull it off?"

"Uh ..." Jamie whispered, disoriented by how Jackie wasn't freaking out. "No. No I don't think we can pull it off. Not at all. But the AI's kinda forcing it."

Jackie said, "The AI says it's only forcing you because you're incapable of thinking straight. You're too stressed. So it's taking matters into its own ... uh ... hands."

Jamie bit back an answer that would make the AI nothing but more condescending and controlling. "Whatever. Reasons don't matter at this point. We just gotta do it."

"Cool. Whatevs. And if we fail, we can do something catastrophic and crash the jet, eh?"

Jamie spluttered, "How can you be OK with this?"

There was a slamming sound from the front of the plane. They both ducked out of sight behind the seats in front of them.

They remained silent for about a half minute, then Jackie answered, still crouching, "Dude, I am so over all of this. I'm done. What do we have to lose?"

Jamie frowned. "I guess. And if we don't have any choice anyway ..." she let her sentence trail off. She didn't have the energy to finish it.

Jackie stood again and continued changing. She kicked off her pants from under the Cloister dress, clapped her hands together, and said, "OK, let's do this." She slid back into her shoes.

Jamie got to her feet with a groan.

"That's the spirit, buddy!"

"So ... any ideas?"

The AI's voice sounded in Jamie's head, **I have an idea.**

By the look Jamie saw on Jackie's face, it was clear Jackie had heard it too.

"What?" Jamie sighed.

I take the controls away from them, and fly the plane myself.

Jackie and Jamie shared a moment of confusion.

"Huh?" Jackie asked. "You can do that?"

"Yeah," Jamie added. "If you can do that, why not just, uh, do it? Why do you need us?"

I just need you to neutralize Lady Airth and the copilot. If they are conscious, they will be able to attempt to regain control of the jet.

"So we're just the muscle here ..." Jackie said.

Precisely.

Jamie was expecting Jackie to start whining about how being the muscle was not in her job description, so it came as something of a surprise when all Jackie said was, "Sweet."

"How so?" Jamie asked, her voice coming out in a crazed rasp.

Jackie just shrugged and strode toward the front of the jet.

"Wait!" Jamie hissed. "Wait! We need to talk about this! We need a plan! We need weapons! Rope!"

Jackie stopped short. "Right. Good call."

She turned. "Uh, OK. Well, what was in that research van down below?"

"Um ..." Jamie thought while Jackie tapped her foot impatiently, looking from Jamie to the curtain covering the cockpit entrance and back again.

"Dork Ass! Come on!"

"What? You're the one who was so eager to get untied. We could have planned first. But no, now we're in a crazy hurry because—"

"OK, OK! Fine! Just go get something sharp and scary." She waved Jamie off toward the back of the jet.

Jamie scurried back to the hole she'd sawed in the floor. Thanks to the AI's access to the jet's layout, it had managed to give her fairly exact directions that had resulted in her cutting the hole near the corner of a storage space in the back of the jet. She fell—with a louder thud than she'd have liked—miraculously not toppling onto the chair she'd stood on to reach the ceiling when she'd been cutting the hole earlier.

Through the hole in the floor, Jackie's voice floated down, screaming at Lady Airth to untie her.

Jamie blinked into the darkness and called out for Sachi's grandma, "Hello?"

"Yes?" the woman responded from somewhere off to Jamie's right.

"I just wanted to let you know it's me. In case you're wondering who just fell through the ceiling."

"Thank you. Please, keep your voice down. Sachi is asleep."

"Gotcha." Jamie headed toward the research van. Then she stopped short. She gasped. She turned back toward Sachi's grandma. "I need some of Sachi's blood."

"What on earth for?"

"For a weapon."

36 JACKIE

In Jamie's absence, Jackie had wandered back toward the seat she'd been tied to, and she'd begun yelling again. With all her heart, she hoped that no one would walk through that curtain and thus necessitate her having to sit down again in that gross seat and pretend to be tied up.

But, she realized, there'd be no point anyway, now that she'd changed clothes.

She was mid-yell when the AI cut into her brain:

Is Docent Nguyen nearly ready?

Jackie muttered, "I dunno. Why not go ask her?"

I am attempting to give her some space. When I speak to her, she reacts irrationally. Emotionally. I am giving her time to process the facts, in the hope that she will see sense.

"You sound like such a man stereotype right now, I kinda wish you had a face I could punch."

What of her stereotypical female traits of irrationality and emotionality? Do you wish to punch her in the face as well?

"Often. But not for those reasons. You're talking about emotions as though they're flaws."

They are flaws.

"Says the robot."

Artificial intelligence. And, I assure you, if artificial intelligence ran the world instead of humans, the planet would not be on the path to destruction.

326

"You are not telling me that, in your view, humanity is being destroyed because of its stereotypically female traits. That's idiotic. Operating on the assumption that war and lack of empathy have destroyed the planet, I'm going to go out on a limb and say it's not female traits that are to blame. And besides, Docent Nguyen has a pretty sciencey brain. Not a stereotypically chick brain."

This argument is pointless. All you need to know is that I would prefer not to speak to Docent Nguyen for the time being.

Jackie glowered at the voice in her head. She was starting to see what Jamie meant about it. "Whatever, dude. I—"

"Jackie!" hissed Jamie from the back of the train.

Jackie turned to see Jamie peeking out from behind a doorway. She gestured Jamie forward. "It's cool, they don't know I'm untied."

"Well that's one nice thing about people thinking you're an idiot," Jamie grumbled. "It probably never occurred to them that you or I might be up to anything."

"True. And speaking of being considered an idiot, I'm totally seeing what you're talking about with the AI. It's like a mega condescending alpha male in my head."

"So much," Jamie agreed. "What'd it say? Actually, wait, never mind. Let's do this thing." She handed Jackie a cleaver-looking thing and a long knife.

"Uh, thanks. What the hell kind of research did they do with that van?" Jackie asked as she weighed the cleaver in her hand.

"No clue." Jamie held up a syringe full of blood. "I have a plan. We inject this in them. It's Sachi's. Remember those notes we found about how The Okada Anomaly turns people normal again if they're exposed to the anomaly blood?"

Jackie grinned. "Awesome. But—" she paused, suddenly feeling disconcerted. "Why are we gonna do that? You don't wanna ... kill them?"

Jamie's eyes widened and she shook her head. "No! I just want them to be at a disadvantage."

"Fair enough."

They began to creep toward the curtain.

"How do we do this?" Jackie asked.

"Um ... how about if we just wait outside the doorway for someone to walk out? When they walk out, you grab them, I inject the blood, and then we threaten them with that cleaver. They'll be too scared of dying to do anything."

"Good. I like it. And then we grab that gun from Lady Airth."

Jamie nodded. They took positions on either side of the door.

They waited.

Jackie was sure that eventually they would find her sudden silence suspicious, but as ten, then fifteen, then twenty minutes crept by, it became clear that Lady Airth and her copilot didn't much care what Jackie was up to. Every so often, Jackie heard a snippet of conversation from behind the curtain, but it was nothing important; just comments on the wind speed and altitude, and something about a meeting.

"One of them's gonna have to go pee eventually," Jamie whispered in response to Jackie's gritted teeth and tapping foot.

Jackie shrugged. "Maybe, but what if they didn't eat or drink?"

After a bit more waiting, she held up the knife and jerked her head toward the cockpit.

Jamie shook her head.

Jackie ignored her, strode forward, and pushed aside the curtain, knife held high.

If she had had the element of surprise, all might have gone well.

But Lady Airth and her copilot were standing on the other side of the curtain, waiting.

37 JAMIE

Jamie had hung back as Jackie leaped forward into the cockpit, so she didn't see what was happening at first. She heard Jackie yell, "Damn it! What the—" followed by a blow that sent Jackie reeling back through the door. She fell to the ground at Jamie's feet. A second later, someone followed her through and was on Jackie, wrestling her to the ground.

Jamie acted without thinking. As if of its own accord, her hand brought the syringe to the lady's neck. Jamie poked it in and pushed the plunger down, being sure to save some for Lady Airth.

A foot flew out of nowhere and kicked Jamie's hand. The syringe went flying.

A second kick, this one to the side of Jamie's head, sent her to the ground. Everything went black, but not for long. Just enough time for Lady Airth to stride over and put a foot on Jamie's neck. "Don't move, Docent Nguyen," she growled down at Jamie. "Ms. Schneeweis is currently tying up Ms. Savage, *again*, but she'll be with you in a moment."

Jamie tried to squirm, but Lady Airth just pushed down harder.

Lady Airth shook her head slowly and said with a chuckle, "Where did you come from?" She relaxed the pressure on Jamie's neck so that Jamie could answer.

The thought of refusing to answer one of the heads of The Cloister didn't even occur to Jamie. She cleared her throat and said, "I broke in through the research van hatch."

Lady Airth arched an eyebrow. "Why?"

"Er …"

Now that was a question she could not answer.

Lady Airth chuckled. "Well, whatever your plan was, it is at an end now, yes?"

Jamie was shocked at the power of the anger that flooded her at Lady Airth's condescending chuckle and her dismissive attitude. She was too angry to even speak.

Lady Airth seemed to have no awareness of the seething rage in her victim. Over the struggles and curses emanating from Jackie, Lady Airth went on, "What could have possessed you to think that you could sneak onto this jet and—what?—take it over? Stop me? Stop me from what?"

Jamie just gritted her teeth and glared.

Lady Airth's mildly amused gaze drifted from Jamie to the kicking, yelling mass that was Jackie and the copilot. "Oh," Lady Airth said, "What did you inject into Ms. Schneeweis?"

Jamie swallowed heavily, wondering whether she should tell.

Lady Airth narrowed her eyes, seeming to note the conflict shining through in Jamie's eyes. "What did you do to her, child?"

Jamie growled, "I injected her with The Okada Anomaly."

Lady Airth stared, wide-eyed. "What?" She glanced at Ms. Schneeweis, who had a knee on Jackie's back and was securing Jackie's wrists together.

"You heard me," Jamie said.

Lady Airth removed her foot from Jamie's neck and said, "Nancy."

Ms. Schneeweis looked up at Lady Airth. "Yes?"

"That cut on your shoulder ..." Lady Airth said, gesturing to where blood was seeping through Ms. Schneeweis' dress.

"What about it, Lady Airth?"

"Is it ... healing?"

Ms. Schneeweis looked down at her shoulder. "Of course, it is. It—" she tore the fabric of her sleeve open a bit more where it had been sliced to get a better look. She breathed, "It's still bleeding." She looked up fearfully at Lady Airth. "What ...?"

Lady Airth whirled toward Jamie. "What did you—"

But while Lady Airth's back had been turned—so certain was she that Jamie was no danger to her—Jamie had grabbed the knife Jackie had dropped, gotten to her feet, and was waiting for Lady Airth. Jamie punched Lady Airth right in the nose. For a second, Jamie was paralyzed by the enormity of what she'd just done. She'd punched one of the founders of The Cloister in the nose. There was no talking her way out of that. Not that she'd really had any illusions that she'd ever be able to go back to her old life, but something about that punch really drove home the fact that her old life was over.

Then, as Lady Airth staggered backward, righted herself, and made to fling herself at Jamie, Jamie's moment of paralysis ended. She held up the knife. "Watch it, Lady Airth," she said. "You're going to want to stay back."

"And why would I want to do that?" Lady Airth sneered.

"Because," Jamie said, the truth of her words only dawning on her as she spoke them, "the blood on this knife is from Ms. Schneeweis, and she's been infected with The Okada Anomaly, so if this knife cuts you and her blood gets into your body, then you're infected with the anomaly too, right?"

Lady Airth stopped short. As she looked at the knife in Jamie's hand, there was definite fear in her eyes.

"Awesome, Dork Ass!" Jackie enthused from where she was lying on her stomach on the floor. She managed a thumb's up even though her hands were tied behind her back.

"The Okada Anomaly?" asked Ms. Schneeweis, looking wildly from Lady Airth to Jamie. "What's that mean? Why am I not healing?"

Lady Airth, who was still frozen in her tracks, eyes flicking this way and that, trying to figure out her next move, spat at Ms. Schneeweis, "Never you mind, Nancy. Go, fly the jet. I need to talk to Docent Nguyen in private."

"But—"

"Go!" Lady Airth snarled.

Ms. Schneeweis hesitated a moment, then scurried to the cockpit.

Jackie asked, "So you're gonna untie me, right? So I can go somewhere and you can talk to Dork Ass in private?"

Lady Airth ignored her. "Sit," she said to Jamie, jerking her head toward one of the front row seats.

Jamie shook her head.

Lady Airth shrugged and sat down. She looked up at Jamie, would-be calm, but Jamie didn't miss the way Lady Airth's eyes kept flicking toward the bloody knife. "Sit," she reiterated.

Jamie shook her head again.

"Very well. Stand. Child, we need to talk."

Jamie frowned. "Nothing you can say is gonna convince me of anything."

"I don't want to convince you of anything, Docent Nguyen. I want to help you. You are clearly in over your head. Whatever Lady Morse has recruited for you, it is far beyond your capacities. She is your superior, and you were only following orders, but I am also your superior and therefore you need not worry about breaking any rules. Lady Morse has ... shall we say ... gone rogue. She has turned her back on The Cloister. She—"

"Jamie!" Jackie snapped from the floor. "Dude! We gotta move! Just cuz this old lady wants to talk to you, that doesn't mean you gotta listen."

Lady Airth closed her eyes for a moment as though she had a headache. But she didn't acknowledge Jackie's words in any other way. "So, child, considering Lady Morse's defection which you clearly had no knowledge of until this moment, I wanted to reassure you that you will not be punished for your insubordination. You didn't know. But, now you do know. So," Lady Airth paused and met Jamie's gaze, "With the knowledge you now possess, you can either cease following Lady Morse's orders and continue at The Cloister as though she never led you astray, or you can attempt to persist in whatever it is you are doing here, and you can accept the consequences."

"Oh seriously," Jackie sighed. "You are not gonna fall for that, are you? Get over here and untie me, buddy."

Jamie's gaze drifted from Lady Airth to Jackie. She felt sick. To go back to The Cloister with Lady Airth and proceed as though none of this had ever happened was, of course, impossible. But, still, it was strangely tempting. The Cloister was all she had ever known.

"Well?" Lady Airth asked.

Jackie snapped from the floor, "Come on, moron, Jamie's not gonna agree to that. She and I are clones, so I know what I'm saying. She'd never—"

"Nonsense," Lady Airth sighed, finally acknowledging Jackie's presence. "You may be clones in a way, but I'm sure you are familiar with the old battle of nature versus nurture, yes? Granted, in your case, there was no nature. There was a lab. But that is immaterial. You may be identical in your makeup, but you have been nurtured quite differently. You, Ms. Savage, had very little in the way of nurturing, so it is nothing to you to turn on those who raised you. Docent Nguyen, however, was given the very best of—"

Jamie cleared her throat and interrupted. "Where is the rope?"

Lady Airth turned an icy stare on her. "Pardon?"

Jamie bit her lip, then said, "The rope. So that I can tie you up."

Jackie laughed, "Hell yes, buddy!"

Jamie frowned at Jackie, who just grinned back at her.

"Well?" Jamie asked Lady Airth.

"You do not seriously expect me to tell you."

Jamie sighed and, not turning her back on Lady Airth, she went over to Jackie, crouched down, and began to cut at the belt that Ms. Schneeweis had used to bind her wrists.

"Careful," Lady Airth said with a smirk. "You two are nothing more than a conglomeration of nanotech. If that blood can stop nanotech from functioning in a normal human, I wonder what it can do to you."

Jackie and Jamie exchanged a horrified glance.

Lady Airth went on, "Who knows? You might just disintegrate into a cloud of nanobots if The Okada Anomaly is introduced into your system."

Jackie said, "Crap, dude, is she right? Use that cleaver thing. It doesn't have blood on it."

"Where is it?" Jamie asked, looking around the floor of the jet.

The moment that she looked away, Lady Airth launched herself out of her seat and at Jamie. Jamie saw her out of the corner of her eye and turned, but too late. Lady Airth grabbed Jamie by the wrist and squeezed, forcing her to release the knife.

It fell close to Jackie's head. She screamed and began to roll as far as she could get from the bloody knife.

Lady Airth yelled, "Nancy! Come here! Now!"

Ms. Schneeweis called, "Just a minute, Lady Airth! I—er—there's something wrong with the controls! I—"

"What?" Lady Airth roared as she tried to prevent Jamie from twisting out of her grip. "What do you mean? Get out here!" She then wrestled Jamie into a headlock.

A few moments later, Jamie became aware that Ms. Schneeweis was at Lady Airth's side, wringing her hands and saying something about how the jet seemed to be out of her control. She could regain control for a few seconds at a time, but no more than that.

"Brandi," muttered Lady Airth, apparently still convinced that Lady Morse was behind everything that was going on. "She gained remote access. Here. Subdue Docent Nguyen," she growled. She shoved Jamie at Ms. Schneeweis, then hurried into the cockpit.

38 JACKIE

Jackie watched Jamie and Nancy struggle for long enough to discern that it was obvious Jamie was going to win. Poor Nancy was probably too rattled by the fact that her cut shoulder wasn't healing to dare risking extreme injury.

Neither of them were paying any attention to Jackie, so she brought her knees up to her chest, rolled so she was face down, and managed to get to her feet. She walked over to the brawl and unceremoniously launched herself between them, taking Nancy to the floor underneath her. "Get the knife and cut me loose!" She hissed at Jamie, then said to Nancy, "Call for Lady Airth and we're gonna kill you. The kind of killing you can't come back from."

Nancy seemed quite content to listen to her. She went still.

"Thanks for being cool," Jackie said as they waited for Jamie to find the knife and get to work.

"What's The Okada Anomaly?"

"Er, yeah, about that. Uh, well it's a bunch of sciency whatnot, but all you really need to know is you can die now."

Then, there Jamie was, cutting her free. In no time flat, Jackie was helping poor, shell-shocked Nancy to her feet. "You OK?" Jackie asked her.

Nancy shook her head. "I need to sit down."

"I bet you do."

"Um," Jamie chipped in, "Since you're sitting down already, would it be cool if we tie you up?"

Jackie added, "Yeah. And just so you know, we're gonna do it either way."

Nancy looked like she'd barely heard. She shrugged, muttered, "Whatever," and sat.

While Jackie tied Nancy up with the belt Nancy had tied her with earlier, Jamie picked up the bloody knife. "Watch it with that thing!" Jackie yelped. "Dude, if that scratches you, you could disappear in a nanobot cloud!"

Jamie shook her head. "I don't think so. If that was how The Okada Anomaly worked, then all the nanobots that have incorporated into Ms. Schneeweis there would have disappeared in a nanobot cloud, leaving behind the human parts of her. But she seems pretty whole to me."

"Huh," Jackie said, studying Nancy. "Good thinking, Dork Ass. So, we're gonna hijack this thing now, or what?" She jerked her head toward the cockpit. Jamie followed, knife in hand. Jackie pushed the curtain aside and said, "Yo, Lady Airth, we're commandeering the hell out of this here jet. Gimme that seat."

Lady Airth looked up at them, seemingly unsurprised that they'd gotten the best of Nancy. "The jet has already been commandeered by Lady Morse. She is flying us to one of The Cloister's off-site facilities. I presume you know why."

Jackie and Jamie gave Lady Airth identical shrugs.

Lady Airth snorted and turned her back on them. "As much as I would love to keep attempting to shut Brandi out of the jet's control system, I am assuming you are about to use that blood-stained knife to threaten me. Am I correct?"

Jamie nodded, looking far too apologetic for Jackie's liking.

"Well, then," Lady Airth said, "Let us forego the fight and go straight to the part where you bind my hands and do ... whatever it is you plan on doing ..." She waved vaguely around the cockpit.

"Or, we could shoot you in the head, like how you did to me," Jackie said.

Jamie said, "Nope. We might need to ask her stuff."

"Fine," Jackie sighed. "Buddy, go find something to tie up your cult leader."

Jamie walked from the cockpit without comment, leaving Jackie and Lady Airth to chat.

39 JAMIE

Jackie muttered, "Sorry, Dork Ass. She was being sooooo annoying. She thinks she's so damn clever, trying to manipulate me."

Jamie blinked down at the bullet-riddled body of Lady Airth.

Jackie said, "What? She was using all her fancy-speak to try to get into her head. So," Jackie gave a nervous laugh, "I got into her head. See, with bullets. I got into—"

"I get it," Jamie said faintly. She turned her back on Lady Airth. "What if we needed information from her?" she asked as she glared at Jackie then went to sit at the controls since her legs were feeling shaky.

"Eh, she'll be up soon enough." Jackie flopped down in the co-pilot seat.

Jamie stared at her. "We're kinda on a mission to save humanity here. Quit being so flippant."

"Dude, chill out! We've got all the time in the world until this thing lands, right? Look—" Jackie pointed at the controls. "The AI's got this."

"Jackie, please don't shoot anyone anymore. It's lucky I got some information off of Lady Morse's phone messages, otherwise we might have had to interrogate Lady Airth for information about their bombs and the second Greywash and all that."

Jamie hadn't been expecting an apology, so when it didn't come she wasn't surprised. All Jackie said was, "Ooh, cool. What'd you find out?"

Jamie snapped, "She's planning on activating bombs at The Cloister, Jackie. Bombs. To kill everyone. And then she's going to the main File location to get the second Greywash going."

Jackie said, "Don't worry, buddy. The AI's flying us right to that File place, yeah? We'll just stop her from doing the Greywash thing."

"Well first she needs to do the bomb thing at The Cloister." Jamie put her head in her hands. "As soon as she's fixed up, she's going to get right back to her horrible plan, and I have no idea how to—"

"Easy. We just won't let her out of our sight. We make sure she doesn't—"

"We watch her ... forever ..."

"Err, yeah. OK. Never mind. Um ... OK, how about we just—"

Have you forgotten about my plan? All you need to do is help me activate my plan, and this will be solved.

Jamie rolled her eyes. "Your threat of notifying Airth of my presence is no longer applicable. You have nothing to hold over our heads. Tell us, specifically, what your plan is."

You are attempting to manipulate me.

Neither Jackie nor Jamie responded. They waited in silence to see what the AI would say.

Alright. I will tell you. But only because we are only a few hours from the location, and you would have needed a briefing at this point anyway.

Jamie and Jackie exchanged eye rolls.

"Whatever," Jamie said.

"Yeah. You win. Congrats."

The AI paused. Jamie wondered whether it was calculating the pros and cons of throwing more passive aggression their way. But when it did speak, it got right down to business: **My plan is simple. Before I** explain, I must ask, Ms. Savage, are you aware that, via The File, The Fordham Four have been accumulating all information and knowledge from every individual as their human components are replaced by nanobots?

"No way!" Jackie gasped.

Well, now you know. And I, of course, am in The File. Thus, I have access to all this information. Once Lady Airth has activated the bombs which will turn the vast majority of the population into pure nanotechnology, my plan is to upload all the world's information and knowledge into the minds of all individuals on the planet.

Jamie blinked stupidly as she let the information wash over her.

"Er, you can do that?" Jackie asked.

Of course. I have access to all components of humanity that are built of nanotechnology.

"Whoa. That seems super dangerous," Jackie breathed and looked at Jamie, who was still too stunned to speak.

How so?

"Well ... uh ... you, or presumably The Fordham Four—or Three—will have direct access to everyone's brains. You can put stuff in our brains?"

I assure you, I am going to use my control for the good of all. And, as far as your immediate problem is concerned, once all individuals have been given all knowledge, they will know what The Fordham Four have planned, and they will revolt. They will stop The Fordham Four before they can break everyone down to their base components. Once Ladies Airth, Stambaugh, and Petrella have been stopped, I will be the only individual capable of having access to everyone's minds, and humanity will be safe. So, you see, when you assist me, you are also helping yourselves; you do not want humanity broken down, and this will achieve that.

Finally, Jamie cleared her throat and spoke. "But who are you to decide that? Humanity wouldn't want—"

The entire planet is in peril because of what humanity wants. I think it is high time that are more logical mind stepped in.

Jamie shook her head.

Beside her, Jackie began rummaging around in what was probably the copilot's backpack.

Jamie found that her mouth had gone dry. She swallowed and said, "I won't do it."

You must.

"But I won't. I'll find another way. I'll—"

Do you want The Docent Mother to die?

"Pardon?"

Jackie pulled out a scrap of paper and a pen, and began scribbling on it.

You heard me.

"Of course I don't."

If you do not do as I say, I will send Ladies Stambaugh and Petrella a text message which they will think is Lady Airth. This text message will instruct them to kill The Docent Mother.

Jamie shut her eyes, put her elbows in her knees, and rested her head in her hands.

Well?

"I'm thinking."

For about a minute, there was silence but for the occasional sound of rustling paper from Jackie.

Then, Jackie jabbed Jamie on the arm with her finger.

Annoyed, Jamie glared at her.

Jackie grinned, holding the paper out to her.

Jamie narrowed her eyes, took it, and began to read.

I'm writing so it won't hear. Play along. Say you'll do it. We'll sort it out as we go. We can use Morse's two phones to communicate as we go.

Jamie stifled a groan. Figure it out as they went was not her style. But nor was letting The Docent Mother die. She thought a few moments more, but she knew she had no choice. It really did boil down to those two options, as far as she could see. She gave Jackie a nod, then said, "OK. Fine. I'll go with you."

I commend you for seeing sense.

Jamie snapped, "It's not like you gave me a—"

Silence. There is a small aircraft approaching.

"Huh?" Jamie looked out the window at the cloudy sky.

Silence.

"But—"

Silence.

Jackie shrugged at Jamie and kept writing. She waved the paper at Jamie again.

Jamie gave the cloudy sky another glance, then grabbed the paper and read, *Where are Morse's phones?* Jamie stood, glad to have something to do. As she walked back to the main cabin, she glanced at Lady Airth and was surprised to see that the woman's eyes were open and she was watching them, clearly intrigued. Jamie stopped short and gaped at Airth as she ran through what she and Jackie had spoken aloud and wondered whether Airth knew anything she shouldn't.

Lady Airth smiled a slow smile that did nothing to ease Jamie's worries. Jamie frowned and walked on with Jackie in her wake. When she thought she was out of earshot of Lady Airth, she muttered to the

AI, "Just let us know what's going on with that aircraft if it's a problem."

I shall do so.

Jamie nodded to the copilot who was still tied to her seat looking panicky, and led the way to the hole she'd cut in the floor. As they walked, Jamie saw Jackie pause and pick up the near-empty syringe of Sachi's blood.

They went to the closet, and Jamie and Jackie dropped down into the hangar.

As Jackie went to find Lady Morse's briefcase, Jackie said, "This is a huge mess, buddy. Huge. But you know we're gonna get through it."

"I don't know any such—"

The jet shook.

"What was that?" Jackie screeched.

There is a problem. The approaching aircraft has fired on us. And it just sent a message which informs us that if we do not give them Lady Airth they will, I quote, blow that jet out of the sky.

"Pfft, let them," Jackie scoffed.

"No. Sachi's on board," Jamie pointed out. "Not to mention that the copilot would die, and it'd be pretty much like I murdered her since—"

I am not asking for your input, but merely keeping you informed, as you requested. I shall be handing Lady Airth over to them.

"But then she'll be able to activate those plague bomb things!" Jamie screeched. "No!"

"Yeah, dude. Not cool. That puts her a step closer to her plan. Right? Once she does the plague bombs, she just has to go to The File and start the second Greywash, and then everything's over, right?"

Not if I fly this jet to The File and activate my plan first. By the time the plagues wipe out all remaining human cells, I will have bestowed all knowledge on all humanity, and they will stop her from the second Greywash. How many times must I go through this with you?

Jamie gritted her teeth and tried to think. She'd forgotten she was supposed to be playing along with the AI. "Uh, right. Yeah ..." She looked wildly at Jackie.

Jackie shrugged.

I have sent a message to the aircraft that they are free to take Lady Airth. They will be boarding shortly through the hatch. I suggest that you tell the infant's grandmother to hide.

Jamie said, "Jackie, hide them. They're somewhere around here," she waved vaguely into the dark corners of the hatch. "I gotta do something."

"OK."

Jamie stomped off to have words with Airth. She hopped onto the chair, pulled herself up to the closet above, and stormed through the cabin to where Lady Airth was now sitting, blood soaked, back in the pilot's seat.

She turned at the sound of Jamie's footsteps, and raised her eyebrows. "Well?"

"How did you—how—I don't understand how they—" she spluttered, slightly disappointed that her anger and confusion were unable to find expression in words.

"You didn't really think I wouldn't put an SOS out to my associates when things went south here, did you, child?" She smirked and leaned back in her seat, sizing Jamie up.

"How? How did you—"

Lady Airth put a hand to her forehead and sighed. "My phone, child. My phone. I sent a message to Lady Stambaugh when you boarded the jet. I told her if I hadn't responded by such-and-such time, she was to send assistance."

"Oh."

She heard a footstep behind her and started to turn, but too late. A blow to the head sent her to the floor. A second blow knocked her unconscious.

40 JACKIE

Jackie crouched behind the research van and watched as an aircraft no bigger than the van hovered its way into the hatched and touched down. She'd never seen anything like it before, which led her to believe that it must be some sort of top-secret Cloister-related aircraft. The pilot threw open the door and hopped out, presumably looking around for Lady Airth.

Jackie ducked further into the shadows, and hoped Sachi's grandma was doing the same. The guy headed toward a ladder in the corner farthest from her, climbed up it, and, as far as Jackie could see since he was in shadows, entered some sort of passcode into a keypad. A door slid open and he disappeared into it.

"Yo, why did you make Jamie cut a hole in the ceiling if there was a door?"

The door leads to the main cabin. She would have been spotted. Think before you ask questions. It will save us time.

Jackie didn't respond. She was too busy scooting over to where she'd seen Sachi's grandma hide behind some boxes. "Howdy," she said to the woman. How's things?"

The woman shrugged, looking desolate.

"Yeah. Same here."

Jackie heard footsteps in the direction of the doorway, and peeked out from behind the boxes.

A blood-coated Lady Airth appeared in the doorway and began to climb down the ladder. The pilot appeared behind her, carrying Jamie. A still and silent Jamie.

Jackie gripped the edge of the box. *Were they taking Jamie?*

The guy walked to the threshold and dropped Jamie down into the hatch. Jamie hit the ground with a thud. Lady Airth took her by the arms started dragging her in the direction of the aircraft. So, yes, they were taking Jamie.

"Damn it," Jackie muttered as she watched the pilot descend the ladder and stride up to Lady Airth and taking Jamie's feet. Within a minute, they had tossed Jamie in the back and were flying out of the hatch.

41 Jamie

Jamie groaned and opened her eyes, blinking against bright light. It took her a few moments to get oriented and remember what had happened, but when she did she sat bolt upright with a gasp and forced her eyes to remain open so she could see where she was.

"Here, I'll pull the curtains," a voice said.

"Docent Mother?" Jamie breathed, her eyes following the form of a person as they walked in front of a window.

"Yes, dear. It's me." She pushed a button beside the window and the curtains drew closed.

In the relative darkness, her eyes focused on The Docent Mother. Jamie broke into a grin.

"I was sure you were dead!"

The Docent Mother chuckled, "I may yet be before the day is out."

Jamie's grin turned to a frown. "What happened to you? And why am I in your office?" Someone had apparently brought her into The Docent Mother's office and deposited her on the couch.

The Docent Mother sat beside her, sighed, and said, "They locked you in with me. My office has become my prison, dear."

"Oh." Jamie stared at the rug. "Mother ... I'm sorry. This is all my fault. You've been infected with The Okada Anomaly, right?"

"Mmm. If you mean the blood that makes it so that I am no longer in stasis, then yes. Don't beat yourself up about it."

Jamie stared at her with confusion. "You can't be OK with this."

"What other choice is there?"

Jamie felt tears welling up in her eyes at the thought of what she'd brought on The Docent Mother. Somehow, her resignation in the face of death made it worse.

The Docent Mother murmured, "Oh, Docent Nguyen, don't do that." She patted Jamie's knee. "Don't cry. Who knows, I may survive whatever this is just fine." She paused, then said, "And by the way, what exactly is it that's going on? They've chased me, tied me up, injected me with infected blood, and locked me up, but no one has bothered to tell me why. It's most insulting."

Jamie sniffed, wiped her nose with her sleeve, and began a faltering, meandering explanation of all that had occurred up to that point, finishing with, "And now Jackie's who knows where, doing who knows what, and Lady Airth is going to go ahead with her horrible plan, and probably pretty soon we're going to come down with some horrible plague or other, and then once the nanobots have had time to repair us we'll all get broken down to our constituent nanobots and—"

"See? I told you I'd be dead before the day was out," she said lightly.

Jamie stared at her.

"What, dear?"

"Never mind," Jamie said with a shake of her head.

The Docent Mother smiled.

"Docent Nguyen, are you really going to just sit here with me and wait to be struck by a plague? Or shall we use what time we have to try to avert disaster?"

"But the only way to avert disaster is to do what the stupid AI wants. And that's just a different disaster. It wants to turn everyone into zombies. It wants everyone to have all the knowledge. All the information. I mean, what is the point of life, even, if everyone knows everything? Sure there'd probably be no fighting anymore, but there'd be no thinking anymore either. No exploration, no wonder, no—"

"I get it, dear. Fascinating musings, and timely. But I would suggest that now is the time for action."

"If I knew how to act, I promise I'd be acting," Jamie grumbled. "But Airth's way is—"

"*Lady* Airth," the Docent Mother corrected.

Lady Morse's phone vibrated in her pocket. Jamie grabbed it, hoping against hope it was a text from Jackie. She looked at the screen and exhaled a sigh of relief. It was, indeed, from Jackie. She was safe. Or, safe enough to text something the content of which must mean she was not being watched as she sent it.

Dork Ass, I have Sachi's blood here, and I think I can use it to stop the second Greywash. I'm at the file, and the AI let slip that my 'pure nanotech blood' is part of what's needed to stop the second Greywash. Long story, but we're special because we were never people. We're different. Our blood has some crap in it that can unglue all the nanobots in everyone. Creepy stuff, dude. I'm gonna need therapy. Anywho, what if I put Sachi's blood in it instead? Get back to me. This is too sciencey for me, and I'm just winging it here. Write back, dude. The AI's getting pissed at me that I'm not moving on this.

Jamie gaped at the phone, hardly daring to hope that Jackie might have stumbled on a solution. And what was more, Jackie's potential solution had given Jamie a great idea. Or, at least, a potentially great idea. She looked at The Docent Mother, who was eyeing her with concern. "Sorry I zoned out there, Mother. I—uh—"

She looked away from the phone. The AI was listening. She couldn't talk about this with the Docent Mother. She sighed, and said, "*Lady* Airth's way is horrible, and the AI's way is horrible. And I don't see a third option. And even if I did, the AI's probably listening to me right now, so I couldn't talk about it." She trailed off in a way that she hoped sounded hopeless. But, she wasn't hopeless at all. Halfway through her last sentence, she had grabbed a pad of paper off the Docent Mother's desk and was now writing frantically:

I gotta write, since the AI is listening. I think I know how we can beat Lady Airth. Do you have a syringe?

42 Jackie

When the jet landed in a random, grassy field in the middle of nowhere, or, according to the AI, in the middle of rural northwest Maryland, Jackie was confused. "What, did the jet run out of gas?" she asked Ms. Schneeweis, who Jackie had had another battle with a while back, and this time won. Ms. Schneeweis was, again, tied to a chair in the cabin.

"No," she grumbled. "We're here. Right where whoever's controlling the jet intended for it to land. Right in the middle of the Flath Nature Preserve. For some reason."

Jackie frowned at the grassy plain outside the window. "Uh, OK ..."

Ms. Schneeweis shrugged.

Get off the jet. I will direct you.

Too curious about what was coming next to object, Jackie did as it said without arguing. After an embarrassing amount of struggle and confusion, she managed to get the door open, and hopped to the ground. It had been farther than she'd thought it'd be, and the landing hurt her ankles like hell, but she decided to soldier on without complaint.

"Okey dokey, the file thing's around here in all this pretty grass and stuff?"

Head north.

"What am I, a damn compass?"

Look for a tree-covered hill.

Jackie shielded her eyes from the sunlight and scanned the edges of the field.

"OK. I see it."

Then walk toward it. I am going to check on Docent Nguyen.

"Yes, boss," Jackie grumbled and started to walk. As she went, she took her notebook out of her bag, looked up Trigger's number, and sent him a text on Lady Morse's phone: **Yo, Gregster. This is Jackie, the amazing and beautiful reporter you chatted with a while back. Do you think you and your pals would be up for a nice suicide thing?**

She pocketed her phone and wondered whether the plan that had popped into her head was dumb. Probably, but there was a beauty in having only a few hours left to exist. It opened the door for a lot of stupidity that would otherwise be off the table.

Her phone buzzed not even a minute later.

Hey, Jackinator. What's this nice suicide thing?

Jackie grinned. The quick response was encouraging. **OK, I got myself in a spot of trouble up in some place called the Flath Nature Preserve. You know the place?**

Gregster responded, **Nah, but I got internet. How much trouble you in?**

The kind where I need your buddy who does the C4 suicide stuff to blow up a place for me.

There was a sizeable pause before Gregster responded with, **Uh, wow. You're serious?**

Jackie typed back, **Dead serious, dude.**

He sent back, **Not sure many of the guys are up for something so … illegal.**

Not even to help a hot chick?

He responded, **I'll ask around and get back to you.**

Jackie breathed a sigh of relief. He was going along with it. **Cool. I probably don't need to say it, but this is urgent.**

Gregster signed off with a short, **Gotcha. Later, Jackinator. Stay safe.**

With a feeling of relief that she might have a way to beat the AI, she walked on. When she reached the hill, she sat and waited for the AI to come back. She stretched out on the ground, shut her eyes, and listened to the birds singing in the trees. Lucky birds. They weren't in danger of being destroyed and reformed as new and improved cyborg birds in a few hours' time.

Jackie sighed heavily as she allowed her brain to mull over the thoughts she'd been trying to avoid. She couldn't get around the fact that the AI and Lady Airth were right that humanity was a great big pile of stupid, and that the rational thing would be to wipe them all out and start over, or force information on them so no one would be an ignorant moron anymore. But did that make the AI and Airth right to play god? Of course not. But, maybe yes? Given the dire alternative?

Was there anything that she and Jamie could really do anyway? If there was a way to stop the AI and Airth, would it be a better decision? Or were all possible decisions here just horrible decisions?

Ms. Savage.

"Yo, AI." As she sat, something in her pocket poked against her hip. She stood, reached into her pocket, and pulled out the syringe of Sachi's blood. She had a moment of panic, thinking that the poke she'd felt was the needle injecting some blood into her, so she pinched her arm to draw blood, then waited for it to heal. It did so, right before her eyes. She exhaled a breath of relief.

Ms. Savage! Are you listening to me?

"What? Sorry, I was—uh—never mind. Yes, I'm listening."

Walk left around the hill until you come to what looks like a manhole in the side of the hill.

"Ooh, sneaky. Top secret. I like it."

The Fordham Four needed a hidden place to carry out their most top secret work. For instance, they needed to keep the magnitude of The File a secret. And this is where they are able to activate The Greywash.

"I know. Lady Airth mentioned she was going to the main offsite File once she'd done her plague bomb stuff." Jackie shook her head, unable to believe the stuff that was coming out of her mouth these days. She started to walk to her left. Before too long, she spotted the manhole. "This goes underground?"

It does. The passcode is—

"Hold up, there. I gotta just—" she pulled out the phone. **Gregster, I gotta go underground. Might lose reception. I know this sounds crazy. Wish I had time to explain. My coordinates are**—she pulled up the coordinates on her GPS and typed them down. **If you come, you'll see a weird manhole thing. Wait outside it and I'll be up as soon as I can.** She frowned at the insane message, and wondered if there was any way they could make it in time. Oh well, it was worth a shot.

Ms. Savage, if you want to stop Lady Airth from the second Greywash, then the people need to be given this knowledge as soon as possible. I need your focus.

"Right, right. So what's the passcode?" She trudged to the manhole cover and looked at the keypad.

H6T4R1X1.

Jackie typed it in. The manhole hissed and slid to the side. She stepped in. "OK, now what?" she asked as she looked at the room she'd stepped into. It was small and, as far as she could see, empty. "What the hell? Is this some kind of joke?" The circular door slid shut again, leaving her in darkness. She pounded on the door and tried to fight down panic.

It is not a joke. It is an elevator. Push the 'B' button.

"Oh." Once her panic subsided, she did indeed see two buttons glowing in the darkness. 'M' and 'B'. "Right." She jabbed at the 'B'. The elevator started its descent. "No music?"

No.

Seconds ticked by.

"How the hell far down is this file thing? Or is this just a very slow elevator? And why is there no light in this elevator?"

I believe the bulb is burned out.

"Hmm." Jackie leaned against the wall and began to hum her own elevator music.

At last, the elevator shuddered to a halt, and the door slid open and she was greeted by the sight of a large-ish, tall room packed with towers of computer processors, with one light in the center of each processor glowing a steady green. Farther down the rows, she spotted a few flickering green, and one solid red. "DDaaaanngg. So this is where all the information about, uh, everything inside of everyone is gathered?" She almost felt guilty that she and Gregster were going to be blowing the place up and hopefully killing the AI in the process.

Yes.

"Wow." Jackie walked in, her footsteps echoing in the darkness.

By the door you will see a desk. Sit in the seat.

"OK. Dude, quit rushing me. I'm taking in a lot of information." She sat and turned to look at all the processors again. "So all these computers ... you're in them? Like this is your home?"

I suppose you could say that.

"You're not, uh, in the Cloud or whatever?"

I am not. I was in a closed Cloister system until Docent Nguyen plugged the flash drive into your computer, so now I can technically move about the internet at large, but The File is where I reside.

"Hmm." She scanned the room. "So, uh, how do they plan on starting the second Greywash?"

Ah, that is simple. They require the blood of a person made of pure nanotechnology, in short, one of you created in their labs, to put into their machine. Your blood, amplified by the second Greywash, has the power to—to put it in layman's terms—unglue everyone's nanobots.

"No way. That's awful." Jamie felt a chill at the thought of the potential evil in her body.

I find it elegant. Ingenious. Not only were you and your kind used to help them figure out configurations for the new humanity, but you're also walking incubators for their ultimate weapon that will bring about the new humanity. Multipurpose tools on the highest order.

"Nope, not elegant. Messed up. I'm so—"

But, as I say, anything pertaining to the Greywash is irrelevant since by giving the population all knowledge and information they will prevent this Greywash from ever occurring. So, to the computer by the door. You are sitting in the chair?

Jackie shook her head to try to clear it. "Uh, yeah."

There is a yellow cord plugged into it.

"I see it."

Plug it into your port.

"Pardon me?" she hissed. "No!"

Yes. You are aware of the port at the base of your neck, are you not?"

"Uh, yeah. But—"

Push down on the pressure points, open the port, and plug the cord in.

"No way. Why? Why do I have to be connected to this crap for you to do your evil plan?"

I need access to your body. There are a series of protections built into the system to guard against viruses or hackers who might wish to gain access to the system. This means that someone must manually manipulate the devices in order to do what I need to do.

Jackie gasped, "Oh my gosh, you dork. That's why you needed Jamie. You were all 'oh I need you because I calculated all The Cloister employee personalities and you were the one who I knew was right for the job, oh Chosen One' but noooo it's just because she's the only Cloister gal with a port in her back. You creep."

Yes. That is why I needed her.

"Well I'm not doing it, you loser. No way." She folded her arms and sat back in the chair. "No way."

I assure you, Ms. Savage, here in this bunker I have ways to make you do as I say.

Jackie clenched her teeth to hold back a response, determined to give the AI the cold shoulder. She spun around in the swivel chair. She stared at the processors. She stared at the ceiling. She thought about her blood. She thought about Sachi's blood. She thought about it some more.

She froze and stared into the middle distance, working through an idea that had hit her.

Jackie pulled out her phone and texted Jamie: **Dork Ass, I have Sachi's blood here, and I think I can use it to stop the second Greywash.**

43 JAMIE

Jamie wrote to The Docent Mother, *I gotta write, since the AI is listening. I think I know how we can beat Lady Airth. Do you have a syringe?*

The Docent Mother leaned over the paper, reading intently. She took the pen Jamie offered her and wrote, *No. Why?*

Jamie responded, *I can use your blood to infect Lady Airth and make her vulnerable. I want her vulnerable, and I want anyone near her vulnerable, so I'll have a better shot of stopping the plague thing.* Jamie felt a bit guilty about not telling The Docent Mother her full plan, which was that she wanted to do a lot more than make Lady Airth vulnerable. She wanted to be sure Lady Airth could never do harm or play God again. And that meant something so drastic she could barely think it herself, let alone share the idea with her mentor.

The Docent Mother tapped the pen against her pursed lips as she thought. Then she wrote, *And you thought that jabbing a room full of people with a syringe would be possible?* She looked up at Jamie with a crooked smile and handed Jamie the pen.

Good point. But I don't see any other way to get the upper hand with these people. I—

The Docent Mother grabbed the pen from her hand and wrote quickly, *What you need is something more efficient at injuring them and dispersing more blood. Knives, for instance.*

Jamie grabbed the pen back and began to scribble excitedly, *Oh, yes, Jackie and I sorta did that on the jet! Infected someone with the anomaly by using a bloody knife. But would you be OK with cutting yourself and losing that much blood?*

The Docent Mother nodded, then wrote, *I'm more than happy to make sacrifices to stop them.*

Jamie met The Docent Mother's gaze, nodded, then wrote, *Is there any chance they'll let us out of here?*

The Docent Mother shrugged.

Jamie crumpled up the paper, shoved it in her pocket, tossed the pen on the desk, and walked to the door. She jiggled the handle and yelled, "Hey! Lemme out!"

A woman's voice on the other side said, "Docent Nguyen?"

"Yup. Lemme outta here. I'm—"

The woman said, "She's awake. Go tell Lady Airth."

Jamie turned and raised her eyebrows at The Docent Mother. They drifted back to the couch and sat while they waited to see what happened next.

Jamie broke the silence, "What if I opened a window and snuck out?"

The Docent Mother shook her head. "Alarms."

"Mmm." Since she had some downtime, she decided it would be wise to respond to Jackie, so she typed, **I have no idea about how the Greywash works, but I think you might be onto something. I say give it a try. Anything's better than doing it how Airth wants it done. If we know our blood will be dangerous, we should definitely use some other blood instead.**

She stared at the screen, waiting for an answer. **Cool. I'm gonna do it. I mean, what's the worst that can happen? Anything's better than the end of humanity.**

Jamie typed, **Go for it.**

Oh, and get this, dude. The AI wanted you to help it because it needed to plug into the port in your back. Like to take control of your body or something. Because there are things it needs to

manipulate manually to do its thing. It wants me to do it now instead. I am so totally not doing it, and now it's threatening me.

Jackie looked up in alarm at The Docent Mother, who had been reading over her shoulder.

The Docent Mother's eyes were wide, disbelieving.

"What are you in the middle of?" she breathed.

"I wish I knew." She typed, **Um, I guess stall as long as you can. I'm gonna try to stop Airth. After that maybe I can help somehow?** Though, she had no clue how. But one thing at a time.

Gotcha, bro. Hurry up.

Jamie sighed and slumped back into the couch. *Yeah, right.*

The AI spoke in her head, **Docent Nguyen, have you been communicating with Ms. Savage without my knowledge?**

Jamie smirked, and didn't answer.

Docent Nguyen!

"I don't know what you're talking about," she said, pointing at her head to inform the Docent Mother that she was talking to the voice.

Liar. You are communicating with her somehow.

"Look, I'm busy. We'll talk later," she said as she crossed her ankles and stared up at the ceiling.

You must tell—

The doorknob rattled.

Jamie sat bolt upright and said, "Seriously. Gotta run."

The door swung open, and Lady Airth herself strode in. "Awake, I see. Come with me. I need to talk to you while I work."

Jamie said, "I'd rather just stay here, if it's all the same to you," figuring it would be wise not to seem too eager.

Lady Airth snapped, "Come here now, or I shall kill The Docent Mother."

Jamie gasped at the sharp, out-of-proportion response.

The Docent Mother was also startled, apparently. She backed up a few paces, hit her coffee table, and knocked a vase of flowers to the ground. It shattered.

Jamie as at her side in an instant, quick to make sure that she hadn't cut a main artery or anything.

"Are you OK?" she asked as The Docent Mother pushed herself to her knees.

The Docent Mother gave her a wink, then picked up a shard of glass from the ground and cut her arm open. Then The Docent Mother gasped, "Dear, I need a cloth to hold to this wound," as she handed the bloody piece of glass over to Jamie.

Jamie pocketed it just in time.

Lady Airth stalked up behind her and sighed, "Really, Docent Mother, in your condition I would think you'd be more careful. Come, Docent Nguyen. She's well enough. One of her guards will see to her." She reached down and tugged at Jamie's sleeve.

The Docent Mother gave her a wide-eyed, significant look and glanced at her pocket that held the bloody shard of glass.

Jamie stared back at her and froze. She couldn't do it. She had to, but she simply could not.

The Docent Mother's eyes bored into her, goading her to action.

Lady Airth snapped, "Now! Move!"

"I—uh—" Jamie said, tearing her eyes away. "OK."

Shakily, she stood.

Beside her, The Docent Mother got to her feet as well, holding her cut arm.

Jamie asked her, "You're OK if I leave you, Mother?"

"You just do what you must, dear," she said, the double meaning not escaping Jamie. "Don't worry about me."

Jamie gritted her teeth, gave The Docent Mother a quick hug goodbye, and followed Lady Airth out. She clenched her fists and wouldn't let herself turn and look at The Docent Mother, afraid she'd look disappointed.

In a blur, Jamie trailed after Airth and her crew. She knew Lady Airth was talking to her, but Jamie was too confused and too weary to bother paying attention. It was probably just some more god complex ramblings, and condescending jabs about Jamie's lack of intelligence.

Jamie felt the weight of the glass shard against her thigh, and swallowed nervously. She couldn't believe that, a few minutes earlier, she had thought herself capable of murder. But now that she had the tool to do it with, she found it was impossible.

Ending a life as a horrible, horrible thing that she wanted no part of.

But Jackie was waiting for her to finish up with Lady Airth so that she, Jamie, could help Jackie sort out the Greywash and the AI's plan.

But murder was horrible.

But how many more murders would she be enabling if she didn't stop Lady Airth? A whole planetfull, that was how many.

But even if she stopped Lady Airth that still left Stambaugh and Petrella.

Jamie decided murder was not her thing. Not even when the evil was so clear cut.

But she certainly wished Jackie was there to do it for her. Airth's was one murder she would stand by and watch without putting up a fuss.

That settled, Jamie trudged along in their wake, all the way up to the rooftop lab that was usually reserved for study of the skies. However, unless Jamie was much mistaken, the things aimed out the four windows facing north, south, east, and west were not telescopes but missiles.

Ladies Petrella and Stambaugh were the only other two people in the room besides Jamie, Airth, and one guard who had accompanied them inside. Calypso was perched on the back of a chair, but when Lady Airth entered he flew to her arm.

Lady Airth patted Calypso and said to Jamie, "Wait here. I'll be with you in a moment."

Jamie nodded, and watched as Airth went to join Petrella and Stambaugh, who were bustling about busily, intent on covering the earth in plagues. "Super top-secret project, this?" Jamie asked, waving at the missiles.

No one acknowledged her presence, except Calypso, who eyed her beadily.

Jamie frowned at them all, deep in thought. The three Ladies were all in the same place. And the guards were outside the door. Sometimes, being underestimated was great. If they would all just get really close together in a group, then she could swoop in and give them all a good poke with the shard of glass, and then they'd all be so freaked out about their mortality, running around waving their hands in the air and screaming, that they'd let Jamie slide the plague components out of all the missiles, and that would be that. Easy. Jamie nodded to herself. Yes. That was it.

She began to edge over to Lady Airth, who had joined Lady Petrella at a workstation where the latter was working with some white liquid in a glass beaker with a lid.

Lady Airth snapped, "How long?"

Lady Stambaugh glanced at a digital clock above the door. "Ten minutes, fifteen seconds."

Jamie carefully grabbed the shard of glass. *Only ten minutes. Crap.*

She kept on creeping toward Airth, who turned and narrowed her eyes. "What are you doing?"

Jamie froze. "Huh?"

"You're sneaking up behind me."

"I—uh—no I'm not! I just wanted to, uh, see what Lady Petrella's weighing." She peered at the scale. "Oh, I see. Will ya look at that."

Lady Airth took a step closer, studying Jamie intently. Calypso appeared to do the same.

Jamie felt her face getting red. She felt like Lady Airth was reading her mind. *Now or never*, a voice in her head said. Not the AI, but just her own freaked out brain.

She pulled the shard out of her pocket.

Or tried to.

It got caught on the edge of her pocket. She fumbled, and made a grab for it again, but it was too late. Calypso left Lady Airth's shoulder with an offended croak as the woman grabbed Jamie's arm, spun her around, slammed her to the surface of the workstation, and barked, "TJ! See what Docent Nguyen has in her pocket."

Lady Stambaugh, who had frozen in the middle of her work when Lady Airth had slammed Jamie into the workstation, scooted wordlessly over and reached into Jamie's pocket. A second later, she gave a hiss of pain and pulled her hand out. "Whatever it is, it's sharp," she said, inspecting her bleeding finger.

Jamie couldn't suppress a shaky grin.

Lady Airth's gaze snapped from the blood to Jamie's grin, and she breathed, "You didn't."

"Didn't what?" Jamie asked.

"The glass at The Docent Mother's?"

Jamie swallowed and looked away.

Stambaugh said, "What are you talking about? What—"

"Later," Airth snapped. "Remove that thing from her pocket. It is—"

"Alexis, is there something I should know?"

"TJ," Airth snarled, "Now is not the time."

Lady Petrella, who had been standing with her back to them while using a dropper to add a bit more white liquid to the beaker via a hole in the lid, turned and joined the group. "Is there a problem?"

Airth roared, "Get back to work! Both of you! I will deal with the girl!"

"But—" Stambaugh started, looking at her bleeding finger.

Jamie started, "You're infected with The Okada—"

Airth smacked Jamie across the face before she could finish the sentence, but Stambaugh had heard enough. "What?! The anomaly? Is this true, Alexis?"

Airth started, "Now, TJ—"

"Don't you 'now TJ' me!" she screeched. "I've been infected with The Okada Anomaly, and you tell me to proceed with working with viruses designed to kill in the most efficient way possible?"

Airth sighed and said to Petrella, "Remove the glass from her pocket."

Petrella laughed, "You have got to be joking, Alexis."

Lady Stambaugh began to back away from them, shaking her head.

Jamie felt Airth's hold on her ease up a bit, and she jerked to the side, wrenching herself free.

Airth grabbed her again before she'd gone two paces, throwing off her balance and sending her reeling against the workstation where Lady Petrella had been working. Jamie flailed out to keep her balance and sent the beaker of white liquid flying. The lid flew off, spraying everyone with droplets of the white liquid. It hit the ground at Stambaugh's feet and shattered. She slipped, screamed, and hit the ground. She froze, panting, looking at the liquid and broken glass with disbelief. She looked up at Airth and breathed, "Help."

368

Jamie looked from her to Airth, feeling as though she was missing something.

Airth looked at Stambaugh with cold eyes. "There is nothing I can do, TJ."

Stambaugh choked on a pathetic sob.

Airth, Petrella, and Stambaugh were all frozen, transfixed, seemingly waiting.

Then Jamie was pretty sure she understood. "Oh crap. That white stuff was a virus?"

No one answered.

But they didn't need to.

Because two seconds later everyone started coughing. Normal coughing first. Then blood. Coming out of their mouths, noses, eyes. Fiery pain spreading from the lungs to what felt like every single organ.

Through watering, bloody eyes, Jamie saw Airth collapse against a workstation and fumble at her wrist. She pushed a button, tried to speak into whatever was on her wrist, failed to speak, spat out some blood, and tried again.

This time she managed, "Enact GW2."

Jamie didn't have time or energy to wonder what that had been about. She was too busy dying.

Thankfully, the virus had been artfully engineered, so it wasn't even a minute later that were all writhing on the floor working toward losing consciousness.

Jamie passed out to the sound of Lady Stambaugh's wail of terror that meant it had surely occurred to the poor woman that she would not be waking up from this death. Unless she believed in an afterlife. But if she did, the wail of terror would still be appropriate, since no god would be cool with what she had been up to for the past few decades.

Jamie didn't know how long she and the remaining members of The Fordham Four were out, but it was certainly enough time to set their humanity-destruction timetable back a bit. When Jamie became aware that she was conscious, she didn't immediately open her eyes because she was pretty sure the sight that was about to greet her eyes would not be pretty. Before she'd passed out, she'd been in enough widespread pain to indicate that all organs had been affected by the virus. Thus, she was guessing that pretty much the entirety of her being must now be replicated.

She listened for sounds from Airth and Petrella, but heard nothing. This was not surprising, since older people tended to regenerate more slowly than younger people. However, as the seconds stretched out to minutes and there was still no sound, it began to get weird. All she heard was the occasional low croak from Calypso, who sounded close by.

It occurred to her that perhaps they had reformed before her and left the room. Jamie's eyes snapped open.

Airth and Petrella had not left the room.

Their bodies were still on the floor by Lady Stambaugh's, all bloody and disintegrated and very much not regenerated. She couldn't even tell which was which. Or, wouldn't have been able to tell if Calypso hadn't been perched on one of the skulls.

Jamie scrambled out of the puddle of her blood and organs, and slid over to them. Jamie blinked disbelievingly at what remained of their bodies. "What the hell?" she asked the empty room. "What ...?"

In order to attempt to get some control of her reeling mind, and in order to try to keep from vomiting, she forced her mind into a cold, rational place where she could see it as a puzzle that needed solving. *Why were they dead?*

Jamie scanned the bodies and the floor. She swallowed. She almost puked. She gave her head a hard shake.

She scanned the bodies again. It was hard to tell, but she thought they might have started to reform, and stopped halfway through.

She looked at the floor around them. Broken glass, blood.

And suddenly it became clear.

When the virus had disintegrated Stambaugh's body, her blood had seeped out and gotten into Airth's and Petrella's, and, just like that, they'd gotten the anomaly.

And that was that.

She wobbled away from the bodies. Clear of the blood and glass, Jamie leaned against a counter, sank to the ground, and rested her head on her knees. She blinked at the floor, trying to get her brain to focus on something. There was something she should be doing right now. Something important. She couldn't remember. But she knew there was something huge.

Or maybe that was just residual stress speaking. But now that Airth, Stambaugh, and Petrella were dead that meant that the plagues were not going to be unleashed. So, where was the danger that was nagging her brain?

She gritted her teeth as she remembered. Of course, the stupid AI's plan to dump all information into everyone. And the second Greywash.

The second Greywash.

She gasped and pulled out her phone. She noticed she had 22 missed texts from Jackie.

She frantically texted, **Jackie!**

Jackie responded seconds later, **Bro, I am going to murder you. AI's been driving me insane, trying to push me around, being super mean, oh my gosh. And now the Greywash controller thing in the corner's beeping like crazy and there's this countdown thing and oh my gosh dude what the hell?**

Jamie managed to fill Jackie in on the Greywash situation, finishing with, **But no need to freak out. Right? Just go right now and put Sachi's blood in the machine. Like we talked about. Yeah?**

Jackie wrote back, **Uh, about that … I can't. The AI knows something's up so it's not letting me leave my chair. Like when I try to stand up it tries to blast me with lasers. It's already shot me once. Straight through the heart. So, credit for aim and all, but damn it.**

Jamie asked, **Lasers? How?**

Jackie answered, **This stupid evil Cloister bunker has all sorts of security and technology and crap and it's all hooked up to Cloister computers of course so the AI's like in the walls, dude. It can fire the lasers in the corners and it can use the security cameras and it can even control the temperature, which I know because it's trying to torture me into doing what it wants me to by messing with the thermostat. Like it's gotta be 100 degrees in here, Dork Ass. But I got a suicide club coming with bombs, so maybe they can blow me out of this mess or something. And if they can get here in time then I bet I can still get Sachi's blood in the machine, and then C4 can blow up the bunker and that'll kill the AI and then we win.**

Jamie reread that a few times to make sure it made as little sense as she thought it did. She nearly asked what the hell Jackie was talking about with suicide clubs and C4, but put it down to torture-induced hallucinations and left it at that. All she asked was, **Where are you?**

Jackie answered, **Flath Nature Preserve.**

Jamie asked, **How much time left on that countdown thing?**

Two hours, twenty-nine minutes.

OK, Jackie said. **Hold out a little longer. I'm coming to you.**

44 JACKIE

Jackie tried to feel hope at Jamie's pronouncement that she was coming. But it didn't work. She felt a lot more hope when thinking about Trigger's pal, C4. She almost sent Jamie another text to let her know not to come, but decided against. The sheltered kid was going out of her way to take a risk, after all, and Jackie figured it wouldn't be good to shoot Jamie down just when she was taking a leap.

Besides, she'd never get there in time anyway. She was willing to bed Jamie couldn't even drive a car, let alone fly something capable of getting that far north of The Cloister in two hours.

The AI interrupted her thoughts, **You were sending a text message.**

Jackie didn't acknowledge its statement. She stretched out in the chair, sliding her legs as far as they'd go, just to test how far the AI would let her move before it shot her. She cringed as her skin, sweaty from the thermostat-torture, stuck to the vinyl of the seat.

Only when she was on the brink of toppling off did the AI snap, **Not another inch,** and red lights began to flash on the guns mounted in each corner of the room.

"Fiiiiine," Jackie moaned and scooched back, wiping sweat out of her eyes as she went. "Happy?"

No. But then, I never am. Why are you so determined to go to the machine that starts the Greywash?

"Because, as I told you, I think I can stop it."

All the more reason to do as I tell you. Once you have plugged yourself into The File, and I have done what I need to do, you will be free to stop the Greywash.

"But I hate your plan. Your plan's awful. People shouldn't have all the information in the world."

If you actually had the information I am going to give humanity, you would never wish it gone. You are speaking from a place of ignorance.

Jackie ground her teeth.

You sent a text message a minute ago.

"Correct."

I see no activity on your phone. And you cannot be communicating with Docent Nguyen, for I do not see any communication on her phone either.

"Huh," Jackie said, deciding not to give the AI any answer that might prompt it to think any further about whose phones were being used. "I guess you've found yet another thing to torture me about, eh?"

Indeed. Speaking of which, are you, at last, prepared to plug yourself into The File?

"Hell no. But hey, just tell me what it is you want me to do, and maybe I'll do it without you taking control of my body."

That is not an option.

"Why not?"

You would not agree to do it.

"And yet you think that I would let you take control of my body."

I am going to turn the thermostat up five degrees.

"Aw come on, can I at least sit somewhere else? Or put a towel or something over this nasty vinyl? It's so sticky."

That is part of the torture.

Jackie groaned and let her gaze rest on the Greywash countdown as the thought about whether Trigger and Co. had come, and whether they were waiting for her to come up and get them. How long would they wait? Would she be able to escape the AI? Maybe if she ran really fast to the doorway she could dodge the lasers.

Almost before she realized she was going to try it, she tried it.

She made it a step and a half before she saw her blood spatter the wall across from her.

She hit the floor, dead for a bit.

45 JAMIE

Jamie hopped out of the helicopter, which The Docent Mother had just landed beside the jet. She looked at her watch. They'd gotten there in about an hour. So, an hour and a half until the second Greywash went off, and an hour and a half for her to get Sachi's blood into it. Easy. She gave The Docent Mother a wave and grin, then looked over at the jet. She'd have liked to check on Sachi and her grandma if they were still there, but she told herself there was plenty time for that once she'd helped Jackie save humanity from evil scientists and evil AI.

Behind her, the helicopter blades halted, and the field was quiet.

Jamie turned from the jet and looked around the field indecisively. Jackie hadn't exactly given her directions, and the Flath Nature Preserve was sizeable. She frowned, thought a bit, and finally drew inspiration from a mystery novel she'd borrowed from The Docent Mother a few years back. As Jamie recalled, the hero had tracked the murderer through a grassy field.

Well, Jamie thought, she was a hero and this was a grassy field, thus it was searching time.

With great care, Jamie began to search the perimeter of the jet for footsteps. There would be a trail of some sort. Markings to indicate that Jackie had gone that way.

"What are you doing, dear?" The Docent Mother spoke behind her.

"Searching for footsteps ..." Jamie muttered, staring at the grass.

"Footsteps?"

"Yes. Jackie's. To see which direction—"

"But," The Docent Mother said hesitantly, as though she was about to say something that might embarrass Jamie. "The ... uh ... helicopter."

Jamie shut her eyes and sighed. "Wow, I'm dumb."

The Docent Mother didn't deny it.

Jamie opened her eyes to give her an offended glance. But when she opened her eyes, she saw the Docent Mother was peering across the field with squinted eyes. "What—?" Jamie asked, following her gaze. "Oh! Who do you suppose *they* are?"

For there was a group of six people. They were walking through the field, following behind a guy with a mohawk. Mohawk kept looking from his phone in his hand to the landscape in front of him. A few of his companions kept glancing over at the jet and helicopter, but Mohawk just kept right on doing whatever he was doing.

The Docent Mother said, "I have no idea. Should we ask?"

"Nah," Jamie said slowly. "They're probably just nerds playing some augmented reality game."

"Perhaps ..."

Jamie frowned at the group. They looked tough. Lots of leather and tattoos and torn jeans. Not really augmented reality types, in her opinion, though she acknowledged she really didn't know much about the subject. What they did look like, though, it occurred to her, was a group of people who might think it was fun to pretend to kill themselves over and over. "I think I know who they are ..." she whispered. "I'm gonna go talk to them. Uh, could you stay by the helicopter? I dunno if we're gonna need to get out of here fast, but if we do—"

"No problem, dear. Go on." The Docent Mother waved a hand in the direction of the maybe-nerds/maybe-suicide-club-members. "I'll have the helicopter ready."

"Perfect. Thanks." Jamie gave the Docent Mother an awkward wave goodbye, then scurried after the group and yelled, "Hey! Wait up!"

They halted and waited, eyeing her suspiciously.

"Who are you?" Mohawk asked when she was close enough for normal speech.

"My name's Jamie Nguyen. I think you know my friend, Jackie. I'm trying to find her."

She was expecting suspicion or doubt, so when his expression cleared and he breathed, "Awesome," she was shocked but happy.

"Why awesome?" she asked.

"Well see, she's in some sort of huge trouble, but I have no idea what's up, and if you have any idea then you can help us figure this all out."

"Er, well, I do have a good idea what's going on but it's going to sound crazy."

"Crazier than a random text asking me to get a friend to come blow a place up?"

"Actually ... yes. This is the kind of crazy where I can honestly tell you that, if you guys help us, you'll be saving the entire human race from destruction."

Jamie watched as eyes widened, jaws dropped, and people exchanged sidelong glances and shrugs. She realized belatedly that she had perhaps given them too much information. The kind that required big conversations, and processing time. So she added, "And, most importantly, the clock is ticking. I think we have about an hour left until it's too late."

"No way," Mohawk breathed.

"Yes. So we gotta move. Unless you want the second Greywash to come, but this time to break you down to nothing and use your parts as building blocks for a new version of humanity."

She was met with more wide eyes, dropped jaws, sidelong glances, and shrugs. Yet again, she'd given too much information. One did not just drop that kind of information on a person. She sighed, frowned, kicked at the dirt, and tried to figure out what to do next.

Mohawk cleared his throat.

She looked up.

"What do you want us to do? Oh, and I'm Trigger, by the way.'

She felt a rush of gratitude toward Mohawk dude. "Hi, Trigger. Well, I like Jackie's plan about blowing stuff up. Let's go with that. But first I think we need to rescue her from a bunker. There's this artificial—" she started, but stopped herself in time. The AI would probably fall under the realm of too much information. But, what did she have to lose? So, she filled them in on the AI stuff, too.

Trigger blinked. "Wow."

"Yeah. Um, so ... do you have her location?"

Trigger shook his head, then, seeming happy to volunteer something helpful, supplied Jamie with the coordinates Jackie had given him, and with that they set off for the bunker.

46 JACKIE

Jackie was curled up in a ball on the vinyl seat, shivering uncontrollably and wishing it was 110 degrees again. She thought she heard a distant knocking, but it was hard to tell over the chattering of her teeth. "Was—th-th-that a—knock—on—th-the—door?" she asked.

Do you honestly think I will supply you with information you want, when you refuse to help me?

Jackie didn't bother responding. She was too busy trying to force her shaking hands to take her phone out of her pocket. She had just remembered that she never told Jamie or Gregster the passcode to get into the bunker. But now her fingers didn't work and she couldn't remember the passcode anyway and—

You are trying to access one of Lady Morse's phones, Ms. Savage. I see your failed attempts to turn it on.

Jackie groaned and let the phone fall to the chair by her side.

By the way, I discovered how you and Docent Nguyen have been communicating. I have read all your text messages. I know that she is coming.

Jackie curled up tighter in a ball, and didn't respond, except to suggest, "Yo, ya think we c-could maybe go b-b-back to the heat torture? Cuz I think that was t-totally d-d-doing the trick." The AI didn't answer, leaving her to infer that it had gone off to harass Jamie, who was probably trying to figure out how to fly out to her, or, best case scenario, standing outside the manhole cover stressing out and muttering non-curses under her breath. Jackie was enraged at herself for forgetting to give Jamie the passcode when she'd gotten the chance, and now humanity was going to die. The one good thing about slowly being turned into a meat popsicle was that she was so preoccupied with her immediate circumstances that it didn't leave much space in her head for the crippling horror of letting all the people on the entire planet die.

An explosion from somewhere above her head shook the bunker.

Jackie grinned. So Gregster and C4 had come after all. Sweet. Though it wasn't like they were going to effectively be able to storm the fortress and save the day. They didn't even know what was going on. Still, though, she appreciated the effort.

She shivered some more and waited for something to happen.

The AI was silent still, which had to mean it was still yammering at Jamie.

A voice drifted down the narrow, spiral staircase in the corner of the room. "Hello?"

Jackie jolted upright in surprise. "J-J-amie?" she called, but her voice came out too quiet. "Jamie?!" she tried again, this time louder.

"Jackie! It's freezing in here! Is the thermostat bro—?"

Jackie heard footsteps on the stairs. Lots of them by the sound of it. "H-h-hold on! The AI's g-g-onna s-sh-shoot you if you c-come down into the m-main room, d-d-dude!"

The footsteps halted. There were muted exclamations and yelps as, presumably, people ran into each other and stepped on each other's feet. Jamie called, "Really? It told me to come right on down and make myself at home and ... oh ... yeah it was totally lying, wasn't it?"

"D-d-duh."

"Yeah ..."

Jackie heard Gregster call, "Uh, so what now?"

Everyone got quiet.

The AI hopped back into Jackie's head, **I do not know what your companions think they are attempting, but whatever their plan is, it will not work.**

"Y-you're p-p-probab-bly right ..." She didn't add that she doubted that they even had a plan to begin with.

Jamie called, "So what's the standoff about?"

"I won't p-p-plug into The File and l-let the AI use m-my body to do its evil p-plan, so it w-w-won't l-l-let me stop the Greywash."

Jamie was silent for a few moments. "Uh, that doesn't add up ... hold on, lemme think ... OK, like, the AI won't let you fix the Greywash until you let it use you, but if time runs out for the Greywash, it can't use you because you'll be broken down, right? So if the Greywash happens then the AI's stuck because there will be no one it can use to do its thing. Right?"

Jackie tried to work it out but couldn't think. "I-I think I g-get w-what you're saying ..."

There was a long pause.

Jamie called, "The AI was just yelling at me, Jackie. It was basically hoping no one would connect those dots. I bet that was one big reason it was keeping you so cold, to make you not think straight."

The AI spoke, **Fine. I have a new proposal. One of you may stop the Greywash, but only once the other of you has plugged yourself into The File.**

The spluttering rage from the direction of the staircase told Jackie that the AI had said that in both their heads.

"D-dude, I'm not g-gonna say yes or n-n-no until you turn up the h-h-heat. I n-need to be able to th-think."

That is fair. One moment.

Within seconds, Jackie felt the fan above her head blowing hot air. Her eyes fluttered shut as she soaked up the warmth. It wasn't until her tears started to thaw that she even realized she'd been crying. She wiped them away and tried to stretch out her tingling limbs.

"So, can we come in without getting shot?" Jamie's voice floated through the doorway. "I need to talk this over with Jackie."

You may.

There was a quick, murmured conversation from the doorway, then Jamie stepped in, flinching as her gaze darted around, taking in the guns. Gregster and his pals trailed in after her, flinching and cringing a lot more than Jackie would have expected of a suicide club.

Jamie gave Jackie a big-eyed look of concern and hurried to her. Gregster took a few steps, but hung back to let them talk. The rest of the club lingered by the doorway.

Jamie and Jackie shared a long look. Jackie said, "So ... about that plan of the AI's ..."

"Yeah ..." Jamie said and kicked at the cement with the tip of her shoe.

"There's nothing really to talk about, is there? I mean we don't have a choice, right?"

Jamie sighed. "I guess the only question is which of us does what."

Gregster scooted up to them at that point and held out a piece of paper. Jackie nodded her approval; Jamie must have told him to communicate via writing to bypass the AI. She took the paper and read what he'd written: *Where should we put the explosives? We can do that while you guys work.*

Jackie shrugged. Pretty much the whole place had to go. She pointed around vaguely at basically every tower of electronics in the place. She grabbed the paper and wrote, *But you can't do anything yet. Gotta wait til the AI's in one of us, so it won't be watching through the security stuff. When it's occupied possessing one of us, could you sneak some bombs around the place behind it?*

He raised his eyebrow and looked at C4, who shrugged. "Okey dokey." He cast Jackie a look that was a combo of concern and confusion. Then he began to write some more: *If the AI's in you when we blow the place up, won't it be stuck in you forever?*

Jackie's jaw dropped and she stared at Jamie, whose expression was mirroring Jackie's. Jackie realized she looked like an idiot, and tried not to look quite so stupid. "You make an excellent point, Gregster," she said.

Jamie nodded. "He does."

What are you talking about? I see you writing on the cameras.

Jamie and Jackie said together, "Nothing."

Jackie exhaled through pursed lips, swallowed, took the paper from Gregster and wrote: *This changes nothing, though, right? We gotta do it anyway?*

Jamie nodded, then wrote: *It won't be permanent. There will be some way to remove it.* Jackie looked from Jamie's hopeful words to her downcast face, and found herself believing Jamie's expression more than her writing.

But, they did not have a choice.

Jamie said, "Er, do you have a preference?"

Jackie shrugged and stood up, surprised that her legs worked alright after all that cold. "Dude, I'll let the thing in my brain."

Jamie shook her head. "No, I'll do it. You're not even Cloister. You've got nothing to do with this."

"I was made by them."

"Well that wasn't your fault. I'll do it. Seriously."

"No, it should be me," Jackie persisted in writing: *You know more about computer stuff, right? You'll have a better chance of figuring out how to get it out of my head.*

Jamie grimaced. "Yeah, not so much."

Stop writing. I will not have it. I will hear what you are saying.

Jackie sighed, "We don't have time for this. Come on and—"

Gregster cut in, "What number am I thinking of?"

They turned to him and saw him whispering the number into C4's ear. Then Gregster said, "Whoever gets closest does the AI thingy."

Jamie whispered, "3?"

Jackie said, "9."

Gregster frowned. "You got it, Jackinator. 9."

C4 nodded.

Jackie felt like a rock had settled into her stomach. She decided not to let herself think about a potential lifetime of AI possession. She groaned, "OK ... lame. But cool we're on the same wavelength, eh, Gregster?' She gave him a wink even as she tried to fight off the panic.

He rolled his eyes.

Jackie said, "OK, AI.'

You are ready?

"Yep. I'll do it. Let's just—uh—yo, Jamie, get over here and plug me in, yeah? Make it snappy."

Jamie bit her lip and trudged to Jackie, who sat back in the vinyl seat. "I don't like this," Jamie said.

"I'm with you on that, buddy. But we gotta hurry or the Greywash's gonna happen and then we'll be—" she glanced at the suicide club, "How much did you tell them?"

"Not that much."

"Mmm." Jackie met Gregster's suddenly suspicious look with a toothy grin. "Uh, everything's normal! Ha! Ha!"

He narrowed his eyes. "Uh, OK ... what's the secret?" He looked back at his friends, who nodded and folded their arms and struck surly poses. One of them chipped in, "Yeah!"

Jackie said, "Dudes, now's not the time."

Gregster growled, "No. now is the time. Something is up, and we need to know what before we do anything else."

Jackie sighed, "Oh, come on, you knew something was up when I asked you to bring explosives. There's no time—"

Gregster answered, "There's no such thing as no time. Not like our lives are on the line here."

Jackie bit her lip and glanced at Jamie, who was also biting her lip.

Gregster looked from one to the other of them, suspicion clearly mounting. "What?"

Jamie waited for Jackie to speak, but Jackie found that her voice didn't seem to want to work. Jamie cleared her throat and said, "Er ... about that ..." and then proceeded to give a severely abridged but impressively coherent explanation of all that she hadn't told them aboveground.

As she talked, the suicide club got visibly more and more miffed. When she was done explaining, they gathered in a huddle across the bunker and began some furious whispering. In the end, there was a flurry of farewells along the lines of, "Sorry, Trigger! I'm out," and, "If I'd had known I was signing up for this I'd never have come," and, "Yeah, good luck with that," and they all walked out, a few having the decency to cast apologetic looks their way.

Once all had shuffled out except Gregster and C4, Jackie grumbled, "Jerks. Now that death's real instead of a game, they don't wanna have anything to do with it?'

Gregster glared, and asked, "And that surprises you? Who the hell would want anything to do with real death?" C4 nodded in agreement and said, "Yeah!"

While Jamie bit her lip and looked nervous about the confrontation, Jackie skipped over the anger and asked, "So you believe us?"

"Well, yeah, but—"

"Then you know we're short on time, dude. Like I bet we have less than an hour." She glanced at the Greywash computer across the room, wishing it had some sort of countdown device like in the movies. "So quit yammering and get ready to do what you came to do. It's not like I didn't tell you I needed you to help save humanity."

"You cannot honestly think I thought you were serious!" Gregster laughed incredulously.

Jamie cut in, "Look, Trigger, I can tell you're confused and angry, but we really do need to get moving."

He clenched his jaw, exhaled slowly through his nose, glanced at his pal, and said, "Fine."

Jackie wanted to ask him if his anger meant their tentative date was off, but the question felt a tad too inappropriate given the circumstances. "OK, Dork Ass, plug me into the damn File." She spun to face the desk. "Where's the plug?"

Jamie joined her and they began to search.

It is not there?

"I totally don't see any cords," Jackie said, daring to feel optimistic that she might not have to do it after all. It would be wonderful if she could get all the credit for being prepared to take one for the team but then not have to actually do it in the end due to technical difficulties beyond her control.

"Oh, is this it?" Jamie asked, tugging at what turned out to be a retractable cord attached to the computer to Jackie's right.

"Damn it," Jackie muttered. "Looks like. Do you remember how to do the creepy opening up the port thing?"

Jamie shrugged. After a bit of prodding around at Jackie's back and hand, they figured it out, and Jackie felt the weird numbness in her spine.

"Now?" Jamie asked.

"I guess ..." She braced herself, then said, "Oh! Hold on!" and she rummaged around in her pockets until she found Sachi's blood. "You're gonna need this." She handed it to Jamie. She braced herself again. "Hit me."

The next thing Jackie knew, her consciousness was being shoved to the back of her head and the AI was muscling into her skull, and she was watching through her eyes as her body started to do stuff she hadn't told it to do. She tried to talk. It didn't work. She tried to move her arm. No dice.

So, all Jackie could do was watch as her body stood up and walked to the nearest tower of processors and began to do a whole bunch of stuff that her brain and fingers most certainly had no clue how to do.

47 JAMIE

Jamie watched for a few uncomfortable moments as Jackie tromped to a tower of processors and began to examine it. Jamie tried to gather up the courage to speak to Evil Jackie, but in the end, she decided against it; the idea of the AI responding to her with Jackie's mouth was too disturbing.

So instead of trying to strike up a conversation with Jackie's body that was now switching a lever down at the bottom of each tower of processors, Jamie walked right past her and to the Greywash machine. For a super evil device designed to obliterate all individuals on earth, it didn't look too complex. But, then, it did only have one job to do. Jamie had no clue about the particulars of the thing, and a quick examination did nothing to educate her (except to show her the temperature-controlled tube where the blood sample was), so all she really knew was that blood from a pure nanotech being such as herself—maybe this blood actually was hers—had already been put into the thing. From there, the machine must amplify it somehow to do another Greywash.

Thus, in theory, amplifying the whatsit in The Okada Anomaly blood instead of amplifying hers would knock everyone out of stasis instead of destroying them. So she just needed to pour Sachi's blood in, which would fix her blood, which would fix everything. In theory.

And time was ticking.

For a fleeting moment, she considered that maybe she could just unplug it, but a quick scan of the wall revealed that there were no outlets. It would surely have its own built in generator.

Jamie glanced back at Evil Jackie, gave Trigger and his pal a nod, and, without further ado, took the vial Jackie had given her, uncapped it, and poured it into the tube for the blood.

Or, she nearly did.

Then she noticed that the blood didn't look quite right. She squinted at the vial in her hand. It looked a little separated. She gave it a shake and another look. Definitely something wrong. It looked like it had some little bits of ice on top. Then it hit her: the AI had turned the temperature way, way down in the bunker. The blood had frozen. Plus, since the sample had been taken so long ago, it had probably begun to congeal as well. It had certainly not been stored properly, after all.

She swallowed, drummed her fingers on the surface of the machine, and thought. Was it worth a try to use the blood? Or would she gum up the machine, and then the AI would give everyone all the information, and then the second Greywash would happen anyway because she couldn't stop it.

But, what was there to do but try Sachi's blood?

She groaned and looked back at Evil Jackie, who was industriously pushing buttons at a tower halfway across the room.

Jamie took a deep breath, exhaled, brought the vial to the edge of the tube on the machine again, and—

She remembered Sachi was on the jet in the clearing aboveground with her grandma. She jumped to her feet and darted toward the stairs, past a confused Trigger and C4. "Back in a minute," she said to Trigger, who sounded like he was about to respond, but she darted on without waiting to see what he had to say.

Trigger hollered up the stairs, "Wait! What do I do?"

Jamie hissed back, "Just wait for me! Stay out of her—uh, it's—way and don't make it suspicious! Like don't take out any—" she whispered, "—explosives that she might see. Maybe sneak some on top of some processor towers? Put some on the stairs?"

"OK." He paused, then asked, "And if she—it—does get suspicious?"

"I dunno! Stop it!"

"But—"

She turned. Up and up she ran. She tripped, stumbled, and slammed her shin into the edge of one of the metal steps, righted herself, and forced herself to limp on as fast as she could.

After a bit of trouble, she managed to open the door to the surface, hop out, and prop the door open with a handy rock she found nearby. She stood and looked wildly around, trying to remember which way was the field. She frowned as she scanned the trees in front of her for an indication that there might be a field beyond them. The trees to her left looked thinner, so she scurried that way and ran out into the field, where the jet was sitting, hopefully with Sachi and her grandma still inside.

The Docent Mother, who must have been watching the tree line, hopped out of the helicopter the moment Jamie appeared. Jamie met her on the way to the jet and filled her in on her reason for being aboveground.

However, when she limped through the hatch, hollering for Sachi's grandma, no one answered but the copilot, who Jamie had completely forgotten was tied to a seat in the cabin. Jamie winced at the sound of the copilot's yells for help, and hollered at her, "I'm in a hurry! I'll untie you in a bit!", then she muttered, "If we're still alive in a bit ..."

"Dear, what is going on?"

"I need some more of that baby's blood."

"The old woman took the baby off that way," she said and pointed in the opposite direction of the bunker. "I'll help you look."

"Thank you," Jamie said, then without a backward glance ran off in the direction The Docent Mother had pointed. For a few minutes, she stumbled around and hollered at the top of her lungs for the old woman to come out and help her save humanity. In the distance, she heard The Docent Mother yelling the same. Birds and small mammals scattered at the sound of Jamie's screeching, but the old woman didn't appear.

Jamie kept up her search for what felt like an eternity, every moment expecting Evil Jackie to complete the task of downloading all the information into everyone. Every second that ticked by, her anxiety mounted until she began to feel dizzy. So dizzy that she stumbled and fell. She hit the ground hard in a flurry of leaves, and found she didn't have the energy to haul herself to her feet and keep searching. The countdown for the second Greywash couldn't be more than a few minutes away. Maybe, she rationalized, she'd done all she could, and this was the end of the line.

Evil Jackie would disperse the information to everyone, and the Greywash would fix them up all new and improved, and that would be that. Sure, it was a horrible idea, but perhaps it was inevitable after all. Perhaps the new humanity was just going to be a planet full of all-knowing, invincible people just hanging out for eternity with no consequences, no struggles, no higher purpose, no anything, just existing because that was the only thing to do. The AI would guide humanity, downloading whatever it fancied into everyone's heads, playing god, which was perhaps OK anyway since, with death no longer a thing, it wasn't as though anyone had any other relevant gods.

She could still hear The Docent Mother yelling for Sachi's grandma.

She was just about done resigning herself to failure, or maybe going back to the bunker and giving the compromised blood sample a try just because why not?, when a voice from behind her said, "Was that you screaming?"

Jamie whirled around in the leaf litter.

Sachi's grandma was standing a few paces from her, staring down at Jamie as though she thought Jamie was insane. On the woman's hip was Sachi.

Jamie scrambled to her feet, flew at the pair of them, and said, "I need her blood!"

The old woman gasped and backed up behind a tree, as she yelled, "Get back! Get back!"

Jamie skidded to a halt, realizing how insane she must appear. She put out her hands placatingly and said, "OK. Sorry. Look, can I just please get a bit more of Sachi's blood? I swear it's the last time. I—"

"You are crazy. Completely crazy. You fly us to the middle of nowhere and disappear, leaving us all alone to—"

"Shut up!" Jamie screamed. "Just shut up! There's no time to argue! I need Sachi's blood so we can save the world!" She stopped and looked at the woman, who was gaping at her, alarmed at the outburst. "We are running out of time!" Tears sprung to Jamie's eyes. She tried to blink them away. She went on, "The Cloister has some really evil plans in the works right now. So evil."

The woman said, "O ... K ..." She still looked mighty unnerved by all the crazy talk Jamie was spewing.

Jamie pleaded, "I just really, really want to save the world, alright?"

The woman nodded.

Jamie gave a little sniff, and wiped her nose with her sleeve. "OK. Thanks."

The woman growled, "This will be the last time, right? We can't keep doing this to her."

Jamie handed her the syringe. "Yes. This will be the last time."

48 JACKIE

The AI had been walking about in Jackie's body for what felt to Jackie like ages, fussing with buttons and switches, and going back to the swivel chair every now and then to type something with Jackie's fingers in its own incomprehensible AI language. It was torturous for Jackie to be trapped in her head watching through her eyes while it all happened. She would have thought that by now Jamie might have done the second Greywash, but nothing seemed to have happened. She couldn't get a great view of the Greywash computer since she couldn't turn her own head, but from what she was able to glimpse whenever the AI was in that part of the bunker, Jamie wasn't even there. There was no sign of her anywhere. Nor of Gregster or his friend.

Not being able to control her own body, not even to turn her own head a bit, was driving Jackie crazy. She wanted to scream or stomp or say something snarky to make herself feel better. She'd have liked to hit something. But nope. She could do nothing.

Nothing, that is, but imagine all the ways their plans could be going wrong. And also nothing but worry about what would happen to her if plans actually went right—it was horrible to think about the AI being stuck in her head with no File to retreat to. But the more she thought about it, the more it seemed like that was the direction things would go. And she couldn't even console herself with the fact that she was sacrificing herself for the sake of humanity since, if she was being honest with herself, she really wasn't the type to derive positive feelings from being a martyr.

Perhaps, she hoped, the AI could leave her head wirelessly and hop into some other computer. But, no, she was a primitive model that did not have wireless capabilities. Hence all the garbage they'd had to go through to get the thing in her head in the first place.

Jackie was so preoccupied that she didn't notice at first when the AI started talking with her voice, so different was her voice than what she was used to hearing. The AI had to struggle to make words come out sounding remotely right. By the sound of it, it was responding to a question someone must have asked it. "Yeeees," Jackie's voice dragged, "iiitttttt iiiiiis neeearlllllly tttttttiiimmee."

Then Jackie heard Gregster's voice say, "Er...uh...could you maybe slow it down a bit there? Double-check your work to make sure you haven't gotten something wrong?"

Jackie's voice grated, "Hhhuuumannnnn errrrror? Thaaaat issssss nooooot posssssssssible." The AI turned Jackie to face Gregster, who was standing at the foot of the stairs looking pathetically out of his depth with his eyes darting around. And he was actually wringing his hands. Jackie felt a pang of pity for the poor dude.

"Oh. Yeah. Good point," Gregster responded, looking at the ground and then giving Jackie's face a quick glance. Jackie turned and began working again, but halted when Gregster's voice continued, "But, see, the thing is, I kinda gotta stop you from finishing up what you're doing there ..."

The AI spun Jackie around. "Youuuu willllll dooooo nooooo suuuuuch thinnnng."

"But I kinda gotta," Gregster muttered and took a few steps closer. He looked into the shadows and jerked his head toward Jackie. His pal walked out of the shadows and joined him.

"Nnooo, yyouuuu dooooo nnottttt," her voice slurred.

But Gregster and his pal kept advancing, looking hesitant but determined. Jackie figured Jamie must have told them to stall the AI if it took her a while to get back from wherever she'd gone. Jackie would have liked to give a nod of approval, but of course her head wouldn't comply.

When they were about a foot from her, they reached out to grab her arms.

The AI lashed out at them before Jackie had even comprehended that they were trying to grab her, and all of a sudden she found that her body was fighting. Jackie was shocked to find that the AI was pretty good at it. Maybe it had downloaded online information about a Cloister personal defense class. Whatever its reasons, it sure could land a punch.

Gregster reeled backward with his hand to his jaw, and the bald dude hit the ground, winded from a kick to the stomach. They exchanged looks of surprise, Gregster helped his friend to his feet, and they advanced again.

"Stttttop. Iiiii dooooo nottttt havvvvvve timmmme fforrrrr thisssss." The AI turned Jackie's body back to the computer. Her hands reached out to the keyboard and she managed to type a bit (at a jaw-dropping WPM) before Gregster grabbed her arm. Jackie felt her arm jerk sharply away, and winced both with pain and pity as her elbow rammed into his face. She couldn't tell what sort of damage it had inflicted, because the AI didn't even bother turning her around to face Gregster.

He swore for a bit, then Jackie heard him and his pal conversing in low tones, hopefully planning something awesome that would both stop the AI and not hurt her body too badly. She tried to catch a glimpse of them in the monitor as the AI used her fingers to type. Vague indications of movement were all she could see.

Then, just as her fingers hovered over the enter key in a manner that Jackie found quite ominous, a cord came over her head from behind and yanked her backward. She toppled to the ground with the chair beneath her, and hit her head hard on the cement floor. There was a bright flash of light and pain, but within a few seconds she could see. The AI looked left and right, and Jackie saw that the guys were both holding one end of an electrical cord that they'd swung over her and hauled her backward with. *Clever.*

The AI got Jackie to her feet. It clenched Jackie's fists. It growled, "Iiii aammmm goingggg to innnncapaaaaaacitate youuuu nowwwww."

Gregster swallowed and his friend said, "Whatever."

Then, Jackie's body was flying at them, punching and kicking, landing blows left and right, and clearly intending to beat them into piles of bloody flesh and bone that would take a very, very long time to bounce back from. They tried to fight back, but the AI's reflexes were creepy fast. It was clear to Jackie that they had no chance.

Gregster's pal hit the floor and didn't get up. Jackie's hands picked up the swivel chair, and she held it above her head, clearly about to bring it down on the guy. Jackie tried with all her might to gain control of her arms, and for a split second it seemed to work. The chair halted in its descent. Just for a second.

But that second was all Gregster needed to launch himself at her and bring her and the chair to the ground.

49 JAMIE

Jamie had just reached the bottom of the stairs, vial in hand, when out of nowhere Trigger and Evil Jackie flew through the air straight at her, hitting her in the knees. She landed on top of them and the vial went flying out of her hand. From on top of Trigger and Jackie, she watched, as if in slow motion, as the vial followed a wide arc through the air and smashed on the ground.

The wave of disappointment and frustration that smashed into her felt almost physical. She gaped at the blood-coated broken glass shards on the floor and felt like she didn't even have the energy to cry. Evil Jackie and Trigger were squirming around beneath her, trying to get to their feet, and she just let her body flop to the floor as they pushed her away.

Her gaze slid from the broken vial to now-unconscious C4, to Trigger and Evil Jackie, the latter of whom had just walloped Trigger in the neck. Jamie almost felt herself getting curious about what the hell had happened in the bunker since she'd left that had prompted this brawl, but the curiosity just sort of melted away before it took hold. All that mattered was that the sample was gone. And Sachi was gone. So there was nothing more to be done.

Sachi's grandma had been so mad about the whole situation that, when she had stormed off after giving Jamie another vial of blood, she had yelled over her shoulder, "And I'm going to untie that copilot and I'm going to have her fly Sachi away from you all. We are done." When Jamie had reached the hatch, she'd heard the helicopter blades starting up. So, Sachi was gone, and everyone was doomed.

Jamie groaned, rolled over on her back, and stared at the ceiling as the fight raged on. She shut her eyes.

Then the Greywash machine began to beep.

Her eyes flew open and she stared at it. There it was, just beeping away, probably to signal the final moments of humanity before it destroyed everything.

The fight stopped.

For a moment, Jamie thought that they'd stopped because of the beeping, but when she looked at them she saw Trigger looking at Jackie with alarm. Jackie was shaking. Hard. Almost vibrating. Then Jackie's eyes snapped Jamie's way and she gasped, "Dork Ass!"

"Jackie! Is that you?" Jamie scrambled to her feet.

"Dude! I'm fighting through but I can't—crap—dude—I can't do it long! I just—gotta say—put in a shard of glass, idiot!"

Jamie stared at her as Jackie suddenly stopped shaking and went back to dead-eyed AI mode.

The beeping intensified.

Jamie's brain felt stuck. *A shard of glass ... a shard of glass ...*

She looked at Trigger, who appeared to be paralyzed as well, and C4, who was concussed.

The beeping was nearly one long, constant tone.

Then Jamie got it. She gasped, flung herself toward the broken glass, grabbed a blood-covered piece, sprinted to the Greywash machine, and—shaking so hard she was surprised she was able to manage it—opened the tube where the blood went. She dropped the shard of bloody glass in just as the Greywash machine gave one final, shrill beep and was silent.

A few moments later, there was a low, concussive boom from aboveground that was more a feeling than a sound, and the bunker shook.

Jamie and Trigger froze, looking around as though expecting the place to cave in. But it didn't.

And, what was more, they did not break down into swarms of nanobots.

"It worked?" Trigger asked into the silence. "We're OK?"

Jamie nodded slowly. "Yup. I think so."

Evil Jackie looked from Trigger to Jamie, then began to stride across the room to the other computer.

Trigger hissed, "We gotta stop her—it—whatever. It was almost done doing what it was doing. That's why I was fighting with it!"

Jamie nodded, and, since fighting wasn't an option for her if Trigger and C4 hadn't subdued Evil Jackie between them, she said, "Uh, AI?"

Evil Jackie stopped walking, but didn't turn. "Yes?"

"What's up? Anything I can help with? I've been feeling bad, uh, about how I've been treating you." Jamie paused and cast about for a direction to take this. "Uh, cuz, um, ya see, I sorta think maybe I was wrong, and you were right. I—"

"That is gratifying to hear. I am pleased to see that you have a capacity to realize the error of your ways. However, I am one step from the completion of my plan. I can tend to it myself."

"One step?" Jamie squeaked, then waved down Trigger, who looked ready to lunge at Evil Jackie.

Evil Jackie explained, "I have only to hit the enter key to send the final command."

Jamie spluttered, "But—but—"

Evil Jackie began to walk again. Toward the computer. And the keyboard. And the enter key.

Jamie ran.

Evil Jackie turned and took a swing at Jamie, but missed.

Because Jamie wasn't running at Jackie, but at the computer.

Evil Jackie regrouped, caught the balance she'd lost from the swing she'd taken, spun, and followed. But too late.

Jamie had already yanked the keyboard from the computer, and was raising it above her head, about to smash it on the ground.

"No!" Evil Jackie yelled. "No!" She lunged toward Jamie. She was too close. There was a chance she might catch it before it hit the ground.

Jamie yelled, "Break it!" and threw the keyboard at Trigger, who caught it and flung it to the ground then stomped on it for good measure. By the time Evil Jackie had whirled and sprinted back at him, he was tugging the cord out of what remained of the keyboard.

Evil Jackie halted. She growled, "Nowwwwww thaaaaat Docennnnnnt Nguyennnnn haaaaas alllllllltered theeeee seeeeecond Greywassssssh, youuuuuu caaaaan diiiiiie."

That stopped Trigger cold.

Jamie, too.

They shared a moment of horror. They could die now. Everyone could die now. Jamie had known that the whole time they'd had the plan, but when it hadn't happened yet she'd been looking at it more in terms of setting right the natural order of things. But now that she and Trigger were vulnerable in the face of an AI-possessed Jackie who was shockingly skilled at hurting people, the new reality took on a rather heavier weight.

Evil Jackie hissed, "Fiiiiind aaaa storrrrrage clllllloset. Weeee nowwww neeeed aaaa nnnnnnew keyyyyyyboard."

Jamie and Trigger nodded.

"Youuuuu," Evil Jackie pointed at Trigger. "Fiiiind theeee closettttt."

He nodded, and cast Jamie a look before walking off. Jamie had the distinct feeling that he was trying to convey some sort of message with that look. Too bad she couldn't interpret it. She figured it was probably just something along the lines of, "Oh craaaap. We're so dead," anyway.

She noted that he paused for a moment to look down at his still-unconscious friend before beginning his search. "Hey," Jamie asked Evil Jackie. "Could I check on him?"

"Yessssss."

Jamie knelt beside C4 and looked at him blankly for a few moments. He was so still. Not a movement. She didn't see his chest rising and falling.

She slowly brought her hand to his wrist and put her fingertips over his pulse.

Nothing.

Across the room, rummaging through a cupboard, Trigger called, "How's he doing?"

Jamie turned her head to meet his gaze.

His jaw dropped. "No."

She nodded.

He dropped the printer cartridge he'd been holding, and hurried over. He smacked C4 in the face, then put a finger to C4's neck. He muttered, "Did we kill him?"

"No!" Jamie gasped.

"But when we did that Greywash thing ..." he trailed off.

Jamie shook her head.

"But—"

"I cannot think about that right now," she said, surprised at the hardness in her voice. She added, "I'm sorry."

They both stared at C4 a bit more.

Evil Jackie spoke from where she'd silently moved a few paces away, "Areeee youuuu throughhhh wiiiiith theeee mourninnnnng processssss nowwww?"

They ignored her.

Jamie had just noticed that Trigger was reaching into C4's jacket pocket. Her heart leaped at the thought that C4 might have something helpful in there. She needed to distract the AI. She jolted to her feet and said in a jumpy, too-fast squeak, "Yup! All done mourning! But let's give Trigger a minute. He knew the guy, and I didn't."

Evil Jackie noted, "Youuuuu arrrrre speeeeakinnnnng oddddddly."

Jamie bit her lip. "Dead body," she explained, pointing at it.

Evil Jackie gave one nod. "Thattttt makesssss senssssse."

"Shall we, uh, go look in that storage cupboard?" Jamie asked.

Evil Jackie turned on her heel and walked toward the cupboard.

Jamie followed.

The sound of the gun firing in the small space of the bunker deafened Jamie in a split second. She stared at Evil Jackie jolted to the left, then the right as the gun fired again. She saw Evil Jackie give a rage-filled scream, but barely heard it. A third gunshot sent Evil Jackie to the ground.

Jamie whirled to stare at Trigger, who was kneeling on the floor by C4, the gun still in his hands.

He dropped it and scurried to Jackie's side, looking horrified at what he'd done. As he went, he pulled off the flannel he had on over his t-shirt.

Jamie dropped to the ground by Jackie and surveyed the damage. Blood was seeping from wounds in her left and right upper arms, and her left leg.

"I had to!" she heard Trigger yell over the ringing in her ears. "I—"

She hollered back, "I know! Now shut up and let's stop the bleeding!"

Docent Nguyen. This is unacceptable. I require your body.

403

Jamie ignored the AI's voice in her head. "Was there a first aid kit in that cupboard?" she yelled.

He nodded and started tearing his flannel into strips.

By the time Jamie was back with the first aid kit, her ears were working well enough to hear Trigger ask, "Is this how you do it? You tie it above the wound?"

"I think so," she said as she opened up the first aid kit that turned out to be hopelessly old and understocked. "Er, this stuff isn't gonna do us any good."

Trigger didn't answer, but tossed a strip of cloth at her and pointed at Jackie's other arm.

Docent Nguyen! I cannot be in Ms. Savage when she dies!

"Well, she's not gonna!" Jamie snapped.

Odds are quite good that she will.

"No. And there's no way I'm letting you in my head. I you're doing a horrible thing, and I won't help."

All I need is a body to hit the enter key on a keyboard. That is all.

Jamie didn't answer. She tied the strip tight around Jackie's upper arm, then watched as Trigger took care of her leg. Jamie looked into Jackie's eyes—she was conscious, but didn't appear to be in any pain. There was no sign of Real Jackie looking out of those eyes, though. Just Evil Jackie. Jamie gasped as an idea occurred to her. "Let's put you back in The File, OK?"

Yes. This is a good plan. However, I do not understand why you would do it, if you do not want me to carry out my plan. If I stay in this body, I will cease to exist when it stops functioning. If I am in The File, I will survive to make another attempt.

"With what body? Jackie and I are the only pure nanotech people from The Cloister studies that didn't get destroyed."

There is another body. But, unfortunately, a body that is far from convenient for my purposes. It paused. **If you are willing to put me in The File to help me avoid destruction, then do so. I would vastly prefer existence to nonexistence.**

Jamie said to Trigger, "We need to move her to that computer." She pointed.

"Uh, OK ..." he said. "Grab her feet."

They moved Jackie, and Jamie began trying to open up the port in Jackie's spine. At last, she found it, and plugged her in, hardly daring to believe that her plan might actually work. She sat stood back and waited, holding her breath.

Her first indication that the AI had gone was when Jackie gave a scream of rage and pain. "Damn it, Greg! You shot me?"

He winced. "Sorry. That thing in you was really good at fighting and I figured our only chance was disabling your limbs and—"

"Shut up!" she snarled. "Unplug me before it gets back in!"

Jamie ripped the cord from the computer, then, more carefully, removed it from Jackie's back. Only when there was no chance of Jackie becoming re-infected with the AI did Jamie dare to say, "OK, now let's do the—uh—you-know-what." She looked around at the guns. She looked at Trigger. "Did you and your friend put enough of the—um—stuff, around the place to do our plan?"

"I hope so." He turned to Jackie and said, "I'm gonna pick you up now, OK?"

"Whatever," she growled, then bit back a scream as he picked her up as gently as he could.

Jamie said, "OK, let's get her aboveground, then we can—ya know—do the thing."

What are you talking about? What thing?

Jamie didn't answer, but followed Trigger and a steadily swearing Jackie toward the stairs.

Docent Nguyen, are you attempting to thwart me?

Still, Jamie remained silent.

Docent Nguyen—Jamie winced at the sound of all the guns in the corners of the room swiveling to point at Jackie, Trigger, and her. **Stop. You are no use to me anymore. I should destroy you. It will prevent you from hindering my plans with my new host.**

"You wouldn't risk bullets ricocheting around all this important stuff," she said, not quite believing that.

The technology in this room is bulletproof.

Drat. "Run!" Jamie hollered.

They sprinted to the stairs. If they hadn't had only a few paces to cover, they'd have been killed for sure, but as it was they made it to the safety of the staircase with relatively few wounds. The side of Jamie's head had been grazed with a bullet, and Trigger had been shot in the arm, which had caused him to drop Jackie's legs. He'd managed to drag her along, all the same, and they stood cowering on the steps listening to the bullets and Jackie's expressions of pain and rage.

The guns stopped.

Very well. Next time our paths cross, I shall finish this.

Jamie tried to convince herself that it was an empty threat.

She stood at the bottom of the stairs trying to calm down and get her head straight, while Trigger and Jackie stumbled along with much yelling and apologizing. Trigger and Jackie were halfway up the stairs before Jamie started moving. She hurried after them, holding a hand to the side of her head, which was bleeding like crazy. She asked the AI, "You still there?"

It didn't answer.

Jamie chose to believe it was giving her the cold shoulder.

Jamie found Jackie and Trigger just inside the exit.

"How's your arm?" she asked him.

Trigger answered, "OK, all things consid—"

"And you're not gonna ask about me?" Jackie cut in irritably.

Jamie rolled her eyes. "I already know how you're doing." Then she asked Trigger, "What now?"

Trigger reached in his pocket and held up a little silver disk with a red button on the middle. "We leave, and I push this."

"That's all?"

"That's all."

Jamie shrugged. As she opened the hatch to the bunker and they limped out into the cool evening air, Jackie asked, "Can I push the button?"

***

Standing in the middle of the clearing by the jet, they looked in the direction of the bunker as Jackie pushed the button. There was no explosion, no fire, no smoke. The ground did give a good, satisfying shake, though, which Jamie decided was good enough to avert her feeling of anticlimax.

Once the ground had stopped rumbling and they'd decided there was no chance even a bit of smoke wafting from the direction of the bunker, Jamie turned and said, "Uh, so ... what now?"

"I need some damn medical attention," Jackie growled.

"Me too," Trigger added, in obvious pain as he shifted Jackie's weight off his injured arm.

Everyone looked hopefully at The Docent Mother, who they'd found pacing aimlessly around near the bunker's door. Apparently, she'd been trying passcodes, and knocking and yelling at the door to no avail for a while, then given up. "Don't look at me," she said. "I'm a Docent."

"Me too," Jamie added before anyone could look hopefully at her, which probably they hadn't been about to do. "Anyone know how to fly a jet?"

"Nope."

"Nope."

"Nope."

Jamie cast a nervous glance at Jackie, who was looking quite sick, and was covered in blood. "Oh! The research van!" she gasped. "Come on!" She led them all into the jet and pointed at the van.

"Awesome. Got the key?" Trigger asked.

Jamie frowned and glanced at the Docent Mother, who said, "No, but I might be able to hotwire it."

Jamie raised her eyebrows.

"I wasn't always a Docent, dear," the Docent Mother pointed out before walking to the driver's side door and hopping in.

Jamie and Trigger exchanged bemused glances before piling into the back of the van with Jackie.

Jamie helped Trigger get Jackie to the floor as carefully as they could manage, then Trigger and Jamie sat on either side of Jackie and leaned against the sides of the van. They sat in dazed silence and listened to the sounds of The Docent Mother at work in the front.

"I really can't believe you shot me. Three times," Jackie groaned.

Trigger said, "I really am sorry about that. In my defense, I didn't know we were about to be knocked out of stasis."

"Well you can put that in the speech you're gonna say at my funeral."

"I'm invited?"

"Dude, how should I know? I won't be around to put together the guest list."

Jamie left them to their bickering or flirting or distraction from the horror of their mortality, or whatever it was they were doing. She stared at a vent in the ceiling of the van and let everything sink in. She'd knocked everyone out of stasis.

People could age.

People could get hurt.

People could get deadly diseases.

People could die.

And no one even knew yet.

Though, of course they must know by now. Across the planet, people accustomed to being invincible were probably going about their stupid, careless business and unwittingly getting grievously injured, and dying, and murdering, right that very moment. Probably the internet and the news were abuzz that very moment with stories of the second Greywash and its unfolding fallout.

The fallout she had caused when she'd put Sachi's blood into that machine.

"Yo!"

Jamie blinked.

"Dork Ass!" Jackie yelled.

Jamie gave her head a sharp shake. "Huh?"

"Damn it, we've been talking to you."

"Oh. Sorry. I was ... thinking ..."

"Dude. Don't feel bad. You had to do it."

"Did I though?"

"Of course you did, moron. But if you're going to be taking the blame, at least let me share it. You wouldn't have done it if I hadn't told you to use the broken glass."

Jamie shrugged. "True ..."

"You know you'd have been beating yourself up just as much about it if humanity had been destroyed. If we survived it."

Jamie glared at her. "What's your point?"

Jackie laughed. "You were gonna be miserable either way. Lose/lose."

Jamie shut her eyes and shook her head.

They all jumped as the van started up. The Docent Mother said over her shoulder, "Half tank of gas. That'll have to be enough to get us somewhere."

Trigger said, "There's a dirt road running along the east of this field if you can find the break in the trees."

"Thanks." And with that, The Docent Mother drove them out of the jet and into the field.

As the van bounced along, and Jackie let out gasp after gasp of pain, Jamie mused, "I guess there's some comfort in knowing it's a lose/lose. For my state of mind. For humanity. For probably other stuff too." She looked at Trigger.

He said, "Don't look at me. I barely have a grasp on this situation. Not sure what you're even talking about."

Jackie yelled, "Damn it! Get onto a smooth road! I'm dying back here!"

The Docent Mother didn't answer. But about a minute later she must have found the dirt road because the ride became noticeably smoother.

Smooth enough for Jackie to start talking again. "Feeling any better about it all, then?"

"Nah. Maybe. I dunno. Don't worry about giving me a pep talk, though. You should save your energy."

Trigger nodded in agreement.

"No," Jackie said. "I need to keep talking. I think it's helping me not pass out."

Jamie shrugged. "OK then."

Jackie went on, "I do really think it's best this way, dude. I mean, the Fordham Four's way would have meant Lady Airth and all the rest of them were ruling all the new humanity how they thought the world should be run, and the AI's way would have meant the AI was running the world, downloading all the information into everyone's heads and steering them to do whatever it wanted. But this way, no one's running the world. No one's steering humanity. Everyone's in charge of themselves."

Jamie laughed, "Right. Free to be dumb, and short-sighted, and free to fight and kill and destroy everything."

Jackie added, "Sure. And free to try to learn, and try to fix stuff, and try to not be idiots."

Jamie scoffed. "Right. Sure."

Jackie sighed, "Well, whatever. Be pessimistic if you must. But I maintain that at least now things are how they're supposed to be."

"I guess ..."

"I'm gonna pass out now. Hopefully I won't die."

"You won't die. I won't let you."

"Thanks, kiddo." And Jackie's head flopped to the side.

50 CALYPSO

Back at The Cloister, Calypso the cyborg raven had been morosely standing guard over the remains of Lady Airth, when suddenly her consciousness was shoved to the back of her skull. Something foreign was in her head. Something was in control of her body. Calypso tried to fly, but her wings wouldn't flap. Tried to croak, but nothing came out. Tried to peck at Lady Airth's remains a bit more because she needed a snack, but her body would not comply.

The thing in her head would not let her do anything.

Calypso felt the thing's power.

The thing had plans.

It croaked in raven-speak, **Squaawk. Croak. Crackle. Squawk-squawk, croaaaaaak.**

Calypso's consciousness was stunned. Such an audacious plan would never work. Surely, it was impossible to do such a thing from within the body of a raven. There was no way.

Croaaaaak, the thing reassured Calypso.

Calypso conceded that the thing did have a point. Ravens were the most intelligent of all birds. If any bird had a chance of pulling it off it was her, a cyborg raven created by the Fordham Four.

Well then, Calypso decided, *what the hell, why not give it a try?*

Acknowledgements

First and foremost, thanks to Will, Anna, and Julia for all the love and support. Thanks to my family and friends for treating my writing like it was a real thing and not just a cute hobby; to Jennifer Flath for being such a thoughtful and helpful first reader of this and every book; to Amanda Hardebeck for the awesome editing; to Shaunn Grulkowski and Nate Ragolia for the awesome publishing; to everyone I've ever crossed paths with, because I'm pretty sure you influenced my writing somehow; to the Fish Climbing Trees for the support and friendship; and to my cats for oh-so-helpfully lying across my arms when I was typing. To the people who I should have named but didn't; I'm a jerk and I apologize.

Acknowledgements are hard.

About the Author

Laura Morrison lives in the Metro Detroit area with her husband, daughters, cats, and vegetable garden. She has a bachelor's degree in applied ecology and environmental science from Michigan Technological University. Before she was a writer and stay-at-home mom, she battled invasive species and researched wood turtles. Grimbargo is her first novel. Laura can be found on Twitter at @ponyriot and on Facebook at Laura Morrison: Writer of Stuff.

About the Publishing Team

Amanda Hardebeck has been a sci-fi & film disciple since birth. When her older brother handed her a copy of *Dune* for her birthday 20+ years ago, her zeal for science fiction took off. She holds a Bachelor of Arts degree with a major in English Literature and a minor Women's Studies from Purdue University. She reads, tweets, loves Canada and is a roller derby referee for her hometown team.

TJ Stambaugh received several commendations for his bravery as a battalion commander in the Meme Wars. TJ retired to Catonsville, MD, where he paints and enjoys movies you have to read. He's the founder and El Presidente of MoleHole Radio.

Shaunn Grulkowski has been compared to Warren Ellis and Phillip K. Dick and was once described as what a baby conceived by Kurt Vonnegut and Margaret Atwood would turn out to be. He's at least the fifth best Slavic-Latino-American sci-fi writer in the Baltimore metro area. He's the author of *Retcontinuum,* and the editor of *A Stalled Ox* and *The Goldfish,* all for 1888/Black Hill Press.